THE LEGAL THRILLER HAS BEEN REBORN FOR A NEW GENERATION WITH THE "FRESH VOICE" (ROBERT DUGONI) OF

ALLISON LEOTTA

The former federal sex crimes prosecutor scores "a recipe for success: a vulnerable, tenacious heroine, surprising twists and turns, and equal parts romance and danger" (*Library Journal*, starred review) in her acclaimed novels.

Praise for

SPEAK OF THE DEVIL

Named Best Book of the Month by Apple and Featured in the iBookstore

"Sexy and brutal . . . convincing and authoritative. . . . An author who knows what she's talking about."

—*Seattle Post-Intelligencer* (Editor's Choice)

"Vivid, explosive."

—*RT Book Reviews* (4 stars)

"Leotta is on fire in the literary world."

—*Deadline Detroit*

"Terrifically entertaining. . . . Leotta is as skilled in ratcheting up tensions as she is in describing delicate moments of contemplation."

—*The Federal Lawyer*

"Allison Leotta doesn't just write about this world. She lives in it and works in it. That's why *Speak of the Devil* comes to life in the most haunting and best way."

—Brad Meltzer

"Taut and fast-paced . . . intelligent, probing, and clear-eyed. Part morality tale, part riveting drama, and very, very good."

—*Washington Independent Review of Books*

DISCRETION

"A first-rate thriller. Leotta nails the trifecta of fiction: plot, pace, and character."

—David Baldacci

"A realistic legal thriller that's as fun to read as it is fascinating."

—Lisa Scottoline

"Beautifully crafted and frighteningly real."

—Douglas Preston

"An assured and authentic voice, and a highly entertaining storyteller."

—George Pelecanos

"Smart and sexy . . . rock-solid plotting . . . top-notch."

—John Lescroart

"Allison Leotta is by far one of the finest new thriller writers today. Chock-full of twists and turns, *Discretion* will have you on the edge of your seat."

—*Strand Magazine*

LAW OF ATTRACTION

Named One of the Best Legal Thrillers of 2010 by *Suspense Magazine*

"Riveting. . . . Leotta joins the big leagues with pros like Lisa Scottoline and Linda Fairstein."

—*Library Journal* (starred review)

"A racy legal thriller . . . taking on a still-taboo subject."

—*The Washington Post*

"Intense and realistic. . . . Leotta is an up-and-coming literary giant."

—*Suspense Magazine*

"Realistic, gritty, and filled with twists and turns. . . . A great read."

—Alan M. Dershowitz

"Suspenseful . . . strikes all the right chords. . . . Impressive."

—*Mystery Scene*

"Sexy, fast-paced. . . . Reminiscent of Linda Fairstein."

—*City Pulse*

"A riveting page-turner. . . . Leotta turns her experiences into visceral prose."

—*Washington City Paper*

"A great ride . . . a shocking end. . . . A stunning debut indicating a bright future."

—Robert Dugoni

BOOKS BY ALLISON LEOTTA

Law of Attraction

Discretion

Speak of the Devil

ALLISON LEOTTA

SPEAK OF THE DEVIL

POCKET BOOKS
New York London Toronto Sydney New Delhi

Pocket Books
A Division of Simon & Schuster, Inc.
1230 Avenue of the Americas
New York, NY 10020

This book is a work of fiction. Any references to historical events, real people, or real places are used fictitiously. Other names, characters, places, and events are products of the author's imagination, and any resemblance to actual events or places or persons, living or dead, is entirely coincidental.

First Pocket Books paperback edition April 2015

For information about special discounts for bulk purchases, please contact Simon & Schuster Special Sales at 1-866-506-1949 or business@simonandschuster.com.

The Simon & Schuster Speakers Bureau can bring authors to your live event. For more information or to book an event, contact the Simon & Schuster Speakers Bureau at 1-866-248-3049 or visit our website at www.simonspeakers.com.

Manufactured in the United States of America

10 9 8 7 6 5 4 3 2 1

ISBN 978-1-4767-9372-6
ISBN 978-1-4516-4487-6 (ebook)

For my parents,

with love and gratitude

"The Mara Salvatrucha, also known as MS-13, is the world's most dangerous gang."

—National Geographic Explorer

SPEAK OF THE DEVIL

1

Anna fiddled with the napkin on her lap and willed her stomach to calm. *Get it together, Curtis.* In court, she was tough. She was fearless. As a sex-crimes prosecutor in D.C., she looked in the eyes of the city's most dangerous men, pointed at them, and described the worst things they'd ever done. But this was different.

This was her life. And tonight she had to execute the most important personal decision she'd ever made.

The Tabard Inn consistently ranked as one of the most romantic restaurants in D.C., which was why she'd chosen it. The evening was warm and clear, and she'd scored a table in the outdoor courtyard. Waves of ivy covered the brick walls; patches of dark sky peeked through a canopy of potted trees. Attractive diners sat around candlelit tables, swirling expensive glasses of wine. The setting was perfect.

Now if the guy would only show up.

Her phone buzzed with an incoming text. She glanced down hopefully, but the message was work-related.

Det. Hector Ramos: Parking near brothel. Heading in soon.

She texted back.

Good. Be safe.

She set the phone down and watched the door, wondering when Jack would walk through—and how it would feel to meet his eyes now that she'd made her decision. He was ten minutes late, which wasn't like him. Maybe he wasn't coming. That wouldn't be surprising, given their recent history. She would either have the most romantic moment of her life or crushing humiliation. She felt like the Bachelorette, only with slightly less cleavage showing.

• • •

Two miles away, Tierra Guerrero counted the lines radiating from the circle of rotten ceiling. Seven. Not a perfect spider, then, but nobody's perfect. She was just glad to have something to look at. The ceilings she worked under became intimately familiar, and the spidery crack provided a welcome distraction.

It was distracting her, even now, from Ricardo's wet grunts in her ear. His red face bobbed a few inches above hers; his humid breath filled her lungs. The bed rocked with his relentless pumping. Most johns were limited to fifteen minutes, but the brothel owner could go as long as he wanted.

Her hips ached from being pummeled against the

mattress all day. She wanted a hot shower, dinner, and a long night's sleep. "Ooh." She ran her fingers down Ricardo's back and tried to sound like a woman overcome with lust. *"Sí, sí, sí."* To her ears, the moans sounded lame, but most dates responded to even the feeblest signs of passion. Ricardo was no different. He squeezed her arms and pumped faster.

The room was small and shabby, lit by a cheap bedside lamp. A sheet hung from the ceiling, separating two sagging mattresses. The privacy curtain was unnecessary at the moment, though—the other mattress was empty. Tierra was the only girl working today, which meant lots of money, but also lots of wear and tear. She glanced longingly at the stack of poker chips on the nightstand. She hoped Ricardo would be fair when she exchanged the chips for cash. She was supposed to get half the money from her tricks, but Ricardo seemed like the slippery type. She sighed and went back to watching the spidery crack. How much longer could he keep this up?

The sound of male voices drifted in from the living room. They were louder and angrier than the usual murmur of men waiting their turn. She glanced at Ricardo, but his eyes were squeezed shut, his face scrunched in ecstasy. His body might be on top of hers, but his mind was far away.

The bedroom door burst open and crashed into the wall. Three young men strode in, all wearing trench coats, all carrying machetes. Tierra tried to sit up, but she was pinned by the brothel owner's body.

"Ricardo!" she screamed.

Too late.

One of the men hitched an arm around Ricardo's neck and yanked him off her. He slammed the owner against the wall, held the machete to his throat, and spoke in a low growl.

"This is for the Mara Salvatrucha."

• • •

The unmarked Jeep Cherokee pulled to the curb two blocks from the brothel. Three of the four officers wore bulletproof vests with the word POLICE stamped in white letters. Only Hector Ramos wore jeans and a black T-shirt. The only Hispanic detective on D.C.'s Human Trafficking Task Force, Hector played the undercover "customer" in many of the brothel busts in the city.

"She's not a lesbian," Hector said, tucking the transmitter into his front pocket.

"Of course she is," said Ralph. "I have proof."

"She said no when you asked her out?"

"Exactly."

"That'd make half the women in D.C. lesbians."

The guys in the back laughed.

"Your mother didn't say no."

"That's the best you got?" Hector said. "Mama jokes? No wonder she turned you down."

"Your mother loved my jokes." Ralph took a swig of coffee. "Seriously, though. Why won't she date police?"

"Lady like that wants a hero." Hector put his real wallet into the glove compartment and stuffed the decoy wallet into his back pocket. "Not a bunch of children."

He knew the guys would talk about Anna Curtis the whole time he was gone. The prosecutor was beautiful, friendly, and single. She was both a diversion and an enigma to the police who worked with her. Hector was considering asking her out himself—he might stand a better chance than most. If this bust went well, maybe he'd ask her to go to the firing range or grab drinks after work one night.

He reached around and patted his lower back. His fingers rested momentarily on the Glock, solid and reassuring, tucked into his jeans. He opened the door.

"You boys gonna be okay in this big car all by yourselves?"

"Get the fuck outta here," Ralph laughed.

"Good luck," called a voice from the backseat. The UC work was the riskiest part of the operation.

"I don't need luck." Hector stepped out of the Jeep. "I got you guys watching my back." He shut the door and walked toward the brothel.

2

Anna watched the restaurant's inner door swing open, and Jack finally strode into the Tabard Inn's courtyard. Broad-shouldered, a couple inches north of six feet tall, Jack always made an impression when he walked into a room. He had smooth brown skin and light green eyes, and wore his head cleanly shaved. Tonight, he'd traded his usual suit for dark jeans and a white linen button-down shirt, allowing her a glimpse of the dark copper skin of his chest.

He walked with easy grace across the brick patio to her. She noticed some other diners—mostly women, but a few men—watching him. Anna stood nervously, causing her napkin to fall off her lap. She leaned to pick it up; when she stood again, Jack was next to her. She tipped her head up to meet his eyes, wondering what kind of reception she would find there. He smiled at her, warily, but with real warmth, and her heart did a happy little dance.

"Hello, Anna." His voice was a deep baritone, incredibly sexy when it was this soft.

"Hi." Being this close to him made her feel a little shaky, in the best way.

They paused, unsure how to greet each other after all this time. She closed the space between them, put her hand on his bicep, and leaned up to kiss his cheek. It was freshly shaved smooth, but his scent was what really got to her. Soap, clean linen, and the fresh peppermint that his daughter put in his pocket every morning. He was the one who pulled her the final few inches into a hug. She rested her forehead against his jawbone, closed her eyes, and let her nose almost graze the side of his neck as she breathed him in.

"It's good to see you," he murmured.

"Yes."

When she opened her eyes, much of the conversation on the patio had stopped. People were looking at them. She cleared her throat and stepped back, feigning nonchalance. She was used to the stares. Jack was African-American, born and bred in D.C., street-smart with a professorial edge. She was blond and blue-eyed, slowly learning to tamp down her earnest Midwestern smile. Even in the diverse District, they drew the occasional double take.

"You look beautiful," Jack said. "Tall."

"You too," she laughed. The four-inch heels she wore with her little black dress were a departure. Even with the extra height, she was two inches shorter than Jack. She felt both glamorous and unsteady.

They sat at the round iron table, the candle throwing soft light onto Jack's angular cheekbones. A waiter came and gestured to the wine list. She didn't know wine, so she just chose a bottle of champagne in the middle. It cost more than she'd normally spend on groceries for a week, but what the hell, it might be the biggest night of her life. Jack raised his eyebrows but didn't comment.

"Thanks for coming," she said.

"Of course. Your call was unexpected—but welcome."

Welcome was good. Welcome meant she had a chance.

During their big fight, Anna had been furious at him. But with the passage of time and the perspective that came with it, she realized that she'd been at least partially wrong. Okay, mostly wrong. But that fight was just a symptom of a much larger problem: that Jack had wanted a long-term commitment, while she remained uncertain.

After they broke up, she was heartsick—but knew it was pointless to rekindle their romance unless she was certain she would stay forever. That was only fair to him and his six-year-old daughter. Now that Anna was certain, she didn't know if he still felt the same way.

The waiter came back with a chilled bottle. He popped the cork and splashed an inch of the bubbly into Anna's flute, then stood looking at her expectantly. It took her a moment to realize she was supposed to taste the champagne. Growing up, it had been a big deal when her mom took them to Denny's. She took a sip and paused, as if making a truly discriminating choice. "Excellent," she pronounced. The waiter bowed slightly and poured champagne into both flutes.

Jack was fighting back a smile. He was ten years older and, it sometimes felt, decades wiser.

"How are things on the ninth floor?" she asked.

"Okay." Jack was chief of the Homicide unit, one of the most prestigious positions in the country's largest U.S. Attorney's Office. He described the challenges of a recent hiring freeze. But Anna found it difficult to process his words. She was staring at his mouth, wondering how he would respond to her Big Question. What if he said no? What if he said yes? She couldn't make it through an entire dinner without knowing.

Jack seemed to sense her distraction. He stopped talking about budget cuts and asked, "What's on your mind, sweetheart?"

The endearment kindled her courage. She took a deep breath.

"Jack, I—" She'd tried different versions of her speech all day. But now the words evaporated. Only the core emotion remained. "I love you. My days don't really seem to happen until I tell you about them. I hate every night we're not together."

She reached into her purse and pulled out the little red box from the Tiny Jewel Box. She slid it across the table.

"Open it," she whispered.

He looked at her for a long moment before sliding the box open. Inside was a men's dress watch. It was the single most expensive item she'd ever purchased. Jack looked up again, his face inscrutable. She plowed ahead.

"I—I know this isn't how this is usually done. But I couldn't come back to you, and Olivia, without being able to tell you that I want to spend the rest of my life with you. So I got you a token. To show you how serious I am.

"I know I've made mistakes. And I'm sorry. I never saw how a good relationship works. But I promise I'll do whatever I can to be a good partner to you, and a good mother to Olivia."

She reached over, pulled the watch out of the box, and turned it around so he could read the inscription on the back: I WANT TO SPEND ALL MY TIME WITH YOU.

"Will you marry me?" she asked.

A breeze ruffled the ivy on the wall next to him. The candle on their table danced, sending a shadow flickering over Jack's face. He rocked back in his chair, opened his mouth, and closed it again. It was rare to see the formidable Homicide chief speechless. She became aware of the stares from the other people on the patio, as the silence stretched into an eternity of heart-pounding, stomach-clenching anticipation. Finally, Jack took the watch from her hands and slowly returned it to the box.

"Anna," he said softly. "No."

3

Tierra curled up on the mattress, trying to cover her naked body with trembling arms. She watched the man holding the machete to Ricardo's throat. The brothel owner was skinny everywhere except his belly, which was so round and fat, it looked like he'd swallowed a basketball. He wore a white undershirt, black socks, and a purple condom, which shriveled and splatted to the floor.

"Gato, please," Ricardo croaked. "Stop."

"Oh, am I hurting you?" Gato replied in Spanish. "Pardon me." He threw an elbow into Ricardo's face. Ricardo's nose crunched, bent, and spouted blood. The two men standing by the bed laughed.

"You think you're hurt now," said the one nearest Tierra. "We haven't even gotten started." This man wore a crazy grin, which widened as he looked down at her. He grabbed a handful of her hair and yanked her across the mattress toward him. She yelped in pain.

"Where are the other girls?" Gato asked. He shifted the machete so the blade lay on Ricardo's chest.

The brothel owner opened his mouth, but nothing came out. Gato sighed and put his weight into the steel; it sliced through Ricardo's undershirt and drew a diagonal red line across his chest.

Ricardo shrieked, "Their car broke down on I-95! Please, stop!"

Gato eased up on the blade. "How unlucky. You believe him, Psycho?"

"It doesn't matter. The unlucky one is this *puta*."

The grinning man called Psycho tightened his grip on Tierra's hair and ran the blade of his machete softly up her thigh. The room tilted and swayed; Tierra thought she might faint.

"Can I go first?" asked the third man. He appeared to be the youngest of the three. "I never get to go first." Like the others, he spoke Spanish peppered with English. His eyes were glassy and unfocused.

"You'll wait your turn, Bufón," said Psycho. "Gato, you want the honors?"

Keeping the brothel owner pinned to the wall, Gato glanced over at Tierra. Instead of the cruelty she expected, she found sympathy in his face. Desperate hope flashed through her. This Gato might actually help her. She pleaded with her eyes. But Gato blinked and looked back at Psycho.

"No, man. I'm handling this *cabron*. You do it."

"My pleasure."

Psycho unbuttoned his pants, letting go of her hair as he fumbled with his zipper. Tierra forced herself not to run. She wouldn't stand a chance if she fought or struggled. No, she'd do whatever these men told her, whatever it took to survive. She'd been screwing strange men all day. Three more wouldn't kill her. She hoped. She looked down submissively, preparing herself for the worst. But she wasn't prepared for what happened next.

A fourth intruder stepped silently through the bedroom door. In his right hand he carried a bloody machete. In his left, he held up the severed head of the *cuidador*, the doorman who was supposed to be guarding the brothel. The *cuidador*'s face was frozen midscream; his ragged neck dripped blood onto the floor.

Tierra shuddered at the head, but the beast who held it terrified her even more. He was dressed like the others, in a trench coat and jeans, but Tierra understood that he was not human. His skin was entirely covered with dark hieroglyphs. His nose was just two nostrils sunken into his face. He had long black hair—and two fleshy horns protruding from his forehead.

He was the Devil.

She was vaguely aware of the warm wetness spreading on the mattress, as she lost control of her bladder.

"*I* am first," the Devil said.

He tossed the severed head across the room to Psycho, who caught it with a grunt and a grin. A line of scarlet droplets spattered the wall. The Devil rolled the machete in his hand and looked down at Tierra. He licked his lips and smiled, revealing a row of gleaming white teeth, each sharpened to a point.

She screamed and screamed, but no sound came out.

• • •

Hector Ramos walked down the quiet street of row houses. Although the sky was dark, the night was warm. It had been a hot day for early October, and heat still radiated from the pavement, releasing the scent of asphalt and motor grease. The usual urban activity buzzed from a distance: cars honking on Thirteenth Street, sirens pealing a few blocks over. A man in a suit hurried past, engrossed in something he was texting. This street was a few blocks from Tivoli Square, a historic complex whose renovation had recently caused a wave of gentrification. But many of the longtime Hispanic residents remained, and this was now a diverse and vibrant neighborhood.

It still had some blemishes, though. The brothel operating on Monroe Street was one of them. The redbrick row house looked like all the others on this street, although it hadn't been fixed up like some of its neighbors. The shutters were peeling, the porch sagged, the windows were caked with filth. Weeds clumped in a mostly dirt yard.

The brothel was small but a nuisance on the block. The neighbors didn't appreciate the stream of men going in and out in regular fifteen-minute intervals. Complaints had been made; a quick investigation launched; a confidential informant reported four girls working ten hours a day in the basement apartment. Last week, Hector had conducted an afternoon of surveillance. Based on the number of men he saw, each girl might be handling a hundred customers a week.

Hector could have brought his anticipatory search warrant to any sex-crimes prosecutor in the U.S. Attorney's Office, but he preferred to knock on Anna's door. Not just because she was pretty. Anna was kind and respectful, even when she was correcting some flaw in his warrant. If this bust went well, he'd have a chance to work with her more.

For now, he focused on the row house. There were two things he always worried about at this stage. First, had the informant lied to him, and was he about to raid some innocent family's home? Second, would someone inside try to kill him?

The "Eyes" of the operation would watch with binoculars, and Ralph would listen through the transmitter tucked in Hector's pocket. A fifth officer was waiting in the back alley, securing the rear door. But the arrest team was a block away, and they couldn't see what went down in the brothel. Once Hector was inside, he was on his own.

He would be quick. Go in, hand thirty dollars to the doorman, establish that he would be getting sex in return for the money. Take his poker chip. A real john would give his chip to the next available girl, who would give him fifteen minutes in return. But Hector would "have to go to the bathroom" first. Then the team would raid the place, arrest everyone inside, and search the house for more evidence. It wasn't easy work, but Hector and his team had the routine down. They did it several times a month.

Of course, another brothel would soon pop up a few blocks from here, part of the game of Whac-A-Mole the police played with pimps and prostitutes. But the good citizens of Monroe Street would be appeased. At least for a few months.

Hector trotted down the concrete steps to the front

door of the basement apartment. A couple of dark-haired kids were putting up Halloween decorations on the stoop next door, talking in mixed English and Spanish. Hector made eye contact with a boy who was holding a little plastic skeleton on a string.

"*Hola.*" Hector smiled at the boy as he knocked on the door.

"Shhh." The boy brought a finger to his lips. "The Devil is inside."

The hair on the back of Hector's neck stood up.

4

A woman at the next table was looking at Anna with pity. That was not the reaction Anna had been hoping to elicit tonight. She felt the blood rushing to her cheeks, burning with the pain of rejection and the embarrassment of having it happen so publicly. The latter was her own fault, for popping the question in a crowded restaurant. She tucked the little red box back into her purse, as if hiding the watch could also hide the debacle of presenting it.

"Anna," Jack said gently. "Wait."

She didn't want him to see the hurt on her face. She looked down at her purse, like she was trying to find something in there. Maybe her dignity.

"I understand," she said.

"You *don't* understand." Jack's voice was quiet but firm. "Look at me."

She met his eyes. Despite everything, she still found them a warm and happy place to land.

"When a couple gets engaged," he said, "they have to tell that story over and over again, for years."

She tilted her head.

"I'm a traditional kind of guy. In our story . . ."

Jack's eyes were twinkling. "*I* want to be the one who does the asking."

He pulled out his own little red box, stood up, and walked over to Anna's chair. Then he knelt down on one knee. He opened up the box and turned it toward Anna. Nestled in the white silk was a sparkling diamond on a platinum band. She found it hard to take a breath.

She remembered this ring. It was the one Jack had pointed out when they were at the Tiny Jewel Box a month ago, following up on some evidence in a case involving an escort who was killed at the U.S. Capitol. When Anna realized he was checking out engagement rings for personal reasons, she'd freaked out. That had contributed to their breakup. Now she was overcome with happiness to see the ring again.

"Anna Curtis," he said, grinning. "I think I know the answer to this question. But I'll go ahead and ask. Will you marry me?"

Anna looked at the man kneeling in front of her. She wanted to take in every detail of this moment, knowing she would replay it for the rest of her life: Jack, holding the ring out like a glittering promise of their future, his green eyes glowing with happiness, his mouth curved into a broad white smile.

"Yes!" The word came out in a hiccup. She realized she was crying. Her hands were shaking, but he held the left one steady as he slipped the ring onto her finger.

They were both standing, arms around each other, her body pressed hard against his. She kissed him as tears streamed down her cheeks.

The sound of clapping brought her back to the present. They pulled apart and saw that the rest of the restaurant was cheering for them. Jack grinned at her. He looked young and radiant and ridiculously happy.

"We should've asked for a bulk discount at the Tiny Jewel Box," he said.

She laughed through her tears, feeling giddy. "When did you buy the ring?"

"Before we even went there for the Capitol case." He took a napkin from the table and dabbed her cheeks.

"And you've been carrying it around ever since?"

"I couldn't bring myself to return it. It's been sitting in my nightstand. That's why I was late. Your friend Grace tipped me off. I ran home and got it."

"Grace! I swore her to secrecy."

"It was all in pursuit of a worthy cause."

He twined his fingers with hers and held up her hand so they could look at the ring on her finger. It sparkled even in candlelight.

"How are we going to tell the office?" Anna asked. They'd kept their relationship a secret until now.

"Forget the office," Jack laughed. "How are we going to tell Olivia?"

His sassy six-year-old daughter was either going to be Anna's biggest fan or her severest critic. But Anna put aside her worries about office politics and family drama. She stepped back into Jack's embrace. She just wanted to bask in the bliss of getting engaged to the man she loved. They'd figure out everything else tomorrow.

5

A moment after Hector knocked, a woman began yelling from inside the brothel.

"Ayúdeme! Ayúdeme!"

Her voice was muffled, but her words were unmistakable.

"A woman is calling for help inside." Hector spoke loudly toward his pocket so the arrest team would hear him through the transmitter. "I need backup. I'm going in."

Cursing under his breath, he pulled the Glock from the back of his jeans, braced himself, and kicked the door to the basement apartment. It buckled open. Hector swung into the brothel, gun first. So much for the plan. There would be no evidence collection, no orderly execution of a search warrant. Not when there was a woman screaming for help.

The dim hallway smelled of cigarettes, latex, and sex. Hector's eyes skimmed the interior and landed on a hulking shape at the end of the hall. One man was crouched over another, rifling through his pockets. The crouching man sprang to his feet, holding a machete. He was young, with the glassy, unfocused eyes of the very high.

"Stop!" Hector yelled. "Police!"

The man raised his machete and charged at him, screaming obscenities in Spanish. Hector had years of training and experience; he'd practiced hundreds of drills—but a guy charging with a machete was still a heart-stopping moment.

Hector fired twice into the man's center mass. The machete clattered to the floor. The guy dropped a couple of yards from Hector's feet. Burned gunpowder overpowered the brothel's other smells.

The sound of gunshots inside the apartment was stunning. Hector had been on the Metropolitan Police Department for ten years; he had fired his Glock countless times on the range and in MPD training. But he'd never shot a person. His ears rang from the noise; his heart pounded from the shock of what he'd just done.

Ralph and the others rushed inside behind him. Ralph knelt down and started cuffing the guy Hector had shot. No telling what damage the shots had done—the man still had to be incapacitated.

Hector stepped around Ralph and approached the prone man whose pockets the machete guy had been going through. His hands and feet were bound with duct tape—but his entire head was gone. Where there should have been a face there was just a pool of blood on dirty carpet. Hector swallowed back a wave of bile and kept going.

The hallway deposited him into a dark and musty living room. The main source of light was a boxy old TV with porn playing on it. "Ah, ah, ah!" the woman on TV moaned, her breasts bouncing frantically as she rode the man beneath her. A cheap plastic stopwatch was tacked to the wall, to track the time each john was allowed. A bookshelf was overturned, its stash of condoms, lube, and VHS porn tapes scattered on the floor. A few dingy couches slouched around the TV. Several of the cushions had been sliced open, and bits of the inner fluff floated through the air.

Another man lay on a couch; he was also bound in duct tape, with a piece of tape over his mouth. This man was alive and terrified. He met Hector's gaze and signaled with his head toward the back rooms.

Hector strode to a bedroom and threw open the door. There were two mattresses separated by a curtain, but otherwise the room was empty. He moved to the next bedroom.

It took him a moment to process the scene. A naked woman curled on a mattress, sobbing. Next to the bed, a grinning man scrambled to pull up his pants, which were tangled around his ankles. A severed human head—presumably from the body in the hallway—was impaled on top of a cheap bedside lamp. It dripped blood onto the lightbulb, which flickered in protest.

Two men in trench coats were fumbling with the lock on the bedroom's back door, which led outside to the back alley. They held a third man, who wore only a bloody white T-shirt and black socks. Hector recognized him from his mug shot—Ricardo Amaya, the brothel owner, the man Hector had come here to arrest.

One of the two thugs was an average-looking Hispanic male, but the other seemed to be wearing some sort of mask. Hector's eyes went to their hands, assessing the threat they presented. Both thugs carried machetes, but unlike the fool in the front hallway, they didn't raise them at Hector. Instead, they opened the back door and stepped outside into the dark alley, dragging the half-naked brothel owner with them.

Hector could see another officer outside in the alley, guarding the rear door. The weird-looking thug hurled Ricardo at the officer. The officer was bowled over; he and the brothel owner fell in a tangled heap to the ground. The two thugs took off running.

Meanwhile, the man with his pants around his ankles was reaching toward a machete on the floor. Hector kicked the machete away and slammed the guy, chest-first, into the wall. Hector cuffed him, then shoved him into Ralph's arms.

"Call for backup," Hector said. "Two Hispanic males with machetes, wearing jeans and trench coats, running west toward Fourteenth Street."

Hector ran through the bedroom's back door and out into the dark alley. He could see the two thugs rounding the corner, more than a block away. He sprinted after them.

6

An hour later, Detective Tavon McGee knelt down in the brothel's front yard. The flashing police lights illuminated a little plastic skeleton lying in the dirt. With gloved hands, he pinched the string attached to the plastic skull and held up the figurine. The little skeleton seemed to dance on its cord as the detective examined it with a flashlight.

McGee filled his lungs with the warm night air, momentarily relieved to study the kitschy representation of death as opposed to the real thing. The scene inside the brothel was a bloody mess. Two corpses: one downed by the double-tap of a police Glock, one duct-taped and decapitated. Three injured: the brothel owner with his chest carved up, drifting in and out of consciousness; a second man, duct-taped and confused; and a naked prostitute, bruised and bloody, sobbing nonsensically about *el diablo*. The three survivors were on their way to Howard University Hospital; the two dead were headed to the Medical Examiner's Office.

The crime-scene techs had their work cut out for them: dozens of used condoms in the garbage can in the bedroom. Blood spattered on the bedroom walls. Broken furniture strewn around the living room.

It was a messy scene, and it was going to be a messy case. Two of the invaders had gotten away. The police involved in the shooting would not be able to work the case. A Use of Force investigation would be launched, to determine whether Hector Ramos's shooting was justified. All of the officers would be placed on administrative leave pending the decision. Their union attorneys might not let them talk for weeks, if not months. McGee would have to figure much of this out on his own.

He was a homicide detective, had been for over twenty years. He was used to sorting out the relationships between the living and the dead.

A movement in the row house next door caught his eye. A dark-haired kid was cracking open the front door and peering out. The boy was maybe five years old, with knobby knees and wide brown eyes.

"This yours, little man?" McGee called. He held up the plastic skeleton. The kid nodded. McGee walked up the steps to the boy's porch. The metal railing around the porch was decorated with dozens of identical little skeletons, as well as black rubber bats and pipe-cleaner spiders. Ghosts made of wispy white sheets hung from the ceiling, twirling slowly in the breeze. McGee handed the little skeleton to the boy. "What's your name?"

"I'm not 'posed to talk to strangers."

"It's okay. I'm the police."

McGee touched the badge hanging from a thin

chain around his neck. The kid still looked worried. McGee knelt down so their heads were almost the same height. Then he smiled, revealing the gummy gap where his two front teeth used to be.

Tavon McGee was 6'4", 290 pounds, with skin the color of espresso beans. He could use his bulk to intimidate witnesses or bureaucrats. But with kids, the key was getting down on their level—and smiling. The gap in McGee's front teeth made children feel like he was one of them. Folks speculated on why he didn't get the hole fixed. Fact was, he'd solved more than one homicide because some child felt comfortable talking to him. No one could argue with the highest case-closure rate in D.C.

The boy said, "My name's Jorge."

"That must've been pretty scary, what you saw next door, Jorge."

The kid looked down at the little skeleton in his hands.

"But I'm guessing you were brave, right?"

The boy met his eyes and nodded.

"What happened?"

"The Devil told me to shush," the boy whispered. "Then he went in there with his friends."

"What do you mean, the Devil?"

The kid held two index fingers to his forehead, simulating horns.

A woman appeared in the doorway. "Jorge!" she cried. "*Venga aqui! Ahora!*"

The kid ran into the house. McGee stood up, his

knees creaking in protest. The woman tried to shut the door in his face, but he stuck a foot into the doorjamb.

"Ma'am, I need to talk to your son."

"No hablo íngles."

She pushed on the door, putting pressure on McGee's foot. He held up his badge and cocked his head. She reluctantly allowed him inside.

Ten minutes later, he walked back out again, with the names and DOBs of everyone in the house—but no further information about the crime next door. Mom refused to allow the kid to talk to him any more. McGee would return tomorrow with a subpoena requiring the boy to testify in the grand jury. But he knew how these things worked. By tomorrow, Jorge's mother would have convinced him that he hadn't seen anything. McGee sighed and brushed a ghost out of his way as he went down the steps.

Hector Ramos came out of the brothel's basement door, leading a young Hispanic man in handcuffs. The handcuffed man grinned at McGee. He'd been smiling all night. It was a strange smile, completely inappropriate for his situation. McGee wondered what the hell was wrong with him. The man wasn't carrying ID and wasn't giving his name. McGee glanced at the tattoos covering his neck, at the two teardrop tattoos by his eye. They'd find out his name soon enough; no way this gangbanger hadn't been arrested and fingerprinted before.

McGee nodded at the Human-Trafficking detective. Hector was known as a solid cop and a dependable teammate. McGee wondered why he hadn't left MPD for a higher-paying federal job years ago. Putting this mope in the cruiser would be the last official move Hector would make for a while, though. McGee doubted the detective would enjoy his time out on administrative leave. He got the impression that Hector was an action guy.

Hector stopped before putting the thug in the cruiser and spoke to McGee. "Gotta show you something." Hector pulled out an evidence bag with a small photo inside it. "I found this in his pants pocket when I frisked him. You know who this is, right?"

McGee took the bag and looked at it. The police flashers bounced red and blue light on the photograph of a woman's face, smiling and beautiful. McGee knew the face, but she was so out of place and unexpected here, it took him a moment to recognize her. He stopped breathing for a moment. Good Lord.

"Mirandized?" he asked Hector.

"Yeah."

"Why do you have this picture?" McGee held it before the tattooed man.

The guy's weird smile grew. "She's my girlfriend, man."

"The hell she is. Where'd you get this from?"

"Go fuck yourself is where. I want my lawyer."

McGee shoved the guy into the back of the police cruiser and slammed the door. He paced the curb and considered calling Jack Bailey. Jack had a right to know. But McGee had heard what Jack and Anna were up to tonight. He didn't want to ruin this night for them.

He put the picture in his pocket. Let Jack and Anna have one night of happiness and celebration. They deserved it. He'd tell them tomorrow.

7

Colorful lights danced across Anna's eyelids: blue, green, yellow, orange, red. She kept her eyes shut. She was warm and comfortable and exactly where she wanted to be. Jack was spooned against her back, both of them naked. She pushed herself backward, snuggling even closer. His lips brushed her ear and his hand cupped her breast. She murmured happily.

The sound of the doorknob rattling sent a shot of adrenaline coursing through her body. She sat up, clutching the sheet to her chest. Sunlight streamed through the stained-glass arch above the picture window, throwing a colorful checkerboard onto the bed and wood floor.

"Daddy, wake up!" called Olivia's high-pitched voice. The knob rattled again. "Why is the door locked? You're gonna be late for work!"

"Okay, honey, I'm coming." Jack sat up, blinking at his alarm clock. "Ask Luisa to make you some breakfast."

"Duh! I already did." Little footsteps trotted away from the door.

Anna smiled at him. "Tough crowd."

"You think so now? Wait till we tell her we're getting married."

"I know. I'm scared."

"Kidding." He kissed her and climbed out of bed. She let her eyes wander over his long, athletic body. "I think she's going to be really happy to hear it. She's been asking about you a lot."

"Mm. That seems unlikely."

Back when Anna and Jack were just friends, Olivia seemed to like her. But the little girl cooled when she realized Anna was taking an important place in her father's heart. Anna tried to win her over, and eventually thought she and Olivia were having a breakthrough. That was right before Anna's big fight with Jack. She hadn't seen the little girl since.

Jack and Anna padded to the bathroom. She felt content and pleasantly achy from their exertions the night before. She loved showering with him again, soaping him up, talking about their day as the steam clouded the shower door. *My fiancé*, she thought, watching him run a razor over his scalp. *My future husband. My family.* The words sent a bolt of happiness through her.

She was done showering first. She wrapped one towel around her head and one around her torso and went into the bedroom. Her phone flashed with a new text message.

Jody Curtis: Well?

Anna called her sister. Jody lived in Michigan, and was all the family Anna had.

"What happened?" Jody answered breathlessly.

"He said yes! Actually, he said no, but then he proposed to me."

"Congratulations! He's obviously a very wise man." Jody made Anna describe the entire night in detail.

"He's amazing," Anna concluded. "Just—the best man I know."

"You're gushing. It's cracking me up. I love it."

"I can't wait for you to meet him. When can you come to D.C.?"

"In three weeks?"

"Great! We can go wedding-dress shopping. You'll be my maid of honor, right?"

"I better be. But I'm not sure that title works. Can I be your maid of dishonor?"

"Perfect." Anna laughed, then quieted. It felt unfair that she should be so happy when Jody was going through a rough time. "How are things on your end?"

"Actually," Jody lowered her voice. "I'm just getting dressed at Brent's house now."

"Jo! I thought you decided no more of his booty calls."

"Oh, Annie. One more walk of shame isn't gonna make a difference."

"You deserve better than this."

"Not everyone finds Prince Charming. Some of us have to settle for the frogs."

"That is so wrong. No one should settle for a frog. Especially not you."

Anna could hear a muffled male voice in the background.

"Gotta go," Jody said. "Love ya."

"No frogs!"

The line clicked.

Jack stuck his head out of the bathroom door. "You dealing with a plague?"

"Yeah, the plague of my sister's ex-boyfriend." Anna sighed and used the towel to dry her hair. She wondered how she could convince Jody to believe in herself enough to stop hooking up with cheating, lying Brent—without coming across as the obnoxious big sister who thought she had the world all figured out.

For now, Anna just had to figure out how to dress for the day. She went to Jack's closet, where a few of her clothes still hung, a remnant of their prebreakup era. She pulled some pieces out, trying to create an outfit from the wardrobe scraps. She'd have to stop by her apartment and get more clothes and her cat tonight.

She dressed in a black pantsuit and sensible pumps—the uniform of female prosecutors—and a lacy ivory camisole that felt fittingly bridal. As Jack buttoned up his shirt, she opened the window shade and gazed out. It was wonderful to be back here, looking at the mature trees and historic homes. She knew this place better than she knew her own apartment in the city. The neighbors, the mail carrier, even the gardeners setting up to mow Jack's yard were familiar.

When she turned around, Jack was knotting a red tie. She smiled at how handsome her future husband looked in a suit.

"Ready?" he asked her.

She might *never* feel ready to face Olivia. But she nodded.

He held her hand, and they walked down the wooden steps of his old Victorian. Anna noticed, as she always did, the picture hanging in the hall by Olivia's room. It was a studio portrait of Jack and his late wife, holding an infant Olivia between them. Nina Flores had been a beautiful police officer, killed in the line of duty four years ago. Jack rarely spoke about it. But Nina's presence was everywhere in the house. Nina was the one who'd painted Jack's bedroom walls red, who'd hung the lacy curtains in Olivia's room, who'd planted the peach tree in the front yard. Anna was very aware that she was stepping into a household that another woman had created. She supposed she would make her own mark eventually. She would try to do it while respecting the woman who'd come before.

They followed the voices to the sunny kitchen at the back of the house. Olivia was sitting at the counter, eating scrambled eggs and toast. She wore a pink T-shirt, and her wavy black hair was in two low ponytails. The little girl had creamy caramel skin and her father's luminous green eyes. They were leveled on her nanny with the intensity of an expert negotiator sizing up her opponent. Luisa stood at the counter, packing lunch into a *Princess and the Frog* lunch box.

"Please, Luisa, can I just have a jelly sandwich? There's enough protein in the cheese stick and yogurt."

"No, *cosita*, we need to get some meat on your bones. Jelly is not enough. How about a turkey sandwich?"

"How about half a turkey and half a jelly?"

Luisa put her hands on her wide hips and frowned at the little girl. "Do you promise to eat both?"

"Of course!" The little girl flashed a winning smile.

"Okay, okay," Luisa grumbled cheerfully. Olivia grinned in triumph. As Luisa pulled the jam from the fridge, she caught sight of them in the doorway.

"Well hello, Miss Anna!" said the nanny. "How nice to see you back here!"

Olivia's eyes lasered to the doorway. They widened when she saw Anna. Anna braced herself for rejection. But the little girl surprised her.

"Anna!" she screeched as she clambered down from the stool. Olivia ran full throttle into Anna's arms. "I missed you!"

Olivia hugged her so tightly, Anna could barely breathe. "I missed you, too." Anna put her arms around the little girl, tentatively at first, then with more confidence. It was the first real hug Olivia had ever allowed her. It felt wonderful. She kissed the girl's soft cheek, and noticed that she was wearing the *Princess and the Frog* barrettes Anna had given her a while back.

Olivia pulled back and held Anna's shoulders sternly while she spoke. "Don't leave us again."

"I won't."

"In fact," Jack scooped up Olivia, "I took your suggestion. I asked Anna to marry us."

"What'd you say?" Olivia searched Anna's face.

"I said yes."

"Yay!" Olivia hopped down from Jack's arms and jumped up and down in circles, clapping. "Yay! Yay!

Can I be a flower girl? Can I help pick the band? Can we invite my friends?"

"Yes to everything." Anna was filled with unexpected joy. She had loved Olivia for a long time. The fact that Olivia loved her back was more than she had hoped for.

A movement in the kitchen made Anna look up. Luisa was crossing herself. Her skin had gone pale and slack. *"Dios mío,"* she whispered.

"What's wrong?" Anna asked. She and Luisa had always had a friendly, easy relationship.

"N-nothing." Luisa shook her head. "Congratulations. I am very happy for you."

The nanny turned to the counter and continued making sandwiches. But her hands were shaking as she spread jam on bread. She whispered something in Spanish under her breath. It sounded like a prayer. Anna glanced at Jack, who shook his head, looking as perplexed as she felt.

8

"Oh my God!" Grace squealed. She held Anna's hand and examined the ring. "It's gorgeous! Gotta be at least one-point-two carats—and on platinum. Girl, he spent a pretty penny on you."

Anna smiled at her best friend. Grace was an elegant black woman with a sharp mind and an impressive collection of designer shoes stashed in her filing cabinets. Two years earlier, she and Anna had started together in the Domestic Violence Misdemeanor unit. The experience had been difficult but rewarding, akin to boot camp—it broke them down and built them back up, and bonded them in a way that few other jobs could. Over the years they'd worked their way up through the office's rotation together, taking on more responsibility and more serious cases. Now they were both senior sex-crimes prosecutors. Grace was the only person in the office who'd known that Anna and Jack were dating. Grace had gone with Anna to the Tiny Jewel Box to pick out the watch for Jack.

"I can't believe you tipped him off," Anna said.

"Look, I love you both, you know that." Grace lowered her voice. "But he's gonna get enough grief from the sisters for marrying a white woman. It'll be fine—don't frown—but he didn't need the additional twist of a reverse-gender proposal. Trust me on this."

Anna nodded, forgiving her friend. She tried to brush away her anxiety at the thought of people judging their relationship and finding her wanting.

"Think of all the money you could've saved on that watch," Grace said, cheerfully changing the subject.

"No, he needed to hear it from me, first," Anna said. "And I like the idea of something from me being with him all day."

"Yeah. Why is it the woman is marked as 'taken' as soon as a couple gets engaged, while the man isn't until *after* the wedding?"

"The same reason women traditionally take their husband's name, instead of vice versa."

"What will you do? Anna Bailey has a nice ring to it."

"I'll figure it out later. The more important question now is: Will you be a bridesmaid?"

"Of course!" Grace trilled, and they hugged some more.

The noise brought more women. Soon Anna's office was crowded with prosecutors, paralegals, and advocates, all wanting a turn looking at her ring. They peppered Anna with questions—who, where, when, and how. Jack was right; she was going to tell this story, and all of its details, many times.

"My goodness, what's going on here?"

The women quieted. The chief of the Sex Crimes

unit stood in Anna's doorway. Carla Martinez, a lovely Hispanic woman with a Puerto Rican accent, looked impeccable as always in a ruffled white blouse, long-beaded necklace, and black pencil skirt. Her dark hair hung in a chic bob. Carla was senior enough to transcend the black-pantsuit uniform of junior prosecutors.

"Anna got engaged," Grace announced.

"Congratulations!" Carla smiled warmly at her. "Who's the lucky man?"

"Jack Bailey," Anna said.

"Oh." Carla's smile disappeared. Carla and Jack had a notorious rivalry, always competing to get the best cases and prosecutors for their two sections. The ongoing turf war between Homicide and Sex Offense was infamous in the office. Carla recovered with a polite nod. "My best wishes to both of you."

Anna thanked her boss, wondering what history lay behind that cool facade.

"Jack's gorgeous!" said a secretary.

"No wonder you got that Capitol case last year," said another prosecutor, only half in jest.

Anna sighed. The snarkiness was part of the reason she'd kept their relationship secret for so long. In many ways, the office was like high school, with a hierarchy based on seniority and laced with gossip. The rotation system—where lawyers moved through ever-more important sections of the office—stoked competition, making everyone talk about who was getting promoted faster. Anna wanted people to appreciate her lawyering on the merits, not see her as a little hussy sleeping her way to the top. Even though she wasn't in the Homicide unit, and Jack didn't supervise her, she knew that people would talk—and that not all the talk would be generous.

Carla held a manila file in her hands. "One of your warrants came in last night, Anna. If you have time, I'd like you to paper it."

"Of course," Anna said. Senior prosecutors typically papered their own cases.

The rest of the women took the cue, murmuring good-byes and shuffling out of Anna's office. Anna took the file from her boss and glanced at the information written on the front of the jacket:

Defendant:	Jose Garcia, aka "Psycho," DOB 3/17/93
Lead Charge:	First Degree Murder while armed (machete) (Jaime Lopez), Felony Murder (B-1), Attempted First Degree Sexual Assault w/a (machete), B-I w/a (machete)
Holds Requested:	B(1)(A) - Dangerous crime / crime of violence
Stay Away/ No Contact:	Tierra Guerrero, Ricardo Amaya
Prior Convictions:	Simple Assault (2012), B&E (2012), Simple Assault (2011)

Anna grimaced as she skimmed the PD-163, which described in broad strokes what had happened last night. Flipping to the next form, she recognized the warrant she'd signed for Hector Ramos. It obviously hadn't gone the way Hector had planned.

"Do we know if the sexual assault was completed?" Anna asked. According to the paperwork, the prostitute had been so distraught, she hadn't made much sense when talking to police on the scene.

"It's not one hundred percent clear, but you can drop the 'attempt' and go with straight sex assault if you get a more solid statement from her."

"Sex kit?"

"Yes, last night."

"Where is she now?"

"Still at Howard University Hospital. She had some pretty severe injuries. Not clear how she got them."

"I'll go talk to her after the initial appearance."

"Good. Focus on finding the two who got away. There's a Use of Force investigation, so don't be surprised if the officers won't talk to you for a while. Tavon McGee's your lead. He'll fill you in."

A few minutes after Carla left, McGee ambled into Anna's office. He carried a McDonald's bag in one hand and tipped his black fedora with the other.

"Good morning, madam prosecutor!"

"McGee," Anna smiled at the big detective. She adored him. Her first big domestic violence trial was with him, and he'd looked out for her ever since. He was also a good friend of Jack's. "You probably didn't get much sleep last night."

"Haven't slept yet." He flashed his gap-toothed smile at her, then lowered his big frame into a chair. His eyes glanced down at her hand. "Did you get engaged?"

"Yes." She looked down at her ring, which sparkled under the fluorescents. A thrill of happiness warmed her. "To Jack."

"About damn time. Congratulations!"

"Thanks." Anna laughed. She hadn't told McGee they were dating—but the detective didn't miss much. "You'll be invited to the wedding. So, tell me what happened with the gentleman called 'Psycho' last night."

"It's a hot mess." McGee handed her a box of chicken tenders and unwrapped a Big Mac for himself. Between bites of his burger, McGee described the brothel raid and the carnage inside. "In the end, there were two bodies. Decapitated doorman. And Hector Ramos shot one of the bad guys."

"Hence Psycho's felony murder charge," Anna said. Psycho was legally responsible for anyone who was killed while he was committing a felony, even if that person was his accomplice. "What evidence do we have on the guys who got away?"

"Lots of usable prints in the brothel, we'll run 'em. But hundreds of guys go in there every week."

"Did they get the bedsheets?"

"Yeah. Also the condom Psycho was wearing, one used condom on the floor—purple—and twenty-five used condoms in the garbage can." He showed her a picture. "Most are gonna be from paying clients."

Anna felt sorry for the poor DNA analyst who'd

have to parse through the seminal swirl at the bottom of the plastic bucket.

"We'll try to flip Psycho," she said. "Get him to distinguish the rapists from the johns."

Anna looked at Psycho's arrest photos. The man had several tattoos; some were gang symbols.

"MS-13," she murmured. The gang was a growing problem in D.C. They were notoriously violent, ruthless, and getting larger every month. "Did you put these tattoos and their meaning in the *Gerstein*?"

"You want me to?"

"Yep."

McGee handed Anna his thumb drive. She stuck it into her computer and pulled up the *Gerstein*, the document McGee would sign under oath, and which would be the basis of detaining Psycho. When Anna argued in court, she would be limited to the facts written in the *Gerstein*'s four corners, so now was the time to include anything she needed. Anna worked with McGee to flesh out the document. As she printed out the final version, she got a phone call from the courthouse. Psycho's case would be called soon.

"Okay." She stood. "Let's go."

"Wait. I gotta show you something." McGee frowned and pulled a plastic evidence bag from his suit pocket. "I don't know that this has anything to do with anything. But you should know—Hector Ramos found it in Psycho's pocket."

She took the clear bag and smoothed it onto her desk. It held a picture of a smiling, beautiful woman. Anna's stomach somersaulted. She'd passed that face in Jack's hallway, hundreds of times. She'd secretly compared her own face to it. The photo was of Jack's late wife.

"Oh my God," she said. "What was Psycho doing with a picture of Nina Flores?"

"He wouldn't say."

"Does Jack know?"

"Not yet. I figured I'd give you two lovebirds a night off."

Anna glanced at her watch. "We'll tell him after the hearing."

McGee nodded, and put his fedora back on. Although he didn't need to come, McGee walked her to the courthouse.

C-10 was the sole courtroom on the lowest level of D.C. Superior Court. It was bigger than other courtrooms and accommodated a larger crowd. Every person who was arrested for a violation of D.C. law was processed here after their arrest. That often included hundreds of people a day.

A thin layer of grime covered every surface. Rows of unforgiving wooden benches were filled with families and friends, looking miserable and washed out under the fluorescents. Between them and the well of the court were two pointless walls of bulletproof Plexiglas. This barrier would stop only the most random of bullets, because there was a four-foot gap between the two Plexiglas walls, for the aisle that led from the audience to the judge's bench. The Plexiglas was just barrier enough to tell the audience that the court didn't trust them, without providing much protection for courtroom personnel.

Anna walked down the gray linoleum aisle toward the front of the courtroom. She tried to keep her thoughts on the case, but she kept circling back to the picture. Why would a thug be carrying a photo of a police officer, four years after her death?

She barely noticed the stench of the courtroom. The defendants were coming from a night in lockup: unshowered, hungover, or still drunk, often in clothes stained with beer, vomit, or urine. For the prostitutes who had to spend the night in skimpy clothing, the government provided Tyvek paper jumpsuits, dubbed "bunny suits." The Marshals wore rubber gloves when they led the defendants in and out, and sprayed Lysol on the hard surfaces every thirty minutes or so. There were no windows in the basement courtroom and the ventilation system was either broken or disastrously weak, so the pungent air hung in a visible cloud, making everything appear grainy. Several audience members held the collars of their T-shirts over their noses.

An old lady reached out and grabbed Anna's sleeve, pulling Anna from her thoughts. The old woman's eyes were cloudy with cataracts. Her gnarled hands trembled.

"Excuse me, miss, can you tell me how much my grandson's bail will be?"

Anna leaned down and whispered, "There's no bail in D.C., ma'am. He'll either be released or held pending a detention hearing. But I can't give you legal advice, I'm a prosecutor. Do you know the name of your grandson's lawyer?"

The old woman shook her head, looking lost. Anna asked her grandson's name, then checked it against the lockup list at the prosecution table: He was charged with homicide—poor grandma. Anna wrote the defense attorney's name and phone number on a Post-it Note, and went back to kneel beside the old lady.

"This is his lawyer, ma'am. I don't see him here—he may be in the back talking to your grandson. If you don't meet him today, you can call and he'll explain everything to you."

"Bless you, dear."

"Thanks . . . take care." There was nothing else Anna could say that would be useful. She was on the side that was trying to put this woman's grandson in jail.

She went to the prosecution table and pulled her own defendant's rap sheet out of the pile left by PreTrial Services. The table was covered with dozens of case jackets, each of which represented a person who had been arrested the day before and was being presented to a judge today. One overwhelmed prosecutor stood at the front of the courtroom, handling all the initial appearances except murders and first-degree sex offenses, which a specialized senior prosecutor like Anna would do.

During the presentment, each defendant heard the charges against him and got a lawyer assigned if he couldn't afford one, which was the case for many of the defendants in the District. The C-10 judge made a preliminary decision, based on the charging documents, about whether to keep each defendant in custody or release him pending trial. If the defendant was held, a full hearing would be scheduled within a few days, when the government would present witnesses.

Today's C-10 prosecutor stood in front of the bench, making a detention argument about a female defendant who was, oddly, sitting in a chair in the well of the court. On closer inspection, Anna saw that the woman was hugely pregnant and panting. She was in labor. Meanwhile, the prosecutor described how she threw a pan of boiling grease on another woman while on probation for another violent crime. The judge sent her to the hospital to have the baby and remanded her to custody after that. The deputies hurried the woman to the side door, where a paramedic stood, presumably with an ambulance waiting nearby. Anna sent up a quick prayer that they wouldn't see that baby here in eighteen years.

She sat in the vestigial jury box—as far as she knew, there had never been a jury or a trial in C-10—and flipped through the criminal history sheet, looking for any information tying Psycho to Nina Flores. There was nothing she could discern from the report. She speculated: Maybe Nina had previously arrested him. Or perhaps he'd had something to do with Nina's death, and the picture was a trophy.

As more defendants were processed, Anna pulled out her phone and cradled it discreetly on her lap. She went online and clicked around until she found a children's book called *No More Frogs*. It was a parable about environmental degradation, but the title made it work for her purposes. She bought a copy and sent it to Jody.

"Lockup number ninety-two," the clerk intoned. "Ninety-two" was the number written in thick black marker on her case jacket. Jose Garcia, aka "Psycho," was the ninety-second person processed in the last twenty-four hours. Anna put her phone away and walked to the well of the courtroom. The regular C-10 prosecutor looked relieved that he would have a few minutes off his feet. Anna smiled sympathetically at him as he sank into his chair at the prosecution table. It wasn't so long ago that she was a junior prosecutor on C-10 duty.

"Anna Curtis on behalf of the United States."

"Steve Schwalm, from Office of the Public Defender, for the defendant Jose Garcia."

Anna nodded at the defense attorney—she'd had some cases against him; he was an excellent lawyer. Despite the stigma associated with public defenders, D.C.'s Office of the Public Defender was one of the best in the country, with lawyers from top law schools tackling cutting-edge issues and getting outstanding results. But the stigma had power. Some defendants rejected their appointed defender and insisted on paying fifteen thousand dollars for a cut-rate private attorney. The public defender was almost always the better choice.

The deputy Marshals brought the defendant through the side door, and Anna looked him over. She would spend the next nine months thinking and writing and learning about him—but she would see him only rarely, during court appearances.

Jose Garcia, aka "Psycho," didn't look terribly threatening at first glance. He was slim and slight—maybe 5'5". Anna was naturally three inches taller than him, five in her pumps. His hair was shorn tight to his head, like a soldier. He wore an orange prison jumpsuit and "pumpkin seeds," flimsy orange prison sneakers. She hoped this meant his street clothes were bagged and in police custody, awaiting DNA testing. That was the way things were supposed to happen, but "supposed to" didn't always play out in reality.

The man had a baby face, but had taken steps to look more menacing: lines shaved into his eyebrows, tattoos inscribed on his neck. On the left side of his neck was a skeleton hand in the shape of "the claw," pinky and thumb up in a symbol that resembled a surfer's "hang loose" sign. On the right side of his neck was a triangle made up of three big black dots. On the back was a large MS tattoo, elaborately drawn to look three-dimensional. Two tattooed teardrops dripped from his left eye, and more tattoos disappeared under his collar.

But the most disturbing thing about Psycho was his wide smile. The expression was so inappropriate for a shackled man being led into court, Anna wondered if she'd have to deal with an insanity defense. The judge noticed it, too.

"Would you like to share what you find so amusing, Mr. Garcia?" Judge Sofia Menendez asked. She was efficient and no-nonsense, a good match for this cattle call of a courtroom.

Psycho opened his mouth, but Schwalm grabbed him by the arm and whispered fiercely in his ear. Psycho nodded and closed his mouth, although he kept smiling.

"He's just happy to be out of lockup and to have a chance to appear before you, Your Honor," Schwalm said.

The judge narrowed her eyes skeptically, then turned to Anna. "What's the government's position on detention?"

"We're asking for a B1A hold. The defendant committed a crime of violence."

"Defense?"

"Probable cause hasn't been established. According to the government, this was a brothel. There's no evidence that Mr. Garcia wasn't just a paying client, whose transaction was interrupted by three men who came to commit these alleged crimes."

"Prosecution?"

"The defendant was clearly with the other three men raiding the brothel," Anna said. "Fifth paragraph, third line. 'The defendant's fingerprints were identified on a machete found by his feet.' Sixth paragraph: 'The man who was shot wore a trench coat, as did the men who fled. A similar trench coat was found in the bedroom.' Four trench coats, four invaders. It's our theory that the trench coats were worn to conceal their machetes, and Mr. Garcia was the fourth man raiding the brothel. Your Honor can also note the defendant's tattoos. They're symbols representing the gang MS-13, also known as the Mara Salvatrucha. The man who was shot had similar tattoos."

"Is that in the *Gerstein*?" the judge asked. She was familiar with the gang; every judge in the District knew that MS-13 was one of the most violent gangs in America.

"Ninth paragraph. Detective McGee notes that the three-dot tattoo is a symbol of the three places to which MS-13 can lead a gang member: prison, the hospital, or the morgue. The MS and the claw are also symbols of affiliation with the gang."

The judge's pen moved on the paper. "I find there's probable cause to believe the defendant committed the crimes charged. He'll be held in jail pending a preliminary hearing, four days from now. I grant the government's request that he have no contact with the victims."

Anna wrote all this on the case jacket. When she looked up, she found Psycho aiming his weird smile at her. It was unnerving. She was accustomed to hostile glares, but the inexplicable grin felt more malevolent and feral. When she met his eyes, Psycho raised his upper lip a fraction, turning it into a snarl. She got the impression that he wanted to jump across the courtroom and tear her throat out with his teeth.

The clerk called lockup number 93. A deputy took Psycho's arm and led him back to the holding cell. Anna shook off her unease.

In the hallway afterward, Anna spoke to the defense attorney. "Can we get your client in to talk?"

"I thought you'd be interested in that. I asked. He says no."

"First one in the lifeboat gets the best seat. I can offer him a good deal."

"He says he'll never snitch. But I'll try again. What can you tell me? What do you want to know from him?"

"Who were his accomplices, what were they doing? And this." Anna took a copy of Nina Flores's photo from the file. "I want to know where he got it, and why he was carrying it around. Even if he just gives me that, we'll be off to a great start."

"I'll ask. If he changes his mind, I'll call you."

"Thanks." Anna wouldn't count on it.

Back at the U.S. Attorney's Office, she headed to Jack's floor. She had to tell him about Nina's photo. But his office was empty.

"He's in court all day, hon," called Vanetta, his secretary.

Anna spent a few minutes chatting about Vanetta's grandkids. But she felt uneasy as she walked away. She wouldn't feel settled until she could ask Jack about the photo. He would have a logical explanation. He always did.

9

Howard University Hospital was a monolithic brick building on the south side of the college campus. Founded in 1862, it was initially called Freedmen's Hospital and provided medical care for ex-slaves. Today, it was a comprehensive level-one trauma center. Anna knew and liked a lot of the staff, but visiting was rarely a pleasant experience. For her, a trip to HUH usually meant a victim was so badly injured that their first meeting had to take place in a hospital room.

McGee flashed his badge at the receptionist, who directed them to the seventh floor. Kerry Hughes was waiting for them there. The older African-American woman reminded Anna of a fireplug: short, solid, and ready for emergencies. Kerry was a SANE nurse—a Sexual Assault Nurse Examiner—whose specialty was collecting medical and forensic evidence of sex crimes by examining the victim. She was bright, knowledgeable, and tireless. Kerry was the only SANE nurse in D.C., which meant she examined every rape survivor who came in for a sex kit. Anyone less dedicated would have quit years ago.

Kerry greeted them warmly and pulled them into an empty room where she handed McGee a small white box containing Tierra Guerrero's sex kit. The kit included combings from the victim's pubic hair, scrapings from underneath her fingernails, and long Q-tips that had been used to swab her orifices. A sex kit usually included the victim's clothes, but there were none in this case because the victim had been naked when the attack began. McGee would send the box to D.C.'s new DNA lab for analysis.

Kerry handed Anna the SANE papers that contained her findings. Anna automatically turned to the third page and glanced at the gingerbread figurine, on which Kerry had marked X's to indicate areas of injury. The figure had X's on her face, neck, chest, arms, back, and buttocks.

"There were also some of the worst internal injuries I've ever seen," Kerry said softly.

Given the nurse's experience, that was saying a lot. Anna turned to the next page, which had a diagram of female genitalia. Kerry pointed to the marks she'd made on it.

"Vaginal tearing at two o'clock, five o'clock, and ten o'clock. Significant tearing to the perineum. And multiple lacerations to the anus. But the *internal* tearing was the most concerning. Her rectum was ruptured. The surgeons had to go in and sew her up. She could have died."

Anna clenched her jaw and examined the photos Kerry handed her.

"Is she okay to talk to us?" Anna asked.

"You can try," Kerry said. "She doesn't speak much English."

Kerry led them down the hall to a small private room. Anna knocked on the doorframe. The young woman in the bed looked over. Anna maintained a neutral expression, but cringed inwardly. The woman's lip was split, and there was a gash across her forehead. Anna also knew the injuries that lay under her hospital gown. Tierra Guerrero was probably quite pretty before her face was beaten. She had long, dark hair and light hazel eyes. Now she looked frightened and exhausted.

"May I come in?" Anna asked.

The woman tilted her head.

"*Permiso para entrar?*" Anna tried. She'd retained enough high school Spanish to make a few moments of polite conversation.

The woman's face relaxed and she nodded. Anna sat in a chair by her head, McGee by her feet.

"*Me llamo Anna Curtis. Soy abogada para los Estados Unidos. Quiero ayudarla.*" This was the Spanish phrase she knew best: My name is Anna Curtis. I'm a lawyer for the United States. I want to help you.

The woman nodded. Anna explained in halting Spanish the self-evident point that her Spanish was not very good—but that an officer who spoke it was coming soon.

"*Gracias,*" Tierra reached out her hand on the bed and Anna held it. Tierra leaned her head back on the pillow and closed her eyes. Anna sat holding her hand in silence for the next ten minutes.

When Officer Enrique Melendez came in, Anna introduced him and gently started the interview. She asked the officer to explain that they were investigating the crimes that took place in the Monroe Street brothel the night before. Tierra nodded, then said something in rapid Spanish to the officer.

He turned to Anna. "She's worried about being deported."

Anna nodded; this was a common enough concern. "As a crime victim, she's eligible for a U-visa, which would allow her to stay in the country legally while the case is pending, for up to four years. I can help her obtain that visa."

After Melendez translated, Tierra visibly relaxed. Anna started asking some easy basic questions, to get her in the rhythm of talking. Soon Tierra was speaking freely, or as freely as she could with the injuries on her face. McGee took notes as Melendez translated. Anna could understand a few Spanish phrases, but mostly had to rely on the officer's translation.

Tierra was born nineteen years ago in Guatemala. When she was five, her parents immigrated without papers to the United States to find work. For the first ten years, Tierra continued to live in Guatemala with an aunt. Finally, when she was fifteen, her parents sent for her. She made the difficult journey and reunited with parents she barely remembered. They were now living in a one-bedroom apartment in Northern Virginia.

While Tierra had been in Guatemala, her parents had two more children. These younger children, American citizens, were the hope of the family. They had lived with their parents their whole lives, and their parents lavished attention on them. Tierra felt like an outsider from the moment she arrived.

When she was seventeen, she left her family's one-bedroom apartment and moved in with a boyfriend. When that relationship ended, she started moving from friend to friend, couch to couch, trying to find a way to support herself.

At this point in her story, Tierra stopped talking and looked away.

"How have you been supporting yourself?" Anna asked, keeping her expression open and nonjudgmental. She knew the answer, but she needed the young woman to be able to say it. Tierra bit her lip. "Please, just tell me the truth. I can help you if you're truthful. I don't prosecute anyone for prostitution. I prosecute people for sexual assault. The only trouble you'll ever have from me is if you lie."

Tierra looked down at her hands. "I sold myself."

Tierra said she'd begun working at brothels a few months ago. She didn't need papers, and the wages were in cash. She didn't have a pimp. She found work easily enough, but didn't have a steady clientele. The men who went to these brothels wanted new girls—*carne fresca*—every week. She'd built connections in the brothel circuit, and was able to move to a new brothel each week, changing brothels every Sunday.

Anna knew the weekly movement was not just to satisfy johns' desire for new faces—it also kept the women alienated, unable to build friends or allies in any location.

"When did you arrive at the brothel on Monroe Street?" Anna asked.

"Just yesterday morning," the officer translated Tierra's words. "Three more girls were supposed to come from New York, but their pimp called to say their car broke down. It was just the timekeeper, the doorman, and me. I handled as many dates as I could. Twenty-four. I was exhausted." She was supposed to have made three hundred and sixty.

"The man tied up on the couch," Anna said. "Who was he?"

"The timekeeper. His job is to kick out the johns after their fifteen minutes are up."

"And the one whose head—" Anna tried to say it without being gruesome. "Who was killed?"

"The doorman."

"Tell me what was happening when the men arrived."

"Ricardo came, a little before closing time. The owner gets any girl he wants for free. I even took off my T-shirt for him. Normally, men have to pay five dollars extra for that. We were in the middle of it, when . . ." She trailed off.

Anna prompted, "What happened?"

"No." Tierra began to shiver. "I don't want to talk about it."

"Why not?"

"*Habla del Diablo, y él aparecerá,*" Tierra whispered.

"Speak of the Devil and he shall appear," Melendez translated.

Many witnesses were afraid that if they testified against their assailant, he would come after them. Anna leaned forward and met Tierra's eyes.

"Speaking about the Devil is the *only* way to fight him," Anna said. "A witness needs to talk about the crime for it to be brought to justice. We need you to tell us about the men who did this."

Tierra shook her head. "Sometimes evil is not done by men. It's controlled by something much more powerful."

"Evil is a result of choices people make," Anna said. "But people can fight it, too. You start by bearing witness against the person who hurt you."

"You don't understand," Tierra said softly. "He's not a person. He had scales and sharp teeth."

"He was wearing a mask?"

"No." Tierra shook her head. "It was his face. His skin was covered everywhere in black marks. His nose was just holes in his face, like a goat. And he had horns."

"What do you mean, horns?"

Tierra pointed to her forehead.

"What were they made of? Steel, wood, plastic?"

"They were growing under his skin. Round bumps, each the size of a small plum."

Anna glanced at Melendez, wondering if he was getting the translation right. "Am I missing something?" she asked him.

"I'm just telling you what she said." Melendez shrugged. "I don't know what she actually saw."

"It was three men, three MS-13 members." Tierra started crying. "And the Devil."

"Okay, it's okay. You're safe now." Anna handed her a box of tissues. "What happened when the men—and this 'Devil'—came into your room?"

Tierra blew her nose. "The Devil was holding our doorman's head. He threw the head to the man called Psycho. Then the Devil . . ."

"Tell me."

"He raped me. Then he used the handle of his machete. He wanted to hear me scream; he liked it. And when he was done, the one they called Psycho started to rape me."

Anna gently asked the details she needed to know for her case. They had violated Tierra vaginally and anally. They used condoms, throwing them in the same garbage can the johns used.

"They hurt me so much." Tierra's sobs were growing louder. "They didn't just want sex. They wanted to tear me up. The Devil said it was to punish Ricardo. For what, I don't know."

"You're safe now," Anna repeated, putting a hand on Tierra's arm. "You can rest and get better. This is a good place. The doctors will take care of you."

"The doctors can't protect me from the Devil."

Tierra was heaving now, nose running, face red. Anna rubbed her arm, trying to calm her. A nurse came in and told Anna they needed to go, the patient had to rest. Anna and the officers stood.

"There are no devils in this world," Anna told

Tierra. "This was a man. We'll do everything we can to find him and make him pay for what he did."

"You are wrong, Miss Lawyer." Tierra spoke between sobs. "You are kind, and you mean well. But the Devil is real. You can't stop him. No person can."

10

Anna was more concerned with mundane investigative challenges than demonic ones. She wanted to speak to the other two victims, but the timekeeper had been released from the hospital and would have to be tracked down. The brothel owner was both sedated and represented by counsel. Talking to him would be complicated, because he had criminal liability of his own. Anna would have to decide whether to immunize his testimony, and how much of a break to offer him for being a victim of a crime when he was also a perpetrator. For now, her best bet was talking to the officers who'd raided the place—if they would speak to her.

As McGee steered the Crown Vic out of the hospital parking lot, she sat in the passenger seat, scrolling through the contacts in her phone.

"You're wasting your time," McGee said.

"You never know till you try." She dialed a number and put the phone to her ear.

"One of these days, experience is gonna beat that optimism right out of you."

"Shh," Anna said, as the phone rang.

"For the record, I'm not looking forward to that day."

Anna smiled at him. McGee drove the rest of the way in silence as she made calls. Occasionally, he rolled his eyes in response to her end of the conversation.

Of the five officers who'd been at the brothel, three did not pick up. The other two told her she'd have to talk to their union rep first. When Anna called the union rep, he referred her to private defense attorneys whom the union had retained for the officers. And when Anna called the lawyers, they asserted their clients' right to remain silent, until they'd been cleared in the Use of Force investigation. Anna understood where they were coming from, but wondered how she was going to prosecute a case without talking to the police witnesses.

Anna tapped her phone against her leg in frustration. McGee continued to steer the car down the city streets in silence. Anna appreciated that he didn't say, "I told you so."

She considered one more possibility. If she could get the FBI involved, she'd have a whole new world of resources. She called her friend FBI Agent Samantha Randazzo. Anna and Sam had worked together on the case involving the murder of an escort in a congressman's office. They'd gotten off to a rocky start, but had grown to like and respect each other. Anna counted Sam as a friend now.

"Randazzo," Sam answered on the first ring.

"Hey, Sam, it's Anna. I just got an interesting new case. Thought the FBI might want to be involved."

"Deets?"

Anna could hear shouts in the background. Sam worked in the Violent Crime unit, and was probably out with her squad right now. Anna quickly filled her in on what had happened at the brothel.

"So you caught one bad guy, but two more got away, your victims are all criminals, and your cops might be, too," Sam said. "Great case!"

"There are some nice potential federal charges," Anna said, trying to sell the case. "Human trafficking and gang activity, so maybe the seeds of a RICO case."

"Some very tiny seeds," Sam said. "The FBI's not taking brothel cases these days unless they're trafficking minors. And you need a pattern of racketeering activity for RICO. Maybe if you can get your friend Psycho to cooperate. Call me in a week, let me know what you've got, and I'll see what I can do. And, stop by the restaurant sometime. My mom is always asking how you're doing."

"Will do," Anna said.

Anna slid her phone into her purse with disappointment. Samantha wouldn't take a dog of a case out of mere affection. It was a catch-22: If Anna wanted the FBI involved, she'd have to make this a stronger case—but it would be difficult to build her case without the FBI's resources.

As they approached the U.S. Attorney's Office, her phone rang, making her purse shimmy in her lap. It was Hector Ramos. She answered and spoke to him for a few minutes. When she hung up, she turned to McGee with a smile. "He's not using the union's lawyers. And he's willing to talk to us, outside the office. I recommended Sergio's."

"Wonders never cease."

McGee drove a few blocks away, to the Italian restaurant owned by Agent Randazzo's family. It was four o'clock when they walked in, and the place was mostly empty, but it still smelled of fresh-baked garlic bread, spicy tomato sauce, and wood-fired pizza.

A young man came out from the kitchen. Tony Randazzo—Samantha's brother—was Anna's age, tall and dark-haired, with the boisterous charm of a man who ran a neighborhood institution.

"Anna!" He came over and kissed her cheek. "To what do I owe this unexpected pleasure?"

"Hey, Tony. I'm just bringing a couple cops to try the city's best eggplant patties."

"You're not here to see me? Then I don't know if we can fit you in." He looked around the empty restaurant and shook his head. "Do you have a reservation?"

Anna laughed as he led them to a four-top by the front window. Anna had loved the food at Sergio's even before she started working with Sam. Now, when Anna came here, she felt like family. It was nice, since her own family—Jody—lived in Flint.

Tony went into the kitchen and came back carrying a plate heaped with eggplant patties, fried calamari, and butterfly shrimp. He set the plate on their table and sat down with them.

"Eat, eat," he said. "My mother's motto."

"These are my favorite." Anna speared a patty. "How are your mom and dad?"

"Good. They'll be sorry they missed you. You look gorgeous, by the way."

"Being engaged suits her," McGee drawled.

Tony glanced at McGee, then down at Anna's hand. She held up her ring.

"Very nice." Tony sighed. "Is this the guy you were 'just getting over' a few weeks ago?"

"Yep."

Tony had asked her out while she and Jack were broken up. Anna turned him down because she was still in love with Jack. Now she was especially glad she hadn't dated Tony. She could still come here and be friends with everyone, without complications.

"Congratulations." Tony's eyes twinkled again with their usual mischief. "I'm sure he'll make an excellent first husband."

"I'm only planning on doing this once."

"Of course. Still, get a good prenup."

"Get out of here," she said, laughing. "Stop trying to jinx me."

"I would never do that." Tony stood with a smile. "I'm very happy for you."

"Thanks."

When he left, McGee looked at her with narrowed eyes.

"He's just a big joker," Anna said.

"He didn't seem to be joking."

"Oh, he's harmless. Try the shrimp."

McGee was soon mollified—or at least silenced—by the delicious food.

Hector Ramos arrived ten minutes later. Anna felt

sorry for him as soon as he walked in the door. He was a good-looking man: a little taller than her, in his early thirties, muscular, with short brown hair and a goatee. He was quiet, but had an easy smile. At least, he usually did. Today, the skin around his eyes had the bluish rings of someone who hadn't slept in a while. His face was pale and drawn, with stubble on his cheeks. When he sat down, Anna nudged the plate of appetizers toward him, but he shook his head.

"Thanks so much for coming," Anna said. "I know you didn't have to."

"I did."

She nodded gratefully. Hector had the most to risk by talking about the shooting. But perhaps he was also the most interested in making a case against the gang whose member he'd shot.

"How are you doing?" she asked.

"Hanging in."

Most cops went their entire career without ever drawing their guns. Officers who actually shot someone often had a hard time getting over it. Many required years of counseling.

Hector waved over a waiter and ordered three cans of DC Brau. "You all drinking with me?" Anna and McGee shook their heads. Hector tried to smile, but it came off as a grimace. "Oh well, I'm not on duty now. Won't be for a while."

Before Anna even had to ask, Hector started telling her what happened the night before, at the brothel. Anna followed up with questions, getting all the flavor and details that weren't in the police reports. McGee took notes. He would testify to Hector's story at the upcoming preliminary hearing, where hearsay was admissible.

"So what did the guys look like?" Anna asked. "The ones who got away."

"I just saw them for a moment, and I was mostly focused on the machetes. One was a medium Hispanic male. The other was strange—his face was covered in dark markings. Probably tattoos, but a lot of them. And there were two bumps, like horns, growing under his forehead."

"A guy like that can't hide for long," Anna said.

"So you'd think. The Latino Liaison unit has been hearing chatter about a devil-man leading MS-13. So far, it's just street talk."

"Do you think you could help a sketch artist? Or ID either of the two guys in a lineup?"

"There'd be no mistaking the devil guy. I'll try with the other. I don't have a clear picture in my head, though. I just saw him for a second, in the middle of all the chaos." He drained his first beer and opened a second. "Do you know who these guys are?"

"That's what we're trying to find out."

"I mean the gang, MS-13."

"Sure. Street gang from El Salvador. Started in L.A., with the immigrants fleeing the Salvadoran civil war. More established Hispanic gangs preyed on them, and MS-13 sprang up as a form of protection."

"Yeah, but the thing you gotta understand is they're not like other gangs," Hector said. "Bloods, Crips, BGF—they're violent, but they make sense.

Other gangs try to make money, and they use violence to protect their drug business or fight over turf. For MS-13, the violence is the whole point of the gang. Their motto is *'Mata, Viola, Controla.'* Kill, Rape, Control."

Anna nodded. The name Mara Salvatrucha translated roughly into "Watch Out for Us Salvadoran Gangsters." Without so many gang niches taken, MS-13 made its name by being the most terrifying, erratic, and brutal. It had gone viral in recent years, establishing cliques in most major American cities. In the last decade, it had gone from a few thousand members to over fifty thousand worldwide.

"A lot of the members get involved when they're just kids. Then they can't get out. The gang will kill you before they let you quit. I feel sorry for them." For a moment Hector's eyes focused on the far distance. Then they returned to cop bravado. "I don't feel sorry for those motherfuckers last night, though. Seeing what they did to that girl. I should've shot them all." Hector pulled the tab on the third beer and drained it. "You can put that in your report."

"That's okay," McGee said. His pen was lying on the table.

Hector crushed the empty can in his fist and looked at Anna. "Have you figured out why that piece of shit was carrying Nina's picture?"

"You knew Nina Flores?" Anna asked, surprised.

"We went to high school together, joined MPD together. She was one of my best friends, until MS-13 took her out."

"I thought she died in an undercover drug buy."

"That's what we all thought. Now I don't know what to think. Let me just say this. If you want to find these guys, look at the cases Nina was working before she died."

Anna tilted her head. What did Nina's old cases—from four years ago—have to do with the brothel raid last night? Hector held her gaze, his eyes haunted but his face hard.

Tony came over, smiling and holding three plates of tiramisu. "On the house! Congratulations on your engagement, Anna."

Anna tore her eyes from Hector's face. "Thank you, Tony."

No one even looked at the cake. The group was remarkably quiet for people who'd just gotten free dessert.

"Okay then." Tony shrugged and headed back to the kitchen.

"You got engaged?" Hector asked. "I didn't even think you dated. Who are you marrying?"

"Jack Bailey."

"Bailey? Christ." Hector stood with a look of disgust. He fished in his wallet for some bills and tossed them on the table. "Do this for me, will you? Get those guys."

He walked out of the restaurant. The door shook from the force of his push.

"What was that all about?" she asked. "What's with the attitude about Jack?"

McGee shook his head, picked up his spoon, and took a bite of his dessert. "I have no idea. But I know who's going to eat his tiramisu."

• • •

Thirty minutes later, Hector walked into his small, quiet apartment. The daylight was fading, but he didn't turn the lights on. Why bother? Normally, he'd be getting ready for work now. Instead, he was benched. Many cops would love some paid days off, but he wasn't that kind of cop. The enforced sloth might drive him crazy.

No, that wasn't true. It was everything else, converging at once, that might drive him crazy. Nina's photo. The secrets he carried. The fact that Anna was engaged to Jack Bailey, of all people. He wanted to punch something. He wanted to crawl out of his own skin.

He went to the bathroom and ran the shower, making the water as hot as he could stand. Pulling off his T-shirt, Hector glared at his figure in the mirror. In the diminishing light, he could see the musculature of his chest, buff from daily workouts. Unlike his arms and face, his torso was pale. Outside of his home, he always wore a shirt of some kind. Even at the beach—or in the MPD locker room. Especially there.

On his right pec were three black dots. On the left pec, over his heart, were the elaborate, crudely artistic initials: MS. The ink was bluish black, stark against his white skin.

The steam from the shower clouded the mirror, obscuring his image. He raised his hand to wipe away the condensation, then stopped, preferring the blurred version of himself. He stripped off the rest of his clothes and stepped into the hot water.

11

Climbing the steps to Jack's front porch always cheered Anna. Lights blazed from the windows of the yellow Victorian. A pumpkin sat on each step, five in all. The garden was abloom with autumn flowers: dark red mums, apricot roses, black-eyed Susans with petals the color of sunshine. Mature oaks and maples wore leafy haloes of orange, yellow, and red. The air smelled of fresh-cut grass with the sweet-smoky hint of burning leaves.

Anna opened the front door but stopped short when she walked into the foyer. It was like stepping into a florist shop. Vase after vase of purple irises covered the front table, the coffee table in the living room, and the counters in the kitchen. There was a vase everywhere she looked. She couldn't help smiling, even as she worried that Jack must have spent a fortune.

As she set down her bag, a furry orange streak hurled itself against her legs. "Raffles!" Anna bent down with surprised delight and picked up her cat. She'd been planning to get the cat from her apartment tonight. The tabby purred and pushed his head under her chin.

When she set down the cat and straightened up, Jack was smiling next to her. He put his arm around her waist, dipped her like a ballroom dancer, and kissed her. For a long time. When he set her on her feet again she felt a little swoon-y.

"Hi," she said, dizzy with happiness. "How'd Raffles get here?"

"I hope you don't mind," Jack said. "I wanted to surprise you."

He led her upstairs to the bedroom closet. All of her clothes were hanging and folded as they had been before their breakup. In the bathroom, her toiletries were neatly laid out. He'd even moved the book on her apartment nightstand to the nightstand beside his bed.

"Welcome home, love," he said.

"Wow."

She turned to Jack and kissed him deeply. This felt like home, and home felt good.

"Luisa's been waiting for you, too," Jack said when they finally pulled apart. "She's staying late tonight to eat with us and make this dinner a celebration."

Anna wouldn't be able to relax completely until she told him about the new case, but she wanted to keep the good mood going. She'd tell him after dinner.

They went downstairs to a table set with colorful plates, another vase of irises, and a mason jar full of flowers and peppermint from the garden. Jack had grilled some steaks, while Luisa had prepared rice and beans and a sweet corn salad. Jack poured wine for the grown-ups and sparkling cider for Olivia, and they all toasted the future of their new family. Eating a home-cooked dinner with three people Anna loved was wonderful, especially compared to the lonely pizza dinners she'd been nuking for the past few weeks. They chatted about their days, joked, and laughed. Luisa had even made a cake for dessert. Anna tried to eat her share, but she was still full from the food at Sergio's.

"They're going to have parent-teacher conferences next week," Olivia said. "Anna, will you come with Daddy?"

Anna was touched by the request. She'd passed the elementary school many times, but had never gone in. She was going to be Olivia's stepmother. A *mother*. That was crazy. Amazing.

"Yes, sweetie, I would really like that."

After dinner, Luisa stayed to help Olivia get ready for bed. When the nanny and child were upstairs, Jack and Anna went to his study and sat on the couch.

"Jack, there's something I need to tell you," Anna said. "It's upsetting."

"Oh no. You're allergic to irises?"

She smiled and shook her head. "This is serious. I got assigned a new case today. Four MS-13 members raided a brothel, raped a prostitute, and beheaded the doorman. MPD shot and killed one, and two more ran off. But they arrested the fourth guy."

He nodded with interest but not shock. He was the Homicide chief, he heard about crimes like this every day. He knew this was not what she had to tell him. He waited while she took a deep breath.

"The guy they arrested had a picture in his pocket. A picture of Nina."

"My wife, Nina?"

Anna cringed. That made it sound like she was engaged to a married man.

"Olivia's mother, Nina, yeah."

"Do you have the picture?"

The actual photo was in an evidence locker, but she had a color copy. She watched Jack's face as she handed it to him. The picture had been cut to about two-by-two inches, so it was just Nina's face, with her long dark hair and radiant smile; there was no context to tell where the picture had been taken. As he looked at the photo, Jack's expression flashed through puzzlement, recognition, disbelief, and anger.

"Jesus. How'd they get this?" He stood and went to the bookshelf. His hand skimmed over a line of books, but he didn't find what he was looking for. "Luisa!"

The nanny came down to the study. "Yes?"

"Do you know where my wedding album is?"

"Oh, let's see, it's supposed to be here." Luisa went to the shelf that Jack had just been flipping through, with the same result. "Oh dear. Things are always disappearing, I swear there's a ghost." Luisa looked through the bookcase, then turned to a different set of bookshelves by the desk. She pulled out a large white album. "Ah, here you go."

Jack took the photo album and opened it on the desk. Anna had never seen these pictures before. She watched as he flipped through photos of his first wedding.

The church had soaring ceilings and thick marble pillars. Family members grinned from the pews, obviously delighted by the match. As she walked down the aisle, Nina Flores wore a shimmery white gown, which skimmed her curves and set off her golden skin. Her long black hair hung in glossy waves and her eyes glowed like tiger's-eye stone. For her wedding day, Nina Flores managed to look both angelically beautiful and ridiculously sexy.

On the next page, a boutonniered Jack waited for Nina at the front of the church. He was beaming. Anna wondered if he would look that happy on *their* wedding day. Their own relationship had been conducted so clandestinely, with so many pressures from work, she'd rarely seen his face light up like this. Did he love Nina more than he loved her? No, of course not. He was just a different man today than the one who'd stood in that church seven years ago. Now his eyes were etched with lines earned from supervising hundreds of homicide cases, from burying a wife, from years of widowerhood and single parenting. Anna loved the man he was today, his reliability, wisdom, and strength. But she felt a pang of regret that she would never know that younger, more carefree version of Jack Bailey.

A few pages later, Jack stopped flipping and drew in a sharp breath. There, among pictures of cheering people throwing rice at him and Nina, was a blank white spot. A ghost of a rectangle showed where the picture used to be. Jack inhaled sharply and placed the album on his desk, now touching it only by the edges. He held up the copy of the photo that had been in Psycho's pocket. Nina's hairstyle and radiant smile in that photo were identical to those on the rest of the page.

The photo Psycho was carrying had been taken from this wedding album. From Jack's study. Anna shivered with the realization that someone had been in the house.

Jack turned to Luisa. Very quietly, he asked. "Do you know how anyone could have gotten this picture from this album?"

She shook her head. "No, Mr. Jack. I don't know."

"You're home all day. I trust you completely. But I need to know who you've allowed in the house, for any reason."

She looked scared. "No one. I mean, Olivia's friends come over for playdates, and their parents or nannies pick them up. Once in a while, a friend of mine comes over, but they do not wander the house alone."

"Tell me about your friends."

She listed a few women's names, none of which Anna recognized. Jack wrote the names down. He looked at the paper, then back up at the nanny. "What about Benicio?"

Benicio was Luisa's sixteen-year-old nephew, who occasionally came over with her.

"Sure, Mr. Jack, you know Benicio stops by sometimes. But he did not take this picture from your album! Why would anyone even want it?"

"That's exactly my question."

"Okay." The nanny looked frightened. "There—there is something I wanted to tell you for a while. But I don't want you to laugh at me."

"What is it?"

Luisa bit her lip and looked at his bookshelves. "Sometimes, things move around in this house."

"What do you mean?"

"Like . . . little knickknacks. They'll be in a different spot in the afternoon than in the morning. Or the papers on your desk will be sitting a little different."

"How long has this been going on?"

"A year or two? I'm not sure. At first, I thought it was just me, being forgetful. Or it was all in my head. Now—I think it's something else."

"What?"

"The ghost." Luisa took a deep breath. "Nina's ghost. I'm afraid she doesn't want you to get remarried."

"Nina would have loved Anna. There's no ghost," Jack said. "There's something worse."

12

Forty minutes later, two uniformed MPD officers walked around the perimeter of Jack's house, checking for signs of forced entry. A crime-scene technician dusted the photo album for prints. Detective McGee spoke to Jack and Anna downstairs while Luisa took Olivia upstairs so the girl wouldn't see all the officers in her house. The uniforms came back into the house, shrugging. "Nothing we could see."

"Check the basement," McGee said.

Jack stood in his study, too upset to sit. Anna stood next to him, her hand on his arm. She hoped her touch was soothing, although it didn't seem to be. His muscles were as taut as piano strings. McGee perched against Jack's desk, a notepad in his hand.

"Do you know when the photo was removed from the house?" McGee asked.

"No."

"When was the last time you looked at the album?"

"I don't know. It's been a while, at least since I started dating Anna, probably longer. Could be two or three years."

"So, far as you know, this photo coulda been stolen three years ago?"

"It's possible."

"Anything else missing in the house?"

"Not that I know of."

"Any things moved?"

"My nanny says things get moved sometimes." Jack shook his head. "She thinks there's a ghost."

"Mm," McGee jotted on his notepad. "How well do you know this nanny?"

"She's been with me since Nina died. She's helped me raise Olivia. I trust her implicitly."

"Sometimes it's the people you think you know . . ."

"No." Jack shook his head. "Not Luisa."

"Does she have family?" McGee persisted. "Friends? People who come over here, visit with her?"

Jack cocked his head. "Her sister comes by from time to time. And the sister's son, Benicio. He goes to Blair High School."

"Give me their full names, addresses, phone numbers."

Jack went to his desk, picked up his address book, and gave the information to McGee. "It wasn't my nanny's family. They're good people."

"Who else is allowed in your house?"

"The usual suburban types. Handymen, grocery delivery guys, plumbers. Olivia's friends, over for playdates. Parents of Olivia's friends. Their nannies."

"Names," McGee said. "Addresses."

Jack flipped through the address book, listing as

many as he could. He handed McGee the list of names that Luisa had given him.

"I'll run background checks," McGee said. "What about Olivia? My nieces are always cannibalizing their mom's scrapbooks. Could Olivia have taken this photo?"

"No. She's not allowed in my study."

"Sometimes a kid's definition of 'not allowed' isn't the same as their parents'."

"Goddammit, Tavon. This isn't about scrapbooking. Someone is stalking my family. Those guys decapitated a man. Why did they have a picture of Nina? A picture from my *den*. I want to know who the hell's been in my house."

"Okay, Chief, calm down." McGee put his hands up in a gesture of peace. He looked over at Anna. "Tell me about the warrant you signed for the brothel. Did you—did anyone—think MS was involved, going in?"

"No. It was just supposed to be a run-of-the-mill bust of a nuisance brothel."

"So it's just a coincidence that these MS guys were in there? Nothing bigger than that?"

"Not that I know of." She turned to Jack. "The guy who had Nina's picture was named Jose Garcia, aka 'Psycho.' Does that ring a bell?"

"No."

"Is it possible he was connected to Nina's death? Maybe the photo is a trophy."

"No. Her death had nothing to do with MS-13." Jack sounded adamant. He put an arm around Anna's shoulders. "I want protection for her."

"I'll see what I can do," McGee said, "but I don't think they're gonna go for that. No specific threat, et cetera."

Jack nodded, knowing he was overreaching. "The house, then."

"Gonna be tough. You don't live in D.C. Only reason we got these guys here"—McGee gestured to the MPD officers emerging from the basement—"is the tie-in to the brothel case. We can try to convince Takoma Park to run some patrol cars past."

"I'll call them myself." As D.C.'s Homicide chief, Jack had connections to all the neighboring police forces. "Meanwhile, Four-D's only three blocks away. Not hard for them to drive a few feet over the line, right?"

If Anna stepped to the edge of Jack's property and peered down the street, she could see D.C.'s Fourth District.

"I'll make sure a marked cruiser drives by tonight."

"Every hour," Jack said. "For the next few weeks."

McGee sighed mightily and put his notebook back in his suit pocket. "Man, you are a tough negotiator. I shoulda had you handle my divorces."

"Thanks, Tavon." Jack pulled Anna closer. "I owe you one."

After the police left, Jack took her hand. "Come on. I need to show you something."

He led her up the stairs to the second floor. They passed Olivia's bedroom, where Luisa was coaxing Olivia into pink pajamas. Jack kept going, leading Anna up a second flight of steps to the attic. She'd never been up here before. He swung open the door at the top of the stairs, leading to a dark, cavernous room that smelled of mothballs, old wood, and uncirculated air.

He pulled a chain hanging from the ceiling and a single lightbulb flickered on. Boxes and old furniture dotted the rough wood floors. Brown-paper reams of insulation lined the walls. Jack shut the door quietly and led Anna to a corner of the attic, where the wooden beams came down so low, they both had to crouch. A heavy black gun safe sat atop an old dresser. The door of the safe had a covered keypad. Jack stuck his hand under the cover and keyed in a pattern.

The door swung open with a creak; Jack reached inside and pulled out a smaller box, which he cracked open. Nestled inside gray foam was a black semiautomatic handgun. He popped out the magazine, then racked the slide and glanced inside the chamber to confirm it was empty. Jack held the weapon, barrel-down, to Anna. She made no move to take it.

"What am I supposed to do with that?"

"Learn to use it. We'll go to the range."

A laugh escaped her throat before she could stop it. "I'm more likely to shoot off my own foot than a robber."

"That's why you go to the range, and take classes about gun safety."

"You know the statistics, Jack. Olivia is more likely to get shot with this than any intruder."

"No, we keep it locked up, and you learn to use it safely. I'll wager those statistics would be different if they only measured homes where a gang member had already broken in."

She nodded. Fair point. "Where did you even get this?"

"It was Nina's."

Anna had no idea that Jack owned a gun. What else didn't she know about him? She looked around the shadowy attic, wondering what was in all the other boxes.

She sank down into an old chair. It sent up a poof of dust, making her sneeze. He handed her a handkerchief. "Thank you." She wiped her nose. "I don't *want* to learn to use a gun."

"Why not?"

She thought, *I'm moving into Nina's house, taking over Nina's family. I don't need to carry Nina's gun, too.* She said, "I've worked on dozens of cases involving civilians with guns. They never end well."

"You're talking about cases where the criminals are armed. You haven't seen a case where the *victim* had a gun, have you?"

"No."

"That's my point."

"When did you become a spokesman for the NRA?"

She was trying to make a joke, but Jack's face remained dead serious. He pulled up another rickety chair next to hers and took her hand.

"Anna, I love you. I'm worried about you. The danger out there is real. I can't go through that again. I can't let Olivia go through it again."

She met his eyes. They were filled with love and a sort of fear she'd never seen there before.

"How did it happen?" she asked quietly. "When Nina died?"

Jack set the gun back in the box and looked up at the wooden beams, as if they might provide a clue. "She was a sex-offense detective with MPD for many years. But a few weeks before she was killed, she got transferred to the power-shift to do drug buy-busts. They made her the UC."

The power-shift was a fancy name for a crappy job—putting in overtime in trouble spots in the city. Going from sex-offense detective to buy-busts was a demotion. As the undercover drug officer, Nina would have dressed like a street addict and bought dime bags from corner boys. It was dangerous work, and it paid less than being a detective.

"One night, after she made a buy, an addict tried to steal the drugs off of her. He put a gun to the back of her head, and shot her."

"Mm." Anna cringed. "Did they catch him?"

"No. MPD investigated, and they threw a lot of resources on it, but they never made an arrest."

He leaned back against the chair, closed his eyes, and rubbed his temples between his thumb and middle finger. His jaw clenched and unclenched.

"I'm sorry," she said. She put her hand on his neck and kneaded his tense muscles.

They sat quietly for a while. Finally, he turned to her. "We'll go to the range this weekend."

"No." She shook her head. "I don't want to learn to use a gun. I don't want it in the house, not with Olivia running around. I'm sorry. Can't we just update the alarm?"

Jack sighed and locked the firearm back in the safe. "You're damn right we're updating the alarm."

He carried the safe down to the second floor and put it up on a top shelf in his bedroom closet. When they came out, Luisa was just closing Olivia's door.

"She's all tucked in," the nanny whispered.

"Thanks, Luisa," Jack said. "Let me walk you out."

As Jack and Luisa headed downstairs, Anna went into Olivia's bedroom. The little girl was awake, watching with big eyes as Anna came into the room and sat on the side of the bed. Olivia curled herself around Anna's knee. Tentatively, Anna reached up and stroked Olivia's hair.

"Anna?"

"Yes, pretty girl?"

"I'm scared of the dark."

"Don't be. Everything is exactly the same in the dark as it is in the light."

"Yeah. But you can't see it so well."

"Good point. Want me to get you a night-light?"

Olivia nodded.

Anna could hear Jack and Luisa talking downstairs, using the low voices adults use when they're upset but trying to keep that fact from children. Olivia strained toward it. Jack's voice was soft but decipherable.

"I don't want you letting *anyone* in the house,

Luisa. Not your friends, not your nephew, not the gardeners. I don't even want Olivia having playdates. Not until we figure out who took this picture, and why."

Anna got up and shut the bedroom door. Moonlight from the window now provided the only illumination in the room. She sat back down on the bed.

"Do you believe in ghosts, Anna?"

"No. I don't."

"Luisa says my mommy's spirit watches over me."

"Ah, well. Spirits are a different matter," Anna extemporized. "I do believe in spirits, but only the nice kind, like your mommy's, who watch out for you."

"Hm. Can you look under my bed?"

"What for?"

"Monsters."

"There's no such thing as monsters."

It was the automatic grown-up response, and Anna remembered how unsatisfying it had been to hear as a kid. So she got down on the floor. As she reached for the flowered dust ruffle, she experienced a tiny shiver of fear. What if there was something beneath the bed? Not a monster but a man, holding a sharpened blade? Ready to grab her wrist. She had a case like that once.

She shook off the vision and lifted the material. Under the bed were a few toys, a doll, and some dust bunnies. Anna let go of the dust ruffle, exhaled, and sat on the bed again.

"All clear."

"How do you *know* there are no monsters?"

Olivia studied Anna's face. This was a serious question, and she expected a serious answer.

"I'm twenty-eight years old. So I've been around for a long time."

"That *is* long."

"And in all that time, I've never seen a monster. I've never met anyone else who has. So I feel pretty confident in saying there are no monsters."

Olivia nodded, somewhat satisfied with the answer.

But Anna was lying, and she knew it. She spent her days fighting monsters. Evil as real as the worst gothic horror. Killers, kidnappers, rapists—on the streets, and in people's homes, and sometimes even under the bed. There were monsters, and Anna was afraid of them.

She continued to sit, patting Olivia's back, as the girl's breaths became slower and deeper. She watched Olivia's cherubic face on the pillow. This was her child now. She would do everything she could to protect her from monsters, real and imagined. She stayed with the little girl until she fell asleep. Then Anna kissed her forehead and left the bedroom, keeping the door propped open to let in the light from the hallway.

That night, Anna snuggled into Jack's body, drawing reassurance from the solid warmth of his skin against hers. His steady breathing helped steady her own. Eventually, she slept. But then she dreamt of all the things she told Olivia didn't exist. A gang of demons, dancing wild-eyed around something in their midst: a creature with horns, cloven feet, and eyes as black as pits. The creature laughed, revealing razor-sharp teeth and a forked tongue, as he bound Anna and Nina to a stake and set fire to them both.

13

Two dozen young men, stripped down to their underwear, crowded around Gato as he stood on a chair in the middle of the cheap motel room. Twenty-four muscular chests, covered in a gallery's worth of blue-and-black tattoos. Forty-eight arms raised, hands clenched in *la garra*, the claw: pinky and index fingers extended in the sign of the Devil's horns. Twenty-four faces all looking at Gato expectantly. The motel room was humid from all the bodies and recycled breath. Gato raised his arms and made the claw, too.

"La Mara," he intoned.

"La Mara," two dozen voices chanted. They threw up the signs: the "M," the "S," the "13," the "L-P-S" for their clique, their hands flying in the gang's elaborate sign language. Gato looked around the room with satisfaction. If Diablo came tonight, he would be pleased.

Once, Gato had loved being Second Word. Out there, he was a landscaper—any asshole could tell him to clip their bushes or weed their flower beds, and he'd just smile and do it. He had no papers; he needed the work. But in here, he was a shot-caller, second only to Psycho. And with Psycho in jail, Gato was First Word. If he had something to say, the homies listened. If a shop owner caused a problem, he decided who would handle it and how brutal they could be. If a rival gang member, a *chavala*, came to their territory, Gato gave the greenlight to have him killed. In here, Gato decided who lived and who died. Only Diablo was more feared.

But he no longer relished the position. Only twenty-one, was he already too old? He didn't like the killings, the beatings, the rapes. He would do what was needed for the gang. He always had. But it was starting to weigh on him. A year ago, he had greenlighted an old friend who tried to come to a *misa* wired up. Now that friend was dead—and the rest of them stripped before each meeting. Most of the bodies were skinny, muscular, and young. Not many MS members made it to old age.

Gato sat down on the only chair. One of the younger homies, Lagrimas, stood behind him. Lagrimas was Gato's Second Word for tonight's meeting.

This was not their usual weekend meeting time, and attendance was light. But Bufón was dead, Psycho was in jail, and decisions had to be made. Diablo had gone back to where he came from—although he would be watching, waiting, ready to return and exact vengeance if they fucked up. They wouldn't see him coming until he arrived, and then it would be too late.

"Psycho needs a lawyer," Gato said. "Not some fucking public defender. How much have we got?"

"Twelve hundred," said Lagrimas, who'd collected the dues.

Not enough. Not nearly enough. Gato looked down at his hands, spreading his fingers so he could see the ink inside the webbing there. The days of heavily tattooed bodies were winding down. The old-timers were covered in tattoos, earned like badges of honor. But law enforcement was onto it. An illegal like Gato couldn't afford big tattoos announcing his gang membership. Immigration officials used the tattoos to establish they were MS, which made it easier to deport them. Gato's tattoos were inside his lips and in the webbing between his fingers and toes. His most obvious tat was the three-dot symbol, inked between his thumb and index finger.

"As of today, rent goes up," he announced. "Every business can pay double what they were paying before. Dues at *misas* are double, too."

There was groaning. This meant more work, less beer and weed.

"We didn't send no money to Araña when he got locked up," Rooster said.

Gato stood up, stepped over a few men, and punched Rooster in the jaw. The younger man fell backward and glared at him, but knew better than to fight.

"You're lucky I'm in a good mood," Gato said. "If Diablo was here, he'd cut you up."

Several men nodded. The last homeboy to talk back to Diablo had been hacked into pieces and fed to dogs. "I wasn't First Word when Araña got arrested. I am now. Any more questions?"

The men were silent. Rooster rubbed his jaw and looked down.

"Good." Gato sat back down. "Since Rooster loves my plan so much, he can put in some work. You have the food carts, Rooster. Lagrimas, you'll take the brothels. Casper, you have the strip malls."

"What if they say they can't pay no more?" Casper asked.

"You tell them the Devil sent us. And they'll answer to the Devil if they don't obey."

The men murmured their agreement. Gato stood up. He was ready to call the *misa* to a close. But Lagrimas leaned over and whispered in his ear. "Buena's up tonight."

Gato nodded. The men could use some fun. There were only three places MS could lead you—but there were benefits, too. This was one of them.

"One final thing," Gato said. "We welcome a new homegirl tonight. Buena."

A cheer went up. The men stood and pushed open the door connecting to the adjoining hotel room, where the girls were waiting. Girls were not allowed in *misas*, although they put in a lot of work for the gang. The girls begged on the streets for the money that paid for hotel rooms; they sometimes sold their bodies to get cash for the gang. But they knew their place. They wanted the acceptance and the glamour, and were willing to do what they were told.

The smell of perfume, marijuana, and beer drifted in from the girls' room. The girls had started the party before them. The homeboys swarmed into the girls' room, and the homegirls swarmed back, until they formed one big party between the two rooms. Music pumped from WILC Romantica 900 AM. Someone threw a red shirt over the bedside lamp, bathing the room in a pink glow.

Gato opened a bottle of Hurricane malt liquor and began to relax. He accepted a joint, and inhaled deeply. He needed this, a chance to think of something besides his friends being killed and arrested.

In one corner, a woman with amateur tattoo equipment inked a tear into Casper's cheek, by his eye. Last week, Casper had killed a *chavala*, earning that tattoo. Homeboys were required to kill *chavalas* on sight. Gato couldn't even recall how many tears he would have now, if he'd gotten one inked for every person he'd killed.

By the bed, Rooster was pulling off Buena's T-shirt. She smiled nervously at him. Rooster ran his thumb down her cheek, then helped her out of her jeans, panties, and bra. Naked, Buena lay on her back on the starched white sheets. She was fifteen years old, with the body of a girl who would one day become a fat woman. But for this moment she was beautifully voluptuous, round and firm as a peach. The party went on, everyone smoking, drinking, and watching the action on the bed. The bass line from the music pulsed through the red light, making Gato feel like he was standing in the middle of a beating heart.

Everyone knew Rooster was in love with Buena, and she with him. Rooster sat on the bed, kissed her gently, and stroked her round breasts. She moaned, and Gato was glad. The rest of the night would be easier for her if she were ready. Rooster pulled off his own pants and climbed onto the bed, arranging himself over his girlfriend. He met Buena's eyes as he entered her. Buena sighed and arched her back.

Gato leaned against the wall and closed his eyes, remembering how it felt with Maria-Rosa, so long ago. The way she smiled at him when he was deep inside her. How it felt to come while looking into her soft brown eyes. Falling asleep with his face pressed into her hair, inhaling the scent of her strawberry shampoo. How much she had trusted him.

A cold beer pressed into his hands made his eyes open. He took the bottle, twisted off the cap, and drank half of it down.

Rooster gasped then stilled over Buena. Closing his eyes, he buried his face in her neck. Casper pushed away the tattoo equipment and stood by the bed. Reluctantly, Rooster pulled out and got up. The two men traded places.

Buena knew what was coming, and she didn't resist. Casper flipped Buena over onto her stomach and pushed his pants down to his knees. Rooster was still pulling his clothes back on when Casper hiked Buena up to her hands and knees and slammed into her from behind. Casper slapped her ass and yeehawed like a rodeo cowboy as he rode her. The other men laughed and cheered.

The rest of the party went on. Two girls danced with three boys in the corner. A couple leaning against a wall shared a cigarette. Rooster walked over and stood next to Gato.

When Casper finished with Buena, Lagrimas took

his turn. He flipped the girl back onto her back, pinned her throat with his hand, and slammed into her with vicious force, making her whimper. But she didn't move to stop him.

Most of the girls Gato knew were like Buena. Enough had happened in her life—she'd been demoralized in so many ways before she met the gang—this seemed like a small price to pay for the acceptance MS-13 offered. Buena gritted her teeth and looked over at Rooster, who gnawed his thumbnail as he watched Lagrimas fucking the girl he loved. Having participated in this ceremony many times himself, Rooster could not object to it now.

When Lagrimas was done, the next homey went. Every one of the men and boys would go, running a little train, a *trenchito*, on Buena. Each would add his own little humiliation to the act. The girl accepted she was property of each of the men, inferior in every way. Girls became part of the gang by being sexed in. Boys were "jumped in" to the gang, beaten by everyone for thirteen seconds.

Gato would be the only man who wouldn't take a turn with Buena. A few of the homies had started to call him Padre—like he was a priest, celibate. That wasn't true—he still did the occasional girl, although it had to be somewhere quiet, somewhere he could close his eyes and imagine she was Maria-Rosa. But he didn't do the *trenchitos* anymore, and he didn't touch the prostitutes at brothels. Still, he couldn't have anyone thinking he'd gone soft. When he first heard the Padre nickname, he beat its creators viciously.

The boys loved sexing in the girls, for obvious reasons. But it was more than just sex. These were boys at the bottom of society's food chain. The world taunted them with their low status, their inferiority, with all the things they would never own or achieve. But at least they were superior to the girls. Here, they had the power.

That didn't make it any easier for a man to watch it happen to the girl he loved. Gato glanced at Rooster, who looked miserable as he stared at the activity on the bed. Gato was sorry he'd punched him earlier. He chugged the rest of his beer, grabbed Rooster by the arm, and led him into the other room.

"It's easier if you don't watch."

14

The next morning, Anna was tempted to stay home with Jack. He was on a mission, making the house a fortress. He'd called a group of ex-cops who owned a security company, and they came over first thing in the morning and started installing metal bars over the basement windows. They put video cameras outside the front and back doors and, inside, mounted a small computer with a monitor showing the video footage. They put in glass-break alarms, door and window sensors, and a panic button on each floor. Anna watched them install one in Olivia's closet, and was glad the girl was already at school. It would freak her out to see this.

Anna wanted to get to work. The photo, upsetting as it was, was a footnote to her investigation. If the case were going to be solved, now was the crucial time in the investigation. The security guys didn't need her telling them which wireless monitoring system to use. So she packed up her stuff and told Jack she was heading to the office.

"I'll drive you," he said. He told the men he'd be right back, then bundled her into his Volvo station wagon. Normally, she loved the walk through the pretty neighborhood, full of towering trees and cars with "World Peace" bumper stickers. The Takoma Metro stop was only half a mile away. The drive took less than two minutes.

She kissed him and opened the car door.

"Wait," he said.

He handed her a little black canister on a key chain. She read the label.

"Pepper spray?"

"Spice up your burrito if Chipotle runs out of Tabasco sauce. Or shoot this at anyone who looks at you funny."

She put the pepper spray on her key chain, kissed him again, and walked to the Metro station. As she rode the escalator up to the elevated platform, she saw Jack, still sitting in his car, watching to make sure she made it up there okay. She smiled and waved at him—and hoped *he* was going to be okay.

As she sat on the train, she took out her phone to check her messages. She saw a notice from Spotify, an app for playing music. She and Jody both subscribed to it, and the settings allowed them to see the songs the other one had listened to. Today, Jody's account read:

Jody is listening to "The Scientist" by Coldplay.
Jody is listening to "The Scientist" by Coldplay.
Jody is listening to "The Scientist" by Coldplay.
Jody is listening to "The Scientist" by Coldplay.
Jody is listening to "The Scientist" by Coldplay.
Jody is listening to "The Scientist" by Coldplay.

Anna shook her head and dialed her sister.

"Hey, Annie." Jody's voice was tired.

"Why are you listening to the world's most depressing breakup song, over and over?"

"It's a beautiful song."

"True. But there are two kinds of breakup songs—the weepy, I'm-going-to-kill-myself-now kind, and the ass-kicking, empowering, dance-around-the-room-in-your-underwear kind. You need to be listening to the strong stuff while you're getting ready for work. It's gonna be in your head all day." Anna scrolled through Spotify, selected "Survivor" by Destiny's Child, and sent the link to her sister. "Okay, listen to this. Three times. That's an order."

"Okay." Jody laughed. Her voice sounded a little better. "How's your left hand? Tired from the weight of that rock yet?"

"Tired from the smackdown it wants to give Brent."

Jody gave a little snort. "Love you. Have a good day, sis."

"You, too. Remember, I can see what you're listening to. 'Survivor.'"

"Aye-aye, captain."

Anna hung up, worried for Jody. Her sister's job on the GM assembly line consisted of lots of repetitive movements—a perfect opportunity for her mind to circle through the post-breakup spiral of nostalgia, sorrow, and self-recrimination. The unpredictable nature of Anna's job presented challenges, but she often appreciated the fact that she could lose herself in it.

By the next subway stop, she saw the Spotify notification:

Jody is listening to "Survivor" by Destiny's Child.

She felt better, and hoped Jody did, too.

When Anna got to the office, she logged on to her computer and found in her in-box the artist's sketches based on Tierra's recollection. One looked like an average young Hispanic guy; he could be any one of a dozen guys Anna passed on the street every day. The other had black scaly skin and nostrils like Voldemort. He looked like a Halloween decoration or a caricature of the Devil. For what they were worth, these pictures would go in the morning crime report, e-mailed to all the police officers in the District.

She spent a good chunk of the morning trying to find a good place for Tierra to stay. She was hoping for a women's shelter with job training and counseling—Tierra needed a support system, not only for the rape, but for the self-esteem and economic issues that had made her turn to prostitution in the first place. But all the shelters and programs were full. Several had recently shut down due to lack of funding. The remaining organizations were overwhelmed and underfunded, barely surviving day to day. Anna called and begged, but there simply wasn't a bed available.

She fell back on the USAO Victim/Witness unit, which would put Tierra up in a motel, under a fake name, for the foreseeable future. It was not ideal. Tierra would get bored and lonely, isolated in a strange place. They would give her instructions for her safety: Stay away from her old neighborhoods, stay off the streets. But Anna knew that without friends, companionship, or daily purpose, witnesses often broke such rules.

Anna once had a case where a woman fleeing an abusive boyfriend was put up in a hotel. But she still longed for the sort of dark masculinity from which she was hiding. She met a stranger in a bar, took him back to her hotel, and was killed by him. Victims of sex offenses and domestic violence needed more than shelter if they were to escape the cycle of violence that shaped their lives.

Anna met with officers in MPD's Latino Liaison and Gang units, seeking information on MS-13 and the strange-looking man who seemed to control it. She learned that Psycho and the dead man, Bufón, were tied to a clique called the Langley Park Salvatruchas, or LPS, based in the Maryland suburbs straddling D.C.'s northeast border. There was street chatter about a "devil" who periodically appeared to stir up violence among the local MS-13 cliques, then disappeared. The Gang unit had gathered all sorts of absurd rumors about him—he drank his victims' blood, he commanded a pack of hellhounds—but Anna got precious few hard facts.

That afternoon, the brothel's timekeeper came in to the U.S. Attorney's Office for a witness conference. Victor Linares was a slight man who looked perpetually afraid. He glanced around her office continually, as if expecting gang members to pop up from behind furniture. He sat on the edge of the seat, next to his anemic-looking, court-appointed defense lawyer. Anna was prepared to talk about immunity—promising not to prosecute Victor for his involvement in the brothel—in return for his testimony against the invaders. But he didn't want immunity.

"I slept through it."

McGee snorted with derision.

"You slept through your hands and feet being duct-taped?" Anna asked.

"I just don't remember what happened."

Anna had him wait in the lobby while she spoke to his defense attorney. "If he says that in the grand jury, I'll have to charge him with perjury."

"He's scared of the gang," said the attorney. "Wouldn't you be?"

Anna thought about the security system Jack was installing at that very moment and nodded.

"Work with him," she said. She'd prefer to wait and have a truthful witness than go forward now, just to have him perjure himself. "Let's talk again in two weeks. If he doesn't cooperate, I will charge him."

She called the witness back into her office. "I'm sending you home today, Mr. Linares. Speak to your lawyer about what's in your best interest here. We'll talk again."

"I'm sorry," the timekeeper said. "Press charges if you want, but I can't testify. Those guys know who I am. You seem like a nice lady, so don't take this the wrong way. Maybe you should think about what's in your own best interest. You don't want to cross the Devil."

Alone again in her office, Anna sat at her computer and, feeling voyeuristic, double-clicked on RCIS, the U.S. Attorney's Office database for investigations. She ran a search for all the cases Nina Flores had been working in the twelve months before she died. Anna had always been curious about Nina, but now she had an official reason to check out her fiancé's first wife.

The search returned a hundred cases. Anna started reading them, one by one. The database contained only a brief summary of each case; if she wanted more information she'd have to track down the physical files.

Nina's caseload reflected a sex-offense detective's usual mix: college acquaintance rapes, prostitutes who'd been violently assaulted, middle-school girls molested by their mothers' boyfriends. Every one of the defendants had a reason to hate Nina. She exposed the worst things they'd ever done, ruined their reputations, sent them to jail, broke up their families. But the police handled thousands of these cases a year. Anna herself had dozens of cases like these in various stages of investigation.

Three cases stood out because they involved known MS-13 members. The first was an MS-13 member who impregnated his twelve-year-old stepdaughter. The girl refused to testify, but DNA testing and birth certificates made the case. He was serving a ten-year sentence in a federal penitentiary in Kansas.

The second was a human-trafficking case: two men accused of transporting fourteen-year-old girls around the region and selling them for sex. The men took them to construction sites and offered them to the laborers. Anna couldn't tell from the database what had ultimately come of the investigation, if anything.

The third was a gang-rape of a fifteen-year-old girl at a "skip party"—a party held by kids skipping school. The database reported that the girl had been lured to the party, where a bunch of MS-13 members had taken turns raping her. She was badly injured as a result. There were several "John Does" listed as defendants. The investigation had been transferred after Nina's death, and eventually "declined" by the next detective, who wrote that the victim was uncooperative and recanting. Anna sighed. A good detective might've been able to get the girl on board again. But some detectives took the easy "decline," and a detective who inherited a case from someone else didn't have the same investment or incentive to put forth the often Herculean effort to keep witnesses cooperating.

She e-mailed the Closed Files unit and asked for all three of Nina's MS-13 cases to be pulled from storage and sent to her. She also asked for the file on Nina's death.

As she walked home that night, pepper spray in hand, she considered whether to tell Jack what Hector had said, and that she was looking at Nina's old cases. He'd always been reluctant to talk about his wife's death. She wasn't sure anything would come of the old cases, and she didn't want to upset Jack any further. She decided not to tell him.

When she got home, Jack showed her how to use the new security system. The only recognizable prints on the photo album had been his and Luisa's. The background checks McGee ran turned up nothing concerning.

"Although a juvenile arrest wouldn't necessarily show up," Jack said.

"Are you thinking of Benicio?" she asked softly.

He shrugged, looking embarrassed. "My mind's been conjuring all sorts of stupid ideas today. Suspecting everyone and everything. Hell, I almost fingerprinted your cat."

She smiled and put her arms around him.

When Anna went to Olivia's bedroom that night—with a new night-light—the girl cheerfully told her the house was now monster-proof. But she still asked Anna to look under her bed.

15

Gato held the cook's face three inches from the grill. The old man stared in terror at the flat metal surface, where beads of oil popped and sizzled. Sweat streamed down the pupusa maker's neck, making Gato's hands slimy. But the man had stopped struggling. At this point, any movement, any slip of the hand, could end with the cook's cheek being charred on the grill like a pork chop in a frying pan.

Gato glanced out the window of the food truck. There was no one in the gas station parking lot. On a typical evening, a constant stream of pedestrians crossed the busy road to get the warm thick pancakes of dough, stuffed with meat or cheese. But not today. The small crowd walked off when Gato and Rooster boarded the truck. No one wanted to mess with MS-13.

The cook's wife whimpered and struggled with Rooster. He had her in a corner, and his hands were traveling up and down her clothes. The pudgy woman had gray hair bundled into a hairnet; her normally smiling face was contorted with fear. She was not the type of woman Rooster was attracted to. But this was not about attraction. It was about power and intimidation.

"I told you, old man," Gato said in soft Spanish. "Rent's gone up. Everybody must do their part."

"We can't," the cook whimpered. "We don't have the money. There just isn't any money."

Gato pushed the man's head closer to the grill. His own hands were getting uncomfortably hot. The old man was shaking. But what almost rattled Gato was the terror in the cook's eyes when he looked at his wife. Rooster had pulled up her T-shirt and was pinching her nipples through her sturdy white bra. She tried to slap his hands away, but this just made him laugh and press himself harder against her. Gato knew if this took much longer, Rooster would become too excited, and would take this woman right here in the truck, even with the side window open. Gato didn't feel like watching that today.

Gato shook the man's neck. His fingers skimmed the grill, burning a knuckle. "Fuck!" Gato screamed, and let go. The man yelped, too. A corner of the man's forehead was seared from the grill. A little circle, like a bright red coin. The old man was trembling all over. Gato's finger throbbed with pain. Inside, too, he was burning with rage and frustration.

"Do you want to see your wife get fucked right here?" Gato screamed.

"No! God, no! Open the cash register, take what you want!"

Gato tried to open the register, but couldn't figure it out. He pushed the cook toward the machine. The pupusa maker punched in some buttons and the drawer sprang open. Inside were a bunch of crumpled bills. Gato pulled them out and counted: $252.

"That's plenty," he said. "Your rent is only two hundred a week."

"Sir, please, you must understand. Everything in here costs money. The dough, napkins, forks, equipment, renting this space to park. We're still paying off this truck. We missed the last two payments to cover your rent. The truck is all we have. If we can't make the payments, we lose it."

Gato grunted as he pocketed the money, keeping the extra fifty-two dollars for all the trouble these *pendejos* had given him. Everyone had a sad story. How hard life is, blah blah blah. He had his own problems to worry about.

"Don't give me that shit. When your rent goes up, you raise your prices. You're a smart businessman. Don't treat me like a fool. And next week it's two hundred and fifty."

"We can't do it!"

"Then we'll bring the Devil."

"No!" The burn on the cook's forehead turned brighter red. "God, no, not the Devil. We'll find a way."

"Yes, you will." Gato looked at the other side of the truck. Rooster was pushing the old woman farther into the corner, unbuckling his belt. Idiot. Sometimes, Gato felt like the only grown-up in the entire gang. He pulled Rooster's shoulder. "Come on. They paid."

"I want a tip."

Gato narrowed his eyes at Rooster. He would not

stand for insubordination, not anywhere, but especially not in front of these suckers. "I *said*, they paid."

Rooster released the woman. She sobbed into her hands. Gato and Rooster hopped out of the back of the truck. The cool night air was a relief after the heat of the truck.

An older woman at the gas pumps watched them nervously as they ambled past. They put their heads down—making it harder for her to see their faces—and clambered up the little embankment to Piney Branch Road. They walked by sprawling garden-style apartments where immigrant families lived several generations to a unit. Gato didn't worry that the pupusa makers would call the police. The couple feared deportation and gang retribution more than they trusted the system.

He and Rooster walked the gravel shoulder as cars sped by on Piney Branch. The swishing vehicles seemed to mock them, showing all they didn't have. Although the gang had managed to build a reputation as the most violent gang in America, almost none of the MS-13 members owned cars. Or houses. The people driving by had been born with all the advantages in life. Gato wanted those things.

"Why'd you make me stop?" Rooster asked.

"Save your shit for Buena."

"That *puta*." Rooster spit on the ground. Gato nodded sagely. After Buena's initiation, Rooster would never be able to look at her the same way again. The initiation often killed the spark a man felt for his girl. But it made the men closer to each other. It made them family. In the end, that was what they all craved. Family.

Gato's mother had been a schoolteacher in El Salvador. His father had worked in the gold mines, until there was a workers' strike. Although he'd been a small boy, Gato vividly remembered the police dragging his father from their home. They never heard from him again. The family continued to live in the two-room apartment in a poor section of Soyapango. The concrete building overlooked bluffs going down to polluted rivers. It wasn't uncommon to see a body sprawled on the slope, having been thrown off the balconies by the gangs who controlled the neighborhood. Gato had the job of going to the communal fountain every day and carrying home clean drinking water. After his father disappeared, Gato's mother worked to support the family, but her teacher's salary never stretched far enough. When Gato was twelve, he and his mother made the dangerous crossing into America in order to find work and send money back home. They got to Langley Park, Maryland, where his mother's brother lived. His mother enrolled him in school and got a job as a nanny. A few months later, she was killed, hit by a car while crossing the street.

Gato's uncle allowed him to continue living in the house, but Gato was barely tolerated there; he certainly wasn't loved. His only real friendship was with Psycho, in his seventh-grade class. Psycho's "family" was MS-13, and the gang welcomed Gato. The thirteen-second beating Gato took to be "jumped in" was worth the friendship and sense of belonging he got in return. Eight years later, Psycho and his band of homies were the only real family Gato knew.

A small voice whispered in Gato's head. *Maria-Rosa could have been your family.*

He strangled the voice, then shoved it into a dark corner of his brain. He wouldn't listen to it. He couldn't. He slung his arm around Rooster's shoulder, and they walked down the road, together.

16

McGee didn't think it would amount to much, but if Anna wanted him to do a walk-and-talk around Langley Park, he would. He spent the day walking up to civilians and talking to everyone who didn't run in the other direction. Some people were known to be helpful to the police, and he made a point of visiting them. Some folks he picked at random. He showed everyone the police sketches, and brought a Spanish-speaking officer to help translate.

He learned that Diablo had developed quite a reputation.

"He's a gangster," said a man pushing a shaved-ice cart. "I heard he chopped up a bunch of kids in El Salvador and sent their arms and legs to the police chief's home. The government don't bother him no more."

"He's the Devil," said a lady working at Señor Pollo. "If he touches your skin, it'll rot."

"I hear he makes the gangs shake down local businesses," said the manager at Pollo Campero. "Not me, no sir. We're fine."

No one admitted any direct knowledge of the gang, or having seen "the Devil" in person. Late in the afternoon, McGee stopped at the pupusa truck at the Sunoco on Carroll and Piney Branch Road. The smell of fresh dough and savory meat mixed with the scent of gasoline and exhaust. Through the window at the side of the truck, McGee could see thc cook, flipping stuffed pancakes on the grill. The man had a nasty quarter-sized burn on his forehead. It was still bright red, must've happened recently. A gray-haired woman worked the cash register.

McGee held up his badge. "Afternoon, folks. Can I talk to you?"

The cook looked nervously around, then gestured for McGee and the other officer to go to the back of the truck. The man climbed down from the truck and met them on the pavement, where they were hidden from the view of people standing on the curb.

"That's a nasty burn," McGee said.

"Yes." The cook touched his forehead. "I had an accident yesterday. Slipped and fell on the grill."

"Just slipped on your own?"

"I'm clumsy." The cook held out a paper bag, greasy with melted cheese. "Two pupusas. On the house."

"Thanks." McGee said. He'd had a snack at every food store he visited. His stomach rumbled in protest of its umpteenth meal of the day, but his mouth watered. "I'm looking into a gang called MS-13, La Mara Salvatrucha. Know anything about them?"

The man looked terrified. "No, sir."

"How about the Langley Park Salvatruchas, the neighborhood clique?"

"No, sir. Sorry."

"Anyone giving you trouble?" McGee asked. "Anything I can help you with?"

"Very kind of you, sir. But, no. We are fine."

The man was lying, but McGee was used to being lied to. He held out his MPD business card. "Nothing's gonna change unless someone's brave enough to talk about it. Call me if you remember something."

The cook looked at the card, puzzled. "Sir, may I ask: Why are so many police coming around, asking about the same stuff?"

"What do you mean?"

The man fished in his pockets and handed McGee another card, almost exactly the same as McGee's. The name on it was Hector Ramos.

McGee smiled evenly at the cook. "What'd Detective Ramos ask you?"

"Same as you, whether I saw anyone from this gang."

"What'd you tell him?"

"That I didn't know nothing. Just like I told you."

"Well, sorry to bother you twice," McGee said. "Detective Ramos and I gotta coordinate a little better, is all. Thanks for the pupusas."

He pocketed the card.

• • •

Hector Ramos lived in an apartment on Ninth Street, in the transitioning Shaw neighborhood. McGee didn't call. He just showed up. Another officer stood behind him as he knocked on the door. McGee had considered doing this alone, but decided he wanted a witness.

Hector opened the door a few inches, but kept the chain on.

"What's up, McGee?"

"Can I come in?"

"Now's not a good time, sorry."

Hector wore a ratty T-shirt and his face sported a four-day growth of beard. McGee peered through the crack of the door. The TV was on, playing a rerun of *Law & Order: SVU*. Beer bottles and a pizza box littered the coffee table.

"It'll just be a minute. I found something today I'm hoping you can help me with." McGee flashed a friendly we're-all-in-this-together smile.

Hector shook his head and ran a hand through his hair; he was obviously uncomfortable keeping McGee out, but determined to do it anyway. McGee noticed that the knuckles on Hector's hand were scraped up.

"Been in a fight, Hector?"

"I gotta go."

Hector pushed the door. He was fast, but McGee was faster. McGee stuck his foot in the doorjamb, wedging it open. He used this move at least once a month on reluctant witnesses—but rarely on police colleagues.

"What have you been doing, Hector?"

"I can't speak to you without my union rep. Now get outta here before I start to think you're violating my Fourth Amendment right to be secure from police intrusion in my home."

"You're gonna get yourself in some trouble, my friend."

"So are you." Hector looked pointedly at McGee's foot. McGee pulled it back. Hector shut the door in his face.

17

The grand jurors didn't like Ricardo Amaya, and Anna didn't blame them. The brothel owner looked like a snake who'd just eaten a dog. He had cold, calculating eyes and a comically round belly attached to an otherwise skinny frame. For his grand jury appearance, he wore three days' worth of stubble, faded jeans, and a T-shirt with a picture of a tie on it. His graying hair was so stiff and spiky with product, it looked like he could use it to shred cabbage.

The Superior Court grand jury was housed in a small room that looked like a classroom in an underfunded community college. The jurors sat at three ascending rows of orange Formica tables. There was no judge or defense attorney. Anna stood in front of the room, next to Ricardo's witness chair. On the other side of Anna was a young pretty stenographer. Ricardo eyed her up and down, as if evaluating what he would charge for her. He'd done the same to Anna.

She was amazed that he could be so lecherous after all he'd been through. He was just released from the hospital two days ago, with forty-six stitches closing up the machete wounds on his chest. You could take the pimp out of the brothel, but you couldn't take the brothel out of the pimp.

Anna needed Ricardo as a witness, but she didn't like him. If the police raid had gone as expected, Ricardo would have been her defendant. He was a bad man who just happened to be a victim of and a witness against men who were even worse. As a prosecutor, she often had to view evil on a sliding scale.

Anna led him through the basics: name, date of birth, where he lived. She was polite, but not friendly. She and Ricardo had an uncomfortable business deal. They were each using the other for their own ends—she to prove her case against the gang members, he to lighten his own criminal exposure. She fronted that to the grand jurors.

"You've agreed to plead guilty to one count of pandering and to cooperate with the government, in return for the government dropping the rest of the potential charges against you, correct?"

"That's right."

Anna led him through the terms of the plea deal. Ricardo was lucky he had a good attorney. Robert Ortiz was a former prosecutor who was now a partner at a large D.C. firm. Ortiz made ten times his prior government salary but he missed the action of Superior Court, so he periodically volunteered for pro bono cases. He was smart and had the experience to know that Ricardo's best option was to cooperate immediately. Anna and Ortiz had hammered out the deal while Ricardo was still recuperating in the hospital.

"What do you have to do in order to get all the benefits in this agreement?" Anna asked.

"I have to tell the truth."

"What happens if you don't tell the truth?"

"I don't get the deal."

Ortiz had prepared him well.

"How do you feel about testifying today?"

"I hate it."

"Why?"

"Because if the gang finds out, they'll kill me."

In here, Ricardo was a "cooperator," but on the street, he was a "snitch." Ricardo was facing so much prison time, he figured it was better to try life on the streets with Anna's deal than years in prison without it.

Anna and her office had taken steps to protect him and keep his cooperation secret for as long as possible, at least until trial. His plea agreement was a public document, but it didn't mention his cooperation. She filed his cooperation agreement as a Sealed Supplement, which was entered on the court's electronic docket but wasn't publicly available. So that the docket entry itself didn't give away his status, every plea agreement in D.C. was filed with a Sealed Supplement. The Sealed Supplements were inside sealed envelopes that were not accessible to the public and not viewable on the court's electronic filing system. For defendants who were not cooperating, the Sealed Supplement merely held a piece of paper that read "This is not a cooperation agreement."

The Victim/Witness unit was also paying Ricardo's moving expenses, to move his family to Havre de

Grace, a small town on the Chesapeake in Maryland. His new address would be unlisted. If he stayed away from his old neighborhood, he would probably be okay.

"Are you familiar with the gang called MS-13?"

"Yes."

"How do you know them?"

"They hang out in my neighborhood. They extort all the Hispanic businesses. They call it 'rent' or 'taxes' or 'protection money.' It just protects you from *them*."

"How much rent was the gang charging you?"

"Less at first, but they kept hiking it up. When it got to a thousand a month, I couldn't pay it no more."

"So what did you do?"

"I just stopped. But a brothel needs protection, so I got a new guy to be my doorman instead. Jaime Lopez, may he rest in peace. He worked for half the price, plus . . . er . . . some freebies, with the girls."

"Did the gang react when you stopped paying them?"

"A few men came by. The ones they called Gato and Psycho. They told me that if I didn't start paying again, the Devil would punish me."

"What did you understand that to mean?"

"I didn't believe that crap. Just stories, a demon from hell, bringing pain and misery through the gang. There'd been many times I missed payments, and the gang did nothing. I thought they were full of shit. I told them to fuck off. 'Scuse my language."

Ricardo only knew their nicknames. He didn't know where they lived, whether they drove cars, or what their phone numbers were. He didn't recognize the photo of Nina Flores. He wasn't able to ID any of the gang members from photo books or help a sketch artist. He was cooperating, but doing as little as possible to earn his credit.

"Do you know Detective Hector Ramos?"

"Is he the one who came in that night, shot Bufón, arrested Psycho?"

"Had you ever met the detective before that night?"

"No."

"Have you spoken to him since then? Or seen him around the neighborhood since the incident?"

"No." Ricardo looked puzzled.

She moved on. "Please tell the jurors what happened in your brothel around eight P.M. on October sixth?"

"It was just about closing time. I was getting romantic with one of my girls." He played with his wedding ring. "When they burst in, I tried to protect my girl. I fought them, and I am very strong. I could of beat them all, if they didn't have machetes."

Everyone was the hero of his own story. Anna saw a couple jurors rolling their eyes.

"Did you know these men?"

"I recognized Gato, Psycho, and Bufón. And they brought the devil-man. He's real. He did the initials."

Ricardo lifted his T-shirt, and pointed to a long diagonal scar, over which "MS-13" had been crudely carved into his flabby pecs. He was sewn up, but not bandaged, and the wounds were still red and puffy. A juror retched and hurried out of the room.

"Did the men say why they were doing this?"

"The devil-man said it was to punish me, make an example out of me for not paying the gang. For turning to others for protection. They hurt Tierra for the same reason, to send a message that I can't protect my girls. Now girls won't work for me!" He paused. "I mean, if I was still trying to run the business. Which I'm not. I've learned, uh, that it's wrong."

"Had MS-13 ever 'punished' you before this?"

"No. They caused trouble, but nothing like this. Not until that devil-man came." Ricardo looked truly afraid.

Ricardo was a jerk—as much an exhibit as a witness—but along with Tierra, made a strong case. Rarely did Anna have a sexual assault with a testifying victim who was fully corroborated by an eyewitness. She'd tell his lawyer to get him a button-down shirt for trial.

• • •

When Anna got back to her office, she found a slim accordion file on her chair. It was labeled IN RE: NINA FLORES. She held it in her hands for a long moment. The office hummed around her, busy and active in the middle of the day. She considered closing her door, but that would make her feel like she was doing something wrong, when in fact she was just doing her job. She sat at her desk and opened the file.

A large envelope contained 8x10 color photos. They were taken at night, and had the shadowy quality of an urban scene lit by a camera flash. Nina Flores's lifeless body lay in an alley. She sprawled on her stomach, arms akimbo, legs bent to one side. Nina's long black hair spread out on the asphalt, her head turned into the sleek waves as if seeking comfort. A dark pool of blood surrounded her head.

Anna set the photos on her desk. Her heart hammered against her ribs. She'd seen plenty of postmortem photos, and was used to the gruesome pictures. But this was different. This was Jack's wife, Olivia's mother. It was the first time the corpse was someone she knew. Although Anna had never met the woman, Nina was present in Anna's life every day. With shaky hands, she put the pictures back in the envelope.

She reached for the next item in the file when her cell phone rang. She jumped, held her hand to her heart, then chided herself: *Breathe.* She answered the phone—it was Jody.

"Hey, Annie! Thanks for *No More Frogs.* It's hilarious."

It took Anna a moment to shake off the case and remember the book she'd sent to her sister. "You're welcome. Put it up on your corkboard, to remind you not to answer Brent's booty calls. How are things going?"

"Okay. He hasn't called, so I can't take too much credit for not answering. But he posted some mobile uploads to Facebook, so I think he's out of town."

"Oh, Jody. You need Net Nanny to block you from surfing for him."

"It doesn't hurt just to look."

"It does hurt, it keeps you thinking about him. Go look at the Brazilian elevator prank on YouTube or something. Or better yet, get out of the house, go ride your bike. Get some fresh air."

"Thanks, Mom. How are *you*? You sound . . . tired."

Anna took a deep breath. Then she told Jody about her case, and the file she was looking through. She described the photos of Nina's body.

"Oh my God, Anna! And you're telling *me* to look away. This is not healthy. Can't you get someone else to do this?"

"I don't want anyone else to do it. I want to find out what happened."

"Touché."

They hung up, neither one of them an inch further from her own obsession, but both knowing the other one cared—which went a long way.

The next item in the file was Nina's death certificate and the Medical Examiner's autopsy report. The cause of death was unambiguous. A single bullet had entered the back of Nina Flores's skull, traveled through the left lobe of her brain, and exited through her maxilla, taking much of the left side of her jaw along with it. Attached to the autopsy report were photographs taken during the autopsy itself. Anna flipped through these quickly, not wanting to linger over images of Nina's corpse stretched on the metal table, her ruined face, her torso split with a Y-shaped incision.

Under the autopsy report were police PD-252 forms, memorializing witness interviews. The police had canvassed the block and spoken to residents to see whether any of them had seen the shooter. Anna read each 252. Twenty-nine people had been interviewed. A few reported hearing the sound of a single gunshot. No one admitted to seeing the shooting. She felt a familiar frustration. No one wanted to be involved. She recalled one case where a man had been stabbed to death on the dance floor of a crowded nightclub as the crowd continued to dance around him. At least twenty people had been within inches of the victim, but not a single person admitted seeing the stabbing.

She flipped to the final document on the right side of the folder. It was a report made by an officer on the scene. Reading the narrative, Anna surmised that the officer had been the "Eyes" of the drug bust, the one whose job was to watch Nina as she did her undercover buy, both for her safety and later to testify about how the drug deal had gone down. The Eyes had been stationed in an abandoned row house, and had watched with binoculars from a window. He called Nina "the UC," the common abbreviation for the undercover officer, and described each unknown person with the letter "S" for "subject." The Eyes described what he'd seen:

> At approximately 2230 hours, the UC approached S-1 and S-2, who were standing on the northeast corner of Benning and G Streets, SE. The UC held up two fingers, then gave $20 in pre-recorded funds to S-1. S-2 gave the UC two small plastic baggies in return. The UC turned away from S-1 and S-2 and walked through the alleyway on the west side of Benning Street. At that time, S-3 entered the alley. He approached the UC, and they appeared to have a short conversation. The UC turned to keep walking, and S-3 withdrew a small

> black firearm from the dip in his pants. He fired one shot at the back of the UC's head. The UC fell to the ground. S-3, S-2, and S-1 all fled from the scene. The undersigned radioed this information to the arrest team, then ran down to the street and gave chase. None of the subjects were apprehended.

Police reports managed to reduce the most dramatic moments in life to mathematically dry prose that seemed more like an SAT logic question. But the ultimate message in this report was clear: Nina Flores was executed while on duty, but the police had been unable to find the man responsible. It was one of eighty-six homicides that had gone unsolved that year.

The fact that none of the subjects were caught, despite the arrest team stationed around the corner, was a serious failure. The "Eyes" was the only person to witness the shooting, and he had never been able to ID the shooter. His report described the subjects as men of medium height and medium build; S-1 and S-2, the drug dealers, were African-American, while S-3, the shooter, was Hispanic. A Hispanic man of medium height and medium build could be Psycho or Gato. Or any one of countless other men on the planet.

Anna looked at the signature block for who had been the "Eyes" that night. She did a double take. It was Hector Ramos.

She took the file to Carla's office. The Sex Crimes chief was on the phone, but signaled for Anna to come in and sit. Carla's office was one story above Jack's and laid out exactly like his: a corner office overlooking the Building Museum. Unlike Jack, Carla had warmed up her office with decorations. A colorful quilt hung on one wall; watercolor paintings were displayed on another. Potpourri perfumed the office, and a bowl of candy sat on her desk. Anna ate a mini Reese's Peanut Butter Cup while she waited for her boss.

Carla was in her mid-forties: beautiful, poised, and a consummate professional. She was the face of special-victims prosecutions for the city, a regular at community meetings. She was known for her compassion, expertise, and competence. But, as far as Anna could tell, Carla had no personal life. She didn't have kids. She didn't seem to have a significant other. Carla had a few peers in the office but most of her contemporaries had left, fleeing in the opposite directions of stay-at-home motherhood or high-paying jobs at law firms. Carla now held a position of prestige and visibility, but she ate lunch alone at her desk.

When Carla hung up, she turned to Anna with a smile. "Hello, Anna. What can I do for you?"

Anna told Carla what she'd learned today. "Something weird is going on with Hector," Anna concluded. "Jack always said Nina died in a buy-bust—but Hector said MS-13 killed her, and told me to look into the cases she was working when she died. He's going around talking to people, even though he's supposed to be on leave. Now I learn Hector was the last person to see Nina alive."

Carla wrinkled her brow. "It was principally his

testimony that led them to conclude her death was part of a buy-bust gone wrong. Finding her picture in Psycho's pocket, maybe Hector's having some doubts."

"Why would MS-13 have been behind her death?"

"Well, this wasn't common knowledge, but I suppose I can tell you. Nina was taken off sex-offense duty after MS-13 greenlighted her. Jack and I were line prosecutors in Homicide back then, and we worked pretty closely." Carla picked up a paper clip and started unraveling its coils. "When she was killed shortly afterward, he took it really hard. He was furious that they couldn't catch the killer. It wasn't long after that, Jack took over the Homicide unit and really shook it up."

"Do you think MS-13 was responsible for Nina's death?" Anna said.

"I don't know," Carla said. "But I do know Hector needs to stand down and let you do your investigation. I'll talk to his sergeant."

Anna thanked Carla and stood to leave. Carla tossed the mangled paper clip into the trash can.

18

Rooster sat on the curb in the parking lot of the ALDI supermarket, waiting for Buena to pick him up in her father's car. The sky was getting dark, but the store's fluorescent lights lit up the patch of sidewalk. Clusters of men and women socialized in pockets of the parking lot and near the bus stop on New Hampshire Avenue. Shoppers periodically came out of the store, carrying groceries and children to their cars. Rooster knew he was in the way, but he didn't move. The shoppers all stepped around him—until a big man with a scraggly beard walked up and stopped directly behind his back.

"Rooster," the man said.

Rooster turned around in surprised annoyance. Most people gave him a wide berth. But the man looked familiar.

"Hector?" Rooster stood to face him. "It's been a long time, man. You look like shit."

"A couple of your homies hit a brothel on Monroe the other night. You know anything about that?"

"I have the right to remain silent." Rooster smirked.

"One of them had this picture in his pocket." Hector held up a copy of Nina Flores's photograph. "I want to know why."

"Anything I say can and will be used against me in a court of law. Right, Hector?"

"Fuck you, Rooster. *Dígame*." Hector took a step closer to Rooster. He had dark bags under his eyes.

"I have the right to an attorney, bro. If I cannot afford an attorney, one will be provided for me."

"The woman is dead. Have some fucking respect and let her rest in peace. Tell your homies it's over."

"I heard you killed a homeboy at that brothel. If you want, I can tattoo you a little teardrop. What would your five-oh friends think about that?"

Hector's fist cracked against Rooster's mouth. Rooster staggered back, and warm salty liquid flooded his mouth. His tongue touched his upper lip and felt where it was split. The blood dripped down his chin.

"Goddammit, this is not a joke!" Hector grabbed Rooster's shirt, spun him around, and thrust his chest against the brick wall. Rooster knew better than to resist. Hector frisked him, but Rooster had nothing.

Rooster looked back over his shoulder. "With all due respect, my friend, go back to D.C. I can't guarantee your safety here in Langley Park."

"Fuck you," Hector said. But he looked toward the parking lot. A crowd had gathered around them.

"Police!" Hector shouted. "Move along."

But he let Rooster go. Rooster turned, straightened his shirt, and spit blood on the ground.

"Good catching up with you, Hector," Rooster said.

Hector turned and walked away.

19

The next morning, Anna and Jack stared at the golden pineapple sitting in the middle of the kitchen table. Sunlight streamed through the windows, glinting off the burnished metal of the faux fruit. Anna turned it around, as if seeing it from all angles would give her a better clue of its meaning. She looked at Jack, who merely smiled and shrugged.

"We need to register," he said.

Anna drained her coffee and got up to pour another cup. She was still getting used to weekends as part of the Bailey family. When she was single, weekends meant sleeping in, going for a run whenever she woke up, maybe stopping by a coffee shop for a latte and a leisurely read of the weekend paper. But, now, Olivia was always ready to start her day at the crack of dawn. Jack was accustomed to the routine, and rolled out of bed around six every morning. He let Anna sleep in, but she was trying to get on board with the early-bird schedule.

Raffles jumped up on the table and poked the pineapple's spiny protrusions with his orange paw. Something about the statue spooked the cat, who mewled and ran away. Anna and Jack laughed.

"How is registering going to solve the puzzle of the golden pineapple?" Anna asked.

"People want to send us stuff. If we don't give them some direction, we're going to get a bunch of these."

"What would we even register for? You have everything a person needs to run a household."

"I certainly don't need any more pineapple statues. Take a look around. Make a wish list. It'll be fun."

"Should we ask Luisa if she needs anything?"

Jack paused. "No. This is our thing. Let's do it ourselves."

Olivia came running into the house from the backyard, her cheeks flushed from the outdoors. She held up a sprig of fresh peppermint. Jack knelt down and Olivia tucked it into his shirt pocket. It was their little ritual, every morning. He chewed the mint leaves throughout the day. To Anna's surprise, Olivia turned and handed Anna a sprig of mint, too. It was the first time the girl had ever included Anna in the ritual. Anna accepted the stem with a lump in her throat.

Thirty minutes later, they were driving to the mall at Tysons Corner Center. Olivia sat in the backseat, singing along to Billy Kelly's "People Really Like Milk." The girl's happy jamming reminded Anna of her sister. As Jack navigated the Beltway, Anna pulled out her phone and checked Jody's status on Spotify. It read:

Jody is listening to "Someone Like You" by Adele.
Jody is listening to "Someone Like You" by Adele.
Jody is listening to "Someone Like You" by Adele.
Jody is listening to "Someone Like You" by Adele.

Jody is listening to "Someone Like You" by Adele.
Jody is listening to "Someone Like You" by Adele.

All the songs had been played last night, until 1:35 A.M. Anna pictured Jody alone at her kitchen table, drinking merlot and looking at pictures of Brent as the song played on repeat. Jody would wake up today with a hangover, a still-broken heart, and the bleak landscape of a weekend with no plans.

Anna had been in the same place. Before Jack, she'd been attracted to a string of bad boys—relationships that never ended well. She knew there was no way out of heartbreak except a straight line through time. Still, Anna wished she could make it easier for her sister. She clicked through some songs, finding the most empowering post-breakup tunes she could. Then she sent Jody the songs and a message.

> Jo—No more sad beautiful songs. This is your morning playlist. Be strong! Love you—Anna.

"Feeling Good" by Nina Simone
"Fighter" by Christina Aguilera
"You Keep Me Hangin' On" by The Supremes
"Before He Cheats" by Carrie Underwood
"I Will Survive" (cover) by Cake

When she looked up, she found the car pulling into a huge Crate & Barrel, just as the store opened at ten A.M. It was a beautiful fall morning, sunny but crisp.

Olivia chanted as they got out of the car. "We're going to register! We're going to register!"

Inside the cavernous store, a saleslady set them up with scanning guns and let them loose. Anna found a set of dinner plates she liked—but when she looked at the price tag on the back, she gulped. As a government worker with law-school loans, she lived frugally. Her old Ikea dishes cost a dollar a piece. These plates were fifty times as expensive.

"Remember," Jack murmured into her ear, "it's either that plate or another pineapple."

Anna shot the plate with her scanning gun. Somewhere in cyberspace, her desire for twelve of the ceramic dishes was noted. He kissed her cheek and they kept going.

Olivia was the most enthusiastic shopper, pointing to gadgets she had no idea how to use: French press, bread maker, double boiler. Anna handed the little girl her scanner and let her shoot them. Part of her was appalled by the gross consumerism of it all. Part of her was entranced by the shiny red KitchenAid mixer. She scanned it.

Jack held up a ridiculous pig-shaped oven mitt. "I want to grow old with you and this."

"Aw, that's so romantic." She laughed.

There *was* something poignant about the activity. This was the juicer she would use to make Jack and Olivia orange juice in the morning. This was the garlic press she would use to make sauce for their dinners. Each little item held its own set of future stories, its own moments of happiness that would define their family.

Anna thought about the fractured family she grew up in—the sound of a belt hitting flesh punctuated her childhood. She understood the generational cycle of violence, how women tended unconsciously to seek out men like their fathers. She'd often worried that she would fall into the same pattern. Marrying Jack was a powerful rebuttal to that worry. She took a deep breath and smiled at him over a plateau of candlesticks.

After two hours, they were done. Anna felt tired but happy. The saleslady did some clicking on her computer, proudly explaining that guests could look them up by bride's name or groom's name, and sort gifts based on price or category. "Voilà!" She handed them the printed registry. Anna folded the papers triumphantly into her purse. There was something very official about being listed together in Crate & Barrel.

After they left the store, Olivia asked if they could go buy her Halloween costume. The adults agreed, and they went to Tysons Corner Center mall. Tucked under an escalator was a seasonal costume store. The front was filled with rubbery masks of demons, zombies, and all variety of Freddy-Krueger-ish monsters. Anna smiled at the sight of two clean-cut boys deciding which gory creature to be. Olivia ran straight to the tiaras and princess dresses. She pulled out a shiny green *The Princess and the Frog* "Tiana" costume. Anna thought that would be the end of it, but then Olivia paused in front of a costume of a witch, complete with a warty green plastic nose. The girl looked back and forth between the princess and the witch, clearly torn.

"I'm not sure if I want to be good or bad."

"Tough choice," Anna agreed.

"Usually, you're very good," Jack said. "Halloween is the one night you get to be somebody else, if you want."

Olivia stood for a few more minutes, then returned Tiana to the rack and pulled out the witch package. She handed it to her father. "Sometimes, it's fun to be bad."

He laughed and went to pay for the witch. As the clerk rang it up, Anna slipped a sexy nurse costume onto the counter. "Sometimes it's fun to be bad," she whispered. Jack's eyes lit up.

That night, after Olivia went to bed, Jack popped some popcorn, Anna turned on the TV, and they cuddled on the couch. They rented the movie *Cloud Atlas*. As the opening credits began to roll, she grabbed her purse from the floor and took out the registry papers. She scanned the list, looking for all the fun things they'd registered for today.

She didn't recognize anything. The lady must have printed the wrong registry. But then Anna started to recognize some of the stuff on the list. Here were the dishes they used every day; here was the big lobster pot that crowded the cabinet beneath the sink. She flipped to the first page. "Jack Bailey" was listed as the groom, but the bride was "Nina Flores." The saleslady had printed out the registry from Jack's first wedding, seven years ago.

The movie started to play. Tom Hanks was on a beautiful Polynesian beach, but Anna wasn't paying attention. She skimmed all the things that Jack had chosen when he and Nina had envisioned the life they would have, the home they would make. It was a fearful contrast, the difference between their expectations and the way their lives had actually played out.

Anna turned to show Jack, but he was already reading it over her shoulder. His face looked pained.

"You okay?" she asked.

He nodded. "I'll call tomorrow and have them remove this one. Are *you* okay?"

"Yeah, of course," she said, although she felt somber. She knew she was taking over a home that had been created before she'd even contemplated having a family herself. She understood her role as a safekeeper of the things that Nina Flores had begun: the house, Olivia, the family. "I wish I knew more about what she was like. What your marriage was like."

He reached for the remote and put the movie on pause.

"What do you want to know, love? I'll tell you."

She had a lot of questions, but the one that came out was, "Why didn't you tell me that Nina was greenlighted?"

He rocked back in surprise. "How did you hear about that?"

"I spoke to Carla."

"Carla." He shook his head. "Why did she bring it up?"

"Hector Ramos did his own personal walk-and-talk around Langley Park. Carla thought he might be looking into how Nina was killed."

Jack's face hardened. "Hector was the Eyes that night. He was supposed to make sure Nina got out of there safe."

"You don't like Hector?"

"He was one of Nina's best friends, and he's supposed to be a solid cop. But when Nina died, I couldn't stand to be around him anymore. I blamed him. And I get the impression he didn't want to be around me, either."

She noticed that Jack hadn't answered her original question. "Why didn't you tell me about the greenlight?"

"Look, any cop faces threats. Nina was threatened by MS-13, but it wasn't the first time she faced that sort of thing, and it's not why she died. She died doing an undercover drug operation."

"Right, but . . . now that we know MS was carrying around her picture, do you still think that?"

"Yes."

He really *wanted* to believe that Nina's death wasn't related to the gang. She couldn't figure out why.

"Do you still miss her?" she asked softly.

"I'll always love her." He looked down at the registry paperwork, folded it, and set it on the side table. "I wish she could see Olivia growing up. But God works in mysterious ways. I mourned her for a long time. Eventually, I moved on. And then I found you."

Jack kissed her gently. He drew her closer, and her body relaxed under his touch. Life was complicated and messy, but his mouth on hers was simple and sweet. She lost interest in watching the movie. They turned off the TV and went up to the bedroom.

20

Adams-Morgan was the type of neighborhood that MS-13 would have owned thirty years earlier. Now the main drag was lined with cute shops catering to hip twenty-something professionals. There was no way Gato could walk into a restaurant like Cashion's Eat Place and demand "rent." The manager, in his skinny jeans and skinny tie, would laugh him off the polished floor and promptly call 911. But a few stores remained from back in the days when Eighteenth Street was a center for recent Hispanic immigrants. These were the shops amenable to the type of business in which Gato specialized. And the neighborhood was diverse enough that he could walk alongside the professionals heading to their brunches, and no one paid him any mind.

Gato strode down the busy street until he got to the Botanica Poderes de los Santos, a little storefront just south of Columbia Road. As he walked in, the door brushed against a fringe of orange raffia hanging from the ceiling. He remembered his mother saying something about raffia—the strawlike fringe was supposed to show that you were entering a sacred place, devoted to the power of the saints or something. For a moment, Gato felt a lick of doubt. He didn't want to anger the saints. He could use all the luck he could get. Then he shook off his concern. *Fuck it*, Gato thought. The only true power in this world was violence—and the fear that came from it.

The door swung closed behind him, shutting out the noise of the street. Inside, the botanica was quiet, with only the soothing sounds of tinkly music and low voices consulting by the counter. The store was spiced with the aroma of fresh and dried herbs, some of which were tied in bunches and hung from the ceiling. This was the basis of the botanica—botany—herbs meant to cure and heal, and to facilitate the power of the saints. To the left was a large ceramic statue of Santa Barbara, riding a white horse. The saint was draped in a chain of fresh flowers, and a profusion of dollars was tucked into her crevices and scattered at the feet of her horse. Behind her, shelves were filled with colorful candles in tall glass cylinders, each with a picture of a saint on it. Gato read the labels on the candles: *Yo Puedo y Tú No*—"I can and you can't." *Tapa Boca*—"Shut up," to get someone to stop gossiping about you. Gato picked up a green one labeled *Chango Macho*—"Mr. Moneymaker." He considered taking it. But no. He didn't need to light a candle to make money. He knew what he had to do. He put the candle back and strode to the cash register.

An old Latina behind the counter was speaking in soft Spanish to a young woman. Gato stepped in front of the young woman and slammed his fist on the counter. A glass globe holding a crucifix in water jumped and splashed. The young woman let out a little shriek.

"I need to talk to you," Gato announced.

The old woman paused mid-sentence, and slowly tilted her head up to look at him. The proprietress was tiny, barely five feet tall. She had curly gray hair that spiraled halfway down her back. Her hands were small, bony, and crossed with ropy blue veins. Gato could kill her as easily as he could make a sandwich.

"I'll be right with you, son," she said. "I'm finishing up with a client."

He put both fists on the counter, narrowed his eyes, and leaned toward her with a glare that had struck terror in a hundred shop owners. Instead of stepping back, she leaned forward and met his eyes. She had one blue eye and one brown. She patted his arm with one of her birdlike hands. "You can have some tea while you wait." The old lady gestured to a ceramic teapot on a small table between two chairs.

Gato blinked, nodded, and went to pour himself a cup of tea. It was peppery with a sweet aftertaste. He wasn't sure why he was standing here drinking it, instead of hurling the teapot across the store, but he was glad none of his homies could see. As he stood with the little teacup cradled in his hands, he listened to the old woman advising her client.

"This is the most powerful medicine for healing a broken heart," the proprietress told the young woman, as she handed her a cellophane bag filled with dried leaves. "Brew it two times a day, every day, for a month. Each time before you drink it, say three things you dislike about Manuel. 'He cheated on me, he is cruel, his morning breath smells like a dog.'"

The young woman smiled slightly and nodded.

The proprietress turned to a shelf and selected a small vial filled with thick golden liquid. "Do you have a good friend who is a man?"

"Yes," said the young woman softly. "Roberto."

"Is Roberto kind to you?"

"Yes. He has always been there for me. He's my best friend."

"Good. This oil is infused with potent herbs. Rub a drop onto the base of your throat each night before you go to bed. As you do, picture Roberto smiling at you. This will calm your mind, and make you dream of Roberto instead of Manuel."

The old lady opened a glass case filled with jewelry and took out a necklace strung with polished blue stones. "Wear this every day. The stones are strong and unyielding. They will steel your heart and make *you* strong, too—so you are not tempted to go back to Manuel. If you see him and feel tempted, touch the stones and remember your *promesa* to your saint—and your promise to yourself. You will not yield." The woman wrapped all three items and put them into a brown paper bag. "In thirty days, you will be cured of this heartache."

"Thank you so much, Señora Zanita," the young woman said as she paid. Gato's eyes were riveted to the cash that changed hands, and he calculated that this store must be making a fortune. Less than the brothel on Monroe Street, but still enough to justify a hefty tax. He decided "rent" should be five hundred dollars a month. The proprietress came around the counter and hugged her customer. The young woman left the store looking hopeful.

Señora Zanita smiled and turned to Gato. She wore a flowing gray dress and several necklaces like the ones in the jewelry case. They were the only people in the store now.

"Thank you for your patience, young man. Come, come. I can see that you are troubled."

"What? No, that's not why I'm here."

"I can read your spirit, son. And I can help."

"Fuck you." He threw his teacup down, shattering it on the tile floor. "I'm here to collect rent. Your business has been skating by, tax-free, for too long."

The old Latina looked down at the ceramic shards and tea dregs scattered at their feet. Then she looked up at his face. Gato saw fear in her mismatched eyes, for just a moment. Then she laughed. She straightened her spine and put her hands on her hips.

"You are a smart man. Why do you think no one steals from a woman who is protected by the saints?" She gestured at a row of figurines. "I can give you something far more precious. Let me throw the shells for you."

She turned and walked to the back of the store. The beads of her necklaces swayed and clicked with her movement. Gato hesitated, then followed her.

The small back room was painted the darkest of blues. Polished white stones were embedded in the ceiling and walls, so the space resembled the sky on a dark night. Carved into the walls were dozens of small recessed nooks where white candles were lit, providing the only light. The scent of eucalyptus wafted from the candles. The furniture consisted of two chairs on either side of a table covered with an indigo cloth. Señora Zanita sat on one side and gestured for Gato to sit on the other. He did, feeling somewhere between intrigued and skeptical.

From a pocket hidden in her dress, Zanita pulled out a handful of shells, the kind you could find on any local beach. She placed them in Gato's hand, then closed his fingers around them. He held the shells, feeling their weight, letting his fingers trace over the ridged ones and the smooth ones, those with tiny points and those with round whorls. After a moment, Zanita cupped her little hands and Gato returned the shells to her. She swirled them around her palms, then tossed them onto the indigo cloth. As she looked down at the pattern the shells made, her long gray curls fell around her face and glowed silver in the candlelight.

"Oh," she said. "I see."

"What?"

She met his eyes. "You have been given a responsibility. A position of leadership or trust. But it is one you don't really want."

"Hmph," he grunted, unimpressed. She could have guessed that just by the fact that he was here to collect rent. "What else?"

"I see a girl. Correct?"

"Go on."

"A beautiful young woman." She looked back

down at the shells. "You loved her very much. And you lost her."

His gut clenched. An image flashed: Maria-Rosa looking up at him as they stood in Rock Creek Park, her eyes crinkled with a smile. His throat constricted, but he kept his face blank.

"It was a tragedy," Zanita continued. "A great tragedy. And you haven't been truly happy since."

"What do you know about happiness?" Gato meant for the words to be a sarcastic growl, but they came out a whisper.

"I know you can be happy again. But you have to take positive steps. You cannot steal happiness. Happiness is a privilege that must be earned—with good thoughts, good acts, and kindness. You live in the world you create."

He felt his head nodding in agreement. This was a truth he had guessed, but ignored, for a long time. She stood and gestured for him to follow her back to the front of the store.

"First, we must choose your saint," she said briskly. She went to a row of ceramic figurines and studied the options. There were women on horses, men on horses, women holding babies, men holding swords. Finally, she pointed to the figure of a man with dark hair and a mustache. He looked like a wily poker player from a Western movie. "*San Simon* might suit you. Many outlaws who practice *Santería* like him."

Gato nodded at the figure, but kept looking down the line of saints. His gaze landed on a skeleton dressed in a hooded white robe and a long set of brown beads.

The skeleton carried a scythe and a set of scales. Gato reached out to touch its skull. Zanita's blue eye grew wider, but the brown one smiled.

"*La Santa Muerte,*" she said. "The Mexican Spirit of the Good Death. She will sometimes help where other saints can't or won't. Yes, I think you are right. This is the *santa* for you."

She took down the figure and handed it to him. Then she selected a deep red candle labeled *Corazón Puro*. "For a pure heart," she said. "Light this every day, and think about the man you wish to become. We all have good and bad inside us. You have plenty of good in you—I see it in your eyes. You must feed and protect the part of yourself you want to be dominant. You can decide to be a good man—or a bad one. Only *you* can make this choice. And it is a choice you must make, a battle you must fight within yourself, every day. But since each day is a new one, each morning offers you a new chance to do the right thing."

She went behind the counter and scooped some dried herbs into a cellophane bag. "For strength," she said. "I see you are already strong in the body. This will also strengthen your heart. Brew one cup every morning. Before you drink it, remember something kind that someone did for you, and how that act of kindness made you feel."

She wrapped everything up into a brown bag and handed it to him. "What is your name, son?"

"Gato."

"Your real name."

"Diego."

"Go with God, Diego."

He reached in his pocket to pay, but she waved off the cash.

"Thank you, Señora Zanita."

Gato left the botanica feeling better than he had in a long time. Out on the sidewalk, red and orange leaves played at his feet. He breathed in the clean, crisp afternoon air. As he walked down the long hill to Dupont Circle, he didn't notice the pricey shops or the young professionals or the sounds of traffic. He thought about whether he really could become the person Señora Zanita suggested. It was a revolutionary idea. It filled him with light, and also a sharp longing. This was an emotion he hadn't experienced in years, and it took him a while to recognize it. It was hope.

Hope felt good.

Only as he was riding the escalator down to the subway did he realize that he hadn't collected any rent.

21

At home, Anna established a new routine. She set her alarm for 5:30 A.M. and was out the door just as Jack and Olivia were rising. The office was empty when she arrived at 6:45, and she found she could sometimes be more productive during the first two hours of uninterrupted concentration than throughout the rest of her workday. Each evening, she tried to leave the office by six. She made it a priority to get home in time for dinner with Olivia and Jack, and to read to the girl before bedtime. Olivia would cuddle next to her, laying her head on Anna's arm.

After the girl's bedtime, Jack would set up his laptop on the kitchen table and work a couple more hours. Sometimes, Anna would still have loose ends from work, but usually she could just sit next to him, sipping a glass of wine, watching an episode of *Mad Men* on Hulu or sneaking a read of *Us Weekly* magazine.

She bought the classic parenting book *Dr. Spock's Baby and Child Care* to help her interact with Olivia. One passage stood out:

It is not your job as a parent to banish all fears from your child's imagination. Your job is to help your child learn constructive ways to cope with and conquer those fears.

She felt reassured. She hadn't banished all the fears from her *own* imagination, but she had ways of coping with them. That was something she could give Olivia, too.

By ten each night, Anna was exhausted. She remembered the days in college and law school—not so long ago—when she'd just be heading out for the night at eleven. But now she was a working mother.

That meant her days were hectic. She had to juggle her personal and professional tasks and learn new ways to be efficient. There was never enough time for everything she wanted to do.

But she was happy. She loved being part of this little family. She realized that happiness wasn't "having it all." No one had it all; that was literally impossible. You couldn't go to the bar with friends at the same time that you read a book to your child at the same time that you worked late on a project. You had to make choices. Happiness came from being content with the compromises you made.

She made compromises between work and family, between Starbucks runs and Candy Land games, between sex and sleep. And she was satisfied with the trade-off. It helped that she didn't have to do it alone. She could work while Jack got Olivia ready for school; he could do the dishes while she and Olivia gave each other pedicures. Anna realized why people referred to their spouse as their "partner."

Sex with Jack had always been good. Despite the darkness that she saw in her profession—or perhaps because of it—Anna appreciated the beauty of two consenting adults giving each other pleasure. And Jack was a generous and skilled lover. But now there was the additional closeness that came from the knowledge that this was her partner for life. It made everything deeper and more intense. She craved him throughout the day, couldn't wait for the moment when she could lock the bedroom door, turn off the light, and start tugging off his shirt. He laughed at her eagerness, but was happy to oblige. Afterward, she slept soundly, curled into his chest.

The stuff they'd registered for started to land on their doorstep via UPS packages with happy congratulatory notes. Nina's old dishes, vases, and utensils slowly began making their way to a "giveaway" pile in the basement. Anna wouldn't have admitted it, but she breathed a little easier with every old dish that went into exile. The house started to feel more like her own.

She noticed herself using the phrase "Jack's house" less and "our house" more. Jack did the same. Her name was not on the title, but her life was centered there. It was home.

The more she became part of the family, the more Anna came to appreciate Luisa. The nanny cooked and cleaned, picked up Olivia from school, and helped her with her homework. Anna realized Jack never could've held the job of Homicide chief without Luisa's assistance. Luisa helped Anna learn the domestic skills that Anna's mother—dealing with her own demons—hadn't passed on. Luisa showed her how to tend to a scraped knee, where the good linens were kept, the secrets to her best recipes. Anna felt like a certified adult when she roasted a whole chicken by herself. Luisa smiled at her approvingly.

One day, Anna got home earlier than usual and found Luisa in the kitchen, lighting a blue candle in a tall glass cylinder. The nanny jumped when Anna walked in. The picture on the candle's label showed a hand extended toward the sky, with five robed figures perched on each finger. The label read, *Mano Poderosa*—"Powerful Hand."

"It's for Benicio," Luisa said. Her cheeks were red; her hands fluttered around as she unnecessarily straightened the salt and pepper shakers. "He's having some trouble in school."

"I hope things get easier," Anna said. The candle reminded her of the music she sent Jody. Everyone had their own rituals for getting through tough times.

"Me, too," Luisa said.

"Is there anything I can do to help?"

"I don't think so. But thank you." Luisa turned to the fridge and started pulling out ingredients for dinner. Anna stood quietly for a minute, then went upstairs to change. When she returned to the kitchen, the candle was gone.

Every morning, walking to the subway, she called Jody. With each passing day, her sister sounded happier and more like herself.

At the office, Psycho's case moved along the criminal-justice assembly line. He was ordered held in jail until trial, which gave Anna some breathing room. She asked that the DNA samples be run through CODIS—the Combined DNA Index System—a national database of DNA profiles of convicted felons. She would have to wait months for results. She ordered the recordings of Psycho's calls from jail, but budgets were tight, and there was no money to have them translated into English. Eventually, she found a Spanish-speaking intern who agreed to transcribe the conversations for a few hours each week in between his other assignments. Since Psycho was making a few hours of calls each day, they would always be behind in monitoring him.

She spoke to the family of the dead doorman. His mother said she didn't even know her son had been working at a brothel—she thought he had a job at a sandwich shop. Anna gave the family information about grief counseling and other services, but came away with little new information for her case.

She sent out subpoenas, bringing in the most relevant witnesses from McGee's walk-and-talk. She heard some interesting tidbits about the gang and how it was preying on the hardworking immigrant community in and around D.C. But she didn't have a breakthrough until Nina's old case files arrived, ten days after the brothel raid.

The first two files came directly from Closed Files. Anna skimmed them—a stepfather's sex assault of his stepdaughter, and a gang-rape at a skip party. Tragic cases, both, but Anna didn't see anything related to her current case. The third box was brought by a secretary from the Fraud section; she said the case had been mothballed in a filing cabinet of George Litz, one of the Fraud lawyers.

The name on the outside of the box was *United States v. John Doe.* Anna pulled open the flaps, took out the folders, and started plowing through the contents. This was the investigation of two MS-13 members pimping underage girls. A Polaroid photo of a victim was stapled to the front of the main file. Her name was handwritten across the bottom: Maria-Rosa Gomez, fourteen years old. The girl was pretty, with auburn hair and deep brown eyes. She wore a sulky pout and a strappy sequined top with a neckline that plunged inappropriately between her little breasts. Behind her, a measuring chart with cheerful children's illustrations showed that Maria-Rosa was 5'3". Anna had seen a version of this same photo in countless cases. One was taken of every child who was forensically interviewed at the Children's Advocacy Center.

Anna opened the file labeled POLICE REPORTS. All of the reports were written by Nina Flores, in crisp, logical prose. The case started out simply enough. An anonymous citizen called 911 to report that two teenage girls were being pimped out of the back of two white vans at a construction site. Nina Flores drove to the site, parked half a block away, and watched. She saw workers going in and out of the vans in fifteen-minute intervals. She concluded that a prostitution operation was being run out of the vans. She approached the vans on foot. One pimp was in the driver's seat of a van and one was standing outside, talking to the other through the window. She identified herself as a police officer, and asked the man on foot for ID. Instead, he jumped into the nearest van and sped off. Later, the van was found, abandoned, a few blocks away. It had been stolen.

Nina heard scuffling inside the remaining van. She drew her weapon and opened the back doors. Inside, she found Maria-Rosa Gomez, wearing a sequined shirt but no pants or underwear. A construction worker was putting on his clothes. Nina arrested him and brought the girl to the Children's Advocacy Center for an interview.

Anna looked up from the police reports. It happened four years ago, but it still made her furious. Pimping a girl out to a series of construction workers. She was filled with a fierce need to find and punish the men who did this. She imagined Nina felt the same way.

Anna dug through the box until she found a CD. It had been hand-labeled with a Sharpie: *CAC, Maria-Rosa Gomez, 9/16/09*, the same day that Nina had approached the vans. Anna popped the CD into her computer.

The scene that came up was familiar. It was an interview room at the Children's Advocacy Center, the one designed for older kids, so the table and chairs were regular-sized. Each wall was painted a different pastel color. A bunch of colored pencils and sheets of blank paper were in the middle of the table. Although the waiting room was offscreen, Anna knew that

Maria-Rosa would have waited among shelves of toys, games, and snacks. The whole place was designed to make kids feel safe, happy, and comfortable.

On the screen, Nina led Maria-Rosa into the room and they both sat at the table. The girl crossed her arms on her chest in the universal teenage gesture: I don't want to talk to you. She was wearing jeans and that horrible sequined top, and her hair looked mussed.

Anna peered at Nina. She'd never seen the woman on video before, never seen how Jack's first wife moved or how she smiled. Anna was struck by how much Nina's demeanor and body language resembled Olivia's. Nina was shorter than Anna, curvier, too. Anna was long and willowy; Nina looked more like a miniature centerfold. She wore dark pants, a clingy white top that showed a hint of impressive cleavage, and a brown leather jacket, over which her long dark hair fell. She looked tough, sexy, and beautiful. Nina pushed her hair back behind her ears as she started the interview

"How are you feeling today, Maria-Rosa?" Even Nina's voice sounded like a grown-up version of Olivia's. It was soft on top but with a tinge of huskiness hinting at a reservoir of strength below.

"Okay."

"I'm going to need you to speak up," Nina said. She pointed at Anna. "There's a video camera there, and it's recording what we're saying. So it needs to be able to hear what you say. Okay?"

Maria-Rosa followed Nina's finger, her eyes growing wide at the sight of the video camera mounted above the door. She nodded reluctantly. Every witness was intimidated by this revelation at first, then eventually forgot that the recording equipment was there.

"There's nothing to worry about." Nina leaned forward, making good eye contact with the girl. "You're not in any trouble. You're not in trouble for skipping school. You're not in trouble for anything you did in the van. You'll never be in any trouble with me, as long as you tell the truth. That's the one rule we have in here. I promise I'll always tell you the truth. And you have to tell me the truth. Can you do that?"

Maria-Rosa met her eyes, briefly. "Yeah."

"First, I want to see if you have any questions for me. What can I tell you that would help you understand this, and feel comfortable with it?"

Anna was impressed with Nina. She'd seen many cops barrel ahead, asking questions of a victim who wasn't ready to answer—prompting them to clam up or lie. Nina was giving her space, creating trust.

"Is my mom listening?"

"No."

"Are you gonna tell her what I say?"

"No. With a couple exceptions, I don't tell her what you tell me."

"What do you mean, exceptions?"

"If your future safety is at risk. Like if you told me your dad was touching you in a way he shouldn't. I'd need to address that, because it wouldn't be safe for you to go back to your house under those circumstances."

Maria-Rosa rolled her eyes. "There's nothing like that."

"Okay. So, tell me about your school. What grade are you in?"

"Ninth."

"What's your favorite subject?"

"Art."

Maria-Rosa started talking: about her school, her homework, her friends. Nina listened actively, making a few comments, asking questions in the right places. The girl grew more relaxed and started to bond with the detective. It was an impressive display. In ten minutes, Anna got a flavor for Nina's personality—and felt a sort of wistfulness as a result. Nina was exactly the sort of cop she would want on her own case. Empathetic, patient, sharp. She knew Jack wouldn't have married someone unless she were special.

"So, Maria-Rosa," Nina reached over and gently touched the girl's wrist. "I see you have a little tattoo here. LPS. What is that?"

"Langley Park Salvatruchas." The girl's voice was quiet, and despite her grown-up shirt, she seemed very young.

"What is LPS?"

"It's my clique."

The girl took a piece of paper and a colored pencil and started drawing a picture. Many young witnesses did this; they were more comfortable talking about difficult subjects when they were looking at something else.

"Did your clique have something to do with why you were in that van today?"

Maria-Rosa nodded and continued to draw flowers and hearts.

"Is that a yes?"

"Yes."

"Tell me about it."

The girl kept sketching silently. She was considering whether to talk, Anna thought, weighing her loyalty to the gang against the repulsive requirement of selling herself to random construction workers. She both wanted to protect the gang and for someone to stop them.

"Everyone needs to put in work," Maria-Rosa said quietly.

"Have you put in this kind of work before?"

"A few times."

"Where?"

"Construction sites. I'm not sure what streets or anything."

"Do you know the cities?"

"One time it was Silver Spring. Another time was Alexandria. A couple times in D.C."

For Anna, those words opened a legal door. The girl had been sold in Maryland, Virginia, and the District. Interstate trafficking of a minor was a federal offense.

"Always in a van, or something else?"

"A van."

"That man who was in the back of the van with you today, when I opened the doors. Had you met him before?"

"No. He was just a construction worker."

"What was he doing with you in the van?"

"What do you think?" Maria-Rosa stopped coloring and looked at Nina. "He paid twenty dollars to fuck me."

The girl was seeing if she could shock the detective. Nina didn't blink.

"And did he?" Nina asked softly. "Fuck you?"

Nina was mirroring the girl's language, a technique meant to build trust and understanding. *You can't shock me*, it said. *I'm still with you. And it's okay.*

The girl kept Nina's gaze. "Yes."

"Is that what you did at all the construction sites in D.C., Alexandria, and Silver Spring? Had sex with construction workers in return for money?"

"Yes."

"There were two vans today. What was the other one for?"

"Another girl." Maria-Rosa started coloring again. "Mercedes. She was putting in work, too."

"Did you or Mercedes get to keep any of the money?"

"No. The guys did."

"The same guys who drove the vans?"

"Yeah."

"Who was driving Mercedes's van? The one that drove away when I came."

"Psycho."

Anna blinked. How many Psycho's could there be? Maybe many in a gang like MS-13. But she'd bet this was the same guy they'd arrested for raiding the brothel.

"Do you know Psycho's real name?"

"No."

"Do you know where he lives?"

"No."

"What about the man who was driving your van?"
"Diablo."

Anna's heart jumped. These were her suspects. She listened intently.

"Who is Diablo?"

Maria-Rosa shrugged. "They say he's the Devil, but I think he's just a mean guy with a messed-up face."

"Do you know where Diablo lives?"

"He comes and goes. When he's not around, we're pretty chill. But when he comes, he wants to see action, make us the 'real' MS-13. He makes everyone put in work."

"What counts as putting in work?"

"Girls have to get money for the gang. Begging or hooking. Boys have to make everyone scared of the gang."

"How do the boys do that?"

A pause. "I don't know."

"Maria-Rosa, do you have a boyfriend?"

The girl shifted in her chair, rearranging her legs. She took a new piece of paper and another pencil. Anna thought, *She's preparing to lie.*

"No," Maria-Rosa said. "No boyfriend."

Anna wondered who she was protecting.

The interview went on for another fifteen minutes. Nina got a little more information, then wrapped up with gentle transition questions about innocuous subjects. She led Maria-Rosa back to the waiting room. The video turned to black.

Anna was sorry to see Nina leave; now that she'd seen Nina in action, her absence made Anna feel as if she'd just lost a friend. She popped the CD out and put it carefully back in its envelope. She wondered why this case hadn't gone forward. It seemed fairly strong from the look of the CAC interview.

The terrible answer came in the next folder. It was labeled MARIA-ROSA GOMEZ GRAND JURY. It began with a copy of a subpoena issued to Maria-Rosa for her testimony to be taken on September 24, 2009. Police reports reflected that Nina called Maria-Rosa three days before her grand jury appearance. Maria-Rosa said that she didn't want to go in the grand jury—that if she went in, the gang would kill her. "And they're going to kill you, too," she told Nina. Nina wanted to put the girl up in a hotel, but Maria-Rosa refused, claiming she was staying "with somebody safe." Nina drove to her house to talk to her, but her parents didn't know where she was. They said she often spent nights out.

The next page in the file was the death certificate for Maria-Rosa Gomez, dated September 22, 2009. Her body had been discovered in Rock Creek Park by a jogger on the footpath that followed the creek. Anna herself had jogged that path many times. Crime-scene photos showed Maria-Rosa's body, curled on its side, on the banks of the river. The bloody body was a jarring juxtaposition to the pretty green of the park in late summertime.

The cause of Maria-Rosa's death was a single bullet through the head, from behind. But the ME's report also listed multiple post-death stab wounds, in a grisly pattern along Maria-Rosa's back. Anna counted: thirteen stab wounds. A sign left by the gang.

Maria-Rosa's murder was three days before Nina's.

After the two murders, the investigation ground to a halt. No suspect was ever identified for the pimping or the murders.

The shameful injustice—the colossal failure of a system Anna was devoted to—screamed from the pages.

Anna looked through the rest of the paperwork for some reference to Mercedes, the girl from the other van. There was surprisingly little information about her. No witness statement, no address, not even a last name. But toward the back of the file was a sealed brown envelope labeled NOT FOR DISCOVERY—not to be shared with defense counsel, should the case ever be charged. Anna opened it. Inside was a business card of a deputy U.S. Marshal and a typed memo to file: "Julia Hernandez's contents removed from file. WITSEC case # 09-1523." A witness had gone into the Witness Protection Program.

The file didn't give any more information about Julia Hernandez or say what she'd seen. But perhaps Anna could tie Psycho to the prior trafficking case and Maria-Rosa's murder. If she could identify Psycho and Diablo as the same defendants in her case, Anna might be able to make a much larger federal case out of the combination. Anna needed to talk to Julia Hernandez.

First, Anna tried Samantha Randazzo again. The FBI agent arrived at Anna's office late in the afternoon. Sam was in her mid-thirties, with long curly black hair and full lips, shiny with gloss. She always managed to make her dark pantsuits look sexy. Today, Sam carried a plastic bag filled with containers from Sergio's: fried calamari, eggplant patties, and a tray of lasagna.

"From Tony," Sam said, setting the bag on Anna's desk.

"Thanks! Tell him I send my best."

"Nah, that'll just encourage him. Fill me in on the case."

Anna told Sam what she'd found over the last two weeks. Sam listened attentively, leaning forward a little more with each development. By the time Anna finished, Sam had her elbows on her knees.

"So you've got interstate trafficking of a minor. The murder of a witness—maybe the murder of a police officer. Then the same two gangbangers raid your brothel when the pimp doesn't pay his extortion money. They rape the girl, kill the doorman. This sounds like something the FBI should be on."

Anna restrained the urge to fist pump.

"There's one more thing." Anna lowered her voice. "But it's totally confidential."

"As opposed to everything else you just told me?" Their entire conversation was subject to the grand jury rules of secrecy.

"Yeah. But the next part is just rumors and speculation, about a decorated member of law enforcement."

"Bring it."

"Hector Ramos is turning up in too many places. My Spidey sense tells me something is off." Anna described everything she'd learned about Hector.

"You do need my help," Sam said. "Give me a copy of the paperwork, and I'll run it past my ASAC."

"Thanks, Sam. I'm doing a reverse proffer with Psycho tomorrow. You want to be there?"

"Absolutely."

The agent took a pile of papers from Anna and stood to leave her office. On the way out, she almost bumped into McGee coming in.

"Hello, ladies," McGee said, tipping his fedora in an exaggerated show of chivalry. Then he pointed his hat at Anna. "You're bringing the FBI in on my biggest case?"

"We might, uh, provide some assistance," Sam said gingerly. "It sounds like the sort of thing we could work on together."

"Well thank goodness!" McGee plopped down into one of Anna's chairs. "I could use the help. This woman's got me running like a racehorse all up and down D.C. and Maryland. You know how many brothels I had to visit?" He paused as Anna and Sam smirked at him. "I didn't mean it to come out that way."

22

Ten days in prison hadn't erased the stupid grin from Psycho's face. Anna regarded him across the tiny metal table in the tiny windowless rooms in the USAO basement. McGee sat at Anna's side, looking uncomfortably squished, his belly pressed against the table because the wall prevented his chair from going back any farther. Sam sat at the head of the table. Steve Schwalm sat next to his client, trying to appear as if he liked him. Psycho wore an orange prison jumpsuit and was handcuffed, with chains shackling him to a big metal bolt in the wall. Sometimes Anna held conferences here with prisoners who were merely handcuffed. Not with Psycho.

Since Psycho's arraignment, Anna and Schwalm had been discussing the possibility of his cooperation. Schwalm wanted his client to do it, but Psycho hadn't moved. Schwalm asked Anna to do a reverse proffer, and she agreed. She'd already given Schwalm all of the information she would list now; the disclosure was required by law. Schwalm could give it to his client himself, but sometimes it helped for a defendant to hear it from the prosecutor. She could give a "scared straight" speech, which was more effective from the mean prosecutor than from the defense attorney, who was trying to build trust with his client.

Anna was willing to give Psycho a break—because she wanted Diablo. In four years, the government hadn't been able to find the man with the horns. Something had to change, and she hoped flipping Psycho was that thing.

"Mr. Garcia," she said. "My case against you is quite strong. You were caught, literally with your pants down, raping a prostitute. There will not only be the testimony of the victim herself, there are several eyewitnesses who can testify about this sexual assault. That includes one decorated MPD police officer."

She didn't mention that she had growing doubts about this police officer.

"We have your semen in the condom. We have your fingerprints on the machete. We have a rape victim with such traumatic injuries she might have died without medical intervention. You're facing First Degree Sexual Assault While Armed—statutory maximum of thirty years to life. Felony Murder, for the death of your friend Bufón—maximum thirty years. And First Degree Murder While Armed, for the death of the doorman—thirty years to life. You aided and abetted, so you're legally responsible for that man's death even if you didn't swing the machete."

She didn't mention the scheme to transport underage girls to construction sites for prostitution, or the death of Maria-Rosa. She didn't have a single witness supporting those charges—yet.

"I'm not here to gloat, Mr. Garcia, I'm just telling you how this is gonna go. And you can ask your lawyer if you think I'm bluffing. He'll tell you I'm not. This is an easy case for me. You're going to be convicted, and you'll spend the rest of your life in jail. Until you die, in a maximum security prison."

The smile did not leave Psycho's face, but he glanced at his lawyer. Schwalm nodded back at him.

"The reason your lawyer suggested we have this talk today is because the law rewards people who begin walking up the path to rehabilitation. In your case, that would mean pleading guilty and cooperating with law enforcement. The judge would take that into account when sentencing you. I'd recommend that you serve thirty years. It's a long sentence, but it isn't life. You'd be fifty-two when you came out. If you ever want to see the world outside of prison again, this is your only chance."

Psycho shifted in his chair, clanking the chains that bound his hands and feet. He shrugged. She couldn't tell if her talk had any impact. Jack was the master of the reverse proffer. He could do a come-to-Jesus talk like no one else, mixing stern rebuke with logic and a fatherly command. She'd seen him make hardened thugs take a deal that no one else could convince them to take.

But Psycho just narrowed his eyes at her and kept smiling. He still looked like he wanted to rip her throat out.

"You have two weeks to decide, Mr. Garcia." She stood up. "After that, the deal is off the table."

When she said goodbye to the defense attorney, Psycho was still grinning at her, but a maniacal sort of fear and hatred had entered his eyes. It wasn't where he needed to be, emotionally. But it was different from where he'd been earlier this morning. She supposed it was a start. The start of what, she couldn't quite tell.

23

The mid-October drive through the Shenandoah Valley was spectacular. Gold waves of foliage draped undulating hills, and purple mountains provided a majestic backdrop. Farmers' stands dotted the country road, their tables heaped with pumpkins, squash, and apples. Olivia's usual car chatter was on mute. The girl sat in the backseat, headphones clamped to her ears, watching *Tangled* on the portable DVD player. The car was filled with the mellow sound of Miles Davis. Jack smiled at Anna as his Volvo station wagon cruised down I-81. She felt more relaxed than she had in weeks.

It took about two hours to get to Blown Away Farm & Inn. A little after five o'clock, they drove down a long, tree-lined driveway, which opened to a redbrick mansion with a white portico and columns. It was a beautiful hotel, and it would be a great place to bring their friends and family. Jack had planned this weekend in the country to scout out places for the wedding. There were lots of stunning places in the city itself, but Anna wanted to be married outdoors. Jack said this area had some of the most beautiful countryside within driving distance of D.C. He'd set up appointments at a few vineyards and farms.

They checked in and were shown to a lovely two-room suite, decorated with antiques. Olivia jumped on her four-poster bed like it was a trampoline until Jack gave her his "stern dad" look. Then she just bounced on her bottom. She was almost as excited as Anna.

As she settled into the suite, Anna felt a lightness she hadn't in a while. It was just a weekend getaway—the case would be there waiting for her on Monday—but it felt good to think about something besides murder, rape, and violence for a while.

An hour later, they went to see the inn's manager. Darlene was a middle-aged white woman who looked surprised when they walked into her office. She might not get many mixed-race couples here in the middle of Virginia. But Darlene quickly recovered her gracious smile and showed them around. The main part of the tour was a wide stone patio at the back of the inn. The day was clear and warm, summer was still fending off autumn.

"This is where most couples choose to have their ceremonies," Darlene said. "Then the cocktail hour is inside the lobby, while we convert the patio to dinner tables and a dance floor."

Anna stood on the patio and drank in the beautiful view. Behind the mansion sprawled a green valley dotted with grazing horses. The valley was surrounded by the blazing autumn trees and the Appalachian Mountains, which reflected the pink light of the setting sun. It looked magical. Anna could picture herself and Jack standing here, promising to love, cherish, and honor each other for the rest of their lives. She met Jack's eyes and saw that he felt the same way. He reached for her hand and they stood gazing out at the view.

"What if it rains?" Olivia asked. She put her hands on her hips and looked up at Darlene.

Darlene answered the six-year-old respectfully. "If there's a chance of rain, we can put up a large white tent over the patio. We can even hang little white lights inside the tent, if you like."

"Excellent," Olivia said. "And we're thinking about a big band. Where would they go?"

Darlene pointed to a grassy space on the side of the patio. After a few more probing questions, the little girl turned to her father and Anna.

"This would be quite satisfactory."

Anna laughed and knelt down. "How do you even learn words like that?"

"I'm just smart."

"That you are."

The next day, they visited more vineyards and farms. Every place was beautiful, green and gold. Anna sampled Virginia wines and savored the long views of countryside, something she couldn't get in Washington. Olivia played with every farm dog and cat they encountered. But at the end of the day, they all agreed that they'd fallen in love with the inn. They went back that evening and spoke to Darlene. They reserved the inn for their wedding on July fourteenth. Anna's heart lurched a little when Darlene blocked out the weekend on her computer. This was really happening.

Later that night, with Olivia sleeping in her adjoining room, Anna and Jack took a bottle of local pinot grigio out to their balcony. The night was warm and soft. They stood watching a huge orange harvest moon rise. Fireflies hovered in the grass below. Anna took a sip of wine and basked in the rare feeling of complete happiness. They talked about whom they would invite to their wedding, and whether they would host a brunch the next morning.

"Next time we're here," Jack said quietly, "you'll be my wife."

He took her face gently between his hands. He kissed her so softly she could barely feel his lips at first. She leaned into him, deepening the kiss, running her hand up the solid wall of his chest. Her breathing quickened, her face flushed with warmth. They left their wine on the balcony and went into the bedroom. The inn had set up their room as if they were already on their honeymoon. Red rose petals were scattered on the bedcovers, infusing the air with sweet perfume. As Jack lit some candles, Anna made sure the door was locked. Then they took off each other's clothes, kissing in between the pieces they shed.

She stepped back so she could look at him, naked in the candlelight. He was beautiful. Without warning, he scooped her up and carried her like a bride over a threshold. She squealed and laughed. "Shh," he said. He kissed her, then laid her down on the rose petals. She was wet and aching for him already. She tried to pull him onto her, but he shook his head.

He walked to the end of the bed, trailing his fingers down her leg as he did. He picked up her foot and kissed each toe, one by one. She giggled. He got on the bed, knelt between her feet, and began trailing slow kisses up her legs. His tongue traced circles on her calves, her knees, her thighs. The warmth of his lips sent ripples of electricity up to her belly. His hands skimmed upward, tracing her hip bones, traversing her stomach, drawing butterfly patterns across her breasts. "Please," she whispered.

"Patience, love," he said. His tongue kept circling higher along her inner thigh, ever so slowly, until she was crying out and straining her hips toward him. His mouth finally found the place she'd been guiding it to. She arched back as he circled her with his tongue. Every other thought left her mind. She closed her eyes, letting herself savor the pure sensory bliss of the man she loved lavishing her with his tongue and lips and fingers. She came with a shiver of happiness.

When she opened her eyes, he was kneeling between her legs, gazing down at her with tenderness. She sat up, smiled, and pushed him back against the bed. She swung a leg over him so she was straddling him. Twining her fingers with his, she held his hands above his head, then leaned down and kissed him, tasting herself on his mouth. Then she sat back slowly and lowered herself onto him. He groaned as his length slid into her, stretching and filling her. She arched her back and moved her hips, bringing him even deeper. He watched her with hooded green eyes. They moved together in a rhythm as intense as it was familiar. She held herself back for as long as she could, until she couldn't take it anymore, and pushed herself over the edge. She felt Jack shuddering under her at the same time.

She stretched herself out, laid her head on his chest, and spread her fingers over his heart. He sleepily stroked her back. She drifted into sleep.

Sometime later, Anna was startled awake by the ringing of her cell phone. She almost let it go to voice mail, but worry drove her hand to fumble around the nightstand. She picked up the phone and squinted at the incoming caller. It was Steve Schwalm, Psycho's attorney. She answered, and Schwalm apologized for interrupting her night.

"But I had to talk to you," he said.

"What's up?" She sat up in bed and glanced at Jack. His eyes were open, watching her. "Did my reverse proffer convince Psycho that he wants to cooperate?"

"Not quite. I'm withdrawing from my representation of Mr. Garcia. I'll be filing something Monday morning."

"Okay. Can we talk about this then?"

"No. It wasn't easy to call you, Anna. I take my duty of confidentiality to my client seriously. But I consulted with an ethics attorney, and we concluded I can and should breach client confidentiality in light of the imminent danger of a future crime." The way he was talking, Anna guessed that he'd already written this in a memo somewhere. "Mr. Garcia has ordered his gang to kill you. You've been greenlighted."

"What?" She tried to shake the sleep and the wine from her head. "What do you mean?"

"I can't go into details about how this was revealed

to me. But it's real. My understanding is that any MS member who sees you may attempt to kill you."

Jack sat up and started putting his boxer shorts back on. Apparently, he could hear the other end of her conversation. Anna tried to get more details from Schwalm, but he said that was all he had to give her. By the time she hung up, Jack was fully dressed and had his cell phone in his hand.

"They put a hit out on you?"

She nodded.

"Christ," he said, and began to pace the room. "I can't believe this is happening again."

Within minutes, Jack turned their charming room into a little command center, from which he called the Marshals, the D.C. police, the local police, and the acting U.S. Attorney. He set up his laptop and started e-mailing people as he spoke on the phone. Anna listened to his end of the conversation as she got dressed. He and a deputy U.S. Marshal decided the B&B was safer than being at home. The local police would drive by the inn throughout the night.

"I want a meeting about Anna's protection first thing Monday morning," Jack said.

"I've got Tierra Guerrero coming in for grand jury Monday morning," she interrupted.

"Make that Monday afternoon." He listened for a beat. "It's definitely credible. Apparently, she really pissed one of them off in a reverse proffer yesterday."

When he got off the phone, Anna poured the rest of the wine, now warm, into their glasses. They sank down on the couch.

"I guess I haven't perfected the reverse proffer yet," Anna tried to joke, although she felt shaky. "This was not the result I was aiming for."

Jack didn't laugh. The muscle in his jaw clenched and unclenched. He pulled her close and wrapped his arms tightly around her.

24

We gotta get a piece of this," Ricardo said. "It's the wave of the future."

"Actually," Victor said, "the Internet's been around for a long time."

"Yeah, but a brothel on the Internets! Now that's something new."

The timekeeper looked at him disbelievingly. "Are you kidding, old man?"

"Why would I kid?"

In fact, Ricardo rarely kidded these days. He spent most of his time worrying. He worried that the gang was going to find out he'd testified against them. He worried about money. It had been almost three weeks since the raid on his brothel. Three weeks without any income. The bills were piling up, and his wife was complaining even more than usual. She was going to be angry that he was out drinking with his friend instead of home helping with the apartment and the children. Too bad.

He ogled the ladies milling around the bars and restaurants of Tivoli Square. This was a neighborhood that knew how to do a Saturday night. It was good to be back in the city, to see women dressed like women, all different shapes and sizes and colors. Tall women in tight jeans, fat women in short skirts, curvy women in clingy blouses. He calculated their worth within seconds of seeing them.

"Hey, lady, I want a piece of that!" he shouted at a teenager in leopard-print leggings. She flicked him off. He laughed.

"See, Victor? That's what makes this city great. You think you see that in Haver duh Grace, or however you fucking say it? No way. It's full of fishermen and farmers."

Ricardo was sick of Havre de Grace. He missed his friends here in D.C. He missed the action and the lights. He missed the food and the women. Most of all, he missed being a big man in town, the owner of a brothel. That's why he'd come back to the District—despite the police warning him to stay away, despite his own fears. He had to see his old neighborhood and the people who knew he was *someone*. He and his old timekeeper were headed to their third bar of the night. Ricardo had seen friends and old customers and was feeling pleasantly buzzed. Seven Natural Lights had washed away many of his worries.

"Worst part is, I got no way to make a living out there. I'm not working on some damn chicken farm."

"I got a job at that shoe store on Fourteenth," Victor said.

"Cramming fat feet into sneakers for minimum wage? No offense, but that's not for me." In fact, Ricardo had no idea how to do anything but sell sex. He told that blond prosecutor that he'd run the Monroe Street brothel for three years. That was technically true—but he had been a brothel owner for almost twenty years. He'd operated in whatever cheap places he could find. When he had rent disputes, or too much competition from rival brothels, or—worst of all—gentrification, he just moved a few blocks and started up again.

But this was the first time the authorities were involved. He had pandering on his record now, and part of his plea deal was "no more brothel." The prosecutor needed his testimony—but would she look the other way if he moved back to the city and started another brothel? He doubted it; she seemed like a bitch. He didn't want to ask his attorney. He wanted his attorney to believe in him.

"That's why I'm thinking about the Internets," Ricardo explained. "You don't need a place. You just advertise online, drive the girl to the customer. Collect the money. No rent, no utilities, no police watching the johns come and go. I got an AOL account. I just need a young kid like you who knows about computers to set the shit up. We'd be partners. Eighty–twenty."

"Yeah, Ricardo, you're the next Steve Jobs."

"What kind of jobs?"

"Never mind."

They turned onto Fifteenth Street, then hopped a low stone wall into Meridian Hill Park. As they walked into the large green space, the noise of the city receded. Tall trees surrounded the park, providing so much foliage it almost felt like the country. Without the distractions of the streetlights and flashing signs, Ricardo noticed the moon: a huge orange circle hanging low in the sky.

"You know, Victor, you should get a plea deal," Ricardo said. "Get this thing behind you, move on with your life."

"Fuck that. They can charge me with whatever. I ain't never saying a word about MS-13 in no courtroom. You see what they did to Jaime? They took his *head* off, man. Took it clean off."

Ricardo nodded. He tried hard not to think about that. He knew that if he hadn't taken the deal, he'd be in jail right now. But once he testified against MS-13 in open court, he could never come back to this neighborhood. If they knew he was snitching, he was dead.

Maybe those assholes would plead guilty, too, and he wouldn't ever have to take the stand. Maybe, if he took the stand, he could claim he forgot everything.

Their shoes crunched on the gravel path. The perimeter of the park was heavily wooded, and it was dark in here, the streetlights blocked by trees. As they walked through, Ricardo heard the crunching of gravel behind him. He glanced back. Several men were walking in the same direction as them. He and Victor walked a little faster.

But the crunching got closer. Were those guys following them? He didn't want to turn and look at them again. But he had to. He twisted his neck, saw that there were five or six men, several tatted up. They'd spread out, so some were behind him, some coming up on either side, like a pack of wolves moving to cut off their prey. Something flashed in one of their hands. A machete? The scar across his chest started to throb. "Victor!" he said.

A man materialized in front of them.

"Hello, Ricardo." It was the devil-man. Horns pointed, sharpened teeth flashing a sharklike smile. The machete made a silky sound as he pulled it from its sheath.

Ricardo ran. He zigzagged through the park without a plan, just the desperate instinct to flee. He tripped over a branch, skinning his chin on the ground. Got up again, bumped right into a man. Felt a blade slice through his shoulder. Thrashed wildly, felt his knee connect with a groin, heard the grunt, kept running. He could hear more of them running behind him, crashing through the brush. His shoulder was on fire, his arm dangling painfully at his side, but he was running scared and running fast.

The end of the park was right ahead of him. On the other side of the trees he could see lights, buildings, people. Safety. There was a large retaining wall where the park bordered Sixteenth Street. He just needed to make it down the wide stone steps and he'd be okay. The staircase was close—he was only a few strides away. His legs pumped at full speed. He was going to make it.

Something heavy slammed into his chest, knocking him down. His palms burned as the gravel tore through skin. He tried to breathe but couldn't; his lungs were stunned by the impact. He hoisted himself to his hands and knees, desperate for air, his chest convulsing ineffectively. He didn't see anyone near him. What had hit his chest?

Then he saw it, rolling away from him like a soccer ball. Victor's head. No longer attached to his body. It thudded to a stop against a stone, tilting to one side, as if asking a question.

Ricardo tried to scream, but nothing came out. His lungs were frozen, his shoulder throbbed, but he hauled himself to his feet. He could see the lights of Sixteenth Street twinkling beyond the trees. So close. He forced his feet to move, although it felt like they were going through water, slow and heavy.

The Devil's face was in front of his. He was no longer smiling. Ricardo stared into the monster's deep black eyes. This couldn't happen now. He had plans. The Internets, the online brothel. His wife. She would . . . well, she might not be too sorry if he didn't come home. But his children! He opened his mouth to plead for his life. Diablo raised the machete above his head. The blade flashed orange, reflecting the light of the harvest moon.

25

Anna stood outside the grand jury witness room, pacing. Although the Constitution imagined the grand jury as a check on the government's power—for no federal criminal charges could be brought unless they were approved by a panel of citizens—in practice, this right was more valuable to the government than to a suspect. The standard for obtaining a grand jury indictment was notoriously low, and the rules of evidence notoriously permissive. But the grand jury was a powerful tool for a prosecutor to build a case. Anna had used the grand jury to lock in Ricardo's testimony, to subpoena surveillance video from surrounding shops, and to obtain medical records of the victims.

Now Anna wanted to lock in Tierra Guerrero's testimony. There was just one problem: Tierra was late. And Anna couldn't reach her.

Anna glanced at her watch: 10:20 A.M. She felt the same worry every time a witness was late, despite how common it was. Tierra was supposed to arrive at 9:30, and they were supposed to go into the grand jury at 10:00. She had already lost her reserved grand jury time.

If Tierra showed up now, Anna would have to bargain with other prosecutors to get another time that day.

Anna had called Tierra's cell phone twice—it went to voice mail. She tried the hotel room—no one answered. In light of the threats to her own life, Anna's imagination was conjuring terrible pictures of what might have happened to the witness.

"Sit," Sam said. The FBI agent reclined in a chair outside the grand jury room, and didn't even look up from her BlackBerry as she admonished Anna. "You're making me nervous."

"Where do you think she is?" Anna asked.

"Four-to-one, she slept in. Three-to-one, she forgot the court date and is off getting a mani-pedi. Two-to-one, she changed her mind, fled the country, and you'll never find her again."

"Can you go to the hotel, Sam? See if she's there or if anyone's seen her?"

Sam sighed. "It's only thirty minutes past her grand jury time. I expect you were raised to be punctual, but you gotta cut civilians some slack."

Anna nodded, forced herself to sit down, and re-reviewed her case file. By eleven, even Sam conceded there was a problem.

"Okay." Sam stood up. "Give me a copy of the subpoena. I'll swing by the hotel."

"Thank you."

Anna returned to her office and spent the next hour trying to get work done. She was feeling off her game, having woken up very early in the Shenandoah Valley and made the long drive in the predawn dark. Jack and Olivia had been mostly quiet—Olivia because she slept, Jack because he was worried. A meeting was scheduled later this afternoon to go over security procedures for Anna in light of the death threat.

A few minutes before noon, Sam appeared with Tierra Guerrero. Tierra wore blue jeans and a big red sweatshirt. Her dark hair was tied back in a ponytail. The woman's face had healed, but her expression was even more miserable than when she'd been in the hospital.

"*Buenos días,*" Anna said, standing to meet them.

"*Buenos días,*" Tierra mumbled to the floor.

"She was at the McDonald's across from the hotel," Sam said drily. "She forgot the court date. And she didn't hear the phone ring when we called this morning. Or see our messages."

Anna met Sam's eyes and nodded. They both knew this was a lie. Tierra had been avoiding them. Anna would get the full story from Sam later. For now, she was just relieved to see her witness.

"Tierra, what happened today?" Anna asked, when the interpreter arrived. "Why didn't you come at nine-thirty like we agreed?"

Tierra shook her head and played with an imaginary fleck of lint on her jeans.

"Is everything okay at the hotel?" Anna asked.

Tierra nodded.

"Have you been going to the counselor?"

Tierra mumbled something in Spanish. The translator said, "The counselor is kind. But it is hard for Tierra to get there."

Anna nodded, recognizing the excuse of someone who didn't want counseling.

"Are you ready to testify before the grand jury?" Anna asked.

Tierra's eyes grew big as the translator repeated Anna's words in Spanish. She shook her head. "No."

"Why not?" Anna asked.

"I have been thinking about what happened. And I was mistaken about what I told you last time."

"Mistaken how?" Anna's stomach clenched. She didn't want to hear the answer. But she certainly couldn't elicit it for the first time in front of the grand jury.

"The man you arrested," Tierra said. "The one called Psycho. He was not with the other three. He was not part of the raid on the brothel. He was a nice man, a paying customer. He came in before the other men. He was having sex with me when the other men arrived and started cutting people up. He was just a john. He's as much a victim as me."

"Tierra, we both know that's not true. That's not what you told me at the hospital. He sexually assaulted you."

"I must have been very groggy from all the pain pills when we spoke before. No one assaulted me."

"Who told you to say this?"

"No one." Tierra's eyes were wide with fear. "I'm sorry for getting it wrong when I spoke to you before."

Anna knew it was pointless to ask her any more questions. The more Tierra talked, the more *Giglio* and *Brady* material she was creating: inconsistent statements, impeachment material, fodder for cross-examination. And the woman was now lying to law enforcement. She needed a lawyer.

Anna's skin was hot with anger. She tried to focus it on the unseen people who'd threatened Tierra, and not on Tierra herself. The woman was clearly terrified.

Tierra's statement was designed to clear Psycho of the sexual assault. Had it been true, it would also get him off the hook for felony murder and the murder of the doorman. If he wasn't part of the gang that raided the brothel, he wasn't legally responsible for anyone's death.

"We should revoke the U-visa," Sam said to Anna. "She doesn't get a visa for lying."

Anna shook her head at the translator; she didn't want this translated.

"No," she said, taking Sam aside. "She's still being victimized. She still needs our help. Maybe she'll come back to our side, start telling the truth again. We might even add an obstruction of justice charge."

"Good luck getting anything useful out of her."

Anna made some phone calls, then met Sam and Tierra in the lobby. Tierra's eyes were red and puffy. She stood when Anna came out.

"Agent Randazzo will go with you to the courthouse," Anna said, handing her some paperwork. "They're going to appoint a lawyer for you. You need to talk about all this with your own lawyer. Also, I think you should talk to a woman from Polaris. Here's her card. She used to work as a prostitute, and she helps other women get out of the trade."

"Thank you," Tierra said. "I have created so much trouble for you. I'm so sorry."

"Be safe," Anna said. "Call Agent Randazzo if anyone bothers you again."

Anna went back to her office to write the *Brady* letter. A prosecutor had an obligation to inform a defendant whenever she discovered exculpatory evidence. Anna hated writing a letter like this, where the exculpatory statements were so obviously false and likely the product of witness intimidation. It would just confirm to Psycho that his efforts to obstruct justice were working.

As she typed, Detective McGee knocked on the door of her office. He wore the world-weary, focused expression of a homicide detective who'd just gotten a new case. But it was more than that. It was a look of sympathy, directed at Anna.

"What is it?" Anna asked.

"It's Ricardo Amaya and Victor Linares—our brothel owner and his timekeeper," he said. "They're dead. Their bodies were found in Meridian Hill Park. Both decapitated. Each stabbed thirteen times postmortem."

26

"You need to come off the case," Jack said. He was gripping his mug so tightly, it looked as though his knuckles were trying to escape from his skin. The remnants of their mostly untouched room-service dinner were pushed to one side of the table.

"That's not an option," Anna repeated.

They'd been going in the same conversational circle for the last hour. Anna could hardly believe Jack's stance. There was no way he would come off a case if *he* were threatened. She was spooked, she was queasy—but she wasn't quitting.

"Of course it's a fucking option! They killed two of your witnesses," he said. "You need to take them seriously when they say they're going to kill you, too. You're a great lawyer, but our office has lots of great lawyers. Someone else can try the case."

"What good does that do? They'll just threaten the next prosecutor."

"I'm not engaged to the next prosecutor."

"You're their chief."

"Goddammit! I'm not willing to risk your safety."

"It's not your call," she said softly.

Jack slammed the mug down and stood abruptly, knocking his chair over. He set it straight, picked up Anna's phone, and strode into the hallway. She was alone for the first time since they'd checked in.

The Marshals had put them in a two-bedroom suite at the Residence Inn by National Airport. Olivia was in one of the bedrooms, watching *Phineas and Ferb* on TV. When Anna and Jack picked her up from school this afternoon, they didn't tell her why they were going to a hotel. They just said the hotel had a pool. Olivia had been pleased.

Jack came back into the room, holding Anna's phone out to her. "Your sister wants to talk to you."

She glared at him, astonished.

"Not cool, Jack." She took the phone. "Hey, Jody."

"Annie? Oh my God! You've been threatened? You've gotta get off the case."

"No, no, it's not really a big deal. I'm not sure why Jack is freaking out so much."

"Not a big deal! You're in a hotel hiding from people who want to kill you!"

"I know, it sounds bad. But you can't just quit a case, or every criminal would make threats."

"That sounds nice in the abstract. Not when it's my sister's life."

"Look, I know a few prosecutors who've had death threats. No one abandons the case. You take a few precautions, get the jerks convicted, move on."

"Jack's wife got killed like this," Jody said.

"Yeah . . ." Anna looked over at him. He was pacing by the window, running his hand over the back of his neck. He was usually the coolest head in any room. She'd never seen him so upset. She needed to go easier on him. "No one knows for sure what happened there."

"Annie, I don't like it."

"Me, neither. But it'll be okay. I promise. How are you? Been to Brent's house lately?"

"Don't try to change the subject."

"I take that as a yes?"

"Anna. Please. Be careful."

"I will."

"Love you."

"You, too."

She hung up, thinking about her own family. For too long, she'd cowered in silence. She'd vowed never again to back down in the face of violence. She wasn't backing down now.

She went to Jack, put a gentle hand on his arm, and led him to the couch, where they sat.

"Don't worry," she said. "It's going to be fine."

"You don't know that."

"A prosecutor can't quit whenever the bad guys threaten them. If we all did that, who would stop the crimes?"

"You sound like me," Jack said. "Four years ago. I was wrong then. You're wrong now."

"What do you mean?"

His face was a mask of pain.

"When Nina was greenlighted," he said slowly, "she wanted to go into Witness Protection. I disagreed. I said what you're saying: You stand your ground and fight. That's what makes America different from places like El Salvador. I thought we could handle things with police patrols at our house, a little protection, and vigilance. Nina disagreed. She said she knew how this gang worked, and they didn't play by our rules. But she stayed. Because of me, she stayed. A week later, she was dead."

Anna realized why Jack had been so intent on believing that Nina's death was a random drug shooting, unrelated to MS-13.

She put her hand on his leg. "Jack, it wasn't your fault."

"It might have been." He closed his eyes for a moment, then looked directly at her. "I can't let it happen again."

"It won't. I'll take every precaution." She listed all the protections the Marshals had enumerated at their meeting today. "We're in a hotel. The Marshals are giving us portal-to-portal protection as we commute. It'll be fine."

If anything, these murders made her even more determined to bring down Psycho and his gang. Not only for what they'd done to Ricardo and Victor, Tierra and Maria-Rosa, and countless girls every year. But for what she suspected they'd done to Nina—and for what that had done to Jack.

A shuffling noise in the doorway made Anna look away from Jack. Olivia stood in the door between the two rooms, looking worried. Anna wondered how much she'd heard.

"Wow!" Anna announced as cheerfully as she could. "How'd it get past your bedtime?"

Olivia shook her head.

"Let's pick out some good books to read, okay?"

The girl nodded solemnly, and allowed Anna to take her hand and lead her back to her bedroom. They went through the bedtime ritual: story, pj's, face washing. Olivia brushed her teeth, spat out the foam, and turned to Anna.

"Why are we in this hotel?" Olivia asked.

Anna considered calling Jack in to field the question. But if she was going to be Olivia's mother, she had to start handling things like this on her own. Stalling for time, she grabbed a washcloth.

"Come here, you look like a rabid dog."

Olivia looked at her foamy mouth in the mirror and giggled. "Arf, arf."

Anna wiped the toothpaste from Olivia's face and wondered what was better: for the girl to feel secure, or for her to know the truth? She wanted Olivia to trust her, to know that when Anna answered her questions, she answered honestly. On the other hand, Anna didn't want Olivia's childhood to be filled with worry and fear; Dr. Spock said it was important for kids to grow up believing the world was generally a good place.

"We're here for work," Anna said. "Sometimes grown-ups have to move around or go to hotels for work. Nobody likes it, but sometimes you have to do stuff you don't really love doing, in order to do the right thing."

"It's not so bad," Olivia said. "The pool's cool."

"Good." Anna rinsed the girl's toothbrush and herded her back to the bedroom. Olivia climbed into bed. Anna wondered if now was a good time to talk about stranger danger, or if that would just freak her out. She turned off the light and tucked the blankets around Olivia's skinny little legs.

"Anna?" Olivia said.

"Mm-hm?"

"You know not to talk to strangers, right?"

Anna swallowed a laugh. "Yes. I do."

"Good."

"Don't worry, sweetie. Everything's gonna be just fine." Anna made it sound so convincing, she almost believed it herself. Olivia nodded and rolled over to her side. Anna sat next to her, patting her gently, until the girl fell asleep.

27

At eight the next morning, a deputy U.S. Marshal knocked on their hotel door. Tracey Fitzgerald was a pretty young Asian woman in a dark pantsuit. She would be the deputy who escorted them to and from work. Anna was disappointed that their deputy was a tiny woman; she was expecting a big man, Tommy Lee Jones from *The Fugitive*. Then she felt ashamed at her own sexism. This woman would do a fine job protecting them. A gun had the same power no matter who was firing it.

Fitzgerald walked them to the parking lot and gestured for Jack, Olivia, and Anna to sit in the back of a blue Ford Taurus. Anna felt strange to be riding in the back, as if the deputy were their chauffeur. Their first stop was Olivia's elementary school. Olivia skipped off to her classroom, and Anna sat with Jack and Fitzgerald as they discussed security procedures with the school principal.

"How are you feeling?" Jack asked Anna as the car pulled away from the school.

"Okay," Anna said. "Worried about Olivia."

"Don't worry," Fitzgerald met her eyes in the rear-view mirror. "Your family members aren't really in danger. They usually just kill the prosecutor."

Jack didn't seem amused, but Anna laughed. She was glad Fitzgerald had a sense of humor. Even gallows humor was welcome at this point.

Jack spent the rest of the ride talking on his cell to the D.C. branch of the U.S. Marshals Service. "I know you're not a babysitting service," Jack said. "But this is about protecting my family." He arranged to have a deputy pick up Olivia from school and bring her to the hotel every day that week. He would leave work early to be with her.

"What about Luisa?" Anna asked.

"It seems like a good week to give her a vacation," Jack replied.

When they got to the U.S. Attorney's Office, Jack rode the elevator with Anna and got out on her floor. She stopped at the door to the Sex Crimes unit.

"You're sweet," she said. "But I'm fine. Go be chief."

He nodded, kissed her lips chastely, and went back to the elevators.

She was glad to go to her office, log on, and start working. Before, her case against Psycho was part of her job. Now it was personal. If he thought killing witnesses was going to get him out of jail, he was about to see how wrong he was. She was going to rebuild this case, and make it even stronger than before.

Anna walked to Carla's office and knocked on the open door. Carla invited her to take a seat.

"I'm hoping to get Psycho's jail calls translated now," Anna said. "I know we didn't have funds before, but now—"

"Absolutely," Carla interrupted. "Get them expedited."

"Thanks," Anna stood to go.

"Actually can you close the door?" Carla said. "There's one more thing."

After the door was shut, Carla said, "So it's Hector. He's on the *Lewis* list."

"Why am I not surprised."

Supervisors had a list of MPD officers who had some potential impeachment issue in their record. Line prosecutors couldn't look at the list, for privacy reasons. But if a prosecutor intended to call an officer as a witness, she had to check with her supervisor to be sure there were no *Lewis* issues. Depending on the issue, she would determine whether to use the officer—and be required to turn over the impeachment material to defense counsel—or to find another witness.

"Turns out Hector has a juvenile assault conviction from Los Angeles. The record is sealed, but I made some calls."

"What did you find?"

"He was arrested for jumping another young man into MS-13. When he was a teenager, Hector Ramos was an MS-13 member."

Anna let that sink in. "I better have somebody follow him."

"I agree. It can't be regular MPD, though. Internal Affairs maybe."

"I'll ask Samantha Randazzo. She's already helping on the case. This is perfect for the FBI."

"Good." Carla met her eyes with concern. "Are you hanging in there?"

"Yeah, I'm fine. Thank you. I just want to get these guys."

"Is Jack okay?"

"You know him. He's a fighter." Anna didn't want to tell Carla, Jack's office rival, that he wanted Anna to drop the case.

Back in her office, Anna called Sam and relayed the new information.

Sam whistled. "You want me to put a tail on Hector?"

"Exactly. And can you interview the people who witnessed Nina's death? The names are in the file. No one admitted to seeing or hearing much, but we should follow up."

"On it."

When they hung up, Anna pulled out the file dealing with Nina's old case with Maria-Rosa Gomez and the underage prostitution scheme. She grabbed the folder marked NOT FOR DISCOVERY and headed to the fifth floor.

The Fraud unit was the ivory tower of the U.S. Attorney's Office. Lawyers in Fraud might handle ten big cases at a time, as opposed to the hundreds in the misdemeanor trenches of the Domestic Violence and Sex Crimes unit. Sex Crimes lawyers spent their days running to court or interviewing emotional witnesses; it wasn't uncommon to see a crying woman rushing down the hall to the bathroom, or an AUSA asking a witness to show a bruised cheek for a photo. But in the Fraud section, people sat quietly before their computers, reviewing documents or drafting pleadings. It felt like a law firm, but with prison-made furniture.

Once lawyers got into the Fraud section, they stayed. Most of the Fraud AUSAs looked like they were approaching grandparenthood, while most lawyers in Anna's section were the young, single, happy-hour crowd. The sense of permanence was reflected in the typical Fraud office decor: diplomas on the walls, Tiffany lamps on desks, oriental rugs covering government-blue carpets. The younger prosecutors, still going through the office's section-by-section rotation, traveled light; ego walls were rare.

George Litz's office was livelier than the rest. Four burly men, all with short hair and dark suits, sat in the guest chairs, leaned against the bookshelves, or perched on the windowsill. They had to be federal agents. George himself leaned back in his desk chair and tossed a Nerf football to the agents as they spoke. He had broad shoulders and an abundance of steel-gray hair. The conversation tapered off as Anna knocked on the open door.

"Hey, George," she said. "I'm Anna Curtis. From the Sex Crimes unit."

She'd seen him in the hallways, but never spoken to him before. He was a generation older, and their work had never intersected.

"What can I do for you?" George and the agents seemed pleased to be distracted by a young woman.

“I’d like to talk to you about the Maria-Rosa Gomez case.”

George glanced at the men hanging around his big office. “I guess it’s about time for lunch, guys. Why don’t you go, and pick me up something? We’ll keep working when you get back.”

The men joked with one another good-naturedly as they filed out of the office. Anna sat in one of the seats, warm from the body before.

“I’m sorry to interrupt,” she said. “I have a rape case. I think it’s related to the Gomez case you handled back when you were in Sex Offense.”

“How so?”

Anna sketched out the broad strokes.

“Those sound like my defendants,” George said. He tossed the football in the air and caught it. “How’d did you get my old file anyway?”

“Your secretary left it for me. There was an e-mail asking about it.”

“Ah. Sorry I missed that.”

“So what happened in the Gomez case?” Anna said. “I can’t tell from the file.”

“Nothing happened to it. The defendants were in the wind.” George turned to his filing cabinets and rummaged through until he pulled out a Redweld folder. He handed it to Anna. She glanced through and saw a draft indictment, charging two John Does, aka Psycho and Diablo.

“You never got their names?” Anna asked.

“We got a million fingerprints from the stolen vans, but they were johns, or the vehicle owner’s, or just not in the system. There was one set from the driver's side door handle—I'm thinking the devil guy—but they weren't in the system either. I was sure he'd be arrested eventually on something else, but nothing ever came in. The case went dormant. Probably went back to El Salvador."

"If so, they're back," Anna said. "And I'm pretty sure I've got one of them in custody."

George almost dropped his football. "Which one?"

"Psycho."

"That's great."

"Yeah. I'd love it if someone from your case could ID them, and we could tie the two cases together. I saw a reference to another witness, Julia Hernandez. What can you tell me about her?"

"I can't tell you, but she saw the whole thing. Once the girl and Flores were killed, the Marshals put Julia into Witsec. Probably living somewhere near a cornfield. I figured if we ever arrested somebody, we'd bring her back."

"Now's that time. How do I talk to her?"

"We'll have to call the Marshals Service. They're in charge of Witsec, they decide whether a protected witness comes in for a meeting."

The team of agents returned to George's office, carrying sandwiches wrapped in cellophane. One tossed a sandwich to George. "Pastrami from New Course," the agent laughed. New Course was a sandwich shop that made a point of employing former offenders. "I told 'em it was for you, so I'm sure they made it extra juicy." The agent mimed jerking off.

George shook his head good-naturedly and turned

to Anna. "I'll make a few calls," he said. "See what I can do. I've got to get back to this—but good luck."

The agents were unwrapping their sandwiches, cheerfully debating whether it was a certain health risk for law enforcement agents to eat at New Course.

"Actually," Anna said, "can you step out with me for a second?"

George looked longingly at his sandwich but stepped into the hall with her. She shut the door.

"I'm wondering," Anna said, "do you know an MPD officer named Hector Ramos?"

"Heard of him. Human-Trafficking Task Force?"

"Yeah, that's where he is now. Four years ago, he was on the power-shift. He was the Eyes on the buy-bust where Nina died. I'm wondering if he ever worked on this case. Or had any connection to it?"

George's face was blank. "Nope."

"Any connection between him and the MS-13 members involved in this case?"

"Don't think so." He opened the door to his office again. "Good luck."

Anna thanked George and left. The smell of sandwiches made her belly rumble with hunger. She considered running out to grab a burrito at Chipotle, but the Marshals had her spooked. They could escort her to and from work, but they couldn't be with her all day, so they advised her to stay inside the U.S. Attorney's Office unless she had a police escort. It was like she was under house arrest. She went down to the vending machines and bought pita chips and a Snickers bar. Lunch of champions.

28

The brief that Psycho's newly appointed attorney filed later that day didn't surprise Anna. The Motion to Change Bond Status, based on Anna's *Brady* letter about Tierra's new story, was a standard effort to get Psycho released from jail. The judge scheduled the hearing for the next morning.

Anna walked to court with McGee. He tried to distract her with gossip, even as he scanned the street to make sure no one was hiding in the bushes with a machete.

D.C. Superior Court was the court of the people. Anna and McGee got at the end of a long line of civilians snaking through the brick patio before the main doors. Lawyers and cops had to wait with everyone else. Inside, the atrium swarmed with people looking at the big electronic board listing courtrooms, mothers dragging kids by one arm, and lawyers having last-minute or first-time conferences with clients on the plastic chairs bolted to the walls. Escalators crisscrossed the atrium, going up six flights. Anna and McGee rode up to the third floor.

Judge Susan Spiegel's courtroom was as tattered as

all the others in D.C. Superior Court. It was windowless, with a low ceiling of stained fluorescent panels. Threadbare mustard-colored carpeting covered the floor. The courtroom was packed with people waiting for their own hearings.

McGee didn't need to be there; Anna could handle this hearing alone. He had volunteered to escort her, though, and she was glad.

Although court personnel usually sat in the first row, McGee gestured for Anna to sit with him in the last row. He wanted the wall at his back.

"Nobody's going to attack me in court," Anna said. "There're metal detectors and armed CSOs."

McGee shrugged and offered her a stick of gum.

The judge took the bench at precisely nine thirty, but Anna and McGee had to wait another two hours, as the judge called case after case before theirs. Anna's attention drifted as alleged murderers, rapists, and robbers had their status conferences, sentencings, and probation revocation hearings. She checked her phone discreetly a few times. Judge Spiegel would yell at her if she noticed.

Anna thought longingly of the federal District Court, across the street, where attorneys got set times for their hearings, showed up, and were done. Once she brought federal charges, the Superior Court case would be dismissed, and she would try her case there.

A little before noon, the clerk finally called, "United States versus Jose Garcia, aka Psycho." Everyone took their places. A deputy Marshal brought Psycho out from the holding cell hidden behind the courtroom. He wore the usual orange prison jumpsuit, and the same inappropriate smile. He didn't look at Anna as he was led to stand next to his lawyer.

"Frank Ciopobi, for Mr. Garcia," the new lawyer said.

"I understand you've been appointed to take over this case. The court is grateful for your service." Despite the shabby courtroom, Judge Spiegel was smart and efficient. But she was perpetually cranky, with a permanent vertical crease between her eyebrows. This introductory politeness was likely the warmest she would be during the entire proceeding. "The defendant has moved to change his bond status. Mr. Ciopobi, what's your argument?"

"At the detention hearing, the defendant was held without bond based on evidence presented by the government. However, all of that evidence is gone. Tierra Guerrero has recanted her prior statements, and admits that my client was simply a paying customer. This admission defeats all charges against my client."

"So it's your theory, Mr. Ciopobi, that your client was having consensual sex in a room in which three strangers with machetes were slicing up the owner of the brothel—and that despite the fact that he was wearing a trench coat, carrying a machete, and is an MS-13 member, your client was not part of the group of trench coat–wearing machete-wielding MS-13 members who decapitated the brothel's doorman, terrorized its employees, attacked a police officer, and fled? Your client was simply in the wrong place, dressed the wrong way, and armed with the wrong machete, at the wrong time?"

"Not exactly, Your Honor. But I don't need to have

a theory. I've got no burden to prove anything. It's the government that needs to have a theory and evidence. And the testimony you just related comes in large part from the brothel owner, who, unfortunately, has passed away. We don't see how the government will prove the story it initially recounted."

"Ms. Curtis?" The judge turned her scowl to Anna.

"We believe Ricardo Amaya was killed by MS-13 in an effort to obstruct this investigation. He was decapitated and stabbed thirteen times—a classic MS-13 signature—three days ago. His timekeeper was killed in the same fashion. If anything, these homicides and Ms. Guerrero's obvious intimidation *add* to the charges we intend to bring against the defendant." She pointed at Psycho. "Letting him go now would reward an organization that's doing everything it can to undermine the system."

"Ms. Curtis," the judge said. "Do you have any evidence that Mr. Garcia was himself involved in your witness's death or recantation?"

"Not yet," Anna said. "But there is evidence connecting him to the gang, and connecting the gang to the murder of the brothel owner."

"How do you plan to prove this case if you don't have your key witnesses?"

Good question. Anna would like to know that herself.

"We're confident in our case, Your Honor. We intend to reveal our evidence and witnesses when required under the rules, but not sooner."

"Please approach, Ms. Curtis. Alone."

Psycho kept smiling as Anna walked up to the bench. The judge turned on the husher so the rest of the courtroom couldn't hear their conversation. "You're presenting this to a federal grand jury?"

"Yes," Anna answered. The grand jury investigation was secret, and could not be disclosed to the defendant—or anyone aside from law enforcement and the judge—until an indictment had come down.

"When do you expect to return an indictment?"

"In a month."

"At which time it will be a District judge's problem, and not mine. Very well." Judge Spiegel turned off the husher, indicating the sidebar was over. Anna walked back to the prosecution table. Psycho was glaring at her as he smiled.

"I find that there is enough evidence to keep the defendant in jail for now. However, I am setting a status hearing for four weeks from today. If this case has been federally indicted by then, Mr. Amaya's bond decision will not be up to me. If it hasn't, then I'll expect the government to tell me how it intends to prove the serious allegations it has charged. So ordered."

The judge had given Anna some leeway, but not much. If Anna was going to keep Psycho off the streets, she needed to rebuild her case against him, quickly.

When Anna got back to the office, she went through the preliminary translators' reports for Psycho's jail calls. Psycho spent a lot of time talking to a woman named Lola, who seemed to be his girlfriend. He called his mother and his grandmother. He talked about family gossip, how he was faring in jail, and all the things he wanted to do when he got out. There was some phone sex. But he never called male friends. And he never mentioned a word about his case. Nothing. Usually, that was the main thing prisoners wanted to talk about.

Anna paused at a telling sliver of conversation.

The girlfriend said, "So, Gato's gonna—"

"Nah nah nah!" Psycho said. "Not now."

The girlfriend started talking about a friend who'd recently had a baby.

Anna realized why there was nothing incriminating on Psycho's jail calls. She picked up her own phone and called Michael Kevin, a supervisor at the D.C. Jail. Kevin was familiar with the contraband that got smuggled into the jail. More important, he liked Anna. She asked if one of his guys could toss Psycho's prison cell, but in a way that Psycho wouldn't know it had been searched. Kevin agreed. Unlike a citizen in his home or office, a prisoner had no expectation of privacy, and the government didn't need a warrant to search his cell.

Two hours later, Kevin called back.

"Found a cell phone under his mattress," he said.

"Great," Anna said. "Can you send me the details? And put the phone back exactly where you found it?"

She spent the afternoon writing an application for a wiretap. It might take a few days for a court to approve the wire, but then the agents could hear what Psycho was saying when he thought no one was listening.

29

Meanwhile, Sam drove to Benning Road and parked her Dodge Durango near the alley where Nina Flores had been killed four years ago. This was a residential block lined with low brick apartment buildings. Sam had been to this street before; it was one that was often named on police reports.

Walking past the alley, Sam noted the spot where Nina's corpse had lain in the crime-scene pictures. This afternoon, there was only some trash and a stray cat.

In the paperwork detailing Nina's death was a list of six witnesses who had seen or heard the shooting. Sam was going to knock on their doors.

The witnesses lived in buildings on either side of the alley. Sam got into the first building by buzzing all of the apartments. Some trusting soul buzzed open the front door. She went in and knocked on the door of the first apartment on the list.

An old lady opened the door and squinted up at her. "Yes?"

"Ms. Jackson?"

"Who?"

"Are you Ms. Ida Jackson?"

"No. Who are you?"

Sam flashed her badge. "How long have you lived here, ma'am?"

"Twenty years, missy. Is that a crime?"

"No. Do you know Ida Jackson?"

"Never heard of her."

"Do you remember a shooting in the alley four years ago?"

"I barely remember what I had for breakfast. I've gotta go, my shows are on."

The door shut.

Sam tried the next five apartments on the list. Two didn't answer. One family had just moved in and didn't know the prior residents. The other two families had lived there at the time of the shooting, but their names didn't match up with the names given on the police paperwork. When Sam asked them if they remembered the four-year-old shooting, they just shrugged. It was so long ago.

Each of the PD-252's—the police witness statements—was signed by Hector Ramos. Sam didn't for a minute believe he had simply gotten the names and addresses wrong on every one. Detective Ramos had lied in his police reports.

Now Sam started knocking on random doors. Most people didn't answer. Some faces peered at her from behind windows, but the doors often remained silent and closed. When someone actually answered, Sam held up a picture of Nina Flores's body in the alley, and asked if they remembered the shooting from four years ago. Everyone shook their heads, relieved to have such a simple and easily negatable question.

She kept knocking. She was looking for one particular woman. Sam didn't know exactly who it was, but she was out there somewhere. On every street, there was one woman who was the neighborhood's eyes and ears. Usually someone who had lived there for decades and had plenty of gray hair. She'd raised kids there, but didn't have any living with her now. She spent her time at her window, looking out on the street, or on her stoop, watching the action. She would ask why the police didn't do more about crime in the neighborhood. She saw everything, remembered everything, and was willing to tell the police what she saw. Sam was going to find that woman.

Her lucky break finally came—but the old woman turned out to be a young man. De'Vone Jones was twenty-eight years old. He had a handsome face, smooth brown skin, and the most impressive biceps Sam had ever seen. His legs were skin over bones, sitting motionless in his wheelchair.

He invited Sam into his ground-floor apartment and wheeled himself to an open spot next to the couch. The way he spun his wheelchair around, the wheels seemed an extension of his graceful body. He had been a tree doctor, he said, trimming branches and cutting down old trees. But a few years ago, a branch snapped and his harness failed. He'd fallen forty feet to the ground. He no longer had feeling below the waist. But he was able to live near the mother of his children, and still be part of his community.

Sam showed him the picture of Nina Flores's body in the alley, and asked about the shooting four years ago. He nodded. "I remember that."

"What do you remember?"

"I was on the computer, right there." He gestured to a desk that abutted a window overlooking the alley. "Heard the sound of a gunshot. One single blast. Unmistakable. Not the first time in this neighborhood. I looked over my computer, out the window." Sam went to the window. It had a view of the alley, including the spot where Nina's body had fallen.

"How much time passed between the gunshot and you looking out the window?"

"No time. I heard the shot and I looked out."

"What did you see?"

"Woman was down, laying in the alley. Pool of blood under her head. Just like in that photo."

"Did you see anyone else?"

"Just one person. A Spanish guy."

"What did he look like?"

"Late twenties, early thirties. Tall. Dark hair and a goatee. Street clothes."

"Which way did he run?"

"He didn't run. He just stood there."

"Just stood there? What was he doing?"

"Holding a gun in his hands. He threw the gun down, next to the body. Then he called someone. Eventually, some police came. They walked away with him."

"The police walked away with the same guy who threw down the gun?"

"Yeah."

"Did you see *anyone* running on the street?"

"No. It was just the lady down, and the guy standing next to her."

"Are you sure that you looked out the window the moment you heard the gunshot? For instance, could you have heard a gunshot, then the shooter runs away, somebody else comes up, then you look out the window?"

"No, it was no time at all. I remember it clearly."

Sam nodded. She wasn't surprised when two witnesses' stories had discrepancies, but this was nothing like the foot chase described in Hector's police report.

"Do you think you could ID the 'Spanish' guy?" she asked. "If I brought you a photo spread?"

"I don't know, it's been so long. Somebody should have asked me that four years ago."

"Yes," she said. "Somebody should have."

30

Gato sat on the second-story balcony of his apartment, his plastic chair tipped backward, his feet on the porch railing. The balcony overlooked a few trees, then traffic-clogged New Hampshire Avenue. The cars revved and honked, their constant noise part of the chill night air. But if he focused hard enough on the trees, he could pretend he was alone in a forest. In one hand, he had a can of Bud Chelada, in the other, he held his cell phone away from his ear as Psycho shouted curses at him.

He watched a squirrel with an acorn in its mouth dart up the trunk of a bare oak. Gato felt a stab of jealousy toward the animal, wishing he could be that free. Instead, he had to run this organization that he both loved and hated. Mostly, he had to live with his own fucked-up self. He drained the last sip of tomato beer and tossed the can over the side of the balcony. He picked up a fresh Chelada from the floor, cracked it open, and took a long gulp.

He rented one room of this two-bedroom apartment from the family whose name was on the lease.

The two parents and their three little kids all slept in the other bedroom.

"And now I have to spend another month in jail!" Psycho's rant was picking up steam. He was furious about his bond hearing in court today.

"I know, homey, I know," Gato said. "We've doubled rents, been trying to collect money to get you a better lawyer."

"How much you got?"

"Almost eight thousand."

"That ain't shit! That won't get me a meeting."

"We just need a little more time," Gato said.

In the past, when homies went to jail, the gang sent no money at all—although they always made elaborate promises of help. But Gato was determined to actually help Psycho.

"And this bitch," Psycho continued in Spanish. "The prosecutor. She pointed at me, homey. *Pointed.* I mean, the disrespect! From a *woman*. I want to tear her up. She needs to be dealt with. Do you hear what I'm saying? You need to change her mind. Have fun with her, whatever. But I don't want to see her again. You understand me?"

"It's not that easy. She's got cops following her around now."

"You're the smart one, Gato. Figure it out. I can't take this anymore. There's no windows here. They got three of us in a tiny room, not fit for a dog. I'm going crazy, man. I mean for *real* crazy."

Psycho's voice had the hint of a scared child in it, which hurt Gato to hear. He and Psycho hadn't set out to be the gang's shot-callers. But time passed, the older guys died or were arrested or deported. Being MS wasn't easy—you had to be strong, and if you wanted to live, sometimes someone else had to die. That was his crazy life, *mi vida loca*. He looked at the three-dot tattoo on his hand. He'd known where MS would take him when he joined.

But now Psycho was asking him to do more than just greenlight the prosecutor. A greenlight was often just empty bravado. According to MS-13 rules, any member was bound to kill on sight a greenlighted person, using whatever weapon they had on them. In reality, it was unlikely any of the soldiers would run across the prosecutor in their daily lives. Even if they did, many would just turn and walk away. It took effort to convince soldiers to go out and kill someone—especially a prosecutor. The greenlight as it stood against Anna Curtis could take years to happen, if it happened at all. If they really wanted it done, it had to be specifically assigned to a man whose job was to hunt her down.

Keeping the phone cradled to his ear, Gato stood and walked inside the apartment. His little bedroom held a twin-sized mattress, a cheap nightstand, and a scuffed dresser. On the dresser were the *Santa Muerte* figurine and the *Corazón Puro* candle that Señora Zanita had given him at the botanica. The candle was not burning right now, but he had been lighting it for an hour every night before bed. In his nightstand was the bag of herbs that Zanita had told him to brew every day. He had followed her instructions, and made the tea every morning, using the time to remember an act of kindness someone had shown him. In the process, he'd realized that, other than his mother, Psycho was the person who'd shown Gato the most kindness in his life.

It was Psycho who had stopped a bully from beating the crap out of Gato when he was a scrawny thirteen-year-old. Psycho who'd brought loaves of his mother's *pan* to school, because Gato was always hungry. Psycho who introduced him to the gang and gave him the only community who cared about him.

They'd known each other almost half their fucked-up lives. Gato barely remembered his siblings in El Salvador. For all his faults, Psycho was the closest thing Gato had to family. He was like a brother—like a father, even. And now he needed Gato's help.

Gato thought of Señora Zanita's words. Each day he could choose to be a good man or a bad man. Sometimes, the choice was not a clear one.

Gato tucked the candle and *Santa Muerte* into a drawer, among his socks. Someone had to put in work for the good of the gang. Someone had to be brave.

"I'll do it," Gato said. "I'll kill her."

31

After just a few days, living in a hotel had become the new normal. Anna learned to use the mini-kitchen efficiently. They kept a semblance of family routine by eating breakfast every morning at the hotel table. At 8:00 A.M., Deputy Fitzgerald knocked on their door and walked them to the waiting blue Taurus. After the deputy Marshal dropped Olivia at school and the adults at the U.S. Attorney's Office, they carried on their days much like before, except there was no leaving school or work grounds.

Jack put Luisa on an extended vacation. "It's too far to have her commute out to Virginia," he told Anna. But then he hired another babysitter, a Polish woman who smelled of cooked cabbage and had to commute almost as far. He wouldn't even tell Luisa where they were staying.

"I think you're being too hard on her," Anna said. "I think your suspicions border on paranoia."

"I'm giving her a paid vacation," Jack said. "Most nannies would love that kind of paranoia."

"Just because she's Latina doesn't mean she's affiliated with the gang."

"I don't need a lecture on racism from *you*."

She stared at him. He rubbed his temples, then put a hand on her shoulder. "I'm sorry," he whispered. "Bear with me." He pulled her gently toward him, and buried his nose in her hair. She stiffened—but his muscles were even tighter, his breathing shaky. He was barely keeping it together. She returned the embrace. They didn't talk about Luisa anymore.

Pets weren't allowed at the hotel. Grace agreed to keep Raffles at her house for the duration. Anna was thankful that her friend was a cat person. She missed having the tabby greet her at the door.

At work, friends started popping by Anna's office as word got out that she'd been threatened. There were worried hugs, and offers to go get her lunch whenever she needed. Folks stopped by with unrequested coffees, cookies, and sandwiches. A paralegal gave her a whistle to put on her key chain. Anna smiled and attached it next to the pepper spray. She was touched by the show of support from her friends and colleagues.

Jody did her best across the miles. Be safe! Jody texted, before sending the song "I Fought the Law and the Law Won."

Sam was investigating the case now, and bringing Anna snacks from Sergio's all the time. With all the food from friends, Anna was afraid she would need a bigger wedding dress.

With the FBI on board, the case was moving with a velocity she hadn't been able to attain before. The murder of witnesses and the threat to her life made it a top-priority case, reviewed by the front office and political appointees at Main Justice. Anna told them she wanted to charge a federal RICO conspiracy, and she got immediate support for the idea.

On Thursday, Anna and McGee headed to the home of Maria-Rosa Gomez. The house was a small Cape Cod with a neat yard. Sandra Gomez answered the door somberly and led Anna and McGee into her living room. A wallpaper mural of a Roman countryside scene covered one wall. The furniture was heavy, wooden, and elaborately carved. Sandra had a plate of cookies out on the table, and asked if they wanted some coffee. Anna took a cup and McGee took three cookies, which seemed to please Sandra. They sat down on the L-shaped couch.

"Thank you for meeting with us today," Anna said. "I expect this must be hard for you."

"I'm sorry Mr. Gomez could not be here today," Maria-Rosa's mother said. "He's working, but . . . he could have gotten out of work. He just finds it very hard to talk about this." Sandra Gomez looked at her hands. "I know as much as he does, probably more."

"I appreciate your help. It appears there might be a connection between your daughter's case and a case that I'm investigating now. If you don't mind, I'd like to ask you a few questions, and I apologize if you answered these already, years ago. But it might be a big help."

"I'm happy to talk to you if it might help catch the person who took Maria-Rosa from us."

Anna asked her some general questions about her daughter.

"Maria-Rosa was a good girl," Sandra said. "When she was a teenager, she had a bit of a wild streak. But she was still a good student."

Sandra showed Anna some of Maria-Rosa's high school report cards—mostly B's and C's, with the occasional A. She handed Anna a school yearbook, and pointed to the smiling photo of her daughter.

"She was beautiful," Anna said. These things were Sandra Gomez's treasures. The papers, photo albums, and yearbooks were all she had left of her daughter.

"Thank you," Sandra said. "She got involved with some boy when she was fourteen years old. She started sneaking out of the house, hanging out late. He was in a terrible gang. I told her to stay away from him, but the more I demanded, the more she wanted to be with him."

"Do you know his name?"

"He went by a nickname. 'Gato.' "

It had to be the same guy.

"Do you know Gato's full name? Or where he lived?"

"No. That's all I knew. She would disappear constantly. I called the police, but they wouldn't do anything till she was gone for forty-eight hours. She would come back, leave again. In a few weeks, she became a shell of herself. She might have been on drugs.

"One day, a kind detective named Nina Flores brought her home to me." Sandra pulled Nina's business card from a folder and set it before Anna. "The detective was very supportive. She told me Maria-Rosa had been assaulted and the police were investigating.

She told me to talk to my daughter about it, to 'open a dialogue.'"

Sandra's eyes filled with tears.

Anna handed her a tissue from her purse. "Do you want to take a break, ma'am?"

Sandra nodded and got up. She used the bathroom, then came back a few minutes later. Her eyes were red but dry.

"Maria-Rosa wouldn't talk to me. She said it was none of my business. I knew that Gato boy had something to do with it, but she said no, he loved her. He would protect her. Three days before she was supposed to testify, she got ready to go out. I tried to stop her, and we had a terrible fight. She left. I don't know where she went. I never saw her alive again."

• • •

Gato wasn't happy to be sitting in the passenger seat while a girl drove. But Buena had a car—at least her parents did. So he was forced to rely on her as he carried out his promise: killing Anna Curtis.

They'd been following the prosecutor since she left her office. So far, Gato hadn't seen a chance. She was in an unmarked Crown Vic, clearly a police car. The big black man driving it wore a dark suit with a bulge at one side. A gun.

But what really bothered Gato was that the Durango was parked on the curb in front of Maria-Rosa's house.

Why the hell were they here? Of all the places in the world. He felt sick to his stomach. He hadn't been back here for four years—not even for Maria-Rosa's funeral. It looked the same as he remembered it. He tucked his hands under his thighs to hide that they were shaking.

"Are you okay?" Buena asked.

"Shut up."

Buena lowered her gaze to her lap. Gato felt a stab of regret, but brushed it away. He didn't care about her. He didn't need anyone's sympathy. He looked back at the house.

Four years ago, he came here every day. He'd only been through the front door once. Maria-Rosa's parents had never liked him. But he would sneak in through Maria-Rosa's window at night and lie with her. Once he brought her into the gang, things changed. At first, he loved to have her hang out with him and his homeboys. But there were no free rides. She had to put in work like everyone else.

Gato chewed the inside of his cheek until he tasted blood. Buena was staring at him again. At least this time she was wise enough not to ask what was wrong. When he met her eyes, she looked away.

He watched the house. The prosecutor and the big police officer were in there for a long time. Gato put his hand on the gun in the dip of his jeans. At some point, the officer would have to leave her side.

"What do we do now?" Buena asked.

"We wait."

32

CakeLove occupied a cute storefront on the corner of Fifteenth and U Streets. McGee pulled the Crown Vic to the curb in front of it. Through the plate-glass windows, Anna could see the cheerful interior, the Halloween decorations, the bright cases full of cupcakes. U Street was lined with hip shops, trendy bars, and happening music venues. People of every age, race, and color mingled here—glamorous urban hipsters, Section 8 recipients, Politico-reading wonks, wide-eyed Capitol Hill interns fresh from their home states. They sipped Frappuccinos, ate at sidewalk cafés, and tried their best pickup lines on each other. Anna and Jack fit right into this diverse center of their city.

She was here to taste wedding cakes, but she felt drained from a day of talking about murder, deception, and gang violence. She just wanted to go home and sleep. Even that wasn't really possible, since "home" was currently a hotel room.

"You need to transition from prosecutor mode to bride mode," said McGee.

She smiled at him. “I wish it was as easy as turning a switch.”

“You got a band?”

“The Bullettes. They’re an all-girl swing band.”

“You got a place?”

“Blown Away Farm. It’s beautiful.”

“Olivia’s got a flower girl dress?”

“Yeah, so cute. White with pink flower petals sewn into the tulle. You should see how adorable she looks in it.”

“There’s the spirit,” McGee said. “You gonna take Jack’s name?”

“Mmm, I’ve been going back and forth. It’d be easier to pick Olivia up from school. It’d be nice to be part of the family. But I’ve been Anna Curtis my whole life. Why should I give up my whole identity for this outdated tradition where the woman becomes property of the man she marries?”

“The woman becomes property of the man she marries? How come none of my ex-wives knew that?”

They laughed. She put her hand on the door handle. “Thanks, McGee.”

“You got a Marshal picking you up?” McGee asked.

“Yep.” She stepped out of the car and walked across the sidewalk into the shop.

• • •

Gato stood in front of the Boundless Yoga studio on U Street, a few shops away from CakeLove. On the other side of the window, a bunch of women on colorful mats stuck their butts up in the air at him. Normally, he would be fascinated by the display, but tonight he was watching the cupcake shop.

He sent Buena home—but he'd made her leave the car. He touched the gun in his pants. He knew it well, had used it over the years to do the necessary tasks for the gang. He would do one more tonight.

• • •

The bell tinkled as Anna stepped into the store. The air was scented with warm cake, melted butter, and cinnamon. Olivia sat on a bar stool at the counter, eating a cupcake from the top down. She had a dollop of pink frosting on the tip of her nose. Anna giggled when she saw it.

Jack turned toward the sound, and a big smile spread across his face when he saw her. "Hello, love." He came over and greeted her with a kiss. "You look beautiful."

"Thanks." After a long day at work, her suit was wrinkled, her ponytail was escaping the confines of the elastic band, and any makeup she'd applied this morning was long gone. It must be true love, she thought, if she still looked beautiful in Jack's eyes.

He led her to the counter, his arm proudly around her waist. "Anna, this is my friend Warren Brown."

Warren was a handsome African-American man with short twists and a big smile.

"The beautiful bride!" He reached over the counter and shook her hand. "So nice to meet you. Jack's told me so much about you."

"You, too." Anna was touched. Warren had been a lawyer, then left his law practice to open CakeLove. It had been wildly successful; he'd had his own show on the Food Network. He and Jack were friends from their law school days. The fact that Warren was personally handling their wedding cake tasting was an honor.

"Anna, you've got to try the strawberry buttercream!" Olivia held out the half-eaten pink cupcake to her. Anna took a bite from the least-ragged part. It was like a frothy strawberry dream.

"Wow." Anna pointed at Olivia's cupcake. "This is it. This is our wedding cake."

"Well, just hold on," Warren laughed. "That's a nice vote of confidence, but you should try a few more."

He gestured for Jack and Anna to sit next to Olivia at the counter, and then he proceeded to bring out twenty different flavors of cupcakes for them to taste. Jack held out a coconut delight and she met his eyes as she took a bite. Anna felt the stress of the day dissolve, swept away by a sugar rush. They tasted cupcake after delicious cupcake. They each had their favorites, which sparked an impassioned debate about the relative merits of strawberry buttercream, chocolate fuzzy wuzzy, and banana split. So they ordered a cupcake tree—a three-tiered platter heaped with cupcakes of each flavor.

As Warren processed the order, Anna turned to Jack. "Thanks for setting this up," she said.

"Thanks for coming." He put his arm around her shoulder and kissed her forehead.

• • •

Gato stood in a dark patch of sidewalk and watched as the woman inside the bright cake shop tasted cupcakes. People flowed past Gato—happy, chatty groups headed to bars and restaurants. They didn't notice him. In the middle of the crowded street, he felt very alone.

This was one of the few times he'd seen the prosecutor out in public without a cop at her side. He could just walk into the cupcake shop, hold his gun to her head, and pull the trigger. The witnesses would be stunned, and he could simply run away. This had worked for him before. "Go," he muttered to himself. "Fucking do it."

Gato walked to the shop and reached for the door. He could see the prosecutor inside, just a few feet away, smiling as she took a bite of another cupcake. Her face glowed with good health and the confidence of someone who mattered in the world.

Halloween decorations hung from the ceiling of the cupcakery. A figure swung on a string just inside the door, moved by an unseen force. Gato glanced at it—and stopped short. It was a skeleton in a robe, holding a scythe. The Grim Reaper—who looked very much like the *Santa Muerte*. His saint stared directly at him.

The man working behind the counter noticed him. The guy walked toward the door, mouthing the words "We're closed."

Gato's fingers remained on the door handle. He could kill this guy, too. The *Santa Muerte* figure swayed, like it was shaking its head. His saint was telling him something. Gato stared at the skull, then shook off his hesitation. He'd make things right with the saints later. Now his best friend was trapped in a windowless shit-stinking jail cell. His fingers closed around the door handle.

The store owner turned the dead bolt. "We open at ten tomorrow," he said through the glass.

Gato's chance was gone. The prosecutor and her family hadn't even glanced at him. Gato turned away from the shop and walked down the block. He sat on the steps of another store and put his head in his hands. He sat there for a long time. When he finally walked back to the cake shop, it was dark and empty.

He got into Buena's parents' car and drove back to Maria-Rosa's house. The lights shone from the living room windows, but Maria-Rosa's room upstairs was black. He shimmied up the tree he'd climbed so many times, four years ago, and fiddled with the broken window lock. The window slid open, and he climbed into the bedroom.

It was exactly the same. Her parents had tidied it up, but they hadn't changed the furniture, quilt, or pictures on the walls. He could imagine Maria-Rosa walking through the door any minute.

He could hear the TV downstairs, her parents talking in low voices. This was idiotic; they could come in here at any moment. But he no longer cared. He climbed onto Maria-Rosa's bed and laid his head on her pillow. He thought he could still smell a hint of her strawberry shampoo. The pillow grew wet beneath his cheek. He lay there for a long time, glad no one could see him crying.

33

Reading the affidavit in support of the arrest warrant made Anna's head hurt. Samantha sat in the chair next to her desk, her face set in grim determination. The warrant was for the arrest of Hector Ramos. It charged him with Nina Flores's murder.

Anna tried to organize her thoughts. She sipped her coffee, hoping the caffeine would sharpen her brain enough to make the right decision. "He's an MPD officer. Ten years on the force, multiple awards."

"And multiple Use of Force allegations. Including one for the brothel, where he shot another MS-13 member. Wonder what he was trying to hide?"

"Why would he kill Nina Flores?" Anna said.

"Because she was greenlighted by MS-13. And Hector is a member of MS-13."

"Why did he shoot Bufón, then?"

"Hector didn't expect to see him there. He was surprised."

"I don't know," Anna said. "Nina was Hector's friend. I've worked with him on a couple cases, and he's good. You're telling me he's a gang assassin infiltrating MPD? Did you get anything from ballistics?"

"Bullet was too compromised to be of value. No prints on the gun, no DNA, either. The gun was sold at a Virginia show to someone without papers. A drop gun. Exactly what an experienced police officer would use to kill someone."

"Or a drug dealer. You don't have enough."

Anna and Sam always had this tension when they worked with each other: Anna was more conservative and deliberate; Sam was aggressive and bold. They balanced each other out, but it wasn't always an easy dynamic.

"Look," Sam said. "We're not going to get a confession before we really confront him. So sign the warrant. I'll bring him in, question him. We'll see what he says. Maybe he'll give us some false exculpatories that show he's lying."

"I'm not arresting a police officer for murder just to see what he'll say. Here's what you do. You've been following him, right? And he's going around hassling MS-13 members, knocking heads?"

"Basically."

"The next time you see him go over the line, arrest him for that. He's off duty—that's a simple assault. Then you can question him."

"Okay." Sam stood. "Bet I can bring him in by tomorrow, latest."

"Good luck," Anna said. "Be safe."

She remembered wishing the same thing to Hector when he went to raid the brothel.

• • •

Pho 14 was a tiny Vietnamese restaurant in Columbia Heights. It specialized in savory beef noodle soup, delicious and cheap. Hector had eaten there before, and liked the brisket soup best. But that wasn't why he was here this afternoon.

He stood across the street, watching through the window. The tables inside the restaurant were crowded with people slurping long noodles out of giant bowls. They ranged from lobbyists to gangbangers. The latter category interested Hector.

He watched a young man paying for takeout at the cash register. The kid had the gang motto *"Mata - Viola - Controla"* tattooed on the back of his neck. Hector knew his nickname was "Casper." He waited until Casper came out of the restaurant and walked west on Park Street.

Hector came up behind him, so quietly that Casper didn't notice until the last moment, and then it was too late. Hector put a hand on the guy's arm, swung him into an alley, and held up his badge.

"Lawyer!" said Casper.

"Not gonna happen, Casper." Hector took the picture of Nina out of his pocket. "Why is your clique carrying this around?"

"Fuck you. I said 'lawyer.'"

Casper put his hands on Hector's chest and tried to push him away; Hector shoved him back against the wall. Casper took a wild swing, which landed with a thud on Hector's chin. Hector threw a fist into Casper's stomach. Casper bent over, gasping for breath.

"I'll ask you nicely one more time," Hector said.

"Why are your homies carrying around Nina's picture?"

"You know why," Casper said, straightening up. He hocked up a wad of phlegm and spit it in Hector's face. They were on each other, brawling up a cloud of fists and elbows and curses. The soup flew out of Casper's hands and hit the brick wall, spilling broth and noodles onto both men.

"Hey, hey!"

Someone was pulling him and the kid apart. Hector turned around in fury, pulling back his fist to hit whoever it was. A pretty young woman with a mass of curly black hair and a dark suit. A tall man in a dark suit and a neat haircut. The woman pulled back her suit jacket, revealing her badge and Glock.

"Samantha Randazzo, FBI. My partner, Steve Quisenberry."

Hector nodded, trying to catch his breath as he wiped noodles from his face. Casper was crouched down, arms over his face, hair slick with soup. Hector asked, "You guys here to help me with my interrogation?"

"No, sir. Detective Hector Ramos, you're under arrest for assaulting this young man. Put your hands where I can see them."

Hector blinked in disbelief, then turned and put his hands against the brick wall. The male FBI agent frisked him. "Clean."

The female agent helped Casper to his feet, then spun him around so that he was facing the wall. "You, too." Casper put up his hands as the male agent frisked him.

"Sir," the female agent said to Casper, "you're not under arrest, but I need you to come in and make a statement."

"I don't know nothing," Casper said. "I ain't never seen this guy before. He didn't touch me."

The woman rolled her eyes and steered him by the elbow. "You can come as a witness, or I can arrest you for making a false statement to a law enforcement officer. Let's go."

• • •

An hour later, Anna stood in the FBI's Washington Field Office, watching through the one-way mirror as Sam spoke to Hector. The detective looked like he'd lost twenty pounds since Anna last saw him, three weeks ago. His beard had grown in thick and luxuriant. He wore a flannel shirt and jeans. He looked like an anorexic lumberjack.

"I can't believe you're bringing me in for this bullshit," Hector said.

"Why are you asking these guys about Nina Flores?"

"I'm investigating. Same as you."

"You're on administrative leave. You're not even supposed to have a burger at the FOP."

"I don't want a burger. I want a beer." His mouth formed something resembling a smile.

Sam ignored the joke. "All right, so tell me what you're investigating. Seriously. This is my case, if you have information or some theory, I'd like to hear it."

"I'm investigating who killed Nina."

"Right. And what have you learned?"

"Nothing."

"You were there when she was killed, right? You *saw* who killed her."

"Right, but I couldn't ID him."

"It's funny, because I've been talking to some other folks who were there. Folks who weren't in your police reports. They also saw the shooter. Gave a description, lemme see." Sam feigned looking down at her pad. "Late twenties, tall, Hispanic male, dark hair, goatee. Of course that was four years ago. He'd be in his mid-thirties now, and he might have grown that goatee into a full beard."

His face grew pale. "What are you getting at?"

"Tell me what you saw the night Nina died."

"You think I killed Nina Flores?"

"I'm just investigating. Tell me what you saw."

"I'm taking five."

On the other side of the glass, Anna nodded. She'd expected Hector to plead the Fifth and stop answering questions much earlier in the interrogation. Sam came out of the room looking frustrated. As Sam slammed the door behind her, Hector stood and paced the interrogation room. His eyes were wild with anger or fear, Anna wasn't sure which.

"Don't say it," Sam said.

"I think you really made a connection there," Anna said. "You have a way with people."

"Shut up. Want to get lunch?"

Anna smiled and shook her head. "I'll order a sandwich for you. You're gonna be stuck in the basement of Super Court. Papering a misdemeanor assault."

34

The house on Greenwood Street had been in foreclosure and abandoned for as long as anyone could remember. A scuffed FOR SALE sign was staked in the yard, sagging sideways. Gato had never seen anyone remotely interested in buying the place. It was a perfect flophouse for the Langley Park Salvatruchas.

The living room had stained yellow carpeting and brown curtains covering the windows. Although it was unfurnished, the house had an overstuffed feel due to the plump trash bags lining the walls. The plastic bags were full of the clothes and toiletries of homeboys staying here, and were kept packed so their owners could grab them and run at a moment's notice. At night, the men would make pillows out of their clothes and sleep on the floor.

Homeboys were hanging around the first floor, waiting for the meeting to start. This was the last *misa*, the weekly meeting of their clique, to prepare for next week's *generale*—a big meeting of all the cliques in the region.

Diablo and Gato stood in the small backyard. It

was surrounded by a tall wood-plank privacy fence. In the darkness of night, Diablo's face looked particularly monstrous. He'd come back to check on things, and was not happy with what he found.

Gato was slightly less scared of Diablo than the other homeboys were. Gato had been in the gang for eight years, since he was thirteen years old. He had known Diablo since Diablo was just another homey visiting from Los Angeles. Over time, he'd seen Diablo transform from a moderately ugly man with many tattoos to the very incarnation of the Devil himself. As Diablo's face morphed, Gato wondered whether he really might have sold his soul to the Devil.

But what he *actually* knew about Diablo was more frightening than talk of demons. Diablo wanted, above all, to be feared. He enjoyed inflicting pain. And he was just as ruthless to homeboys as he was to *chavalas*, if the homeboys didn't obey orders.

Diablo had his hands in his pockets; his weight was on one foot as the other tapped the ground, a dangerously casual stance. Gato couldn't tell what Diablo was thinking, but he knew it wasn't anything pleasant.

"You knew she was greenlighted," Diablo said softly in Spanish.

"Yes," Gato answered.

"In fact, you were the one who was supposed to put in the work."

"I volunteered."

"Exactly. You saw the woman."

"Yes."

"And you had a gun."

"Right."

"So the part I can't understand is, how is it possible that you are here—and she is not dead?"

Gato looked down at his feet, shuffling around in the dirt. His failure to kill Anna Curtis was a barefaced breach of their code. Sometimes it took a while for a greenlight to happen—but Gato had no excuse. He'd been right there, with a weapon.

Diablo didn't care whether the prosecutor was guarded by police, or whether killing her would have meant Gato being arrested or killed himself. Those risks came with the territory. As a younger man, Gato had thrilled at those risks.

And Diablo would laugh if Gato tried to explain about the *Santa Muerte* in the cupcake shop. Diablo had grown up during the Salvadoran Civil War. As a child, he'd seen bodies stacked ten high. He had been given a rifle and told to kill anyone who came onto the family farm—and he had done it. After seeing his own family killed, Diablo had survived by preying on others. How could you explain "You can choose to be a good man" to someone who wanted to be the Devil?

Diablo was becoming the heart of the gang. And Gato was outgrowing it. The violence wasn't fun anymore. He knew now what he was risking. Not his freedom, not even his life. He was risking his soul.

"Maybe I shouldn't be MS anymore." Gato looked up from his shoe. "Maybe I should leave the gang."

"You know the three ways out of MS-13. Jail, hospital, or morgue. You aren't in any of those places."

"I don't know if I can do this anymore."

Gato took the gun from his waistband and held it out. Diablo looked at it for several seconds before stepping forward to take it. He played with it in his hand, and Gato had the distinct impression that Diablo was considering shooting him in the head. Instead, Diablo slung an arm around his shoulder.

"This saddens me," Diablo said. "But I am not surprised. We have known each other for many years. I know you have a soft heart."

Gato waited for the "but," but it didn't come.

"Come on," Diablo said. "Let's go inside."

They walked back through the sliding glass doors and into the house. They went down to the basement, to an empty room with a concrete floor and a few bare bulbs overhead.

Boys and men milled about in the basement. They were stripped down to their underwear. They fell silent when they saw Diablo. Diablo rarely came to their local *misas*. When he was there, it was serious.

Gato and Diablo took off their clothes, and Diablo started the meeting. When Diablo was here, he was the First Word; Gato was Second. Everyone threw up the claw, intoned *La Mara*, and handed in their rent. They spoke of a drive-by shooting last week and of the money coming from local businesses. Finally, Diablo turned to Gato.

"I am told that we have a member who failed to execute a greenlight when he had a chance."

Gato looked out at the crowd of men, all glaring at him. They knew who Diablo was talking about. Buena's story had gotten around.

"I've thought about what to do with this member. I considered greenlighting him myself."

Gato's heart hammered in his chest. The basement suddenly felt hot and sweaty.

"But I have known him for a long time. He has always obeyed before. Now his heart grows soft. Let's see if a *calentón* will harden it. And then, we will give him one more chance to do his duty."

Some men nodded, others grumbled. Not all would have given Gato a second chance. In the past, Gato was the one who had imposed discipline—his homies expected discipline from him. Several men surrounded him, and he was pushed into the middle of the room.

Gato didn't struggle. He knew it would be useless. He had been through this before. He could do it again.

He was pushed down to the cement floor, and Diablo started to count.

"Uno."

Fists pummeled Gato's back, elbows rained on his head. He curled into a ball to try to protect himself, but felt someone pull his arms and legs so he was stretched out. A bare foot kicked him in his stomach. Gato retched with pain.

"Dos. Tres. Cuatro."

Diablo was counting slowly. The count would go to thirteen, but Diablo could make it last for seconds or minutes.

Gato felt his lip split, felt his forehead gashed open. Arms, feet, and fists slammed into him. Pain saturated every part of his body. Blood poured from his forehead into his left eye, making the world appear a red blur. All he could see were tattoos, furious faces, flying fists.

"Cinco."

A swift kick connected with his rib cage and made a cracking sound. He wondered how many ribs were broken. Gato felt himself slipping away, the world receding until it was just a loud crimson spot in a world of black silence.

And then he was in another time, another place—but the same thing happening to him. Gato was thirteen years old. He was being jumped in. It was the only way a boy could become a member of MS-13 and he desperately wanted to join. He wanted the family, the friendship, the excitement. Psycho had counted for him then, and made the thirteen seconds go by quickly. The homey who counted for you was important, like a big brother.

Gato had known he was being jumped in for life. At thirteen, he didn't understand what life was.

The crimson spot grew bigger, pushing aside the blackness, until it was fully the world he lived in today, full of homies kicking and beating him.

"Doce," Diablo said. *"Trece."*

The pummeling stopped. One final kick knocked Gato onto his back. He looked up through the red haze and saw the Devil looking down upon him. He felt flashing waves of nausea and pain. There were voices, but he couldn't hear them over the ringing in his ears. *This is what I'll see when I die*, Gato thought. *I'm already in hell.*

Diablo's face loomed in front of Gato's, the horns

shimmering red in Gato's blood-soaked view. Diablo took out the gun and pointed it at Gato's face.

"Do you understand why you were punished?" Diablo asked.

Gato managed a weak moan.

"Good. You're forgiven. You will kill the prosecutor. Otherwise, it's you who will be killed."

Diablo tucked the gun into Gato's pants. The blackness crept back in again. Gato closed his eyes and welcomed its warm and obliterating embrace.

• • •

Diablo stood over his fallen homeboy. He had seen this before and would see it again. Gato had lost the taste for blood. It was too bad. But Gato had given his word, and he knew where MS would bring him. There was no backing out.

But there was little that could be done with a member who wanted to leave. Gato was a liability. If arrested, he might snitch. He could never be trusted again.

Diablo took Rooster by the arm and steered him upstairs and out to the backyard. He shut the sliding glass doors so they were alone outside.

"You have to put in some work," Diablo said. "I have two tasks for you."

"Okay, *jefe*," Rooster said. "What?"

"If Gato doesn't kill that *puta* in a week, you kill Gato. And then you'll become Second Word."

Rooster took a deep breath and nodded. Diablo knew killing one of your own homies was difficult.

But Rooster followed orders. And at nineteen, he was fairly senior in the Langley Park Salvatruchas. He was ready to take on greater responsibility.

"Okay," Rooster said. He looked up hopefully. "But Gato will do it."

"I know he will," said Diablo. "That brings me to the second task. After he kills the prosecutor, you kill him anyway."

35

Anna waited expectantly just outside the TSA security perimeter. Soon, Jody came wheeling her suitcase through the terminal, staring up at National Airport's soaring steel-beamed ceiling. When she saw her sister, Jody broke into a trot. They met each other with fierce hugs and a few squeals.

"Oh my God, you look great!"

"*You* look great!"

It was akin to complimenting their own selves, since they'd always been mistaken for twins. Jody had the same blond hair and blue eyes as Anna, the same lanky limbs and ready smile. But their lives were carving them into different shapes. Jody was muscular from installing instrument panels into GM trucks all day, while Anna was more willowy, from a job that required little heavy lifting. Anna still wore her suit, having left the office early; Jody wore jeans, well-loved hiking boots, and a puffy red jacket. The biggest difference in their looks, though, was the long scar that ran across Jody's cheek, from the edge of her mouth to her ear, the worst remnant from their childhood.

"Let me see the hardware!" Jody held up Anna's hand. "Wow. Nice."

Anna took her sister's bag and they talked and laughed out to Jack's car, parked in the garage. Anna drove Jack's station wagon the short distance to the Residence Inn. She had booked a room for Jody on the same floor as them.

"I wish you could see the house," Anna said, as they walked into the anonymous gray hotel room.

"Me too."

"Let me tell you about the security precautions." Anna explained the Marshals' portal-to-portal security. "I get a ride to and from work. Otherwise, we're on our own."

"My life could use a little danger." Jody struck an exaggerated boxer's pose. Anna laughed.

She was glad Jody had come, despite everything. Anna felt ten degrees happier with her sister in town. They were each other's entire family. Their mother had died in a car accident years earlier. They hadn't seen their father since they were kids—and they had no desire to change that. There were a few cousins scattered in Michigan, but no one with whom they kept in touch regularly. Now that Jody was here, Anna felt like she could begin wedding planning in earnest. While Jack was at work and Olivia was in school, Anna was taking the rest of the afternoon off to be with her sister.

As Jody unpacked, Anna asked her about Brent.

"You know—I'm good," Jody said. "I'll always have a soft spot for him. But it's under control. Mostly."

"What does 'mostly' mean?"

"Sometimes I wish there was no Internet. Breakups must've been so much easier before you could watch your ex's life online. But I haven't looked in two weeks."

"That's great."

"The playlists helped."

"I'm glad."

After Jody unpacked, they headed to Hitched, a dress store in Georgetown where Grace's cousin worked. To avoid the inevitable twenty minutes of jockeying for a parking spot, they took a cab, which got stuck in traffic. They bailed out a couple blocks from the store. As they walked down the brick sidewalk lining Wisconsin Avenue, Jody exclaimed, "Cute neighborhood!" The hip little shops, nestled in historic storefronts, were decked out for Halloween with sparkly designer pumpkins and glittering skulls. Huge baskets of bloodred mums crowned black iron lampposts. The trees lining the street were at the height of their fall glory.

But Anna couldn't fully relax and enjoy the sights. Although her rational side knew it was unlikely that she'd run into a gang member—they had no reason to expect she'd be here—she was on guard. More than once, a figure partly seen from the corner of her eye or a person coming out of a store made her jump. She had walked these streets many times before, but never noticed how many doorways, alleys, and corners there were for an assailant to hide behind. Jack had argued that she shouldn't go out—but she needed some time to just feel like a normal bride. The Marshals said she should use caution, but she didn't have to stay locked up in the hotel every day.

Grace was waiting for them outside of Hitched. She and Jody greeted each other with happy exclamations and hugs. Although they'd been talking on the phone for weeks, plotting an engagement party, this was their first in-person meeting. Anna's heart was full of happiness as she watched two people she loved become friends.

Inside, the elegant little store was lined with rows of white dresses. Yards of satin, silk, and lace surrounded them, overwhelming in their variety, despite the monochromatic scheme. Jody flipped a price tag hanging from a sleeve and gaped at the number written there.

"Are these made of gold?" Jody whispered. Most of their childhood clothes had been purchased at Meijer, a Michigan superstore which also sold washing machines, groceries, hamsters, and shotguns.

"Shh," Anna whispered back. "We can go to David's Bridal after this."

Grace introduced them to her younger cousin, a saleswoman named Mia, who looked curiously at Jody's hiking boots but otherwise was as poised and polite as could be.

"So," Mia smiled at Anna. "Tell me what you have in mind?"

"Okay," Anna looked at the three female faces around her. Everyone was listening intently, like she was about to reveal the secrets of the universe. "It's going to be a summer wedding, outdoors. So something light and not too formal. Not too much lace or beading or frills. Something . . . simple."

"Elegant," Grace said.

"Inexpensive," Jody said.

Mia smiled at them all. "We can work with that. Why don't you pull some that you like and I'll bring a few ideas."

Twenty minutes later, Anna found herself in a large dressing room, wearing just her panties and stepping into a silky white slip. Grace and Jody sat in ornate chairs, debating the merits of strapless gowns. A dozen white dresses lined the walls. Mia came in holding another.

"I have a good feeling about this one," she said. "It's an Amsale, very elegant. But this is the floor sample of a discontinued line, so you'd pay less than a quarter of the price."

Both Jody and Grace nodded approvingly.

Mia held the dress open and Anna stepped in. Mia zipped her into it, pinning the back with clothespins. Then Mia had her step up onto an octagonal dais, and turned her to face the mirror. She heard Jody and Grace gasping—and she saw why. The dress was gorgeous. It was strapless, made of ruched ivory satin that clung down her torso to her hips, then fell in gentle scooped waves to her feet. It was simple and elegant, and although her bare shoulders seemed shockingly exposed on this chilly October afternoon, it would be perfect for an outdoor wedding in July.

Mia clipped a gossamer veil to the back of her hair. Suddenly, Anna looked like a real bride. Someone more serene, beautiful, and wise than her real self. She experienced the dizzying sense of being in the middle of a memory she would have for the rest of her life. Every other part of wedding planning felt somewhat abstract. But there was something about wearing a wedding dress that insisted this was actually happening: the sensory experience of satin against skin, the tug of gravity on the garment that was heavier than anything she'd worn before, looking in the mirror and seeing herself transformed from an ordinary woman into a storybook princess.

She heard sniffling and looked over. Grace was beaming, but Jody had tears in her eyes. "I wish Mom could see you now." That got Anna crying, too. Mia expertly produced two Kleenexes and stood back while the sisters held each other. When they dried their eyes, Jody said, "That's the one. Your dress."

"Is this too much, though?" Anna asked. Mia cocked her head. "This is my fiancé's second wedding. He has a daughter. So I'm not sure if I should wear something . . . more second-wedding-ish? Like a white suit?"

"Mm-mm." Mia shook her head. "You're a young woman. This is your wedding, it's your day. Look at you. You're a bride."

The words inflated a bubble of happiness in Anna's chest. She tried on another twelve dresses, all beautiful, but none with the same effect as the first. When she was putting her work clothes on again, Grace spoke quietly with Mia outside the dressing room, then came back in and announced that Mia could discount the dress even more, if Anna took it tonight. That clinched it. Back in the showroom, Anna thanked Mia and handed her a credit card. They made arrangements for Anna to come back for fittings.

Anna, Grace, and Jody walked out of the store and into the darkening night. On the sidewalk, people hurried home from work, their footsteps tapping cheerfully on the bricks. Anna felt content and tired and hungry. Trying on all the heavy dresses had been a surprising workout.

"See," Grace said. "I told you Mia would do right by you."

"She's wonderful," Anna agreed. "Thank you for setting that up!"

They hugged their goodbyes. Grace and Jody exchanged logistical information for the engagement party the next night: what time Jody would come over, what she should bring. Then Grace waved goodbye and caught a cab.

"She's really cool," Jody said, as they watched the taxi drive off. "I like her."

"I know, right? I just hope you like Jack as much."

The two sisters walked to Dupont Circle, chatting and window-shopping along the way. As they turned north on Twentieth Street, they began hearing the murmur of a big crowd. The streets were blocked to traffic with orange striped barriers. Anna and Jody had to push their way through a thickening crowd of people. And then the parade rounded the corner, preceded by the blaring sound of Cher's "Believe." The music came from a huge elaborate float, which was covered in men dressed as glamorous women, wearing sequined dresses, feather boas, enormous BeDazzled hats, and seven-inch-high metal-studded platform shoes.

"The Drag Races!" Anna shouted to her sister.

"The what?"

"Drag queens have a parade through the city around Halloween every year. Actually, they call it the High Heel Races these days. More politically correct, I guess."

"Seriously?" Jody gawked at the raucous parade. Dozens of floats followed the first. Confetti whirled in the air as the crowd applauded the men in their glittery outfits. With expert makeup, long wigs, and shimmery stockings, many of the drag queens looked more feminine and beautiful than the biological women standing on the sidewalk. Everyone danced and cheered.

"This hasn't made its way to Flint yet?" Anna asked.

"I'm not sure Flint is ready for this."

"Everybody fantasizes about being someone else. It's fun to have one night where we celebrate that."

"It's weird."

"I'm in favor of any event in D.C. where everyone has fun and no one gets hurt. I'm glad you got a chance to see it."

"Um . . . okay."

A drag queen dressed as Kathy Griffin threw candy at their feet. A float full of guys dressed as the "YMCA" characters boomed past, with men in chaps, police costumes, and Indian-chief headdresses exuberantly making the letters with their arms. A guy in a slinky evening gown walked two pugs in sequined tutus. Jody laughed. Eventually, her toes began to tap to the music.

"I want that guy's shoes." Jody pointed to a pair of sparkly red stilettos. "And his legs."

"That's the spirit."

They watched until Anna's phone buzzed with a text.

Jack: You ok?

She realized she was late for dinner. She was sorry to make him worry. She replied,

Yes, fine, on my way.

Anna and Jody pushed through the crowd. A few dour protesters stood on the edge of the parade, holding up signs about sodomites, evil, and eternal damnation. Anna shook her head at them. From where she stood, evil was the exact opposite of the parade. Evil existed when one person tried to hurt another. The protesters were roundly ignored.

"That was fun," Jody said, as they hurried up Connecticut Avenue.

"Yeah," Anna smiled at her sister. "I'm glad you think so."

Outside the dancing crowd, the night was dark and chilly. Anna hugged her coat tightly to her chest and leaned into the wind as they navigated a crosswalk.

Truth be told, she was a little nervous about this

dinner. She was about to introduce the three most important people in her life. She hoped they would like each other. You don't just marry a man—you marry his family, and you marry your two families together. They become a unit: for holidays, birthdays, and big events, and for those times when you need someone to babysit, celebrate with, or mourn with. They become the source of your recipes and gossip, the sounding board for your political views. Jody had little choice in the matter—but she would now be spending Christmases and Thanksgivings and who-knew-what-else with Jack and Olivia. Anna hoped Jody would like the new family she was being brought into. If she didn't, holidays were going to be awkward.

Al Tiramisu restaurant was cozy and warm, full of good smells and bustling with waiters carrying plates heaped with pasta. Jack and Olivia were already seated. Jack stood and smiled when they walked in.

"Is that him?" Jody whispered.

"Yeah," Anna said.

"I approve."

"You haven't even met him."

"You want a debate?"

They went over to the table, and Jack and Jody greeted each other with a handshake that turned into a hey-we-should-be-hugging-right? embrace. "You look radiant." He kissed Anna, then held her at arm's length to study her face. "You're actually glowing." She smiled; she'd felt all glowy since leaving Hitched. They sat down. Olivia had drawn a picture for Jody, which was presented and accepted with great ceremony. Jody had brought Olivia an MSU Spartan sweatshirt, which was similarly received.

"So, I understand I have to earn your stamp of approval," Jack said. "What can I tell you?"

"Do you have a brother?"

"I'm an only child."

"Damn." Jody covered her mouth. "I mean, too bad."

Olivia giggled.

"Seriously." Jody put on a stern face and looked at Jack. "Do you love my sister?

"With all my heart."

"You gonna treat her right?"

"Like a queen."

"I know you already do. I know you make her happier than I've ever seen her. I know she thinks you're pretty much the best man on the planet." Jody smiled at him. "I approve."

"Phew!" Jack wiped his hand across his brow in an exaggerated show of relief. They all laughed.

Olivia ordered a baby pizza; the grown-ups ordered homemade pastas, fresh fish, and a couple bottles of wine. The food was good and the conversation was easy. Anna sat back and watched all the people who now constituted her family chatting, laughing, and having a good time. She felt a wave of pure contentment, and she made a conscious effort to be fully present in the moment, savoring it. It had taken her a long time to get to this point. But she'd made it. And this was what life was all about.

36

After weeks of bureaucratic wrangling, the Marshals finally agreed to let Anna meet Julia Hernandez, the mysterious witness who had gone into the Witness Protection Program after Maria-Rosa was killed. But the meeting was on the Marshals' terms. They refused to bring the witness downtown—too dangerous, they said. The meeting would be at the Days Inn on the outskirts of the city. And it was scheduled for five P.M. on the evening of Anna's engagement party. When Anna tried to move it, they said they could try again in May. Anna told them not to cancel—she would be there.

"No worries. I'll see you at Grace's," Jody said as Anna changed from jeans to a dress.

"I wish I could help you set up."

"Nah, this is better. The bride shouldn't be chopping onions."

Anna got Jody a cab and climbed into Deputy Fitzgerald's Taurus. Fitzgerald drove up I-395, then through the surface streets downtown. Usually, Anna liked to prepare for a witness interview by reading everything about the witness, but the Marshals hadn't shared Julia's statements with her. Anna hoped Julia would be able to identify Psycho and Diablo at the construction site as the same two men who raided the brothel.

Agent Fitzgerald drove east on New York Avenue, toward the edge of the city. The farther out they got, the scruffier the street became, lined with cheap motels, warehouses, and vacant lots, all punctuated with chain-link fences. The dull gray sky provided a fittingly bleak backdrop for the ruined urban landscape. For decades, politicians talked about upgrading this street, which was a main artery into D.C. and many tourists' first impression of the city. A new Metro station had spruced up one section of the road, but most of it remained gritty and unimpressive.

The Days Inn was a squat motel long past its prime of life. A plastic bag swirled through the mostly empty parking lot. Cars on New York Avenue sped past, their drivers hardly noticing the sad structure. It was the sort of anonymous place where the Marshals could keep a witness unnoticed.

"Days Inn The 'Hood," Fitzgerald muttered.

Samantha's black Durango was already parked in the lot. The FBI agent climbed out of the SUV as Anna got out of the unmarked Taurus. Anna had asked Sam to be with her during the meeting, to take notes and witness the interview. Fitzgerald would wait in the car; her job was just to transport Anna.

"You set?" Sam asked. "They're ready for us."

"Great," Anna said. "Let's meet Julia."

They walked up the outdoor steps to the second floor, then halfway down the outdoor hallway. A man in cargo pants and a short-sleeved plaid shirt was waiting outside the door. He introduced himself as Deputy Marshal Jeff Cook. Sam pulled back her jacket, revealing her FBI badge. The Marshal nodded and unlocked the door. They all walked into the room, and he shut the door quickly behind them.

The motel room felt warm after the chill air outside. It was dimly lit, the shades drawn. Anna's eyes took a second to adjust to the low light.

"Ms. Curtis, Agent Randazzo," said Deputy Cook. "Let me introduce you to Julia."

Anna turned with a smile toward the woman who sat at the desk. Her smile vanished as she recognized the woman.

It was Nina Flores.

37

Anna felt like the wind had been knocked out of her. She could barely breathe.

The woman was in her late thirties, ten years older than Anna. She looked a little older than in the pictures, but she was still as beautiful, with golden skin and shiny black hair now cut in a chin-length bob. Nina's amber eyes grew round with surprise, in a way that made her look a lot like Olivia.

Anna put a hand on the wall to steady herself. She realized why the Marshals had set up the meeting here rather than at the U.S. Attorney's Office—so no one would recognize Nina and see that she was still alive.

Some part of her noticed that Samantha's mouth was gaping open. Sam had been friends with Jack for a long time; she had probably met his wife. Hell, Sam might have been at Jack and Nina's wedding.

Nina looked as shocked as Anna felt. The two women stared at each other. Anna felt like she was in a surreal dream. Nina was the first to recover. She stood and turned to her handler.

"I can't talk to her," Nina said. "She's dating my husband."

"I'm engaged to him," Anna said. "You're supposed to be dead."

Nina's eyes flashed down to Anna's left hand—to the ring on her finger—then narrowed. Anna noticed Nina had used the word "husband." Not "ex-husband," or "ex." Husband. It was a proprietary word.

"So," Deputy Cook looked back and forth between the two women. "I take it you ladies know each other."

"I've seen your death certificate." Anna couldn't take her eyes off of Nina. "I've seen pictures of your autopsy."

"I was at your funeral," Sam said. "I saw your *corpse*. Where'd that come from?"

"The Marshals," Nina said.

"Hector Ramos will be mighty relieved to hear you're alive," Sam said.

"Hector? Why?"

"I just questioned him as a person of interest in your murder."

"Christ. Hector was my best friend. Still is, I suppose, though we haven't spoken in four years. He helped me set it up." Nina shook her head. "What a mess, what a goddamned mess we made of all this."

Anna stared at her. Who did *we* encompass?

She took a deep breath. "Does Jack know you're alive?"

Nina looked at her silently. Her eyes went up and down Anna's figure, like a prizefighter sizing up an opponent. "No, he doesn't. Not yet."

"You can't tell him," the deputy said.

"I'm not agreeing to that," Anna replied, keeping her eyes on Nina. "How do you know who I am, anyway? How do you know about me and Jack?"

Nina sighed, and sat on the bed. She rubbed her temples between her thumb and middle finger. Anna had seen Jack make the same gesture countless times, and she wondered whose move it had been first, and which one of them picked it up from the other.

"I couldn't stay away," Nina said. "I was supposed to, but I had to see my daughter. My family. I've been back half a dozen times, watching the house. I saw you there."

Anna remembered what Luisa said about things being moved around the house.

"Did you come inside?" she asked.

"Once or twice," Nina replied.

Anna had dismissed Luisa's belief about a ghost in the house. But in a real way, there had been.

The deputy shook his head, conveying disapproval, but not shock. Nina must have admitted this to him at some point. It was a terrible breach of protocol—Witsec witnesses were never supposed to go back to their old neighborhoods. Apparently, the breach hadn't been enough to get her kicked out of the program.

Anna and Nina stared at each other silently for several minutes. Finally, Sam stepped forward. "I don't think this interview is going to happen today."

"Right," Deputy Cook said. He turned to Anna. "But, ma'am, you can't tell your boyfriend . . . or her husband . . . or *anybody* . . . that she's alive. That could put her life at risk."

Anna stared at him. She'd bought her wedding dress yesterday. She'd ordered a cake.

"I have to tell my fiancé. The engagement party is tonight. He needs to know that his . . ." Anna's voice trailed off.

"His wife," Nina said. "The mother of his child. Is still alive."

"Jack doesn't need to know anything," Sam said. "The less you tell him, the better. C'mon, Anna."

Sam turned to the deputy Marshal as she shepherded Anna out the door. "We'll reschedule this."

"We'll have to see if we can bring the witness back," Deputy Cook said. "It takes a lot of resources."

Sam and Anna walked out into the night. The air outside the hotel room was thirty degrees cooler, but Anna hardly felt the change. She walked, in a daze, down the hall, down the steps, to the unmarked Taurus. Deputy Fitzgerald was still sitting in the driver's seat reading a newspaper, exactly as she had been when Anna left, as if the whole world hadn't just collapsed.

38

Anna was vaguely aware of Sam waving Fitzgerald off and saying she would escort Anna herself. Sam bundled her into the passenger seat of the Durango and drove off. Anna stared at the Jersey barriers floating past on New York Avenue, as she tried to process what had just happened. Sam was silent, giving Anna the space she needed to recalibrate her life.

A few things suddenly made sense. Hector Ramos hadn't hurt Nina—he'd been standing over the body in the alleyway because he was staging a "crime scene" to help his friend fake her death. MS-13 wasn't carrying Nina's photo as a trophy—they suspected she was still alive, and still had a greenlight out on her. The photo was for the members to be on the lookout so they could kill her on sight.

But no matter how much she turned it over in her head, there was one question Anna couldn't answer. She turned to Sam.

"Why would a woman fake her own death and not tell her husband?"

Sam shook her head. "I'm trying to figure that one out myself."

"How could a mother make her child go through that?"

"Not everyone has the same maternal instinct."

"Okay. But *how* would she even do it? I know Witsec would get her a new name, ID, social security number. Relocation. But a corpse? Autopsy photos?"

"That's the easy part." Sam sped through a yellow light. "That's what they do. I had a case where they relocated a man, his wife, *and* his mistress—without the wife knowing. The guy wouldn't leave without her. Here, they'd just need an unclaimed body with similar specs to Nina. The Marshals have jurisdiction over the entire country, so they'd have some choices. Not so hard, then, to set up the 'crime scene' and 'autopsy' photos. 'Identify' her with fingerprints and Hector's testimony. It's clever."

"It's horrible," Anna said. "Jack and Olivia thought she was dead all these years. They thought they buried her."

"I know. I was there."

The street flew past in a blur of chain-link, neon, and cement. The sun was in the last throes of setting, casting long gray shadows across the world.

"What am I gonna do, Sam? I just ordered my wedding invitations."

"Am I invited?"

"Of course. With a guest."

"Thanks." Sam turned north onto Thirteenth Street. "Look, this isn't a dilemma. Jack and Nina are done. There's a death certificate. Legally, that's as good as a divorce. Just keep planning your wedding."

"I can't do that without telling Jack that his wife is—"

"Stop," Sam held up a hand. "If you're planning to breach Witsec procedures, don't tell me about it beforehand. I'd have an obligation to report it." She glanced sideways at her friend. "Hypothetically speaking, though, I don't think anyone would blame you if it just slipped out in the heat of the moment."

Anna glanced at the clock: It was 5:28. Her engagement party would begin in one hour and thirty-two minutes. She wasn't sure she could get through it.

"Sam, can you pull over?"

Sam nodded and pulled the Durango to the curb. Cardozo High School was on their right, sitting at the crest of a big hill. Anna got out and stood on the sidewalk. The city spread out before her, its lights shimmering below. In the distance, the U.S. Capitol and the Washington Monument were lit with spotlights. Anna noticed neither the lovely view nor the wind whipping her hair against her face. She stood, arms crossed over her chest, trying to breathe, trying to clear her head. She couldn't seem to get a really good lungful of air.

Sam came and stood next to her.

"You want me to cancel the party?" Sam asked softly. "I can make the calls."

Anna looked out at the city and tried to focus her thoughts. Eventually, she became aware of the cold, the wind, and the strands of her hair stinging her cheeks. Her sister had come to town for this. Her best friend had been planning this party for weeks. Caterers had been hired; they were probably at Grace's house right now.

"No," Anna said. "I'd like to go to my party."

Sam nodded, and they got back into the car. Anna directed her to the lovely residential streets of Woodley Park. She would compartmentalize the news, let Jack enjoy the party, and try to enjoy it herself. She would tell him afterward. She dreaded the idea.

Grace's house was a historic white four-square with gray shutters and a red door. Sam parked in the driveway and insisted on coming in to help set up.

"You're a guest," Anna said. "Come back at seven."

"I was practically raised in a restaurant," Sam said, climbing out of the Durango. "I nail appetizers. Besides, you should have someone with you who knows what's going on now."

"Thanks, Sam."

"You're early!" Grace greeted them at the door with a smile and cheek kisses. "Come on in, I have a couple spare aprons."

She led them into her beautiful house, all shiny wood floors and crown moldings and impeccable taste. Crystal vases were filled with ivory roses. Glass globes held smooth gray stones and white candles waiting to be lit. Everything was festive, elegant, and happy. Raffles was curled up on a dove-gray couch. When he saw Anna, he mewled and ran over. She bent down so he could give her a furry head butt.

Grace brought them to her enormous kitchen, where Jody was laying tiny champagne grapes on a tray of cheese. "Hey!" Jody looked up. Holding her damp hands in the air, she came to give Anna a hug, but then stopped in front of her sister. "What's wrong?"

"Nothing," Anna put on her best happy voice and made the hug happen. "What smells so delicious in here?"

Soon, they were all in female-in-kitchen autopilot mode. Anna sliced strawberries, Jody washed dishes, Sam arranged a mound of shrimp on ice. Grace instructed the caterers on where to set up silver warming dishes. Her husband was a partner at one of the downtown mega law firms; she was expert at throwing fancy events.

Jack arrived fifteen minutes before the party was set to start. He came into the kitchen, kissed Anna, hugged Grace and Jody, and greeted Sam with a surprised high five. He handed Grace a bottle of Veuve Clicquot and a bouquet of tiger lilies and thanked her for hosting the party.

"So," he turned to Anna and popped a strawberry in his mouth. "How did your meeting with the Witsec witness go?"

She glanced at Sam. "Very interesting. Julia was not at all what I expected."

"They never tell you the real story for these witnesses," Jack said. "Let me guess. A construction worker who got a sex-change operation and has a new identity as a female hairstylist? True story, I had a case like that once."

"Let's talk about it after the party. Here, carry this to the living room." Anna handed him a crystal bowl full of berries.

Soon, the guests arrived, and the house was filled with the happy sounds of a party. People chatted, forks pinged against china, crystal flutes clinked as champagne was poured into them. Anna stood with her arm tucked into Jack's elbow as they made their way through the crowd, greeting everyone, accepting congratulations.

Her mind kept flashing images of Jack and Nina as a young couple, hopeful, in love. Standing at an altar, making their vows to each other. In the hospital, after Nina gave birth to their baby girl. Anna wasn't sure Jack would still want to go forward with their wedding once he learned his wife was alive. Anna tried to shake off these visions and portray the happy bride she wanted to be, graciously accepting good wishes. She'd deal with the rest later.

Daniel Davenport, the defense attorney on the Capitol homicide case, came over to shake hands and offer his congratulations. Rose Johnson, who'd been a witness in one of Anna's domestic violence cases, gave her a hug and a Hallmark card. A couple of Jack's cousins had come to town, and Anna put on her best face for them. She could feel them sizing her up. Jack didn't have much family in D.C. He was an only child, his father had never been in the picture, and his mother had been a transplant from North Carolina. Anna hoped she was making a good impression on the few family members who'd made the trek.

Marty Zinn, the acting U.S. Attorney, dinged a fork against a wineglass. The room quieted, and Marty gave a funny speech about Anna and Jack's interoffice relationship. Anna made sure a smile stayed on her face the whole time. He presented them with a faux conflict-of-interest waiver signed by the Attorney General. Everyone laughed and clapped.

Jack stepped forward and held up his hands.

"This is a wonderful occasion." His deep voice commanded the room. "Anna and I both want to thank you for coming to celebrate it with us."

Jack had a great presence in a courtroom, and was even more compelling in a room full of people who were just there to see him. He looked handsome and confident, and she felt a stab of possessiveness. This was her fiancé. They'd gone through a lot to be here. *Mine*, she thought. *This man is* mine.

Jack thanked Grace for throwing the party and inviting everyone into her beautiful home. The room filled with cheers and clinks as everyone drank a toast to their hostess.

"And now I'd like to propose a toast to my fiancée." He beamed at Anna. The rest of the crowd raised their champagne glasses. "I'm so lucky to have this woman. Many of you know the tragedy my family went through four years ago. I might never have recovered from it, if I hadn't met such a wonderful person, and fallen so deeply in love." He looked down directly at her. "Anna, I love you. Thank you for making me the luckiest man in the world."

The room erupted in cheers and clinks. He took a sip and leaned down to kiss her. His lips were warm beneath the cool drops of champagne. When he pulled back, she had tears in her eyes. His brows knitted.

"I'm just so happy," she said.

He smiled and handed her a cocktail napkin. She

dabbed at her eyes. After the speech, more people came up, offering them congratulations. Anna put on her best glowing-bride smile. She accepted all the good wishes with cheer and laughter. When she teared up one more time, she passed it off as the misty eyes of a bride. If there was one thing Superior Court taught a prosecutor, it was how to keep from crying when things were falling apart.

As the night wore on and the liquor flowed, the inevitable war stories were trotted out. Legal blunders, mistaken identities, flashes of brilliance, strokes of dumb luck. McGee started telling a story involving Jack, a murder at a strip club, and a one-legged pimp. Anna took the opportunity to slip through Grace's kitchen, out the sliding glass doors, and onto the back porch. The night air was shockingly cold as it hit her skin. The view of the backyard was black on black, tall trees topped by the night sky. She walked to the edge of the porch, put her elbows on the railing, and took bracing gulps of the cold air.

• • •

Gato stood in front of the big white mansion with the red door. From a dark spot at the side of the house, under a weeping cherry tree, he could see both the front walk and the back porch. He kept watch for the lady prosecutor.

His whole body ached, he was covered in bruises, and conflicting thoughts battled in his mind. "You live in the world you create," Señora Zanita had said. "Happiness cannot be stolen . . . it must be earned."

But if he didn't kill the prosecutor now, the gang would kill him. No one had to tell him that; he'd been around long enough to know.

Part of him wished they would just do it, put him out of his misery. Even more than the bruises from the beating, his head hurt from the constant struggle to be someone he wasn't. He was too good to fit in the gang, but too evil to fit anywhere else. In his pocket, his hand brushed against the gang's handgun. He imagined how the cold barrel would taste if he put it in his mouth.

He could see dozens of people through the brightly lit windows. There was some kind of party happening inside. Everyone was having a good time, talking, eating, drinking. Their laughter heightened his solitude. Their warmth made him feel even colder. He hated them. He wanted to be them. He knew he never would.

He stood under the weeping cherry tree and waited for his chance. It came at around ten o'clock. The sliding glass doors at the back of the house opened and the prosecutor came out, onto the back porch. She was alone. She walked to the edge of the deck, put her elbows on the railing, and brushed something from her cheek.

Gato climbed the wooden steps to the deck, making no noise. His nickname meant "cat" for a reason. The woman's back was to him as she stared into the blackness. Gato's fingers closed around the gun.

39

Nina sat at the cheap motel table, staring without appetite at the Wendy's takeout that Deputy Cook had brought her. Cook sat across from her, looking worried at her failure to eat anything all day. He was her handler, and knew her better than anyone else at this point. He was the only person in her current life who knew she wasn't the woman listed on her driver's license. She'd come to a decision, and he needed to know.

"Jeff, after I testify, I want to come out."

"You gotta stay in the hotel for your own safety."

"No. I mean come out of Witsec for good. Give up this 'Julia Hernandez' identity and be me again."

"I don't think that's a good idea. It's not safe. As long as Diablo's out there, MS-13 has a motive to kill you."

"I know. But I never thought I'd be gone this long. I can't live like this anymore. I need to be with my daughter. And my husband."

"I thought you hated him. You wanted to go into Witsec without him."

"I did hate him. But that was a long time ago. I

always thought, once the case was over, I'd come back and we'd try again. Now he's about to get remarried."

"I'll see what I can do," Deputy Cook said. "It's gonna be rough."

Nina nodded. "For everyone."

40

Anna reached down to the cooler on the deck and grabbed a Bud Light from the ice. Champagne was nice, but she was a Flint girl at heart. She would go back into the house, try to relax, and do her damnedest to enjoy her party. She turned toward the glass door, but stopped when she saw movement to the side.

Anna turned to see a figure—out of context but familiar—step onto the porch. It was one of Jack's gardeners, a handsome young man with liquid brown eyes. An angry red scab ran across one of those eyes now, closing it. His face was puffy with purple bruises, and the left side of his mouth was so swollen, it looked like he had a jawbreaker wedged in the side of his cheek.

"Diego," she said. "My God, what happened to you?"

She grabbed a handful of ice from the cooler, wrapped it in a napkin, and held it out to him. He didn't move to take it. He kept his hands in his jacket pockets.

"Here," she urged. "Put this on your cheek. It'll help bring the swelling down."

She'd dealt with enough black eyes to know. He slowly took one hand out of his pocket, reached for the improvised ice pack, and put it to his cheek. He flinched as the pack touched his purple skin. His other hand remained in his pocket.

"Ms. Curtis," he said, "you are very kind. I will remember you next time I brew my tea."

She had no idea what he was talking about.

"Do you work here, too?" she asked.

He shook his head, staring at her silently. His one good eye grew moist; a single tear welled up, leaked out, and ran down his cheek. He moved the ice pack to catch it.

"What's wrong?" she asked.

"Why were you at Maria-Rosa's house the other day?" he replied.

"What?"

"What did her mother say? Does she blame me?"

Her eyes went to his hand holding the ice pack. She saw the three-dot tattoo in the webbing between his forefinger and thumb. Her heart hitched.

"What are you doing here?"

He pulled a black handgun from his pocket. She stared at it as her mind flashed to a self-defense class she'd recently taken— What could she do against a man with a gun? Nothing. Her pepper spray was in her purse, sitting in Grace's front closet. She thought about the handgun locked in Jack's safe. She desperately wished she had listened to him and was carrying it now. Her heart was pounding so hard, it seemed to be trying to break open her rib cage and escape.

"They sent me here to kill you." He set the ice pack on the railing. "For the Mara Salvatrucha."

She opened her mouth, but her voice was trapped in her throat.

Gato raised the gun, and pointed it at his own head.

"Don't worry, Ms. Curtis. I'm not gonna do it. I just want to die a good death, like my saint, *la Santa Muerte*."

She shook her head. "No, Diego. Suicide isn't a good death."

"The gang's gonna kill me anyway. If *they* do it, it will be long and painful."

"No. We can protect you."

"I'm no snitch." The gun shook in his trembling hands. "I wish I was a better man, but it's too late for me."

"It's not too late," she said softly. "You might have made bad choices before—but every day is a new chance to do what's right. This is your chance, Diego."

"You sound like Señora Zanita."

"Just put down the gun. Right there on the rail. And then we can talk. I promise, I'm not going to let anyone hurt you."

He looked at her for a long time, tears streaming down his face. The gun shook so much, she was afraid Gato would fire it and take off half his skull unintentionally. He finally lowered his hand and set the gun on the porch railing.

"Good," Anna exhaled a breath she hadn't realized she'd been holding.

She picked up the gun and banged on the sliding

glass door. Sam was the only one in the kitchen, talking on her cell phone. She came over and slid open the door.

"Hey, Anna, what are you—?" Sam saw the gun in her hand, and Gato crying on the porch. She put down her phone, stepped outside, and placed a hand on her own weapon. "What the hell?"

"Agent Randazzo, this is Diego, also known as Gato. He was my gardener—and apparently, MS-13. He wants to turn himself in."

"Put your hands on the railing and spread your legs, sir."

Gato did as he was told. Sam frisked him, finding fourteen dollars and a prepaid cell phone in his pocket. "You don't mind if I look through here, right?" She tucked the phone into her pocket without waiting for an answer. She put a pair of handcuffs on him.

Anna found Grace inside and asked if there was a spare room she could use. Grace looked puzzled but showed her to the laundry room. Anna and Sam waited until the kitchen was clear, then led Gato there.

Through the living room doorway, Jack saw the strange procession. He left his circle of friends and followed them into the laundry room. Sam shut the door, muffling the sounds of the party. Anna heard a *meow* and looked to the corner. Raffles sat on a pillow, apparently banished here for the party. The cat came over and rubbed himself against her legs.

Gato sank down on a folding chair and put his head in his cuffed hands. He was still shaking. Anna tentatively reached out and put a hand on his shoulder. He didn't flinch or move away. She patted him. "There, there." She sounded like her mother. "It's gonna be okay." Jack looked at her quizzically.

When Gato's shaking subsided, he looked up at Anna.

"If I talk to you, tell you about MS-13, can you get me out of D.C.? Can you fake my death, like Detective Flores?"

"What do you know about Detective Flores's death?" Sam asked.

"Soon as we greenlighted her, they said she died in some drug bust."

"So?"

"We're not stupid. Why do you think I got the job as their gardener? To watch the house, and see if she was really dead. One day, I saw her in the neighborhood. She'd changed her hair, but it was her. I stole a picture from the house, and we carried it around, in case anyone saw her again. So they could kill her for real."

Jack made a choking sound.

"Nina—is alive?" He staggered back, catching himself on the washing machine. "My Nina?"

Anna cringed and nodded. She reached for his hands, but they were gripping the washing machine so tightly, it looked like he wanted to strangle the appliance—or he needed its help to stay on his feet. He stared at her, shaking his head. She dropped her own hands to her sides.

"I was going to tell you," she whispered. "After the party."

Sam looked at them. "Why don't you two go and talk. If you send McGee in here, he and I can chat with Diego."

Anna's stomach churned, but she did what she was trained to do: She managed the crisis. She put on her best poker face, wended her way through the party, and took McGee aside. She quietly explained that he was needed in the laundry room. Then she led Jack upstairs to a big empty bedroom. Gato's confession was not the way she'd hoped to break the news to her fiancé.

She locked the bedroom door, took a deep breath, and turned to Jack. He looked lost and shell-shocked. They stared at each other across the expanse of beige carpet. Muffled laughter and the sound of a popping champagne cork floated up from the living room. Their engagement party continued without them.

"I'm sorry you had to find out like this, Jack."

"How long have you known?"

She glanced at her watch. "About three hours."

His face softened and he nodded. In a corner was a sitting area: two chairs flanking a little glass table. She gestured toward it, and they went over and sat.

"Do you want the short story or the long one?" she asked.

"Everything. I have to know everything."

She took a moment to gather her thoughts, then launched in. He met her eyes as she spoke, but he seemed to look through her, as if he were seeing something else: a memory or a dream. She described all that she'd learned about Nina, starting with her suspicions about Hector, going through the information in the case files, and concluding with the surprise in the motel room. When she got to the end, she paused, remembering the Marshal's instruction.

"Actually," she said, "they told me not to tell you that Nina was alive. They said—"

"Goddammit!" Jack slammed his fist onto the table.

Anna flinched. The tabletop fractured, sending a web of cracks radiating across the glass surface. A thin trickle of blood ran down the side of his hand. He didn't notice.

"I can't fathom all the people who must have lied to make this happen. My friends. Colleagues. People I've worked with every day for the last four years, keeping this from me. Not you too, Anna."

"I didn't and I won't."

He stood and paced the room.

"I *buried* my wife. I told my daughter that her mother was dead." His voice grew strangled. "Over and over, I explained to Olivia why Mommy was in heaven."

Anna fought back her own tears. She looked around until her eyes landed on a box of Kleenex. She went over and pulled out a few tissues, then brought them to Jack.

"You cut yourself."

He glanced down and finally noticed his bleeding hand. He took the wad of Kleenex and pressed it to the wound. His deep voice was shaking when he spoke again.

"What am I going to tell my daughter?"

She shook her head. "I don't know."

"She'll think I lied to her, all these years. She'll never trust me again."

"You're a great father. Olivia knows that."

He drew her into a tight embrace, burying his head in her hair. His body convulsed with quiet, shuddering sobs. She realized she'd never seen him cry before. Her heart hurt to hear it, and to feel how much he was fighting it still. She stroked his back and murmured soothing words whose sound was more important than their meaning. Eventually, he quieted. His breathing evened out. She closed her eyes and rested her cheek against the tight muscles of his chest. His heart thundered under her ear.

"God, I'm relieved she's alive." His voice was steadier now. "But I can't believe she put Olivia and me through this."

Anna tried to think of something that would ease his pain.

"I don't think that many people lied to you," she said.

"How do you figure?"

His arms loosened, and they both sank down on the edge of the bed. She looked up at his face. It seemed to have aged five years in the last five minutes.

"As far as I can tell, only Hector and the Witsec agents were part of it."

He shook his head. "The Medical Examiner herself told me Nina was dead."

"Okay, but—how did you identify the body?"

"I went to the ME's Office. We went through the usual procedure: I sat in the office and they showed me a Polaroid picture of her face. It was—destroyed." He grimaced. "I asked to see a PD-860, and they had one ready. It was clearly a match."

Anna nodded. The PD-860 was an MPD "Request for Comparison of Fingerprints" form. As a police officer, Nina's fingerprints would be on file, making for an easy comparison with the prints of the dead body.

"Hector probably prepared that," Anna said. "His name was all over the file. The ME only knew there was a dead woman—the identity came from Hector. Did you actually see the body?"

He lifted the tissues and looked at his hand; the bleeding had stopped. He crumpled up the Kleenexes and threw them into a garbage can.

"I had to see her. Even though it's not standard procedure. I went downstairs; they knew better than to try to stop me. She was on one of those steel gurneys, her whole body covered in a sheet. I could see her hair peeking out at the top. At least, it looked like her hair. Her left hand was the only part of her that was uncovered. I saw her wedding ring." His voice choked up again. "I held her hand. It was so cold. I held it, and I knelt down next to her. And I begged for her forgiveness."

Anna blinked back her own tears. "Why should she forgive you?"

He met her eyes but stayed silent for a long time. The muscle in his jaw throbbed.

"I thought it was my fault, Anna."

She stared at him.

"There's more to Nina's leaving," he said. "I should have told you this before, but it's not something I'm proud of. It's something I'd rather forget."

A knot of dread twisted through her stomach. She both feared and couldn't wait to hear what he had to say. She put a hand on his arm, both to comfort him and brace herself.

"When Nina wanted to go into Witness Protection, she wanted to go without me."

"Why?"

"I had an affair." Jack grimaced. "Nina found out. She was furious and had decided to leave me."

Anna felt like she'd been punched in the gut. Jack had an affair? She thought he was the perfect man. Infidelity was not something she'd thought him capable of.

"She wanted to go into Witsec." Jack's voice sounded like boots on gravel. "With Olivia—but not me. I told her no. I couldn't allow that. Witsec relocates you to another city, and you can never see or talk to your family or friends again. No phone calls, e-mails, nothing. I couldn't give up all contact with Olivia. I guess Nina decided to go without me *or* our daughter."

Anna took a moment to process this. "Did you suspect that she hadn't actually died? That she'd gone into Witsec instead?"

"No. And not just because every piece of evidence I saw—every person I spoke to—confirmed that she'd been killed. Because she loved Olivia so much. It never crossed my mind that she would leave her."

Anna couldn't understand that, either. "Who was the affair with?"

He looked at her, looked at the wall, looked back at her again. "Carla."

"My boss, Carla? Carla Martinez?"

"Yes."

Anna's hand dropped from his arm.

"We were working on a double-homicide case," Jack said softly, "spending all our time together. Nina and I were drifting apart. After the baby, our sex life was close to nil. Nina was barely home, caught up in her own investigations. When we did talk, it was to fight. Except for Olivia, everything I did on a daily basis was connected to Carla. When Nina was threatened by MS-13, it was right after she'd learned about my . . . mistake."

Anna suddenly understood Carla's coolness when she learned Anna and Jack were together. Carla had always been very warm and supportive of Anna—except on the subject of Jack.

"How long did this go on with Carla?"

"I don't know. A few months. It ended when Nina was killed. I could barely look at Carla anymore after that."

Anna stared at him. How could all this history surround her, and she be unaware of it? She felt like a child walking through a park filled with flowers and statues, not realizing it was a cemetery.

"Were you ever going to tell me you dated my boss?"

"I'm sorry," he said. "This was the worst thing I ever

did. I cheated, and it killed my wife. At least, I thought it did. It's not something I enjoy talking about."

He hung his head and rubbed his temples between his thumb and middle finger.

Anna took a deep breath. She could chew him out, but what good would that do? Her rebuke wouldn't be any more persuasive than four years of crushing guilt. He was human, he'd made mistakes. But his mistakes were in the past—and they were sins he'd committed against Nina, not her.

Anna had regretted that she didn't know the younger version of Jack. But there were benefits, too. He'd made mistakes and learned from them. Those mistakes had shaped him into the man he was now, a man she trusted and admired. The man before her was wiser and better than the one who'd married Nina. And he was going through an incredibly hard time.

"I forgive you," she said. She meant it, although she didn't really have standing in this matter. "Sometimes good people do bad things. That doesn't mean you're a bad person."

He smiled ruefully. "You sound like a defense lawyer."

"Don't tell anyone downstairs," she said. "You'll ruin my reputation."

"God, I don't deserve you." He traced her jaw with his thumb. The anger in his eyes was gone. He cupped both her cheeks in his hands. "I love you, Anna. So much."

He kissed her with gentle urgency. When they pulled apart, he continued to cup her face, gazing down at her as if he were studying some rare and precious treasure.

"What's our next step?" Anna asked.

"We go downstairs and ask Grace where I can buy a replacement table." He nodded toward the sitting area. "Then we try to enjoy what's left of our party. We'll figure out the rest tomorrow. Together?"

"Together," she agreed.

He took her hand, and they went back down to the party. Although their mood was grim, she felt closer to him than she had all night.

41

When Anna woke the next morning, they were in their normal sleeping positions, she on her side, Jack spooning her from behind. From the silence in their suite, Anna guessed that Olivia was still sleeping. Anna was a little hungover from the champagne last night, but felt safe and warm pressed against Jack. She turned to face him, expecting to find him sleeping. His green eyes were open. She wondered if he'd slept at all.

"I have to see her," Jack said.

Anna's heart skipped a few beats. "I'm not sure the Marshals will let you."

"They'll let me." He spoke with the confidence of a man who'd been in law enforcement a long time and knew his way around an agency.

"She's been hiding from you all these years. Maybe she doesn't want to see you."

Her words were unkind, but she wasn't sorry. What she said was true. Nina didn't deserve Jack, and he should be able to see that. And . . . Anna was nervous about how Jack would feel when he saw his wife.

"Maybe she doesn't want to see me. But she doesn't

have much choice now." Jack sat up and ran his hand across the stubble of his head. He looked exhausted but determined. "I want to see her as soon as possible. Today, if I can make that happen."

"Today?" Her heart fluttered again. "She's been gone for four years. Why the rush?"

"It's hard to explain what it was like, living with the guilt. Now that I know she's alive, I won't be able to do anything else until I see her."

She nodded but felt sick at the idea of Jack meeting Nina in some hotel room. In the years since Nina had "died," Jack had practically canonized her—in his memory, she was the perfect wife and mother, dead because of his mistakes. Anna had never thought herself the jealous type, but, she realized, she'd never really been tested on that front before. She'd never loved someone as much as she loved Jack, or worried about losing him.

"I'll come with you," she said.

She could read the struggle on his face: He didn't want her to come—but he didn't know how to tell her. She smiled back at him. She wasn't giving him an easy out. Finally, he nodded.

"Okay."

She tried not to let him hear her sigh of relief.

They went through the motions of a "normal" hotel morning with Olivia. But it all felt different to Anna, like a routine coming to its end. How long could Anna play mother without telling Olivia that her real mother was alive? How long would Jack stay with her now that he knew his first wife was alive?

While Jack showered, Anna focused on talking to Olivia about school, making her breakfast, and packing her backpack. They went into Olivia's room to pick an outfit, and Anna looked at the picture of Nina Flores that sat on the nightstand next to Olivia's bed. The framed smile that used to seem sweet now seemed to gloat. When Olivia went to the closet to get her boots, Anna turned the frame around.

She helped the little girl put on her coat and her cutest hat, a knitted tiger with ears. Jack came out of the shower, clean-shaven and dressed. Anna gazed at the two of them, trying to emblazon the scene in her memory. This was her family. At least for today.

"Let's take a picture," Anna said. She set the camera to auto, pulled Jack toward her, and posed with her arms around the girl. "Someday we'll want to look back and remember when we were a family living in a hotel."

"Cheese," said Olivia.

• • •

Anna drove Jody to the airport later that morning. The sky was gray, tossing down sporadic handfuls of rain. Anna had to keep readjusting the windshield wipers. She could feel Jody watching her worriedly. She told her sister the rough outline of Nina's discovery—without mentioning the circumstances of her fake death, or the fact that she was in Witsec.

"I hate to leave you now," Jody said.

"I'm fine." Anna smiled as convincingly as she could.

Jody kept looking at her. "What are you gonna do, Annie?"

"About what?"

"You know what."

"What's there to do?"

"Stop playing dumb blonde. I know better. Are you gonna postpone the wedding?"

A wave of heavy rain hit the windshield with a clatter. Anna put the wipers on high. They swished furiously back and forth, slicing through the downpour.

"No."

"Don't you think Jack might need a little time to come to grips with this?"

"He hasn't mentioned it."

"Right, because men are so communicative."

"Hey, just because Brent can only talk about the Lions and beer doesn't mean Jack can't speak up if he needs me to hear something."

"Ouch."

"Jo, I'm sorry." Anna slowed the car and wished she'd put the brakes on her tongue instead. "That was terrible. I don't mean to take this out on you. I'm really sorry."

"It's okay. You're under just a little stress. Death threats, wedding planning, trial prep, ghost wives." Jody looked out at the Potomac River, flowing dark and angry to their left.

They drove in silence for a while, each sister mulling how to get the conversation back on track, neither wanting to end the visit with a fight. The rain stopped, and the wipers began squeaking across dry glass. Anna turned them off and steered the car onto the airport exit ramp.

"What would you do?" she asked quietly.

"Me?" Jody said. "I'd do the wrong thing, that's for sure."

Anna pulled the station wagon to the curb in front of Terminal B. All the guys she'd ever dated flashed before her eyes, and the image was like the depiction of human evolution, starting with a chimp, going to a hunchbacked caveman, and ending with a tall man walking upright. Jack was the best man she'd ever known. She adored him. And the fact that they were getting married was a testament to her own evolution.

"I'm in love with him," Anna said. "I'm not going to let him go."

"Okay." Jody nodded. "Then fight like hell to keep him. Whatever you do, I've got your back."

"Thanks, Jo." Anna blinked back tears. "I love you."

"You, too."

They hugged tightly, then hauled Jody's suitcase from the back of the station wagon. A minute later, Anna watched her sister's puffy red jacket disappear into the cavernous mouth of National Airport. She stood next to the car, letting the cold October drizzle spatter her face.

"I was supposed to kill her," Gato said, pointing at Anna.

"Yeah, we got that," Samantha said.

Anna noted the reassuring bulge where Sam's gun was holstered by her side. Anna sat next to Sam in a conference room of the U.S. Attorney's Office. Across the table sat Gato and his newly appointed lawyer. After a long night of questioning by Sam and McGee, Gato had been arraigned in a sealed courtroom and appointed counsel this morning. The judge understood their purpose, and appointed a sharp-eyed lawyer named Seth Pinsky, who was known for being a good defense attorney for cooperators. Pinsky would secure the best possible deal for Gato, because the prosecutors knew Pinsky would help his client be the best possible witness: principally, making sure he avoided the temptation to lie, minimize, or cover up.

"So why didn't you kill me?" Anna asked. "Why are you sitting here, talking to me instead?"

"I don't want to kill anyone anymore." Gato was bruised and handcuffed, but looked more peaceful than the night before. "I'm done with MS-13. I want to get back on the right side of things."

Anna consulted her internal truth detector. After years of listening to people's stories, she'd developed a fair ability to sort fact from fiction. She believed Gato was telling the truth now. If she called him to the stand at trial, he would be a terrible witness—she was sure he'd done awful things that a jury would hate. But he could offer testimony no one else could.

If the case went to trial, Anna and Sam would have to work many hours with Gato and his lawyer to prepare his testimony. Anna was not naive about Gato's willingness—or ability—to tell the unvarnished truth.

As valuable as it was to hear about a crime from an insider, a cooperator's description of events could not be relied upon uncritically. He might embellish or downplay his role in the crimes; he might omit or have suppressed unflattering details; and he might offer self-serving or unbelievable justifications for his own actions. Gato's testimony had to be scrupulously checked, probed, and tested against the other objective evidence.

"Okay," Anna said. "So tell me about the people who want to kill me."

They spent the day talking to Gato. He told them about how he became an MS-13 member. He told them about the various cliques in the area, and who belonged to which group. He spoke of shootings and robberies, assaults and rapes. He described his rise through the ranks of the Langley Park Salvatruchas, the gang's operations, and their raid on the Monroe Street brothel.

"I didn't know Diablo was going to cut the doorman's head off," Gato said. "But I wasn't surprised."

"Tell us about Diablo," Anna said. "What's going on with his face?"

"He did that to himself. It helps his power in the gang. I met him before he did it, back when he just looked like a man—and he still spooks me."

"How did he do it?"

"Operations. He got a surgeon in El Salvador to do it for him. He had the horns implanted in his head, and his nose operated on. It took a long time to cover his whole face with tattoos. He got his teeth filed down."

"It helps him because some people think he's really the Devil and has supernatural powers," Anna said.

"Yeah, but it's more than that. Diablo always felt like he had the Devil in him. The doctor let him look on the outside like he felt inside."

"How did he get to be so powerful in the gang? Was it just his appearance?"

"No." Gato tapped his chest. "It's what's underneath. In a gang full of crazy fuckers, he is the craziest of all. You never know what he's gonna do."

"Did Diablo have anything to do with Maria-Rosa's death?"

"He greenlighted her. He knew I loved her. Whoever killed her deserves to die." He stared at the table, then seemed to shake himself. "For this kind of information, how much time am I gonna serve?"

"It'll be a long time, and it depends on a lot of factors. But with your cooperation, it'll be a lot less than Psycho and Diablo. And you'll serve it in a jail for cooperators, out of the general prison population."

"What if I could help you capture all of them—the whole gang?"

"The more you assist law enforcement, the more credit the court will give you."

Gato looked to his attorney. "Go ahead, tell them," Pinsky said.

"Thursday night," Gato said. "Halloween. There's gonna be a *generale*."

"What's that?"

"Big MS meeting. Not just our clique, but men

from all along the East Coast. Diablo, and maybe a hundred homeboys will be there."

"Where?" Sam asked.

Gato shrugged. "No one will know till the day before. And they won't tell me if I'm in here."

"Would you be willing to wear a wire?" Sam asked.

"Can't wear a wire to a misa or *generale*. We strip. I told you, we're not stupid."

Sam and Anna exchanged a glance. There were other options.

"We'll see what we can do," Anna said.

42

By the time the meeting with Gato ended, the setting sun bathed the sky in a deep rose glow. But for Anna, the most challenging part of the day was about to begin. She and Jack climbed into the back of the unmarked Taurus, and Deputy Fitzgerald drove up New York Avenue for the second time in twenty-four hours. Anna eyed the cheap motels and scrappy lots with distaste. They were going to meet Nina.

Her fingers tapped nervously on the car seat. She hoped Jack and Nina hated each other, that their old fights and controversies would flare up immediately.

Deputy Fitzgerald parked in the lot and escorted the two of them to the motel door. This time, Anna knew whom to expect on the other side. She just couldn't anticipate how her fiancé would react to that person.

Deputy Cook let them in and locked the door behind them. Nina stood in the middle of the room. She looked slightly different than she had yesterday. Anna realized with a sinking heart that the woman was wearing makeup. She wanted to look nice for Jack.

Jack stood still for a moment, gazing at his wife. Nina stood looking at him.

They both moved at once. Jack folded Nina into his arms. Nina rested her head on his chest.

"Oh, Nina," he breathed. He didn't seem to notice that Anna was behind him, still standing by the door, one hand to her broken heart.

"Jack," said Nina. "I'm sorry."

"I'm sorry, too. Thank God you're okay."

To Anna, it felt like they held on to each other for hours. In reality, it was probably a few seconds. Nina pulled back and looked at Jack.

"You look good," Nina said. "How have you been?"

"Fine. How about you?"

"Awful. I made a terrible mistake, Jack. I should never have left my family."

"You thought you were protecting us."

"I could have done it differently. The last few years, it felt like I really was dead. I gave up on you—I left Olivia—I lost everything that made my life worth living."

"I would have come with you," Jack said softly, "if you'd asked."

"I know. But I was so angry about you and Carla. I didn't want you. I'm sorry."

"No, I'm the one who should be sorry. I betrayed you. That's not the man I wanted to be. You deserved better."

"It's okay, Jack. I forgave you a long time ago. Now I just blame myself."

Anna coughed, inartfully.

Jack looked back at Anna as if just realizing she was there.

"You've met my . . . er . . . you've met Anna?"

"Yes." Nina nodded coolly. "She seems like a lovely young girl."

"We're engaged, Nina. To be married."

"I've heard."

"You were dead. I moved on with my life."

"Of course. I wish all the best to both of you." Nina looked like she was going to cry.

Agent Cook broke the silence. "I was married once. Didn't work out, though. I'm sure your marriage will work out much better. At least, one of 'em will. I'll just shut up."

"How is Olivia?" Nina asked softly. "My baby."

"She's six. She's a wonderful, bright little girl. She thinks her mother is dead."

She thinks I'm her mother, Anna thought.

"I did this for Olivia," Nina said.

Anna wasn't sure exactly what this meant, but the emotion on Nina's face erased any doubt Anna had about the other woman's maternal instinct. Anna glanced at Jack, and saw that he was tearing up.

"Can we have a moment, please?" Nina said.

Anna realized the woman was talking to her. She glanced at Jack. He nodded. She got up, and Deputy Cook walked her out of the room. He closed the door behind them, and suddenly he and Anna were out in the cold, dark night. Jack and Nina were on the other side of the door, talking about . . . whatever.

"You can go ahead home, ma'am," the deputy Marshal said, pointing down the outdoor hallway. "I'll make sure Mr. Bailey gets a ride when they're done."

Anna walked to the blue Taurus. Moments later, Deputy Fitzgerald was pulling out onto New York Avenue. The motel receded in the distance. Anna glanced out the window and saw Cook standing on the balcony, lighting a cigarette, apparently having decided that Jack was harmless and could be allowed to speak alone with Nina.

Anna pictured the two of them, alone in the motel room, overwhelmed with emotions. She wished she hadn't allowed herself to be shuffled away so quickly.

43

Anna sat in their darkened hotel room, waiting. An episode of *Breaking Bad* played on the TV, but she wasn't following it. It was her second pay-per-view rental of the night, as she tried to distract herself from the fact that Jack was still at the motel with Nina. It wasn't working. She gazed out the window at the dark city. The headlights of cars passing on the street below grew ever sparser as the night wore on. She waited for Jack to return home. She wondered if he would.

He finally arrived, at a quarter to two. He entered the hotel room quietly, maybe hoping not to wake her.

"Hey," she said. She turned off the TV.

"Hey."

She wanted to ask him a hundred questions. Do you still love her? Did you kiss her?

But she knew this would not help her cause. Instead, she walked over to him, put her arms gently around his neck, and kissed him softly on his lips. She did not detect the taste or smell of another woman on him.

"You doing okay?" she asked.

He sank down on the couch, and she sat next to him.

"I don't know how I'm doing," he said. "I'm—God, I was so relieved to see her. After all those years. The guilt. It's—gone."

"Good."

"But now—I'm angry. I know I shouldn't be. But I had a funeral for her. I stood at her grave and lowered a coffin into the ground. I went through her clothes, one by one, and gave them to Goodwill. Olivia was too young to understand, so she kept asking for her. Every night for months. She would stop, and then one day, out of the blue—is Mommy coming home today? It killed me, every time."

Anna nodded and kept silent. He needed to work out his own emotional process. And she'd learned an important lesson in court: Shut up when things are going your way.

"But Olivia and I got through it. Time passed. I moved on. I met you. Everything was good again. But now that scab has been ripped right open."

"I think she's a foolish woman," Anna said. "To have given you up. But I'm glad she did."

"I love you," he said. The words were a balm.

"I love you, too."

She pulled him into her arms and held him for a long time. She wished she could press "pause" on the moment.

When Anna awoke the next morning, she reached automatically for Jack, but found an empty spot on the bed. She opened her eyes, and found herself alone in the room. Groggily, she padded to Olivia's room, opened the door, and peeked in. The little girl was still asleep in her bed, looking angelic and peaceful. Anna followed the sound of running water to the bathroom. Jack was washing his face in the sink. He was wearing just pajama bottoms, and she watched the muscles in his back rippling under his taut brown skin. He dried his face on a towel and turned to her grimly.

"Good morning," she said. "What got you up so early?'

"I've been thinking all night," he said. "Olivia needs to see Nina."

"Um." She stalled, trying to clear the cobwebs of sleep from her mind. "Are you sure? I mean, Nina is in Witsec. Her whole existence is a secret. Can you really expect a six-year-old to keep a secret that big?"

"Olivia is precocious. She can do it. Anyway, MS-13 knows she's alive. The 'secret' thing is pretty pointless now."

"Maybe it would hurt Olivia more, though? To know her mother left her?"

"We can explain it."

Anna wiped the sleep from her eyes, and wondered whether the "we" referred to Jack and her—or Jack and Nina.

"I'm sorry," Jack said. "I shouldn't have sprung this on you. I've been thinking about it all night. I'll make some coffee and we'll talk."

Fifteen minutes later, she sat with minty fresh

breath and a mug of steaming coffee in her hands. She felt more awake, but not any happier about the prospect of Nina meeting Olivia. It meant Nina was probably around to stay.

"What's the plan, Jack?" She spoke softly so she wouldn't wake the little girl. "Are we still planning our wedding? Or are you getting back together with Nina?"

He met her eyes with resolve. "You and I are getting married."

"Is Nina staying in Witsec? Is she going back to Nebraska after the trial?"

"I don't know. It's been difficult for her. She misses Olivia terribly. I'm not sure she can go back."

"I thought you were angry at Nina," Anna said, trying not to sound hopeful.

"Furious is more like it. But that doesn't change the fact that she's Olivia's mother."

"Didn't she leave because she thought that her presence was somehow putting Olivia in danger? Has that threat gone away?"

"It will if you can catch Diablo and win your case," Jack said.

"Maybe we should wait a few more months to see how it all plays out, then," Anna said. "It would be terrible if Olivia saw her mother, then Nina had to go back into hiding because Psycho got acquitted or Diablo got away."

Jack got up and kissed Anna on the forehead. "I'm counting on you not to let that happen. Anyway," he brought the coffeepot to the table and refilled her cup.

"I can't do it. I can't keep from my little girl the fact that her mother is alive."

Anna thought of her own mother, who died in a car accident when Anna was in college. If her mother were alive today, Anna wouldn't want to miss one second with her. There were so many things she would want to tell her. So many questions she wished she'd asked when she still had the chance.

"I understand," she said.

Jack looked relieved. "Thanks, Anna."

In two days, Anna had a lot of work to do. The MS-13 *generale* was tomorrow night. If they were going to record the meeting, they had to get ready immediately.

After dropping Olivia off at school, Anna went into the office. Staring at the papers on her desk, she kept picturing Nina, taking Olivia from Anna's arms. Anna tried to shake it off and lose herself in the legal issues.

The first was how to record the *generale*. They couldn't wire up Gato. Button-sized video cameras could be worn on a shirt or installed in a cell phone, but there was little that could be secreted on a man in his underwear.

If they could find out where the *generale* was going to happen, they could wire up the room. So far, though, Gato had only been told that the *generale* would be held in Wheaton Regional Park, and someone would tell him where to go when he got there. That didn't help Anna and Sam. Wheaton Regional Park included many acres of pavilions, picnic areas, playgrounds, and trails through woods. There were administrative buildings, a butterfly conservatory, a carousel, and a mini-train that chugged through the grounds. The FBI couldn't wire up the whole place.

The wiretap that Anna had gotten on Psycho's smuggled-in-jail cell phone was finally up and running as of this morning, and it paid off. Later that afternoon, Psycho got a call from a man he referred to as "Rooster," who mentioned that he would be guarding the *generale* in the Train Room. That was a large room overlooking the tracks of the mini-train. Olivia had been there for a birthday party last year.

The room itself could be wired, and the conversation in it recorded. But they had to be smart about it. The government could only record the talk without a court's wiretap order if one party to the conversation consented to the recording. Otherwise, they'd have to get a court order authorizing them to wire up a public place. Such a wiretap application had to satisfy a high legal burden—one they likely couldn't meet on such short notice.

Sam's Ops Plan called for plainclothes FBI agents in cars in the parking lot and pavilions throughout the park. They would monitor the meeting using infrared binoculars and pole cameras to see who was coming and going.

"So they'll know when Gato is inside?" Anna asked.

"Right."

"And you can remotely control the recording devices in the Train Room?"

"We can."

"So you can record only when Gato is in the room, and we have our consenting party."

"Exactly."

"Have Gato arrive early, stay late, and stay close to Diablo."

Anna didn't want to miss a word Diablo said. In years of looking for him, this was the first time the government knew where he was going to be before he got there. And he was leading a big meeting of the gang—that evidence would be gold in a RICO prosecution against him. They had to get it.

The plan called for Diablo to be arrested immediately after the *generale*. Anna drafted an arrest warrant and affidavit, and Sam took it to the home of Magistrate Judge Gallagher, the duty judge that weekend. The judge called Anna to ask some questions, and Sam made edits to the affidavit. When the judge was satisfied, she signed the warrant.

The FBI would set up the recording devices in the Train Room late tonight. Meanwhile, Sam was gathering up a small army of agents and local police. Depending on what was said at the *generale*, they might be able to arrest dozens of MS members. They needed almost a hundred agents to be on hand. Sam borrowed FBI agents from the Baltimore, Richmond, and Charleston Field Offices, and police from Montgomery County. McGee hooked a bunch of MPD officers with the lure of overtime.

Sam's coup de grâce was getting the "eagle"—a law enforcement airplane that would fly overhead and monitor the ground using thermal imaging cameras.

This was going to be one of the largest regional FBI operations of the year, and Sam set it up on two days' notice. She clearly loved it.

A small voice reminded Anna that all the work she did to arrest Diablo brought Nina one step closer to meeting Olivia and getting back together with Jack. Anna kept working and tried to ignore that voice. She didn't want to give it the power of contemplation.

44

Act like it's a first date," Agent Samantha Randazzo said. "Listen more than you talk."

Gato nodded. He wasn't sure he'd ever been on a "first date" the way she meant, but he could listen. He felt like he'd been listening to Agent Randazzo for hours. He felt sick with nervousness. He was ready to be done with this.

They were inside a big warehouse on Georgia Avenue, which the agent was calling the "command center." Shelving units had been pushed to the walls and the big space in the middle was parked up with dark-tinted Suburbans and police cruisers. Cops in suits and uniforms filled the place: drinking coffee, talking, typing on laptops sitting on collapsible tables. Gato got more than one curious or suspicious glance.

"Some cooperators get nervous and chatter," she continued. "That doesn't help us. You want to get the *other* guy talking. Ask questions. Follow up on the answers. Talk about crimes you guys have committed in the past, but in a way that's part of the conversation—not in a way that seems weird."

Gato nodded. The phone the agent had given him

looked like every other prepaid cell phone he'd bought at 7-Eleven. But she said there was a bug in it to record everything, and GPS to track him.

"When you do talk, speak slowly and loudly. But naturally. If you're keeping the phone in your left pocket, try to angle yourself so that your left hip is closest to Diablo, to better pick up his voice. But don't do it in a way that looks funny."

Gato tried to imagine angling his hip toward Diablo in a way that wouldn't look funny, but pictured himself posing like a Victoria's Secret model.

"It won't be an issue," Gato said. "We have to strip. There's no way the phone will go in with me."

"Just in case. If there's any way to keep it on you, do. It'll help us know that you're safe, and let us track where you are. And if a gang member asks you to get in a car, don't! If they bring you somewhere else, it might be to kill you. What's your exit strategy if they try to get you in a car?"

"Um . . . I'll say I gotta take a piss?"

"Good."

Gato knew there was no "exit strategy." If they asked him to "take a ride" and he tried to avoid it, they'd just kill him right there. He didn't mention that to the agent. She'd been role-playing all sorts of different scenarios with him, giving him tips, and coaching his answers. If he didn't have an answer, or she didn't like his answer, it would mean more talking.

"If we positively ID Diablo," the agent continued, "we'll wait until the meeting is over and arrest everyone. You'll be arrested, too, for your own safety, so no one will know you're cooperating. Most of the officers out there won't know you're the cooperator. They'll treat you like everyone else. That means if you resist, you'll get your head smashed, so don't go acting up. You'll be processed just like everyone else, but when your friends are being divided up to be housed, you'll go into protective custody."

He nodded. He didn't like taking orders from a woman, or hearing her talk about smashing in his head. But such was his life now.

"Most importantly," the agent said, "try to act natural."

"Okay," he said although nothing he'd done over the last few days felt natural at all.

Finally, she said it was time for him to go in.

"Remember," she said as she opened the warehouse's side door. "If you get into any trouble, say 'I wish my brother were here.'"

He didn't have brothers in America and couldn't imagine using the line. But he nodded and walked out. As soon as the door shut behind him, it closed out the world of lights, laptops, and police chatter. He was alone, in the dark, cold night, with only a cell phone to protect him. He took a deep breath and started walking.

• • •

In the hotel room, Olivia pulled on her conical black hat, completing her witch costume. She already wore the long black dress and had the warty rubber nose attached over her cute little one. She clutched a plastic jack-o'-lantern for collecting candy.

"You are the cutest witch ever," Anna said.

"I am not cute." Olivia looked offended. "I'm scary. I have powerful magic."

"Ah, right." Anna held up her hands in mock horror. "Please don't turn me into a bat!"

"You'll have to do what I say."

"Anything."

"Bring me some candy, peasant."

Anna grabbed a pack of Skittles and handed it to Olivia. The girl nodded with witchy satisfaction and dropped it into her pumpkin.

Jack opened the door and they all walked into the hallway. He was somber and tense, knowing what was going on in Wheaton Regional Park, unable to do anything to help.

Anna was sorry that the little girl couldn't have a normal Halloween. Takoma Park would be full of kids running down the sidewalks now, yelling "Trick or treat" from house to house. But it was too dangerous for Olivia to be walking the streets tonight. Anna had set up a Halloween scavenger hunt around the hotel suite, which they'd do later. For now, the three of them walked to the front office of the Residence Inn. The manager had invited Olivia to trick-or-treat there.

Anna checked her cell phone for the sixth time that night. No messages, no texts. At this point, her role was minuscule. She could only wait, ready to answer the phone if a legal issue came up. Sam would only call her in the most dire of circumstances, since Anna's legal advice would likely rein in her options. Sam preferred to make the decisions herself, and leave it to Anna to justify them in court later.

The hotel manager was a sweet old lady who'd taped cardboard ghosts to her office door. On her desk was a bowl filled with glow sticks and mini Snickers. The office already held a few other parents and kids who were stranded at the hotel for their own reasons. There were two little princesses, a Batman, a Devil, and a zombie. Olivia stopped walking and stood outside the door.

"It's okay." Anna put a hand on her shoulder. "Go ahead."

"It's a *Devil*," Olivia said. "He's a bad guy."

Anna and Jack frowned at each other. Despite their efforts to shield Olivia, the girl had heard and understood too much of what was happening. Anna knelt down and put a hand on Olivia's arm.

"It's just kids in costumes. They're pretending to be bad for the night. But underneath they're nice kids. Same as you."

Olivia stood looking at the other children several minutes. Finally she nodded. She took Anna's hand and walked into the office to collect her treats.

• • •

Gato trudged down Arcola Street, which led away from busy Georgia Avenue, passed through a modest suburban neighborhood, then ended in Wheaton Regional Park's big parking lot. To the left was the wooded park with its series of pavilions, playgrounds, and picnic tables. Ahead of Gato was the shuttered carousel, the ticket office, and the building that held the Train Room.

On summer days, the park was filled with families having cookouts or birthday parties, and the happy sounds of children on the carousel. Gato had come here once with Maria-Rosa. It seemed like a lifetime ago. In a sense it was. Maria-Rosa's lifetime. She and Gato had spread out a blanket and picnicked on fried chicken and cinnamon-laced *horchata* from Pollo Campero. Then Gato lay down, and Maria-Rosa fitted herself into the crook of his arm. They gazed at the light blue sky through the trees, pointing out animal shapes in the clouds and talking about how they would decorate a house of their own.

Tonight the sky was black. The park was empty and silent.

He shoved his hands deeper into his pockets, trying to warm them as he walked through the lot. He didn't see any police. Agent Randazzo told him that there would be undercover agents watching the whole thing. But he only saw one couple in a car, and they looked like they were here to fool around. If the FBI was here, he could not see any sign of it. His fingers gripped the cell phone like a lifeline.

The Train Room was in a building with offices, bathrooms, and, downstairs, the miniature train "station." A homeboy who worked the night shift as a janitor had a key. Gato walked up a long wooden ramp to the building's entrance. Through the windows, he could see twenty to thirty men and boys already inside.

Rooster sat on a stool, fully dressed, in front of the door. Gato greeted him, and they threw up the *garra*, then the "M" and the "S," and the "13."

"Everyone's gotta take off their clothes," Rooster said apologetically. "Even you, homey."

"No problem."

Gato undressed down to his briefs and piled his clothes and shoes on top of a bench. A bunch of piles were there already. His skin puckered with goose bumps as the cold air hit it. He held on to his cell phone.

"You know you can't bring it inside," Rooster said.

"Right."

Gato tucked the cell phone into his shoe. So much for the FBI's stupid plan. He began to walk toward the room, but Rooster put out a hand to stop him.

"I was wondering," Rooster said. "Did you kill that prosecutor?"

The question had a tinge of malice to it, but Gato had prepared an answer. "I'm close. I followed her, but she was always with a police officer."

"Diablo's not gonna wait forever."

"He won't have to. Soon. I'll get her soon. Don't worry."

Rooster shook his head and shrugged, but didn't move to let him pass. He just stared at him, with a sad look on his face. In that moment, Gato realized that Rooster had been assigned to kill him. Diablo's second chance was no chance at all—but Gato hadn't expected the assignment to be handed out so soon. He'd have to make his own second chance. Gato picked his cell phone out of his shoe.

"Rooster, do me a favor. This wasn't cheap, I don't want to just leave it here. You're staying out here, right? Hold on to it for me."

Rooster nodded, then dropped it into the pocket of his puffy winter coat. He would stay outside, keeping watch, during the *generale.* Gato hoped the FBI could still listen.

• • •

Inside the warehouse, Sam and six FBI agents clustered around a computer. They were the brains of the operation. Throughout the park, they had eyes, ears, and muscle. Gato's phone was working, but it was no longer on his person. Sam radioed the guys in the parking lot.

"Keep good eyes on our CI. He doesn't have his phone anymore."

"Copy that. CI just entered the Train Room."

She nodded to Agent Steve Quisenberry, who sat at a laptop. Quisenberry clicked on the keyboard. The sound from the recording devices in the Train Room began transmitting. The team leaned forward to listen.

45

Gato opened the door. The Train Room was a large space lit tonight by a few small electric lanterns, creating a soft yellow glow in a few patches of the otherwise dark room. Homeboys in underwear stood in clumps talking softly. Some were from the Langley Park Salvatruchas or neighboring cliques, but there were many MS-13 leaders from around the East Coast. Two walls had large windows, from which Gato could see the mini-train tracks and parking lot. He hoped that meant the police could see inside. As Gato walked in, his bare feet crunched on something. The entire floor was covered in a large blue roofers' tarpaulin. At the moment, it was just catching cigarette butts, but MS wasn't known for its prim housekeeping. Gato guessed what kind of mess they were expecting. Still, he walked in.

He looked around, hoping to see Diablo, but the man was nowhere in sight. There were many "old heads"—grizzled older leaders covered in tattoos in the old style. The younger generation of leaders were here, too—some still just boys.

Men continued to arrive. Gato talked to some of his

homies from the LPS, but he was distracted. Eventually, an old head from the Sailors Locos Salvatruchas called the meeting to order.

"*La garra*," the room intoned.

They threw up the signs, "MS" first, then each clique leader adding his clique's sign. The representatives from each clique went around the room saying their nickname and the clique they represented. Gato guessed there were eighty men here now, with leadership from every clique up and down the East Coast.

They blessed a new clique: the Dover Salvatruchas, spun off from a group in Wilmington. The men celebrated their new homeboys and laughed about a recent article branding MS-13 the most dangerous gang in America. That would help recruitment.

After twenty minutes, Rooster, still dressed in his jeans and winter jacket, opened the door and held it ajar. A second later, Diablo entered, gesturing for Rooster to follow him inside the room. Diablo wore only black boxers; his entire body was covered in tattoos, head to foot. His long dark hair streamed down his back, his horns stood proudly on his forehead. He smiled at the men, baring his sharpened teeth. The crowd cheered at the sight of him.

"We come here tonight to celebrate what we've achieved," Diablo said in Spanish. "And to figure out how we can do better."

The men roared, clapped, threw up the claw.

"One thing to celebrate is our increased rent. We are now getting almost a hundred thousand dollars a month from businesses in the D.C. area. People have heard our reputation, and they pay. And we have killed many Eighteenth Street *chavalas*. That gang is growing weak here. That is something we can be very proud of."

Another loud cheer.

"But we have a long way to go. Many businesses still thumb their noses at us. They don't believe us capable of carrying out the threats we have given them. We must show them we are merciless. We punish those who do not obey. *Anyone* who doesn't obey."

He turned and picked up a machete from the floor. Then he drove it right through Rooster's stomach.

"If you don't complete a greenlight," Diablo said, "you will be greenlighted yourself."

In profile, Rooster's eyes bulged and a look of horrified shock crossed his face. He was perfectly still for a moment. From the side, Gato could see the pointed blade of the machete coming out of Rooster's back. A few puffs of down floated out of the slice in the back of his winter jacket; a bubble of blood expanded from his nostril. His bright eyes dulled. Diablo yanked out the blade, and Rooster's body collapsed onto the tarp.

"Bring me Gato!" Diablo's eyes gleamed with pleasure as he held the bloody machete above his head.

Gato turned to run, but a dozen hands were on him, grabbing and dragging him forward. "I wish my brother was here!" Gato yelled. "I wish my brother was here!" But everyone else was yelling, too, and he doubted the FBI could hear his voice in the ruckus. He fought and thrashed and tried to escape but couldn't. Rough hands carried him to the front of the room.

They shoved him down to kneeling in front of Diablo, then down farther, until he was lying on his stomach. They pinned his hands and legs. Someone stepped on his head, pressing his cheek onto the blue tarp. He could feel the cold floor beneath it. He stared sideways, and Rooster's lifeless eyes stared back at him.

He could feel the breath of his homies on the back of his neck, gasping from exertion as they held him down. From the direction of Rooster's body, he saw a line of blood snaking around the blue plastic. It carried a cigarette butt in its path. Gato watched the butt float past someone's boot.

"Rape, kill, control," Diablo shouted. "This is what makes us strong. But to control, you must have discipline. Once discipline breaks down—if we make empty threats—we will not be able to control our own members, much less the community."

Gato thought about Maria-Rosa. He wondered if he would see her in heaven, if he'd managed to make a place for himself there. Probably not. He had too much blood on his own hands.

"This is for the Mara Salvatrucha," Diablo said.

But instead of the blade on his neck, Gato felt the floor shaking. Then he heard the boots, dozens of them, and loud voices yelling in English and Spanish. He saw the bright lasers of high-beam flashlights dancing around the room. The hands released him as the homies turned to flee. In the noise and confusion, Gato was alone, unrestrained, lying on the tarp next to Rooster. Gato didn't move.

As the chaos swirled around him, Gato closed his

eyes, let his cheek rest on the bloody tarp, and tried to remember the strawberry scent of Maria-Rosa's hair.

• • •

McGee burst into the Train Room behind three FBI agents; more MPD officers and FBI agents were behind them. The officers poured into the room, surrounding the group of almost-naked, tattooed men. "Get down!" McGee yelled. "Police, everybody down!"

There was one machete at the front of the room, which was quickly secured by an officer. The gangbangers looked fierce, but they were obviously unarmed. Men in their underwear were no match for law enforcement agents with long guns and bulletproof vests. The thugs put their hands in the air. They got down on the ground. They complied.

Except for one man, who sent a chair flying through a plate-glass window. McGee swung the flashlight mounted on his rifle toward the figure. He was wearing just black boxers and had no weapon in his hands. The man had horns, nonstop tattoos, and nasty sunken nostrils.

"Diablo," McGee said. "They warned me that you were handsome, but my my, you are absolutely breathtaking. Hands up. *Manos arriba!*"

Diablo looked calmly at McGee, then down the line of officers who had guns pointed at his heart. "Adios," said Diablo. He smiled, gave a little wave, then leapt through the smashed window. He landed like a cat on the railroad tracks below, and started running down the tracks in his bare feet.

McGee lowered his weapon. "Fuck."

McGee couldn't shoot an unarmed man in the back. He peered out the broken glass and contemplated making the jump himself. There was no way his knees would survive. He turned, pushed through the door, and ran out into the night. Several agents followed.

Diablo had disappeared. There was just darkness, bare trees, and empty playground equipment. Riderless swings creaked and swayed on their chains.

• • •

"No!" shouted Samantha. She swatted a box of Chips Ahoy! off the table. Innocent cookies went flying through the command center. Diablo was in the wind. The arrest team was spread out in Wheaton Regional Park, but could find no sign of him. They were calling in dogs, but without Diablo's base scent, the dogs were unlikely to find him among all the other human smells.

She turned to the MPD sergeant whose men were supposed to have surrounded the building. "There was no perimeter!" she shouted.

"We covered the doors. We didn't think anyone would go out a window," he said sheepishly.

Sam wanted to cry, although she would never do that in front of her team. It didn't matter how many other MS-13 members were arrested tonight. If Diablo got away, her operation was a failure.

Sam looked around the warehouse. There were eight agents and officers from various police agencies manning the command center: running the phones, audio equipment, and computers. She made a quick decision. She put two fingers in her mouth and whistled loudly. Everyone looked up.

"I need a skeleton crew to stay here," she announced. "Bob, Angela, you hold down the fort." She turned to the other six officers. "We're going into the park. Maybe Diablo will try coming out on this side, through Georgia Avenue."

The six blinked—they all thought they had desk duties tonight—but they nodded. They hastily put on tac vests and checked their weapons. Sam pulled on a radio headset. "And I want a radio connection to the eagle, right away." Sam led them out of the overheated warehouse, into the cold night. The parking lot behind the warehouse was bordered by trees, the back end of Wheaton Regional Park.

She directed her team to spread out—two agents going northward into the woods, two south. "Eagle, what have you got for me?" she asked into the radio.

"Not much is showing up on the thermal imaging," came the response over her radio. "Maybe—try fifteen degrees south, about five hundred yards ahead of you."

She and Quisenberry went into the forest ahead of them, heading slightly to the left, adjusting their bearings at the direction of the officer with the thermal imaging equipment in the aircraft. They walked as quietly as possible on the carpet of dead leaves. Their weapons were drawn, their eyes skimmed over tree trunks and brush. With each step, the night got blacker. The sound of traffic on Georgia Avenue faded into a distant hush, replaced by the sounds of the forest. An owl hooted. Night animals scurried around in the canopy. She and Quisenberry kept going, stepping around boulders and downed trees. They'd been partners so long, they moved as a unit without having to speak.

"I've lost you under the tree cover," the officer in the eagle said in Sam's ear. "But you're close. Stay alert."

In the darkness, Sam thought she saw a glimmer of movement behind a tree trunk. She narrowed her eyes, lowered her chin, and focused on it. Human, half naked. Quisenberry saw it, too. Sam nodded at him.

Quisenberry went left, she went right. As they crept closer, the man in the woods darted from the trees and started running leftward. Sam saw his whole body then, the inked flesh, the dark hair flowing behind him, the horns. He wore only dark underwear. Flying through the forest, barefoot and snarling, he looked like a creature from a twisted fairy tale. The agents sprinted after him. Sam jumped over roots and rocks, praying not to trip or fall, but to catch this monster and bring him in.

Quisenberry made a flying leap and tackled him. Diablo fought back. The two men became a thrashing pile of limbs and curses. Sam pointed her gun at them but didn't dare fire it. She heard Quisenberry shout in agony, and saw Diablo lift his mouth from her partner's shoulder. Blood dripped from teeth that had been filed to triangular points. Diablo snarled bloodily at Sam.

Fuck it, she thought. *That qualifies as armed.* "Steve, move!" she shouted. Quisenberry rolled to the side, giving her a clear shot. Diablo tried to scramble to his feet. Sam fired twice. The devil shuddered, then stilled.

46

The FBI arrested eighty-two MS members, eighty-three if you included Gato. Many were in leadership positions in cliques from as far away as New York and New Jersey. The arrests closed out warrants pending in multiple states. The biggest fish of all was Diablo.

He survived the two bullets, although his hip and femur were fractured. He recuperated in a hospital, under heavy guard.

The press loved his mug shot, airing it over and over. The image played on a primal fear. He looked like the monster from children's nightmares, the one every child suspected was hiding under her bed, whose existence every parent had to deny. "MS-13 Devil" trended on the Internet for days after the arrest.

Anna worked every waking hour for the next ten days, sorting things out. Eighty-two men had to be charged and arraigned, or released. Some were willing to be interviewed. Their information was disseminated among federal and state law enforcement agencies.

Men who were wanted in other jurisdictions, but not chargeable in D.C., were extradited. The U.S. Attorney's Office in Virginia—which had a formidable reputation for fighting MS-13—got a chunk of prisoners. So did the feds in Maryland, New Jersey, Delaware, and New York. Main Justice's elite Organized Crime and Gang Section took some of the defendants. State prosecutors in Maryland charged Diablo and a few others with Rooster's homicide and Gato's attempted homicide. DOJ's Office of International Affairs received extradition requests from El Salvador and Guatemala.

Navigating the bureaucratic maze gave Anna a welcome distraction from her even more complicated personal life. Now that Diablo was in custody, she knew Jack wanted Nina to meet Olivia. But he waited patiently while Anna worked to sort everything out. He was supportive, giving her coffee in the morning and advice in the evening. He rubbed her feet and massaged her shoulders—and didn't mention Nina. For now.

Anna kept her own case, charging Psycho, Diablo, and Gato with a RICO conspiracy predicated on the prostitution and murder of Maria-Rosa Gomez, the extortion of the brothel, the rape of Tierra Guerrero and the murder of the brothel doorman, the murders of Ricardo and the timekeeper, and the murder of Rooster. RICO—the Racketeering Influenced Corrupt Organizations Act—provided extensive criminal penalties for crimes committed to benefit a criminal organization. Even if a member hadn't committed a particular crime himself, he could be prosecuted if he was a member of the organization and knew about or participated in a pattern of criminal activity on behalf of the organization. Anna had a strong RICO case.

The charges against Gato were just for show—so no one would know he was cooperating, at least for now. She'd already hammered out the plea deal with his lawyer.

George Litz, the AUSA from the Fraud section, wanted back in on the case. Anna forgave him for not telling her who "Julia" was—he'd had a duty to maintain Nina's cover in Witsec—and happily accepted him on board. She could use the help.

A week after the *generale*, MPD's Internal Affairs Branch released their Use of Force report for the brothel raid. IAB concluded that Hector's shooting had been justified. In addition, his misdemeanor assault case involving "Casper" was dismissed, based on Agent Randazzo's report that Casper had started the fight. IAB still put a letter of reprimand in Hector's file, but he was allowed to come back to work. Anna was relieved for him. She also wanted to see whether, despite his thick disciplinary file, he might be a useful witness in her trial.

Hector agreed to meet Anna in her office the following week. When he arrived, he was still pale and thin, but he'd shaved off the lumberjack beard and had a neat button-down shirt tucked into khakis. He took a seat next to McGee. Anna hadn't invited Sam to the meeting; the presence of the FBI agent who arrested him would make this already-awkward meeting even more awkward.

"Thanks for coming," Anna said to Hector. "Is your attorney here?"

"I don't need one."

"Atta boy," McGee said. "Screw the lawyers."

Anna shot McGee a good-natured glare, then focused on Hector. "I'm glad you were cleared."

She thought Hector would be angry at her. She had suspected him in Nina's death, and her suspicions led to his arrest. She was prepared for him to gripe at her.

But he said, "I'm sorry, Anna. I was out of control, going around messing with those MS members. I was worried they were still hunting Nina."

"You don't have to apologize."

"I do. I should've stood down and let you handle it. I wanted you to stop them—but I didn't know how much I could tell you, with her being in Witsec. The Marshals said I couldn't tell you anything. I felt like I was the only one in the world who knew the whole truth—and could take care of things. I took it too personally. I was wrong."

"I understand," Anna said. "I'm not blaming you or judging. But I could use your help. You probably heard—we made a big MS bust a couple weeks ago."

Hector nodded.

"If possible, I'd like you to be a witness in the trial. The jury is going to want to hear your testimony. But first I need to know—what is your connection to MS-13?"

McGee looked at him pointedly. Hector shifted uncomfortably in his seat.

"I was jumped into the gang when I was fifteen, living in L.A."

"Are you still a member?"

"No!" He lowered his voice. "No. When my mom found out, she freaked. She sent me to live with my grandmother in D.C. That was ages ago, before MS had any real presence here. At the time, I hated her for moving me. But she was right. It got me away from the gang."

"Do you know some of the MS members here?'

"A few of the older ones, I met back in the day. Most of them, no. I just found them from asking around."

"What's your connection to the gang now?"

"Nothing. Well, maybe I have a chip on my shoulder with them. I take their shit personally."

"If you testify, you'll be cross-examined about all of this. And about your shooting and your arrest for assault. It could be embarrassing."

"It's all right. It's the truth. It might actually be a relief to have it all out there."

He smiled at her. It was the first real smile she'd seen on his face since he'd come to get the warrant signed for the brothel raid.

"Can I ask you a question?" Hector said.

"Sure."

"You still planning to marry Jack Bailey?"

She held up her left hand, showing the ring there. Hector smiled ruefully.

"What do you have against him?" she asked.

"Nothing, it's just—it was just the whole situation. I hated that he didn't appreciate what he had. Nina was—she *is*—just incredible."

"So I hear." It was Anna's turn to smile ruefully.

After two weeks, Anna's hours started to normalize. She wondered when Jack would raise the subject of Nina visiting Olivia. But it turned out to be Olivia who raised the issue, albeit unknowingly.

It was a chilly mid-November morning, but their hotel room was warm and scented with fresh-brewed coffee. They all sat at the breakfast table. Olivia ate Cheerios; Anna and Jack nursed coffees and swapped sections of the *Washington Post*. They were still at the hotel, but not for much longer.

"Guess what?" Jack asked Olivia.

"What?"

"We get to move back home in a few days."

"Yay! Will we get Raffles back?"

"Yes." Anna smiled at her.

"Is Mommy's spirit still at our house or did she get lonely and go away while we were gone?"

Anna paused with the coffee mug halfway to her mouth. Jack looked to her. She took a deep breath and nodded.

"Honey," he said to Olivia. "I have to tell you something. It's surprising, but it's wonderful."

"We're getting a puppy?" Olivia slurped a spoonful of cereal.

"Even better. Your mom is alive."

"What?"

"She's been living in another city."

Olivia put the spoon down and folded her arms across her chest. "Why?"

"Sometimes grown-ups have to do things for work. Even if they don't want to."

"Yeah, Anna told me that's why we're staying at the hotel. I don't think I like work." She narrowed her eyes at her father. "Did you know? Were you lying to me the whole time?"

"No." Jack grimaced. "I just found out myself."

"So she tricked you? That's bad. She's bad."

"She's not." Anna spoke for the first time. Both Jack and Olivia swiveled their heads toward her. "She loves you, Olivia, very much."

"Mm," Olivia said. She was skeptical about whether Nina was a good person. But she wasn't as shocked about Nina being alive as Anna had expected. The girl was still at the age of magical belief: in monsters and fairies and dead mothers who turned out to be alive. "So is she coming back to live with us?"

Jack hesitated.

"No," Anna said. "She's not."

47

The next morning, Olivia insisted on picking out the perfect outfit. She tried on, then discarded, six different dresses before finally settling on a black skirt and purple turtleneck with little flowers embroidered at the sleeves. She directed Anna to put her hair up, then down, then in pigtails. Anna fastened a barrette and hoped this was the one. Olivia tipped her head this way and that as she studied her reflection.

"Good. Thanks, Anna."

"You're welcome."

Anna set the brush down and turned to leave. But Olivia grabbed her wrist, stopping her. The little girl looked up at her with wide, frightened eyes.

"What if she doesn't like me?"

"She loves you. You're her little girl."

"Then why did she leave me?"

Anna sat so her eyes were level with Olivia's. She didn't want to fight Nina's fights, but she couldn't let the girl think her mother didn't want her.

"She missed you all this time."

Olivia climbed on Anna's lap, snuggled her head

under Anna's chin, and sucked her thumb, which she only did when she was tired or worried. Anna held her quietly.

When Jack had arranged everything so quickly, Anna thought the girl should be given more time to digest the news before meeting Nina. But seeing the worry on Olivia's face, Anna realized that the sooner she saw her mother, the better.

Jack was pacing by the hotel room's window when the knock came. Anna's stomach roiled but she smiled reassuringly at Olivia. The girl held her hand as they stood by the couch. Jack strode over and opened the door. Deputy Cook was in the hallway with Nina, but he didn't come inside. Nina walked into the suite and the door shut behind her.

They stood in a triangle, silently taking each other in. Olivia clung to Anna's leg. Jack stood awkwardly by the door. The little girl stared at, but did not move toward, the woman whose face she might or might not remember, but whom she'd seen in thousands of pictures.

Nina came forward and knelt down by Olivia. The woman's eyes were full of wonder and love. "Hello," she said softly.

She reached out to touch Olivia's arm. Olivia stepped back and squeezed Anna's thigh even tighter. If it were her neck, Anna wouldn't be able to breathe. The girl made a strained whimpering sound. Nina's eyes welled up with tears.

Anna remembered the time she'd been forced to meet with her father, during a supervised court-ordered visitation. She was eleven, and her sister was nine. After what he'd done, Anna and her sister refused to talk to him; they turned their backs on him. They did that during every visitation the court ordered, until he finally gave up. Anna hadn't seen him since. She didn't regret it.

But Olivia would regret it if she didn't go to her mother now.

Anna leaned down and gave Nina a hug. "Nina, hello!" she said, forcing her voice to sound cheerful and light. "Nice to see you."

She could feel the other woman's body stiffen against her embrace. Neither of them wanted to touch the other. But the gesture had the right effect on Olivia. Her arms stayed around Anna's legs but relaxed their grip. If Anna was okay with this new woman, Olivia figured she might be okay, too.

Anna said, "Who's up for some Candy Land?"

And so they started their reunion with board games. The four of them played Candy Land and Hungry Hungry Hippos and Operation. By the time they were operating on the poor fat fella, Olivia was laughing and chattering with Nina, even giving some mild trash talk when Nina's tweezers buzzed on the funny bone. Anna glanced at Jack. He smiled at her thankfully.

They ordered room service for lunch, hamburgers and ice-cream sundaes. Over semimelted rocky road, Olivia asked Nina her first serious question.

"Why did you go away all this time?"

"Oh, honey." Nina put her spoon down. "I thought it would be best for you."

"Because I'd been bad?"

"God, no. To protect you. From bad guys who wanted to hurt me. I was worried they would want to hurt you, too. But if they thought I was gone, you'd be safe."

"Will they want to hurt me now?"

Anna felt a flash of anger at Nina. Anna and Jack had deliberately left talk of bad guys and danger out of their conversations with Olivia. They didn't want the girl to be terrified.

"The bad guys can't hurt you now," Nina said. "Because they're in jail. And Anna is going to make sure they stay there."

Olivia looked to Anna, and Anna nodded as convincingly as she could.

"So wait a minute," Olivia said to Nina. "They haven't had their trial yet, but you still decided to come back? Are you sure that's a good idea?"

"I hope it's a good idea," Nina said softly. "You're my little girl, and I love you more than anything else in the world. I really needed to see you."

Olivia looked at her skeptically. Her spoon was on the table. Liquid ice cream dripped out of the glass dishes.

"Let me show you something," Nina said.

She pulled a small photo album from her purse and handed it to Olivia. The girl opened to the first page. It showed Nina in a hospital bed, gazing at a tiny bundle in her arms as if it were the most precious and extraordinary thing she'd ever seen. Jack stood next to her, his hand around her shoulder, as he looked proudly into the eyes of his infant girl.

"Is that me?" Olivia asked.

"Yes. That was the best day of my life."

"Mine too," Jack said. His voice was low and soft. He brushed a thumb across the corner of his eye.

"Wow," Olivia said. She kept turning the pages, looking at photos of her baby self getting her foot inked and stamped on her Sibley Hospital birth certificate. Suckling at Nina's breast. Sleeping in Jack's arms while Nina gazed proudly on. The pictures progressed until Olivia was two years old.

Anna tried to swallow back the lump in her throat. This was a connection she could never share with Olivia.

By the time Nina had to leave, Olivia had grown decidedly warmer toward her. She held her mother's hand as they walked to the door. Nina knelt down.

"Can I come visit you again?" Nina asked.

"Yeah, that'd be fun," Olivia said. She put her arms around Nina's neck and gave her a hug.

When Nina stood, she turned to Anna. "Can I talk to you in the next room for a moment?"

"Um, sure."

They went into the other room and Nina shut the door.

"Thank you for your help today," Nina said.

"You're welcome. I think she really started to warm up at the end."

"I agree. And I don't want to waste any more time. I've already lost four years. I want to see her as much as I can. I'd like to arrange to visit twice a week, if there's no objection from you."

Anna hated the idea. At the same time, she noted that Nina was clever. Anna didn't have an official say in who got to visit Olivia—but she had Jack's ear, and she was living with Nina's daughter. She could make things easier or harder for Nina. Nina knew Anna's buy-in would make it happen, and happen smoothly.

"I don't know," Anna said. "Is that really what's best for Olivia right now? Maybe you should wait until things are more stable in the case. What if you get close to her, then go into Witsec again? She would be devastated."

"Is it really Olivia you're worried about?" Nina asked.

"What does that mean?"

"I think you don't want me to see Jack. You're afraid of the feelings he still has for me."

"He doesn't have any 'feelings' for you except resentment," Anna lied.

"Now you listen to me," Nina stepped forward, golden eyes flashing. "You seem like a nice girl. I can tell my daughter cares about you. But she's *my daughter*. And I have sacrificed *too much*." Nina stopped and took a deep breath. This was clearly not the way she meant the conversation to go. When she spoke again, her voice was softer, her eyes pleading. "Please don't stand in the way of me seeing her."

"I just want what's best for Olivia. In all honesty, I worry that you're going to hurt her again. Someone needs to look out for her."

"Everything I've done," Nina's voice rose again, "I did for her."

Anna shrugged and held her hands up in question. It didn't look that way from where she stood.

"Let me show you something," Nina said. "I took a copy of this with me to Nebraska, to remind myself why I was there."

She dug through her purse, took out a folder, and handed it to Anna. Anna opened it with curiosity. Inside was a child's drawing of a stick figure with horns. The name JOEY was written in child's block letters in a corner.

"What is this?"

"I went to pick Olivia up from the Montessori," Nina said. "An older child had drawn this; it was up on the board. I asked Joey what it was a picture of. He didn't give a clear answer."

A chill crept down Anna's back. "Did you tell Jack?"

"I did. He thought I was using the drawing as an excuse to take Olivia from him. He said that Joey was always drawing pictures of monsters, had been for years. That was true. But my instincts told me it was more. My child was in grave danger.

"The gang had threatened me, but the fact that they might have gone to Olivia's school was far more terrifying. I wanted to take her with me into Witsec, but Jack said no. He wanted me to forgive him for the affair. He said we could get a new house, a new preschool, have the Marshals protect the family. But that wasn't enough. The only way I could protect her was to die myself—for them to think that they couldn't get to me through her."

Anna looked down at the drawing. The idea of

Diablo stalking Olivia was terrifying. Anna wondered how far she would go to protect the girl in the same situation. Something inside her shifted so dramatically it was almost a physical sensation. It was the way she thought about Nina. Before, she'd been able to dismiss Nina as selfish. She'd run away in order to save herself, leaving her husband to pick up the pieces. Her action probably contained a hint of revenge, too, getting back at Jack for cheating on her. But, in fact, her "death" had been a most selfless act. The woman had given up her life to protect her child's. Living in Nebraska, with no family or friends to whom she could tell her real name. Knowing her daughter was growing up, but unable to see it. So homesick, she snuck back to her house to watch her daughter from outside the windows. If we are the sum of the choices we make, Nina was, on balance, a good person. And that made Anna's position more tenuous.

"I won't stand in the way of you visiting her," Anna said softly.

"Thank you." Nina exhaled.

They went back into the other room. Nina embraced the girl one more time, then turned to Jack. They stood a few feet apart, and met each other's eyes steadily.

"Nice to see you, Jack."

"You, too, Nina."

They didn't hug or even shake hands. But there was a current of warmth between them, a spark that had been ignited by their memories of Olivia's birth and nostalgia about their past union.

Anna opened the door. "Goodbye," she said.

48

Jack's yellow Victorian always looked beautiful, but on Christmas Eve, it looked magical. Outside, the trees were strung with white lights, sparkling through the fresh snow on the branches. A laurel wreath adorned the door. Inside, Anna had wrapped the banister with spruce boughs, pinecones, and red velvet ribbons. A Christmas tree blazed in the living room, and stockings hung from the fireplace, where a fire danced. In the kitchen, Anna gave Olivia the task of putting baby carrots onto a plate with other raw vegetables and scooping hummus into a serving bowl. Costco mini-quiches baked in the oven. Raffles purred and rubbed against Anna's leg. She reached down and scratched the cat's neck.

It was great to be living in a house again, to have a full fridge rather than a mini, to have her whole wardrobe, to have her cat back. She was always looking for signs of danger, though, jumping at imagined MS members lurking in the bushes. There had been no problems in the month since their return. Still, a police car was assigned to drive past the house a couple of times each night. Anna flinched whenever the old house creaked. She and Jack were fastidious about turning the alarm on at night.

Luisa was back working full-time. If she felt the burden of Jack's former suspicions, she did not mention it.

"Let's set out milk and cookies for Santa," Olivia said.

"Good idea," Anna said.

They arranged four Nutter Butters on a plate, then set the plate and glass of milk on the hearth by the fire. Olivia smiled at Anna and took one of the cookies for herself.

"Shh," Olivia said, "don't tell Santa."

"I think he already made his list and is somewhere over Europe. There's no changing who's naughty and nice now."

"It's like I have immunity."

"Sort of," Anna laughed. "You're going to be ready to take the bar when you're nine."

"I'm not going to be a lawyer. I'm going to be a police officer."

Jack came downstairs, looking cozy and handsome in a green sweater that matched his eyes. He kissed Anna, ruffled Olivia's hair, and took one of the Nutter Butters.

"Hey!" Olivia protested. "That's for Santa!"

He smiled and put it back.

The doorbell rang, and Anna's chest tightened. A week ago, Jack had asked her if it would be okay to invite Nina. Anna had hesitated. "She doesn't have anywhere else to go," Jack had said. Anna felt sorry for her, and agreed.

Jack opened the door and Nina smiled up at him. Her cheeks were rosy from the cold; her shiny dark hair danced around her face. In a red scarf and fur-lined boots, she was a picture of holiday cheer. She held huge bags overflowing with presents and food.

"Merry Christmas!" Jack said. He kissed her lightly on the cheek. "Come in."

Nina waved at the deputy Marshal who'd walked her up the steps, and he disappeared back into his car. Kinda selfish, Anna thought, making a deputy Marshal work on Christmas Eve. Then she chastised herself for being selfish.

There was a flurry as Jack took Nina's coat and bags and Olivia hugged her and started peppering her with questions. Anna and Nina greeted each other quietly, without hugging. Now that her coat was off, Anna saw that the woman was wearing jeggings and a red sweater that hugged her curves. She had big breasts and a tiny waist, and she looked devastatingly sexy. Anna wished she'd worn her push-up bra.

Soon, Nina set up shop in the kitchen. When she'd heard that they planned to order their Christmas dinner from HoneyBaked, she insisted on making a home-cooked meal instead. Nina pulled out a bunch of groceries, including, to Anna's dismay, a raw turkey. A turkey would take hours to cook. How long was the woman planning on staying?

"Do you want to help me make stuffing?" Nina asked Olivia.

"Yeah!" Olivia loved any excuse to use kitchen gadgets.

Nina cooked up a storm. She moved about the kitchen with grace and confidence. She knew where everything was—of course she did, she'd put it all there. After the turkey was stuffed and in the oven, she had Olivia help her make appetizers. Soon, there was shrimp wrapped in bacon, Brie and cranberries wrapped in phyllo dough, rare roast beef sliced onto brioche rolls. Anna tried to busy herself, but could only rearrange the raw vegetables around the hummus so many times. Jack and Olivia ate like they hadn't had a gourmet meal in ages—which was probably true. The Costco quiches sat untouched and dejected on their plate.

"Oh, the flowers," Nina said, pulling out a bouquet from one of her bags. She opened a cabinet and peered around without finding what she was looking for. "Where's the red vase? I loved that vase."

If you loved it so much, Anna thought, *you shouldn't have left it.*

Nina turned to her. "Do you know where the red vase is?"

"No," Anna said. "Sorry."

Nina looked forlorn. Anna retrieved a blue vase and handed it to her.

"Anna and Daddy got that vase for their wedding," Olivia said. "We all registered together." The little girl watched her mother for a reaction.

"How nice," Nina said coolly as she put the stems in the vase. "How is the wedding planning going?"

"Great," said Anna and Jack, at the same time.

They smiled at each other. Nina paused in her flower arranging and looked at them wistfully.

In truth, Anna wouldn't characterize the wedding preparations as "great." The wedding was in early July, just over six months away. Jack insisted it was going to happen. They had a plan, he said, and they were sticking to it. But he no longer took the affirmative steps he had in the past. Now Anna was the one setting up appointments. When she'd taken him to a flower shop, he seemed distracted and indifferent. To the florist, he probably seemed like any other groom, just a guy who had no interest in flowers. But to Anna, who had seen him tackle every detail so enthusiastically before, the change was notable.

Nina finally declared dinner ready and they sat down for the elaborate meal. There was turkey and stuffing, green beans almondine, cranberry sauce, and a marshmallow-topped sweet-potato casserole, which Jack eagerly dug into. When he took a bite of it, he practically purred.

"Oh, man, this is my favorite," he said.

"I remember." Nina smiled.

Anna thought longingly of that HoneyBaked ham, which wasn't seasoned with the best memories from a failed marriage.

After dinner, Olivia unwrapped the presents from Nina. She squealed with delight and hugged her mother after each one. The two had grown close since they reunited in November.

Olivia went off to try on a new pair of leggings. The three adults sat together in the living room. The silence stretched out, punctuated by the crackling of the fire in the fireplace. Without Olivia as a buffer, the awkwardness of the situation was inescapable. Raffles settled himself on the couch near Nina, and Nina sneezed.

"I'm allergic to cats," she said.

Jack shooed the cat off the couch and handed Nina his handkerchief. Anna clucked for the cat to come over, but Raffles, apparently sensing that this was not a good place to relax, fled from the room.

"So, how are you enjoying the holidays?" Anna asked Nina.

"Very well, thanks." Nina said. "How's the case going?"

"Well."

At this point, the case was slow and deliberate, more likely to cause paper cuts than bullet wounds. The trial was scheduled for June, six months from now.

"It looks like several of the East Coast cliques fell apart after the bust," Anna told Nina. "The cliques that remain are smaller and weakened. The stragglers are 'clique-ing together,' joining forces, but with Diablo and so many leaders out of the picture, they're hobbled."

"That's wonderful!" Nina said. "It makes me more convinced that I'll be able to come out of Witsec after the trial."

"Cheers to that," Jack said.

He raised his mug, and they all toasted with hot cocoa. It tasted bitter in Anna's mouth.

After what felt like a very long night, Nina finally left. Olivia played with some of her new toys while Anna and Jack cleaned up the dishes. It was almost midnight when the kitchen was back in order. Anna wiped her hands on a dish towel and went into the living room.

"Okay, kiddo," she said to Olivia. "Time for bed."

"I'm still playing."

"If you don't go to sleep, Santa can't come."

"He'll come."

"Come on, sweetie."

"You're not my mommy!" Olivia shouted. "My mommy gave me these toys and she would let me play with them! You can't tell me what to do."

Anna stood frozen in place.

Jack strode in. "Don't you talk to Anna that way. Let's go, Olivia. Right now." He looked at Anna sympathetically. "Sorry, love."

She managed a weak smile. While he put Olivia to bed, Anna went down to the basement. It was poorly lit and ten degrees cooler. Anna's eyes skimmed over the shadows, looking for an MS member hiding behind the hot-water heater. But the only sound was the hum of the boiler, the only movement a spider wrapping a cricket in its web. She was alone.

She went to the table that held all the old stuff Anna had designated as the "giveaway" pile. The red vase sat near the front. She picked it up and looked at it for a long time. Then she dropped it in the garbage can.

Back upstairs, she and Jack took turns at the bathroom sink. As she dried her face on a towel, he put his hand on the small of her back and rubbed it.

"Don't worry about Olivia," he said. "She's just testing the new boundaries. You know she loves you very much."

"I know."

"And so do I."

She sighed and tilted her head up to his. "Yeah?"

"Yeah."

"You don't miss the sweet-potato casserole?"

"Actually, I do. You're a terrible cook."

She laughed and swatted him. They went to the bedroom, where he sat on the edge of the bed to take off his socks. She sat next to him.

"Do you still love her, Jack?"

He paused, socks in hand. He crumpled them together and threw them into the hamper, then turned to her.

"Part of me will always love her," Jack said slowly. "There were a lot of deep emotions in that relationship—positive *and* negative. A lot of loose ends that never got tied up. I still feel guilty for how bad I mucked things up, what I put her through." He cupped her cheek with his hand. "But I love you very much, Anna. And you're an innocent party here. You just fell for someone you mistook to be a nice guy. You believed in me. And you don't deserve to have to cancel your dream wedding because of that."

She looked at his face, trying to understand what he was really saying. There was a temptation to hear only what she wanted to hear. But this wasn't the full-throated endorsement she'd been hoping for. Perhaps Jack was looking for a graceful way out. At the very least, he was grappling with some seriously conflicting emotions. Anna might regret, in the years to come, marrying a man who hadn't resolved all his issues with his ex-wife before he said "I do." A sensible woman might step down, cancel the wedding, and give him the space he needed to figure things out.

Instead, she leaned over and trailed her lips along his neck. She slid her hand up his leg, massaging his thigh. Their clothes came off quickly, and she pushed him back onto the bed. He groaned as she slid his length into her mouth. She wasn't the mother of his child; she couldn't cook worth a damn. But she loved him with all her heart. She lavished him with her tongue and lips; her fingers played along the crevices that drove him crazy. With his every moan, her advantage grew.

49

"Ladies and gentlemen of the jury, this is a case about terror. It's a case about death. It's a case about a gang whose very motto was 'Kill, Rape, Control.' "

Anna stood before the jurors, without a podium or notes, talking to them in the same tone she would use to explain a legal concept to her sister. She tried to make the complicated facts easy to digest, building a foundation for "beyond a reasonable doubt" brick by brick. The jurors listened attentively, eyes widening as she described the crimes.

AUSA George Litz and Agent Samantha Randazzo sat at the counsel table next to the jury box. A paralegal sat beside them, ready to call up the government's exhibits on the flat screens in the courtroom and in front of each juror's chair. Transcribed conversations, surveillance video, and hundreds of photographs would be displayed on the screens. Behind their table was a trial cart with six boxes of physical evidence—the machete and trench coats from the brothel raid, the bloodstained blue tarpaulin and machetes from the Train Room, and similar exhibits that would make the government's terrifying narrative real.

A wooden rail, waist high, separated the well of the courtroom from the audience. McGee sat in the first row; Nina sat in the back. As the case agents, they were permitted to remain in the courtroom throughout the trial, even though they were witnesses. Usually, case agents sat in the front row, but Nina's eyes held fear as she looked at the defendants. She wanted her back to the wall. The rest of the audience was packed with press, members of the public, and attorneys and staff from the U.S. Attorney's Office.

"And it's a case about two men," Anna continued, "men who are responsible for crimes ranging from rape to prostitution, from extortion to the murder of government witnesses." Anna turned and pointed across the courtroom at the two defendants seated at the defense table. "Jose Garcia, also known as 'Psycho,' and Dante del Rio, also known as 'Diablo.' "

The defense attorneys had done their best to clean up their clients. Psycho was dressed in a suit and tie, and wore thick-rimmed glasses with no prescription. His lawyer had obviously coached him to keep somber in front of the jury—there was no sign of his crazed smile. He even wore concealer over the tattoos on his face and neck. Anna considered objecting to the cover-up, but decided against it. She had pictures of the tattoos, and was looking forward to showing the jury that Psycho was trying to fool them by wearing makeup to court.

There was little that could be done to make Diablo appear less frightening. He had a haircut, and now wore Justin Bieber–like bangs covering his horns.

He wore a button-down shirt and dark slacks. But no amount of concealer was going to hide the tattoos covering his entire face, or reconstruct the Voldemortish nostrils. He sat in a wheelchair, because the gunshot wounds had not healed entirely in the prison infirmary. His defense attorneys took advantage of the disability to position the chair so Diablo's back was to the jury. Although it was normally considered an advantage that the government got the table next to the jury box, Diablo's counsel was glad to have their client as far from the jury's view as possible.

At the mention of his name, however, Diablo twisted in his chair and stared at Anna. His eyes were black pits, cruel and furious. He grinned, baring his sharpened fangs. His snarl drew gasps from the jurors. Anna paused in her speech and stared at him, hoping all the jurors would notice the display. She could see Diablo's attorneys grinding their own teeth in frustration. She almost felt sorry for them—she imagined he was not an easy client. She met Diablo's gaze and stared back at him coolly. *You do not frighten me. I'm in charge here.*

Three Courtroom Security Officers sat in chairs behind the defendants' tables; another CSO sat next to the court clerk, in front of the judge. Anyone coming into the courtroom to watch the trial had to check in with a guard outside the door. The CSOs would check under the lawyers' tables every morning for concealed weapons. The attorneys had even been instructed not to use fountain pens so the defendants couldn't turn them into makeshift knives.

Anna recited the rest of her opening statement from her position a few feet from the jury box. It had taken days of writing, reciting, editing, and re-reciting the speech until it sounded natural and unrehearsed.

Anna had charged six members of the Langley Park Salvatruchas with a conspiracy to commit RICO violations. Casper, Lagrimas, Cabron, and Gato had already pleaded guilty; only Diablo and Psycho were left. If convicted, they faced life in prison.

Diablo glared at Anna throughout her opening statement. He seemed not to care whether he was convicted—at least, he made no effort to appear docile in front of the jury. Anna ignored him. She'd been stared at by defendants before. She kept her speech focused on the facts the government would prove. Some of her description was general, to avoid identifying her witnesses. Given the fates of some of the witnesses in this case, the judge had granted a protective order permitting the government not to disclose the witnesses' identities in advance. The defense would only receive the witnesses' prior statements and impeachment information after each witness testified. It was certainly a disadvantage to the defendant, but with three witnesses killed, the judge was taking no chances.

Halfway through her opening, however, Anna saw something she was entirely unprepared for. As she was describing how a detective investigating Maria-Rosa's death had her own life threatened, Jack put his arm around Nina's shoulder. He leaned his head toward hers and whispered something into her ear. Nina smiled. Anna lost her train of thought. She ad-libbed, waiting for her mind to recall the passages she had practiced.

"The detective wasn't killed," Anna said, "but in a very real sense, she had her life taken from her. She lost her husband and daughter. It's a life she will never be able to . . . to regain fully." Her mouth had gone dry—the next words wouldn't come. She walked to counsel table and took a sip of water, pretending to consult her notes.

The moment passed. It all came back, as she'd practiced it. Regaining her rhythm, she concluded her opening statement.

But instead of listening to the defendants' opening statements, she kept replaying her stumble over and over in her head. "She had her life taken from her . . . a life she will never be able to regain." *Because of me.*

• • •

Diablo listened to his own attorney pathetically tell the jury about the government's high "burden of proof" and the standard of "beyond a reasonable doubt." The translator's voice repeated the words in Spanish into the earphones on his head—as if he didn't understand the first time how pointless they were. When they arrested him, eight months ago, he still had Rooster's blood on his hands. The whole night was captured on audiotape. This trial was just for show. He was going to jail for a long time.

He didn't mind. He had given the same advice to many homies: Jail wasn't punishment, it was finishing school. MS-13 was stronger in prison than on the street. Diablo would be as feared, respected, and influential in prison as anywhere else. Maybe more so.

But this trial was still important for one reason: Diablo would learn who was snitching. The police reports explained that there was a recording device in Rooster's pocket. It figured—Rooster had always been bitter about the way the gang treated Buena. Diablo was glad to have killed him. But Rooster might not have been the only snitch. Diablo would sit through the trial and see who was testifying against him. Whoever snitched would die in prison, he would make sure of that.

And there was one more thing he had to do before they took him away. It was the reason he was still in this wheelchair, months after his injury. He had to get that bitch.

He stared at the prosecutor, sitting so smugly next to the jury. She would suffer. He couldn't wait to slash that pretty face—to plunge his homemade knife into her pale throat. Savoring the image, he met her eyes once more, licked his lips and smiled, revealing his gleaming white teeth, each sharpened to a wicked point.

His foot tapped the footrest of the wheelchair, where the shiv was hidden inside the hollow metal.

50

Nina testified during the second week of trial, and her testimony was a sensation. She wore a white sundress with a little white sweater, and although Anna's July wedding was only a month away, it was Nina who looked like the glowing bride. She testified simply and softly about the emotional events of the last four years. The jury leaned forward to catch her every word. They loved her. At one point, Anna glanced back into the audience and saw Jack in the back row, riveted by the testimony. Anna's stomach dipped with a nervousness she didn't usually feel when Jack sat in on her trials. He met her eyes and smiled reassuringly.

That evening, Anna, Sam, and George Litz stood around Anna's laptop on a long table in the war room, a conference room on the same hallway as Judge Emerson's courtroom. The room was crammed with exhibits, documents, reference books, and snacks.

The trial team clicked through the Web editions of stories about the day's testimony. By reading the impressions drawn by journalists and bloggers, Anna hoped to get some insight into what the jury was thinking.

Petula Dvorak's article in the *Washington Post* ran a headline that could have fit just as easily in the *Washington City Paper's News of the Weird* column: "Dead Detective Testifies Against the Devil." In less than a thousand words, it was a compelling portrayal of a woman so dedicated to justice that she risked her life to fight the gang. It depicted Nina's decision to go into the Witness Protection Program as a terrible and noble sacrifice, made to protect her young daughter and husband from harm. Thankfully, the press didn't yet know the identity of the "dead" detective's former husband—or the fact that he and Anna were engaged.

"I think the story came out pretty good," Sam said. "It sounds like we've got a strong case. And it doesn't mention you at all."

Anna nodded, relieved. But the relationship between Nina, Jack, and Anna was common knowledge in the U.S. Attorney's Office. It was only a matter of time before Anna's personal life became a piece of a salacious news story.

"Oh, we got your wedding invitation in the mail the other day," George said. "Thanks! BJ and I will be there."

"Great," Anna said. She tried to muster the proper amount of enthusiasm. She liked George and his wife a lot, and was glad they could make it. Lately, though, Anna felt like she was portraying the emotions of a bride as often as she was actually feeling them.

That evening, they had their last witness conference with Gato. Anna and Sam sat in the a small conference room in the Marshal's Office so a deputy could bring Gato up an internal elevator from lockup in the basement without the public seeing him. Across a tiny table sat Gato, his lawyer, and a deputy Marshal. Gato was in shackles and leg irons, cuffed to the leg of the table. It was a precautionary measure taken with all prisoner-witnesses, but it made the power dynamic in the room perfectly clear.

Anna had been through plenty of meetings with Gato as they prepared for his testimony. This was the last chance she'd have to prep him before he took the stand. They went over the highlights of his testimony, and he was as consistent as he'd been before. Anna was pleased. He was going to be a good witness. She was ready to wrap up.

"The most important thing is that you be completely honest," she said. "Your testimony doesn't help us if you lie. And if you don't tell the truth, or don't tell the whole truth, your entire plea deal will be voided."

Gato looked at her with big eyes. He turned and whispered to his lawyer.

"Can we have a minute?" asked Pinsky.

Anna had a sinking feeling in her stomach. She nodded, and she and Sam walked out. Thirty minutes later, Pinsky opened the door and invited them back in.

"Just to be clear," Pinsky said, "now that Diego has pled guilty and is cooperating, he's immunized for whatever he tells you about his career in MS-13, as long as he's truthful." Anna nodded. "Diego, tell Ms. Curtis what you just told me."

Gato glanced at Anna but when he spoke, he looked

down at his hands. "Ms. Curtis, you know I loved Maria-Rosa. When she went to the police, Diablo put a greenlight on her. I begged him not to do it. I said she wouldn't testify, she'd say whatever I told her to. He didn't care. She had betrayed us."

Gato spread out his fingers on the table and stared at the three-dot tattoo.

"Then what happened?" Anna asked.

She tried to keep her voice neutral, although she knew she would hate the answer. Why, she wondered, just once, couldn't a trial go as planned—with the witnesses saying what you expected? There was always something. In the dozens of cases she'd taken to trial, not a single one went down without some sort of surprise in the middle or immediately before. The only question was how bad the surprise would be. She clenched her jaw and waited to hear this one.

• • •

Gato felt all the eyes in the room on him. He continued looking at his hands as his mind went back to the last day he was ever happy. It was four years ago. He and Diablo were alone in a cheap motel room, before a *misa*. At seventeen, Gato was still a bit starstruck to have a private audience with the gang leader. Diablo rubbed the bumps on his forehead as if in deep concentration.

"You have the potential to be a great leader," Diablo said. "If this turns out right, you would earn the position of Second Word. You would earn the respect and gratitude of your homies. And you would earn *my* respect. So tell me, Gato. Let's say you were Second Word. What do *you* think needs to be done?"

"I don't think she'll say anything to the police."

"She already has."

"She won't say anything else."

"You know that's not true." Diablo shook his head. "She's going into the grand jury in three days."

"She'll take it all back. She'll say she lied before."

"Think, Gato. If she couldn't handle being questioned in the pretty pink room at the children's center, how will she do when they threaten to charge her with perjury?"

Gato looked down at his feet. Diablo was right. Maria-Rosa was soft and scared and inclined to "do the right thing." She would testify against Diablo and Psycho. Against the whole gang, maybe even against him. She knew all the terrible things Gato had done.

"It's not your fault," Diablo said. "She brought this on herself. I know you love her. But if you don't do it, one of your homies will. Someone who doesn't care about her. They can be so cruel. Is that what you want to happen to her?"

"No," Gato said, fighting back tears.

"They will find her, Gato, and she will suffer. There's only one way to protect her from that kind of pain. You know what you have to do."

That night, Gato and Maria-Rosa spread out a bed-cover in a corner of the motel room. Many people lay around them, in similar nests of bedding on the floor. Under a sheet and the cover of darkness, they made love. She wrapped her legs around his waist and buried her face in the crook of his neck.

"I'm scared," she whispered.

"Don't worry," Gato whispered back. "Everything will be fine. I'll keep you safe. I love you."

"I love you, too." She arched toward him, bringing him deeper inside of her. He sighed as he came. Then he held her, stroking her back softly until she fell asleep in his arms. He laid his head on the silky blanket of her hair and breathed in her strawberry scent.

The next morning dawned clear and warm. He suggested they go outside and enjoy it. They went to Rock Creek Park, holding hands as they walked down the path next to the creek. The birds chirped and hopped from tree to tree.

They got to a place where a historic stone house stood over a waterwheel covered in moss. The water babbled over rocks. Maria-Rosa smiled at him as she stood on the bank of the creek. She turned to watch the wheel as it gurgled and spun. Gato looked around them. They were alone, surrounded by trees and brush.

He took the gun from his pocket and pointed it at the back of her head.

In the conference room, Gato looked up from his hands. His attorney, the FBI agent, and the prosecutor were all staring at him. The tears streamed silently down his face, making a pattern of splotchy circles on the tabletop. He didn't try to stop them.

"I did it," Gato said. "I babysat her the night before. I made her feel safe. And then I killed her."

51

The next morning, Diablo sat in his wheelchair at the defense table, fuming as he waited for the trial day to start. He knew the trial was winding down, and he had lost patience with it. No MS-13 member had testified against him. So far, the case had been based almost entirely on the testimony of police officers, crime-scene technicians, fingerprint experts, and other law enforcement personnel. He had sat through an entire day of tapes and blurry surveillance video of the two-hour *generale*. The dry experts were punctuated with gory autopsy photographs and cause-of-death testimony from a series of medical examiners. A few citizens had testified to MS-13's extortion—a couple of pupusa makers, a local bookmaker—but it was chickenshit stuff, nothing worthy of his wrath. Perhaps Rooster, whose pocket held the bugged cell phone, had been the only traitor in MS-13's midst.

By sitting peacefully through the trial, waiting to see who would testify, Diablo had wasted too many opportunities to kill that bitch. Three or four times over the past ten days, she perched her posterboards of crime-scene diagrams and photographs on an easel right in front of his table. Every time she walked to the easel, he gazed at the soft nape of her neck and tapped his foot softly on the footrest of the wheelchair, where the shiv was hidden. But he'd let every opportunity pass.

His lawyers were never told in advance who the witnesses would be, but they'd been told yesterday to expect only a handful more witnesses. Diablo didn't know how many more chances he would have with the lady prosecutor. He was done waiting. The next time she walked to the easel, he would kill her.

• • •

Anna sat at the prosecution table feeling exhausted and wrung out. She hadn't slept well the night before, turning Gato's confession over in her mind. She had known, before, that he'd killed people. In the last few months, he'd told her about the *chavalas* he'd murdered. His various crimes were sorted into a binder, ready to be turned over to defense counsel; she had organized her direct examination of him to front these crimes to the jury. But murdering the woman he loved was a different order of evil, and one that shook Anna. She considered not calling him as a witness. But no one else could provide the insider's view of the gang or describe step-by-step the crimes that Diablo and Psycho had committed. The jury was entitled to his testimony. They would learn everything about him, probably hate him, and decide whether to believe him. She thought they still would.

"The government may call its next witness," the judge said.

She stood, took a deep breath, and said, "The government calls Diego Carlos, aka 'Gato,' to the stand."

A door at the side of the courtroom opened, and Gato was led to the witness stand. He was dressed in his orange prison jumpsuit. Anna had opted not to ask his lawyer to dress him up for the jury. Let them see that he was in prison, where he belonged. Gato placed his right hand on a Bible held by the courtroom clerk.

• • •

Diablo's fury rose up within him. Gato had been the most loyal soldier Diablo had. Gato had killed his own girl for MS-13. And now he was betraying them. He was disrespecting Diablo. In front of Psycho and the world. Diablo should have killed Gato himself, with his bare hands, that day at the *misa*. His body shook with rage.

"Do you swear to tell the truth, the whole truth, and nothing but the truth, so help you God?"

Keeping his hand on the Bible, Gato looked over his shoulder and stared at Diablo. "So help me God."

Diablo's fury hit the boiling point. He reached down to the footrest, pulled out the knife, and jumped over the table.

• • •

Anna was watching the jurors' faces, seeing how they reacted to the cooperator taking the stand. She saw the horror reflected there first. Juror number seven, an older lady in a cardigan, suddenly opened her eyes wide and shrieked. Anna turned in the direction the juror was looking.

Diablo leapt out of his wheelchair and over the defense table. He charged toward the witness stand, holding an improvised knife. The courtroom clerk dropped the Bible, screamed, and ran. Diablo barreled into Gato, knocked him to the ground, and plunged the blade into his chest.

The four Courtroom Security Officers reacted instantly. One rushed to the judge and hustled him out of the courtroom; the other three ran to Gato's aid. As they struggled to pull Diablo off, he kept stabbing Gato. A CSO drew his sidearm, but there was no good shot in the jumble of innocent and guilty bodies.

Jurors and spectators fled screaming from the courtroom, streaming out the side and back doors. Finally, the three CSOs managed to pull Diablo off Gato. They cuffed Diablo and hauled him back to the holding cell. Gato lay on the thin beige carpeting, still. The knife and the Bible lay next to him.

Another flash of movement made Anna look toward the defense table. In the distraction of the melee, Psycho was running out of the courtroom.

"He's getting away!" Anna shouted.

Sam and the last CSO ran after him. Anna could hear the screams from the hallway as the chase went through it.

Anna ran over to Gato and knelt next to him. Someone said, "An ambulance is on its way." Gato's chest was covered in blood, and there were multiple punctures in his orange prison jumpsuit. He was struggling to breathe, making a gurgling sound as he did. He met her eyes.

"Tell—" He choked on his own blood, then tried again. "Tell Maria-Rosa's parents I'm sorry."

Anna took his hand and squeezed it. "You're gonna tell them."

He closed his eyes. He didn't open them again. Anna held his hand until the EMTs burst in. They bundled him onto a stretcher and rushed him out of the courtroom.

She stood up. Her hands were covered in Gato's blood. She thought back to the night, on Grace's back porch, when Gato turned himself in. How he said he wanted a "good death." How she promised he would be safe.

Someone asked if she was okay. She nodded yes, but started shaking uncontrollably.

Anna turned to the audience section, and looked for the one person who could comfort her. There was Jack, in the back row. He stood holding Nina, rubbing her back, as Nina cried into his shirt. He murmured soothing words into her ear.

Anna stood frozen in place, unable to look away from the sight of Jack comforting his wife.

52

The next day, the two defendants stood in handcuffs and leg irons, shackled to each other and attached by chains to their tables. Both wore stun belts under their clothes. Diablo had a black eye from his struggles with the CSOs. Psycho's nose was cantilevered to the left; he had been tackled to the ground in the courthouse lobby by a pack of CSOs and police officers. The defense attorneys looked as demoralized as their clients—but they still had one last fight left in them.

The jury box was empty for this argument, but the courtroom was packed. The security detail had doubled.

"We move for a mistrial, Your Honor," Diablo's attorney argued, "because these jurors will be unduly prejudiced by the sight of my client allegedly stabbing the witness."

"And seeing my client leaving the courtroom," Psycho's attorney said.

"A new trial must be held with a jury that won't be tainted by what took place in the courtroom yesterday."

"Government?" asked the judge. Two deputy U.S. Marshals now sat in chairs in front of the bench.

"The court cannot reward these defendants for what happened yesterday. There's ample case law holding that a defendant cannot manufacture a mistrial by committing crimes in front of the jury. Otherwise, every defendant would have incentive to do so. Moreover, the jury may consider what they saw in court yesterday as evidence of the defendants' consciousness of guilt."

Anna started citing case law on the point. But the judge held up his hands. He'd heard enough.

"The motions for mistrial and severance are denied. The assault on a witness and flight from the courtroom is certainly prejudicial, but they are even more probative of the defendants' consciousness of guilt. I'll give the jury reasonable limiting instruction. Ms. Curtis, I understand you had a few more witnesses. Are they still absolutely necessary?"

Anna could tell that the judge believed her evidence was overwhelming, and he just wanted to get the trial over with. By killing Gato, Diablo had made her closing arguments for her. But assuming the defendants were convicted, there would be an appeal, so she had to make sure she had sufficient evidence of all the elements of the charged crimes. She and George would condense and spin through their final day of testimony.

"We'll be brief, Your Honor."

"Then bring in your next witness. Let's call in the jury."

Anna elicited the rest of the testimony before lunch. The defense had no witnesses.

The lawyers gave their closing arguments in the late afternoon. Anna saw the jurors giving Diablo and Psycho looks of hatred and fear as Anna recounted the evidence against them. She called up pictures of the dead bodies on the flat screens in front of the jurors. With gloved hands, she held up Diablo's bloody machete. When the trial started, she thought this would be the most dramatic piece of evidence in the trial. Now that the jurors had seen Diablo kill someone with their own eyes, it seemed like a quaint relic.

Defense counsel gave their closing arguments, valiantly doing the best with what little they had. At four o'clock, the judge sent everyone home for the night, declaring they could all use a rest. The jury would get its instructions and begin deliberating tomorrow.

Anna and George packed up somberly and headed back to the office. Sam asked if Anna wanted to go get a drink, but she declined. Now that her work in the trial was over, she needed to focus on a deliberation of her own.

• • •

Deputy Fitzgerald dropped Anna off at Jack's house. The yellow Victorian was dark and empty; she was the first person home. As she walked in, Raffles ran into the foyer and rubbed his head against her leg. She patted the cat, feeling strange to be alone in the house—usually, she was the last one to arrive. She felt like an intruder. She picked up the mail from the floor in front of the mail slot. There were three new wedding RSVPs. She brought them to the kitchen, poured herself a glass of merlot, and took everything to the study.

This room had become wedding-planning headquarters. Boxes from Crate & Barrel were stacked in a corner, awaiting the moment when Anna would have time to unpack them. On the desk was a folder holding the finalized dinner menu and contracts for the band, CakeLove, Blown Away Farm & Inn, and the florist. A stack of RSVP cards sat next to the folder, along with a handwritten tab—so far, there were 108 yeses and 39 no's. Anna sat at the desk and opened the new RSVPs. All were yeses: from Jack's secretary, Vanetta; acting U.S. Attorney Marty Zinn; and one of Anna's Michigan cousins. The cousin had written a note on the back: *So excited for you! Just bought airline tickets to DC!* Anna added three marks to the "yes" column of the tab.

She took a sip of wine, leaned back in her chair, and looked at the array of wedding gear. Her life was intertwined with Jack's now. And the wedding was no longer just about them. It had a momentum of its own. Their friends and family had set aside the weekend, spent money on presents and travel. She picked up an RSVP card and ran her fingers lightly over the embossed text.

Anna's wedding dress was hanging in the closet upstairs. After two sessions with the seamstress at Hitched, it fit her like a tight hug.

She turned to the bookshelf and took out the white photo album that held the pictures from Jack's first wedding. She flipped through the book, taking in the images of Jack and Nina: smiling, ecstatic, surrounded by friends. Looking at it was like pressing on a bruise.

Anna heard the front door open, and Luisa and Olivia's voices filled the house. Soon came the clattering of pots and dishes as the nanny made dinner. Olivia chatted from the counter as she did her homework. A little while later, Jack's footsteps strode through the foyer. He greeted his daughter with a kiss, then went upstairs to change. No one knew or expected that Anna was home; she'd been working late every night of the trial. The family continued their evening as usual, perfectly able to go on without her. The light outside the windows faded; the room grew dark. She was so caught up in her thoughts, she didn't notice.

Anna is listening to "The Scientist" by Coldplay.
Anna is listening to "The Scientist" by Coldplay.
Anna is listening to "The Scientist" by Coldplay.
Anna is listening to "The Scientist" by Coldplay.
Anna is listening to "The Scientist" by Coldplay.
Anna is listening to "The Scientist" by Coldplay.

When she came out of the study, Luisa had gone home and Jack and Olivia had gone to bed. Anna went upstairs and peered into Olivia's room. The little girl looked like an angel in her sleep. She'd had a tumultuous year. But she was a strong kid, loved by many people, and she was going to be fine. Anna kissed her forehead softly.

Then she went to Jack's room, took off her clothes, and climbed into bed. Jack was asleep on his back, one arm crooked above his head. She fitted herself into him, rested her cheek against his chest, and drew comfort from the warmth of his skin against hers. She couldn't sleep. She listened to his heartbeat under her ear.

The next morning, the judge gave the jurors their instructions, then sent them back to deliberate. Anna sat in George's office with Sam and McGee, trying to make chitchat, trying to pass the time. Waiting for a jury to come back was the closest thing to purgatory on earth. Lunchtime came and went.

George started to worry. "What could be taking them so long?" Anna told him not to fret, the jury had a lot of counts to get through. Inwardly, she knew any number of things could have gone wrong. A gang member might have gotten to one of them. There could be a crazy holdout juror, or one fearful for her life.

If the jury hung, would Nina still come out of witness protection? Or would she have to go back to Nebraska?

At four, the call came from the courtroom clerk. The jury had a verdict. Everyone walked back to the courthouse. The moment when a jury filed into the box after reaching a verdict was always a nerve-racking one for a prosecutor, no matter how strong her case. "Be seated," the judge said. As they sat, several of the jurors nodded at the prosecutors but didn't look toward the defendants, always a good sign.

The foreperson stood and read the verdict form. Diablo and Psycho were pronounced guilty on all counts.

The judge thanked the jurors for their service and set a sentencing date. Everyone knew the sentencing was a formality. The two defendants would go to prison for the rest of their lives.

As they were led back to the holding cell, Diablo turned to snarl at Anna one final time. She looked him in the eye. "Good luck, sir," she said. She turned to pack up her boxes of evidence.

53

An hour later, Anna stood on the roof deck of the U.S. Attorney's Office. The summer evening was warm and soft, and a light breeze ruffled her hair. She looked out in the distance, over D.C. Superior Court and private office buildings, at the shining white obelisk of the Washington Monument. She heard the door swing open behind her, and glanced back toward it.

Carla walked out onto the deck and stood next to her. "Congratulations on the verdict."

"Thank you."

Anna felt ten pounds lighter now that the case was over. DOJ's Capital Crimes section would consider whether to seek the death penalty for Diablo's murder of Gato in the courtroom. Anna might be a witness in that case, but she wouldn't be a lawyer on it.

"This isn't much of a celebration," Carla said.

"I'm meeting Jack for dinner in a bit."

"That sounds better."

"I just needed some time to decompress before I go."

"I can tell you're upset, Anna. Don't blame yourself

for your witness's death. It's terrible, but there was nothing you could have done."

"It makes me sick to my stomach. But thank you."

"Is anything else bothering you?" Carla asked.

"It's just been a tough trial."

"Seeing Jack with Nina must have been difficult."

Carla met her eyes, and Anna found empathy there. She had avoided talking to her boss about Jack. The whole thing was so awkward. But if there was anyone who would understand the entire situation, it was Carla.

"I love him," Anna said. "But, I see him with Nina, and . . ." She couldn't finish the sentence.

"He loves you," Carla said softly. "It's very clear."

"He loves her, too. It's like a bad episode of *Sister Wives.*"

Carla smiled and looked out at the city. "After Nina 'died,' I thought Jack and I would be together. He hadn't made any promises, but I imagined . . . Anyway, it didn't happen that way. His feelings for Nina were too strong. And he felt responsible for her murder—like he and *I* were responsible. He wouldn't talk to me anymore. For a while, I was bitter. He was more devoted to Nina *after* her death than he'd been while she was alive."

Anna listened with interest. For her, it had been the opposite. Everything was fine when Jack loved his *late* wife—that sort of love didn't take anything away from his relationship with Anna. But now that Nina was back, it didn't really work.

"It was hard to compete with a ghost," Carla said. "But you won't have that problem."

"No," Anna said. "I have to compete with a woman who's come back from the dead. Which isn't so easy, either."

Carla gave her a small, sad smile. "If you ever need someone to talk to, I'm here for you."

54

The Tabard Inn was just as beautiful tonight as it had been nine months ago, when Anna asked Jack to marry her here. She walked into the ivy-covered courtyard, feeling like that was a very long time ago. Jack sat at a candlelit table. He looked gorgeous. When Anna got to the table, he smiled and stood to greet her with a kiss. She closed her eyes and savored the feel of his mouth on hers. She inhaled his clean, peppermint scent.

"Congratulations, love," he said.

"Thank you."

They sat and Jack poured her a glass of champagne from a bottle chilling next to the table. "To justice," he said.

"To justice."

They clinked and sipped. The June night was warm and clear, with a light breeze that skimmed across her skin.

"You did a great job at trial," he said. "I'm proud of you. You've really come into your own as a lawyer."

"Thank you. I learned from the best."

She drank all her champagne and held her flute out

to him. Jack poured her more. Around them, the other diners chatted and ate. The world went on, despite the turmoil in her own life.

"Jack, we have to talk about what happened in court yesterday."

"I know." He set down the bottle and looked at her. His face was pained. A breeze made the candle flicker, throwing shadows across his cheeks. "I'm so sorry. When I saw you standing there, looking so shaken, it broke my heart. I should have gone to you before Nina. It's just—she was terrified, seeing those guys who wanted to kill her, running free in the courtroom."

When Jack had finally noticed Anna standing in the middle of the courtroom with Gato's blood on her hands, he left Nina's side and went over to Anna. He gave her his handkerchief and put an arm around her shoulder. He stood next to her as the CSOs figured things out and sent everyone home for the night. He shepherded her to the house and ran a hot shower for her, then brought her hot tea. But nothing could change the fact that, when things got crazy, the first person he protected and consoled was Nina.

"I understand," Anna said. "You were reacting on instinct."

He nodded.

"And that tells me what I need to know. Jack—" She drained the second glass of champagne, set it down, and met his eyes. "I love you. I always will. But I can't marry you."

"Anna, no." He reached for her hand. "Don't do this."

"I don't blame you." She tried to smile. His hand felt warm and comforting. "You didn't set out to hurt me. And you can't help the way you feel. It's natural. She's your wife. The mother of your child. You love her, and you need to see if you can make it work this time."

"I love you, too."

"It's not enough." Her throat was so tight, it was hard to get the words out. "I need someone who loves me more than anyone else."

He looked down, as she knew he would. Because he couldn't say it.

"She's a good woman, Jack. I hope you guys can make a go of it. Olivia would be really happy."

When he looked up again, his eyes were filled with tears. Anna tried to take a deep breath, but her chest hurt too much. She studied his face one last time. She wanted to remember the details, knowing she would replay this over and over in her head: the last moment they were a couple, rather than two separate pieces. Then she drew her hand from his and pulled off the engagement ring. She set it on the table near his hand. She stood up.

"Tell Nina the red vase is in the basement. I almost threw it out, but that would've been wrong."

She walked out of the courtyard, through the restaurant, and out the front door. She held her tears back until she was out on the sidewalk, striding away from the Tabard Inn. Then she let them stream, unchecked, down her cheeks.

She walked through the city, without a plan for

where she was going or what she was doing, driven only by the need to put some distance between herself and Jack so she wouldn't run back in there and take back everything she'd just said.

She walked for a long time. The tears eventually stopped coming. They left salty tracks on her cheeks.

Anna didn't know how long she'd been walking when her purse buzzed with an incoming text. She pulled out her cell phone. It was from Sam:

> At Sergios. Come over 4 celebratory calamari & drinks. I promise to fend off Tony for you.

Anna put the phone back in her purse. She found a Kleenex and wiped her cheeks.

The night was warm and beautiful. The devil was in jail and she was alive. She had good friends and she could use a stiff drink. She flagged down a cab and climbed in. "To Sergio's, please."

ACKNOWLEDGMENTS

Although this book is a work of fiction, it is based on real cases prosecuted by my former office and the U.S. Attorney's Offices in Maryland and Virginia. I am grateful to the prosecutors and officers with whom I worked and talked—both for their heroic efforts at keeping our community safe, and for their generosity in trusting me with their stories. Anna's courage in facing MS-13 was drawn directly from how these folks confronted real danger with strength, humor, and grit. Thank you to Det. Steve Schwalm, Det. Bob Freeman, Det. Kenny Carter, Det. Maria Flores, Det. Wanda Fields, Judge Stephanie Gallagher, Lynn Haaland, Michelle Zamarin, Kate Connelly, Keri Barta, Ken Wainstein, Lou Ramos, and Kelly Higashi. A tip of the hat to my colleague across the river, Zachary Terwilliger of the Eastern District of Virginia, who has spent the last several years prosecuting MS-13 gang members, and whose skills at trial I watched with much admiration. Special thanks to law enforcement superheroes Glenn Kirschner, FBI agent Steve Quisenberry, and "Ed," walking encyclopedias of crim-pro knowledge and generous sharers of jaw-dropping true stories.

Thank you to Georgetown University professor Joseph M. Murphy, author of *Botanicas*, for sharing his unmatched knowledge about the practice of *Santería* in American botanicas. Thanks to Judge Algenon L. Marbley for his extraordinary mentoring, counsel, and support. Thanks to Christy Purington for tutoring me on Spotify. Thanks to Derrick Brent, my co-clerk, friend, and all-around wise man, for insights on Jack's point of view.

The longer I work in publishing, the more I understand how crucial a good agent is. I am fortunate to have one of the finest. Amy Berkower is wise and warm, and has the remarkable talent of bringing out the best in everyone around her. Amy: thank you for believing in me, fighting for me, and continually teaching me how to excel both as a writer and businesswoman.

My editor, Lauren Spiegel, must possess some kind magic which allows her to give me sharp editorial suggestions while leaving me happy, enlightened, and excited to sit down and write. It helps that she's a friend. Lauren: thanks for choosing Anna, for sagely guiding her development over three books, and for making the entire process so fun.

I am grateful to the terrific team at Touchstone, who greeted *Speak of the Devil* with such enthusiasm and worked so hard to make it a success. Sincere thanks to Susan Moldow, Stacy Creamer, Michael Selleck, Liz Perl, Sally Kim, David Falk, Shida Carr, Meredith Villarello, Brian Belfiglio, Marie Florio, Cherlynne Li, Ana Paula De Lima, Mary Nubla, Charlotte Gill, Wendy

Sheanin, Paula Amendolara, Colin Shields, Tracy Nelson, Chrissy Festa, Janice Fryer, Emily Remes, Eric Rayman, Paul O'Halloran, Alanna Ramirez, Chris Lynch, Tom Spain, Josh Karpf, Aline Pace, Jim Thiel, Marcia Burch, and Ashley Hewlett. Special thanks to Carolyn Reidy for her support and editorial guidance.

I'm indebted to Sandi Mendelson and Claire Daniels for matchmaking my blog with the *Huffington Post*.

My good friends and beta readers helped my story and helped me remain a sane and happy storyteller. Anna would have been planning a sad little wedding if not for the thoughtful intervention of Jessica Mikuliak. She, Lynn Haaland, Jeff Cook, Jen Wofford, M.R., and Jenny Brosnahan are each high-powered professionals who took time from their own busy practices to assist significantly in improving this book. I'm grateful for their friendship—and that I don't have to pay their hourly rates.

Unlike Anna, I am blessed with a wonderful family. I owe much to my lovely, incomparable mom, Diane Harnisch, and my dad, Alan Harnisch, whose work as a federal prosecutor inspired me to become one. Much love and thanks go to my awesome sisters, Kerry and Tracey; my sweet stepmother, Laurie; and the entire Harnisch/Reis/Hughes/Fitzgerald/Amsterdam/Levitis/Leotta clan, who make delicious holidays, pretend my absentminded daydreaming is a lovable quirk rather than an annoying character flaw, and never fail to pack any bookstore where I'm signing.

To my two little boys, I love you so much. I'm delighted that you both love books as much as I do. Reading to you at night is the highlight of my day, and it's so exciting to watch you learn how to read yourselves. I hope that one day, you will read this book and be proud of your mom. Since I don't want to explain its contents to you anytime soon, I hope that day will be far, far in the future.

And to Mike: my unfailing ally, most trusted critic, brilliant adviser, and indispensable partner. I'm the writer, but you're the one who always knows exactly what to say. Life is complicated and challenging, but also wondrous and fulfilling; my life wouldn't be nearly as wondrous and fulfilling without you.

Keep reading for a sneak peek of
the next Anna Curtis novel from
Allison Leotta

A GOOD KILLING

COMING SPRING 2015!

1

When I was fifteen, my favorite place in the world was the high-jump setup at the school track. The bar provided a simple obstacle with a certain solution. You either cleared it or you didn't. In a world of tangled problems with knotty answers, that was bliss.

I guess it all started out on that field, the summer before my sophomore year. That's when I fell in love with Owen Fowler. I never could hide how much I wanted that man.

That's why everyone immediately thought I murdered him. Watch any TV crime show, and the person who says "I couldn't have killed him—I loved him!" is the one who did it. Nothing fuels hate like love gone wrong. So when the coach went up in flames, people naturally looked to see if I was holding the match. But I swear: I didn't kill him.

You don't believe me, Annie, I can see it in your eyes. But I'll tell you everything, exactly how it went down. You probably won't agree with what I did. You definitely would've done things differently. But by the end, I hope you'll at least understand.

So—ten years ago. The athletic field was the most beautiful place in Holly Grove. A girl could feel like she was part of something good on that rectangle of perfect grass, surrounded by bleachers shining silver in the sun. Come fall, the football players would own the field, and the stands would hold ten thousand screaming fans. But in July, the stadium was empty, and the kids who went to Coach Fowler's sports camp got to use the spongy red track that circled the field. The air smelled of fresh-cut grass, the clean sweat of a good workout, and the occasional whiff of Icy Hot. To this day, I still love the smell of Icy Hot.

And I loved the feel of the high jump itself. That moment at the peak, as my back sailed over the bar and I looked straight up at the sky—suspended above the earth, touching nothing but air. Like I could detach from the physical world with all its problems. For a second, at least. I was free. It was my little piece of heaven.

You know what I mean, right? You were a pretty good sprinter yourself. What'd you place in the two hundred meter? Eighth in the state? But track didn't mean the same to you. You'd found another way out. By the time I turned fifteen, you'd already accepted that scholarship to U of M. That summer, you were just killing time before college, hanging out at the track a lot. You told Mom you went to watch me, but you were really there to flirt with Rob. Don't fuss, you know it's true. He was a hottie. And not just because he'd been starting quarterback that year—king of the town! He was objectively hot. Guess he peaked early.

You know why he suddenly got interested your senior year, right? After all those years of not knowing your name? No offense, but. You finally grew some boobs. My own chest didn't show signs of catching up any time soon. The high jump was the one place where my resemblance to a wall was still an advantage.

I was aiming to break your school record for high jumping. Six feet, one inch. I thought if I broke it, people would finally start calling me "Jody" instead of "Anna Curtis's little sister." I remember the day I first believed I could do it: July 15, 2004.

I was trying to figure out why my jump had stalled. I was doing everything right, but it just wasn't taking. I tried again: stood at my starting place and sprinted toward the bar. I hit my mark and rounded the turn toward the mat: five strides, pivot, jump! I flew backward, arched my spine, and kicked my feet up. But something was off, I knew it even before my butt knocked down the pole. As my back hit the mat, I heard the bar clatter to the ground, and Rob laughing in the distance.

I said, "Fuck."

"Watch your language, young lady."

Coach Fowler stood next to the mat, which was a surprise. He was the head of the whole camp and mostly stayed with the football team, leaving the lesser athletes to the lesser coaches. The thrill of him noticing me was canceled by the fact that it was when I'd messed up.

"Sorry, Coach!"

I jumped off the mat and fetched the pole. We set it on the risers together. He was tan and tall, with an athletic build and that aura of authority. The sun threw golden glints off his blond hair. He must've been forty at that point, but he was way cuter than the teenage boys he coached.

"You're a good jumper," Coach said. "You could be great—but you have to really want it. Do you really want it?"

I looked over where you and Rob were sitting. Rob was tugging on the tie of your hoodie. The coach followed my gaze.

"Your sister's a good runner. Fast, determined, scrappy," he said. "Jody—you're better."

I blinked with surprise. He knew my name. And . . . not many people thought I was better than you at anything. He reached over and pulled my hand away from my cheek. I hadn't even realized I was touching my scar.

"It's barely noticeable," he said. He cleared his throat and pointed to my pink chalk mark on the ground. "The problem is your approach. Your mark is too close. You shot up this spring, so your stride is longer. You need room to stretch out those long legs."

I tried not to blush at the implication that he'd noticed my legs. Coach took a piece of blue chalk out of his pocket and drew a line on the ground, about three feet behind my pink mark. He also moved back my starting mark. "Try that."

I trotted to the new starting place, feeling the blue nylon of my team shorts brushing against my glamorously long legs. I looked at the coach's marks and wasn't sure I could do it. I glanced at him, and he nodded. You and Rob stopped talking to watch me. I took a deep breath, squinted at the high-jump bar, and sprinted toward it. I reached the coach's mark and counted off my curve, demanding my legs cover as much ground as they could with each stride: one, two, three, four, five. Pivot. Go!

I jumped. And I flew.

I knew it was perfect the moment I took off. I felt it in my legs, my hips, my spine. I soared back over the pole with inches to spare. Suspended in the air, I looked at the bright blue sky and the soft white clouds and felt a moment of perfection.

I landed on my shoulder blades and let myself somersault backward. A few runners broke out into applause. You yelled, "Go, Jody!"

I jumped on the mat. "Yes!"

"There it is!" Coach yelled. "Good girl! Do that at a meet, and we'll be putting your name up in the gym."

I bounced to the edge of the mat, and Coach met me with a high five. Then he held out his hand to help me down. I took it, feeling honored, shy, and electrically happy. His grip was steady and strong. Dad had never held my hand like that. Coach's fingers tightened around mine as I stepped down, then opened to release me. But I didn't want to break the connection. I kept holding on to his hand for a few seconds after he let go.

2

Anna felt a gentle nudge on her shoulder but kept her eyes closed. Another nudge followed, more insistently. She smelled fresh-brewed coffee and heard morning birds chattering, but all she wanted was to stay curled in warm oblivion. She closed her eyes tighter, determined to hold on to her sleep. It was like trying to hold on to water; the harder she squeezed, the faster it slipped away. She cracked an eye.

The unfamiliar bedroom was bright and lovely, decorated in expensive neutrals. Her black pantsuit was draped neatly over an ivory chair. She glanced down and saw that she was wearing only her bra and panties from the night before. She became aware of a dull headache, throbbing with each beat of her heart. Blinking, she pulled the blanket to her chest, sat up, and tried to remember how she'd gotten here.

A pair of warm brown hands handed her a steaming mug of coffee. Anna looked up at the hands' owner. Her friend Grace smiled down at her.

"You look like your hair got caught in a blender," Grace said.

"I feel like it was my whole head."

At least she understood where she was: Grace's guest room. The night before came back in a series of images that grew blurrier toward the end: placing her engagement ring on the table at the Tabard Inn; walking through Dupont Circle with tears streaming down her face; meeting Grace, Samantha, and the detectives at Sergio's restaurant to toast the jury's verdict in the

MS-13 case. And wine. Endless glasses of wine, which, despite Anna's wholehearted efforts, had succeeded in blotting everything out for only a few short hours.

And left her with a massive hangover. She groaned and rubbed her temples. Grace handed her two Advil, which she gratefully swallowed down with coffee. It was sweet and milky, which coaxed a smile through the blur. Her life was a mess, but at least she had a good friend who knew how she took her coffee.

Anna spotted her cell phone on the nightstand. She had two "unknown" calls from a Michigan area code, and a string of worried texts and calls from her fiancé. Correction: her ex-fiancé. She let the phone thump back down.

"I would've let you sleep longer," Grace said, "but you have a phone call."

"Jack?"

"Who else?"

Anna shook her head, which was a mistake. She wondered how long it would take for the caffeine and ibuprofen to kick in. "We're done."

"He tracked you down here," Grace said. "That doesn't sound 'done.' That sounds kind of romantic."

"He's the Homicide chief. If he can't locate his ex-fiancé, he should resign."

"I didn't want to hit you with this, but . . . he's distraught. And you know he's not the distraught type."

Anna plucked unhappily at the blanket. She wanted to talk to him—she wanted it like a dieter wants cupcakes. But there was nothing left to say. She knew Jack loved her. He loved another woman, too.

"Please tell him I'm fine, and I'm sorry, and I can't talk to him now."

"Okay, sweetie."

Grace handed her a box of Kleenex and left. Anna

banished a rogue tear, as her phone buzzed from the nightstand. It was the "unknown" caller from Michigan again, the same 313 area code as her sister. She blew her nose and picked up.

"Hello."

"Hi, Anna? It's Kathy Mack. From Holly Grove High School?"

That was another world, and Anna needed a moment to get there. She stared at the ceiling until her memory caught up with the conversation: Kathy was an old friend of her sister's. Anna saw her occasionally, when she went home to visit Jody in Michigan. They'd never traded phone calls.

"Kathy—hi! Is everything okay?"

"Actually . . . no. There's a lot going on here. I don't know where to start. I guess I should start with this: Coach Fowler died. He— Some people are saying he was killed."

"Oh—that's terrible."

Anna sat back against the pillows. Since she was a kid, Coach Fowler had been a major figure in her hometown, leading Holly Grove's football team to the state championship several times. He was the most successful member of their community, and one who gave back. His recommendation helped Anna get a college scholarship and out of their small, rusting town.

"It is terrible," Kathy said, "but that's not exactly why I'm calling. See, the police want to question Jody."

"What? Why?" The coach had mentored Jody in high school, but that was ten years ago. As far as Anna knew, they hadn't been in touch since then.

"I have no idea," Kathy said. "And no one can find her. The police went to her house, but she's not answering her door. I've tried her number; she's not picking up."

"Thanks for calling me," Anna said. "I'll try her now."

They hung up and Anna dialed her sister's number. She got an automated message she'd never heard on Jody's phone before: "The person you're trying to reach is no longer available." It didn't let her leave a voice mail.

Anna's chest tightened. She was always vaguely worried about her little sister. For the last few months, they hadn't spoken as often as usual. If Jody were in trouble, Anna might not even know.

She welcomed a reason to get out of town for a while. Get away from Jack, D.C. Superior Court, and the inevitable sympathy from everyone she'd have to uninvite from her wedding. She could take a couple days off. Prosecutors often did after a big trial.

She swiped through her phone, tapped the Expedia app, and clicked on a last-minute deal to Detroit. Then she called Kathy back. "Thanks for calling, Kathy. I'm flying to Michigan this afternoon."

3

As soon as the airplane screeched to a halt on the runway of Detroit Metro Airport, Anna powered up her phone and tried to call her sister again. No luck. Her headache was receding, but the worry in her stomach grew.

She got off the plane and hurried past a wine bar, golf shop, and day spa—besides the casinos, the airport housed the most sophisticated commerce in Detroit—and took the escalators down to baggage claim, where she looked for Cooper Bolden. Kathy had arranged for Cooper to pick Anna up. He'd been a friend in high school, a sunny, bookish kid whose family owned a farm on the outskirts of the county. She hadn't spoken to him in ages. Last she heard, he'd become an Army Ranger and gone to Afghanistan. She scanned the area for him now, looking for a tall, skinny boy with knobby knees and flapping elbows.

Standing against a pillar, scrolling through his phone, was a man with a chest like a Ford 350. He wasn't wearing glasses, and his black hair was shorter, but under a couple days' worth of stubble was a familiar lopsided grin.

"Cooper?"

He looked up and she could see his eyes: light blue rimmed with indigo. She rushed forward to hug him. He stumbled, laughed, and hugged her back.

"Anna. Hi! Easy."

"Easy? You're three times as big as you were in high school."

Cooper laughed. "Maybe only twice as big." He pulled up the jeans on his left leg, lifting the hem. Below was a silver prosthetic limb. "Compliments of the Taliban."

"Oh, Coop. I'm sorry."

"It's okay. They didn't get the best part of me."

"Your spleen?"

"No. My enormous"—he held his hands two feet apart—"intellect."

"Of course."

"You look great," Cooper said. "Just like I remember you. Except more . . ."

"Weary?"

"No. Grown-up."

Anna grabbed her suitcase off the conveyor belt. When she packed it, two days earlier, she thought she'd spend a few nights at Grace's house, in the process of moving out of Jack's. Now she had the dizzying sensation of being a nomad, with no true home anywhere on earth. For the last year, she'd lived with Jack and his six-year-old daughter in their pretty yellow Victorian. After their engagement, Anna started calling it "our house." At Jack's urging, she'd begun to make it her own: rearranging where the mugs were kept, registering for silverware. But now she'd have to find her own apartment. She had to go to that pretty yellow Victorian and pack everything up, deciding which things to take and which to leave forever. She'd see all Olivia's toys and first-grade artwork and know that she had no claim to them. Because, much as she wanted to be—as often as she'd gone to parent-teacher conferences, braided the girl's hair, pored over parenting books trying to figure out the right answer to every six-year-old question—she wasn't Olivia's mother. Without Jack, she was nothing to Olivia. She was just a woman with a suitcase and a hangover.

Cooper took the bag from her hands. "I got it," he said.

She came back to the present and glanced at his leg. "But—"

"Can't stop me from being chivalrous."

She'd had a hard breakup, but he'd lost a limb for his country. It put things in perspective. Normally, she'd insist on carrying her own luggage, but now she just said, "Thanks."

As they walked toward the parking lot, she saw that Cooper's gait had changed too. It used to be a long, loping bounce, like a frisky colt finding his balance. Now his stride was shorter, more deliberate, and with a little hitch that could be interpreted as a swagger if you didn't know better.

"Have you heard from Jody?" Anna asked. "I still can't get ahold of her."

He shook his head. "All I know is the police want to interview her."

"I wish she'd called me. I'm a lawyer."

"I expect she knows that," Cooper said with a smile. "And she doesn't need a lawyer. She'll be glad to see her sister, though."

"I hope so. Can we go right to her house?"

"Sure."

In the parking garage, she followed him to a handicapped parking space and reached for the door to a gray sedan. He shook his head. "That's not mine." He walked to the other side of the sedan, where a huge black Harley-Davidson sat in a motorcycle spot. She glanced at the bike and then at Cooper's prosthetic leg.

"Don't worry. There's a double amputee riding across America." He strapped her bag to a luggage rack and handed her a helmet. "He was fine when he started, but he lost both legs in a motorcycle accident."

She laughed, weighing the risk to her life versus the risk of hurting his feelings. She'd never ridden a motorcycle before and was mildly terrified. She reached for the helmet. Cooper opened a saddlebag and pulled out a black leather jacket, similar to the one he was wearing, and held it out to her. But it was mid-June, warm and balmy.

"No thanks," she said.

"It's to protect your skin if we have a crash."

"Oh, that's reassuring."

She put on the leather jacket. It smelled of cedar, cherries, and the faint hint of another woman's perfume. Cooper straddled the front seat. She climbed onto the seat behind him and grabbed the metal handles on the sides of the seat, leaving a wide berth between their bodies.

Cooper glanced back. "Don't be shy. Scooch up nice and close and hold on to my waist."

She hesitated, suddenly wary. Who picks someone up from the airport on a motorcycle? What if she'd had more luggage? She met his clear blue eyes and found only earnestness there. She slid forward and put her arms around him.

He started the engine and pulled forward. As the motorcycle drove past the parked cars, her heartbeat quickened. She was very aware that she had a large man between her legs, her breasts pressed against his back, and a giant engine humming beneath her. She could feel Cooper's lean muscles beneath his leather jacket. She wasn't cheating on Jack, she reasoned. First: she was just getting a ride. Second: she and Jack were done. Third: she hoped she didn't die.

Anna tried to pay for parking, but Cooper beat her

to it. He pulled out of the parking structure and onto the service road. Anna could reach out and touch the car in the next lane—which would take her arm off. As he pulled onto the highway's on-ramp, Cooper yelled, "Ready?"

"Yeah," she lied.

The bike roared up to Michigan's 70 mph speed limit. She held tight to Cooper's waist. The motor filled her ears and the pavement flew under her feet. She wondered how it would feel if her body hit it. The bike angled low into a curve, and Cooper swung between her thighs. Her adrenaline surged. She was scared and thrilled and very aware of being alive.

Halfway between Detroit and Flint, Cooper slowed the bike and took the exit ramp marked "Holly Grove." Anna's grip relaxed, but her chest tightened. She'd been relieved when she left this town, and she never liked coming back. The only thing she really loved here was her sister.

Cooper passed through the historic downtown. It must have been charming once, but it wasn't used for much these days. The courthouse and city hall still looked respectable enough, but the storefronts in between were mostly vacant and dilapidated. With each auto factory that closed, the town took a hit. And the commerce that still remained in Holly Grove was in the suburbs. Cooper continued out there, passing subdivisions anchored with strip malls, big-box stores, and massive parking lots. He turned onto a smaller cross street, leaving the commercial strip behind.

As they came up to the curve before Holly Grove High School, Anna noticed an acrid smell, growing stronger. The football stadium came into sight, and she stared at it in shock.

A burned-out car was smashed into the center of

a blackened circle at the bottom of the stadium's cement wall. The ground beneath it was an oily scab of scorched earth. The top of the stadium appeared unscathed, with the word *BULLDOGS* still gleaming in blue and silver. The charred smell was so strong it was like sticking her head into a recently used barbecue grill. Yellow crime-scene tape surrounded the area. A few police officers lingered around the perimeter.

Cooper pulled the bike to the shoulder, put down the kickstand, and took off his helmet. The roar of the engine was replaced with the chirping of insects. She took off her helmet, too, smelling fresh-cut grass, ashes, and gasoline.

"What happened?" she asked.

"This is where Coach Fowler died," Cooper said.

"How?"

"He came around this turn. Guess his car was going pretty fast. Crashed right into the stadium. His car went up in flames. He didn't make it out."

She climbed off the bike and walked to the edge of the yellow tape. A cop on the other side glanced over but didn't shoo her away. She guessed the crime-scene work was done and they were just waiting for a tow. Cooper stood next to her.

The car was a classic Corvette. A few spots of blue paint were still visible, but most of the outside was burned black. The hood was smashed in so far, the car looked like a pug. A circular web cracked the windshield in front of the driver's seat.

Anna looked at the ground between the road and the stadium. There was a dirt shoulder, a section of grass, and then a cement apron abutting the concrete wall. There were no skid marks.

"You know what's weird?" Cooper said.

"Other than Coach Fowler crashing right into his

stadium, without making any apparent attempt to stop?"

"Cars don't generally explode on impact. I mean, it happens sometimes, but it's not like the movies. It's rare. And when cars do catch fire from a crash, there's usually a more heavily burned area where the fire started, like around the battery or gas tank, and then some less burned parts. But the coach's car is blackened all around. To me, cars look like this when someone has taken serious steps to make it happen."

"How do you know so much about burning cars?"

"I saw a lot of them in Afghanistan." Cooper ran a hand through his short black hair. "I was in one."

Anna glanced up at his face. He was looking at the stadium, but seeing something else. Before she could respond, a police officer came up to them. "Help you?"

"Actually, yes, sir." Cooper straightened and put a hand on Anna's shoulder. "We're looking for my friend's sister, Jody Curtis. I understand you are, too. Do you know if she's been located?"

"She's at the station now."

"Is she okay?" Anna said.

"Seems so."

"Thank God." She was flooded with relief. "What's she doing at the station?"

"Being interrogated," the officer said. "In connection with Coach Fowler's death."

That made Anna pause. *Questioned* was one thing. *Interrogated* sounded a lot more adversarial.

"Thanks, Officer." She turned to Cooper. "Can we head to the station?"

"Let's go."